Dystopias and Utopias on Earth and Beyond

Caught as we are in a grave climate crisis that seems more irreversible with every passing year, our literary portrayals of the future often feature the dystopian collapse of the world as we know it. Science fiction explores how we got here, while pointing toward a more hopeful path forward. From an ecofeminist perspective, a core cause of our current ecological catastrophe is the patriarchal domination of nature, playing out in parallel with the oppression of women. As an alternative to dystopian futures that seem increasingly inevitable, ecofeminist science fiction helps us conjure utopias that promote environmental sustainability based on more egalitarian human relationships.

Dystopias and Utopias on Earth and Beyond: Feminist Ecocriticism of Science Fiction explores the fictional worlds of such canonical novelists as Margaret Atwood, Octavia Butler, Ursula K. Le Guin, Doris Lessing, and Joan Slonczewski, as well as those of lesser-known science fiction writers, as they collectively probe humanity's greatest existential threats. Contributors from five continents provide compelling analyses of far-future dystopias on Earth that are all too easy to imagine becoming reality if humankind's current trajectory continues, as well as provocative insights into science fiction utopias set on idyllic planets orbiting distant stars, which offer liberatory alternatives that might someday be actualized in the real world. By examining the links between the destruction of the environment and the domination of women, *Dystopias and Utopias on Earth and Beyond* provides the tools to counteract those intertwined oppressions, helping create a foundation for a truly habitable world.

Douglas A. Vakoch is President of METI, dedicated to Messaging Extraterrestrial Intelligence and sustaining civilization on multigenerational timescales. As Director of Green Psychotherapy, PC, he helps alleviate environmental distress through ecotherapy. Dr. Vakoch is editor-in-chief of the book series *Space and Society*, as well as general editor of *Ecocritical Theory and Practice*. He has explored ecofeminism in six of his other books, including *Ecofeminist Science Fiction: International Perspectives on Gender, Ecology, and Literature.*

Routledge Studies in World Literatures and the Environment

Series Editors: Scott Slovic and Swarnalatha Rangarajan

For more information about this series, please visit: https://www.routledg e.com/Routledge-Studies-in-World-Literatures-and-the-Environment/book-series/ASHER4038

"In an era of planetary crisis, *Dystopias and Utopias on Earth and Beyond: Feminist Ecocriticism of Science Fiction* offers a smart, urgent alternative to our collective downward spiral, not only offering fiery critique of our selfish and self-destructive present but galvanizing, positive visions of 'what futures we might hope for.'"

Gerry Canavan, Associate Professor of
English, Marquette University. Co-editor of
Green Planets: Ecology and Science Fiction

"Ecofeminist writers have long used science fiction as a futuristic and sometimes other-worldly medium through which to imagine and energize social and ecological solutions in this world, the one we inhabit here and now. Doug Vakoch's latest collection encompasses a dazzling array of international scholarly voices, considering the work of eminent and less-well-known women science fiction writers from the 19th century to the present. This book is an exciting and timely contribution to the field of ecocriticism."

Scott Slovic, University Distinguished
Professor of Environmental Humanities,
University of Idaho

"With twelve distinctive chapters that explore various ecofeminist dimensions of both dystopic fictional worlds and science fiction utopias of distant planets, this impressive new collection makes us imagine the worst and the best of times here on Earth: a world in environmental turbulence or ecological equilibrium. Only when the oppression of women and the exploitation of the more-than-human environments vanish, is the second option more likely to be our reality."

Serpil Oppermann, Professor of Environmental
Humanities, Cappadocia University. Co-editor of
International Perspectives in Feminist Ecocriticism

"I highly recommend this collection of insightful studies of imaginative fiction addressing human and nonhuman communities. The feminist perspective helps us envision ways to sustain our global ecosystem beyond the many threats of our present day."

Joan Slonczewski, Professor of Biology, Kenyon
College. Author of *A Door into Ocean*

"*Dystopias and Utopias on Earth and Beyond* presents work by a diverse group of scholars whose analyses together demonstrate how feminist authors have mobilized the genre tools of science fiction both to caution and to hope. Especially at a time like ours—a time of great social and environmental distress—readers will come away from this book with a reinforced appreciation for the critical and creative insight of Octavia E. Butler, Ursula K. Le Guin, and others in the canon of feminist and ecological science fiction."

Eric C. Otto, Professor of Environmental
Humanities, Florida Gulf Coast University

Dystopias and Utopias on Earth and Beyond

Feminist Ecocriticism of Science Fiction

Edited by Douglas A. Vakoch

Routledge
Taylor & Francis Group

NEW YORK AND LONDON

First published 2021
by Routledge
52 Vanderbilt Avenue, New York, NY 10017

and by Routledge
2 Park Square, Milton Park, Abingdon, Oxon, OX14 4RN

Routledge is an imprint of the Taylor & Francis Group, an informa business

© 2021 selection and editorial matter, Douglas A. Vakoch; individual
chapters, the contributors

Library of Congress Cataloging-in-Publication Data
A catalog record for this title has been requested

ISBN: 978-0-367-71623-3 (hbk)
ISBN: 978-0-367-71629-5 (pbk)
ISBN: 978-1-003-15298-9 (ebk)

Typeset in Sabon
by Deanta Global Publishing Services, Chennai, India

To Ursula K. Le Guin,
for *The Left Hand of Darkness*

Contents

Illustrations

Contributors

Nicole Anae graduated from Charles Sturt University with a BEd and DipT before earning her PhD through the Faculty of English, Journalism, and European Languages at the University of Tasmania. Her research explores historical and contemporary encounters between the self, embodiment, and culture with a view to examining issues of identity and performance. She is a senior lecturer in Literary and Cultural Studies at Central Queensland University and has also worked at the University of South Australia (Mawson Lakes), the University of the South Pacific (Laucala Bay Campus in Suva, Fiji), Charles Sturt University (Wagga Wagg), and the University of Southern Queensland (Springfield).

Izabel F. O. Brandão is a professor of literature in English and contemporary Brazilian women writers at the Federal University of Alagoas, Brazil (now retired). She has edited or co-edited several books about women writers and feminist criticism and has published extensively both in Brazil and elsewhere (France, England, Italy, Spain, and the US). She co-edited (with Ildney Cavalcanti and two other scholars) a feminist anthology in translation titled *Traduções da cultura: perspectivas críticas feministas – 1970-2010* (*Translations of Culture: Feminist Perspectives 1970-2010*). In 2019 she edited (with Laureny Lourenço) the book *Literatura e ecologia: trilhando novos caminhos críticos* (*Literature and Ecology: Tracking New Critical Paths*), published by Edufal). She is also a poet.

Ildney Cavalcanti earned a PhD in English studies from the University of Strathclyde and completed postdoctoral studies at the University of Cardiff. She is an associate professor at the Faculdade de Letras of the Universidade Federal de Alagoas (Brazil), where she coordinates the research group Literatura e Utopia. Her interests include English studies, gender studies, queer studies, feminism, science fiction, utopianism and dystopianism, and posthumanism. Her latest publication is *Utopias Sonhadas/Distopias Anunciadas – Feminismo, Gênero e Cultura Queer na Literatura* (2019), an anthology of critical essays edited in collaboration with Luciana Calado Deplagne.

Amy Chan Kit-sze is an associate professor in the English Department at Hong Kong Shue Yan University. She is also the Director of the Master of Arts Programme in Interdisciplinary Cultural Studies and the Associate Director of the Technoscience Research and Development Centre. Her research interests include Deleuzian studies, technoscience culture studies, gender studies, Buddhism and Daoism, science fiction studies, and literary studies. She co-edited the books *World Weavers: Globalization, Science Fiction, and the Cybernetic Revolution* (2005), *Science Fiction and the Prediction of the Future* (2011), *Technovisuality: Cultural Re-enchantment and the Experience of Technology* (2015), and *Deleuze and the Humanities: East and West* (2018).

Michelle Deininger, PhD, teaches English literature on Cardiff University's Pathways to a Degree scheme, which equips mature students with the skills to undertake undergraduate study. She completed her undergraduate studies at Oxford and Cardiff University, before undertaking an MA and PhD at Cardiff. Her doctoral thesis, which was awarded AHRC funding, mapped a tradition of the female-authored short story in Wales and uncovered a number of authors and texts that had been previously neglected or forgotten. She has recently completed a chapter on the Eco-Gothic in Elizabeth Gaskell's short fiction for *Victorian Ecocriticism: The Politics of Place and Early Environmental Justice* (Lexington, 2018) and is writing a book with Claire Flay Petty (Cardiff Met) titled *Scholarship and Sisterhood: Women, Writing and Higher Education*.

Julia Kuznetski (née Tofantšuk) is an associate professor of British literature at Tallinn University, Estonia. Her research and teaching interests include contemporary British and Anglophone literature, art and culture, women writers, gender and feminist criticism, diaspora studies, ecocriticism, and ecofeminism. She is the author of a number of publications in these areas, including a co-edited book (with Silvia Pellicer-Ortín) *Women on the Move: Body, Memory and Femininity in Present-day Transnational Diasporic Writing* (Routledge, 2018); "Transcorporeality, Fluidity and Transanimality in Monique Roffey's Novel *Archipelago*" in *Transcending the Postmodern: The Singular Response of Literature to the Transmodern Paradigm*, edited by Susana Onega and Jean-Michel Ganteau (Routledge, 2020), as well as "A Journey Through Eco-apocalypse and Gender Transformations: New Perspectives on Angela Carter's The Passion of New Eve" in *Transecology: Transgender Perspectives on Environment and Nature*, edited by Douglas A. Vakoch (Routledge, 2020). Kuznetski is a member of ASLE, FINSSE, ESSE, Estonian Women's Studies Center, Lexington Books' Ecocritical Theory and Practice Advisory Board, a founding member of the Tallinn University Gender research group, and a reviewer for *Ecozon@: European Journal of Literature, Culture and Environment*.

Patrick D. Murphy is a professor emeritus of English at the University of Central Florida. He earned a BA in history from UCLA in 1973, an MA in English from California State University, Northridge in 1983, and a PhD in English from the University of California, Davis in 1986. Recent publications include *Persuasive Aesthetic Ecocritical Praxis* (Lexington Books, 2015) and "Pessimism, Optimism, Human Inertia and Anthropogenic Climate Change," special climate change issue, *ISLE: Interdisciplinary Studies in Literature and Environment* (2014).

Iris Ralph is an associate professor in the English Department of Tamkang University. She holds a BSc from Monash University, a BA (English) from San Francisco State University, and an MA (English) and PhD (English) from The University of Texas at Austin. Ralph's areas of specialty are Australian, UK, and US literature; ecocriticism; animal studies; and posthumanism. Her publications include book chapters in *Doing English in Asia* (Lexington), *Ecocriticism in Taiwan* (Lexington), and *Ted Hughes* (Palgrave Macmillan). Ralph has published journal articles in *AJE: Australasian Journal of Ecocriticism and Cultural Ecology*; *Neohelicon*; *Tamkang Review*; *William Carlos Williams Review*; *Cowrie*; *CLCWeb*; *Journal of Ecocriticism*; and *Kritika Kultura*. Her book *Packing Death in Australian Literature: Ecocides and Eco-Sides* was recently published (Routledge, 2020). Ralph currently is serving as the editor-in-chief of the *Tamkang Review*.

Irene Sanz Alonso is an adjunct professor at the University of Alcalá (Spain) and a secondary school teacher. She finished her PhD in 2014 with a dissertation titled *Redefining Humanity in Science Fiction: The Alien from an Ecofeminist Perspective*. She is a member of the Spanish research group GIECO (Grupo de investigación en ecocrítica) and the secretary of the online journal *Ecozon@*. Her main fields of research are ecofeminism, animal studies, science fiction, and fantasy.

Gemma Scammell graduated in July 2017 with an MA in Creative Writing and English Literature from Cardiff Metropolitan and is now working full time on her PhD. Previously, Scammell taught an adult learning creative writing class for the local authority and is now working part time as a widening access tutor for Cardiff Metropolitan University. She is a member of the Association of Writers and Writing Programs. Her research interests include social spaces, psychogeography, the fiction of Haruki Murakami, posthumanism, and ecofeminism.

Vandana Singh was born and raised in India and currently lives in the Boston area, where she is a professor in the Department of Physics and Earth Sciences at Framingham State University, as well as a science fiction writer. Although her PhD is in particle physics, in recent years she has been working on the transdisciplinary scholarship of climate change, focusing on innovative pedagogies. Singh's short fiction has been widely published to critical acclaim, and many of her stories have been reprinted in Year's Best collections. Her North American debut is a second short story collection, *Ambiguity Machines and Other Stories* (Small Beer Press), which was No. 1 on *Publisher's Weekly*'s Top Ten in Science Fiction when it came out in February 2018, and it earned praise from *Wired*, *The Washington Post*, and *The Seattle Times*, among others. *Locus Magazine*'s Gary K. Wolfe refers to her as "one of the most compelling and original voices in recent SF." She has collaborated with Arizona State University's Center for Science and the Imagination three times, twice on climate change–related projects. Her first collaboration led to the start of her academic work in the area, resulting in a case study of Arctic climate change as part of a program award from the American Association of Colleges and Universities, for which she traveled to the Alaskan North Shore in 2014. She has been an invited panelist for the National Academy of Sciences working group on interdisciplinarity in STEM, and has taught in and/or co-led summer workshops on climate change for middle and high school teachers.

Christy Tidwell is an associate professor of English and Humanities at the South Dakota School of Mines & Technology. She has published in *ISLE*, *Extrapolation*, *Americana: The Journal of American Popular Culture 1900 to Present*, and *Femspec*, as well as multiple edited collections. Her work largely focuses on speculative fiction, environment, and gender. Tidwell is co-editor of *Gender and Environment in Science Fiction* (Lexington Books, 2018) and of *Fear and Nature: Ecohorror Studies in the Anthropocene* (Penn State University Press, 2021).

Hatice Övgü Tüzün received her BA in English Language and Literature from İstanbul University and her MA and PhD from the University of Kent (UK). She spent eight years as a faculty member of the Department of English Language and Literature, Beykent University and then moved to Bahçeşehir University, where she has been a faculty member of the Department of American Culture and Literature since 2008. She has published articles on Victorian and modern literature, Turkish literature, science fiction, travel writing, and the political novel. Her recent research interests include posthumanism and emotions in literature. She is currently Chair of the Department of American Culture and Literature at Bahçeşehir University.

Debra Wain holds a PhD in Creative Writing. Her research interests include women, food, and culture, which she has investigated through her creative practice of writing short fiction. Her work has appeared in publications such as *Meniscus* (winner CAL Fiction Award), *Journal of Post-Colonial Cultures and Societies*, *Verity La*, and *Tincture*. She is a current sessional academic at a number of Australian universities. She has presented her research on the roles of food in fiction at the Third International Food Studies Conference and at the Australasian Association of Writing Programs Conferences.

Karl Zuelke, MFA, PhD, is director of the Writing Center and the Math and Science Center at Mount St. Joseph University in Cincinnati, Ohio. He also teaches literature, writing, and environmental studies there. His MFA is from Indiana University and his doctorate is from the University of Cincinnati. His doctoral dissertation is an ecocritical exploration of four genres of nature writing and science writing. He has published eco-critical articles on Terry Tempest Williams in *Exploring the Literary Landscapes of Terry Tempest Williams* and Pierre Teilhard de Chardin in *Ecocriticism and Religion* (forthcoming), as well as creative work in a variety of journals including *The Antioch Review, ISLE*, and *The Journal of Kentucky Studies*. Zuelke has been a long-time member of the Association for the Study of Literature and Environment (ASLE) and the Society for Literature, Science, and the Arts (SLSA) and has presented numerous papers at those conferences and others. His latest projects include a creative/critical blog, *Dreaming, Singing*, daily creative med-itations or critical engagements with the 385 poems included in John Berryman's *The Dream Songs*. He is also at work on a novel about place, industry, and environmental degradation, set in Dayton, Ohio.

Foreword

Ecofeminism and Speculative Fiction: A Writer's Reflection

I shouldered my rucksack, took a deep breath, and stepped up with my right foot. The mountain path was strewn with pine needles. I was a city-bred kid from the subtropics a few hundred miles south, so for me, pine trees were strangers. I slipped and fell heavily forward, which was fortunate because to my left the mountainside dropped away into a green nothingness. But my glasses bounced off my nose and fell, apparently endlessly, into the valley far below.

I was part of a group of some 15 students, most of us teenagers from Delhi, trekking through the Himalayas to study the Chipko movement, one of the most remarkable social justice-environmental movements in the world. It was the summer of 1980; on the other side of the world, Charles David Keeling had been recording rising atmospheric carbon dioxide concentrations for 22 years, but climate change was still decades away from public consciousness. At the age of 17, I was aware of biodiversity loss from habitat loss, and had a vague notion that all this was somehow connected to social injustice. As I scrambled to my feet after that stumble, wondering how I would manage without my glasses for the two weeks that remained of our trip, I didn't know that the trip would have a paradigm-shifting impact on my life, that it would enable me to *see* in an entirely different way.

The Chipko movement (Guha 1989) was more than an environmental movement; it was also a struggle for self-determination (including rights to forest produce) for the rural people of the region that had begun in 1964. In 1974, the now legendary Gaura Devi and 27 other village women confronted loggers in Reni village, who had been sent to cut trees for a government auction. When discussions failed, the women put their arms around the trees and successfully prevented them from being cut (hence "chipko," which means "to stick to" in Hindi). The movement spread all over the Uttarakhand region of the Himalayas.

Six years after the pivotal event, we were there to learn, and to witness the remarkable waves of change and resistance that were spreading through the region. During the 20 days or so that we were in the mountains, we went from village to village with our Chipko guides, traversing paths through forests and over mountain ridges, right up to 10,000 feet. Most of the places were remote enough that the inhabitants had never seen city folk before, nor did they know about the things we take for granted in cities such as electricity, TV, coffee. But this was their world, where such things were irrelevant. We experienced the tremendous hospitality of the rural poor, and were witness to their deep knowledge of the land. We found that the difference between a "Chipko" village and one still untouched by the movement was dramatic—in the former, there were active women's councils, where the agenda could include anything from forest protection to the education of girls to the problem of illicit liquor. Men were involved too—in fact many of the leaders were men, Gandhians like Chandi Prasad Bhatt and Sunderlal Bahuguna (who had invited us), for example. But women were the backbone of the movement. In the villages still untouched by the movement, we could see the difference—people were ground down by their struggles, and there was a palpable sense of defeat. We had the privilege of traveling with Chipko villagers to such places and witnessing some transformations. In one instance we were joined by a local poet, Ghanshyam Raturi, who is now famous as the poet of Chipko. As we traversed a windy alpine meadow above the tree line, he taught us his songs of resistance and praise, songs that I remember to this day.

Among the revelatory moments of my Chipko experience—and there are several—one stands out. Near the end of our trip, we were in a high mountain valley, where a meeting of several Chipko villages was taking place. Speaking to the crowd was a woman with greying hair. She spoke strongly, and with passion, fists pounding the air. I was standing at the back of the crowd. I felt something shift inside me at that moment, a crack in my conception of the world that would take years to understand and articulate. It was in fact several years later, when I read the Western feminists such as Betty Friedan, that I realized the significance of the moment. Despite the fact that my grandmother had taken part in the freedom struggle against British colonialism, and despite other familial examples of women's agency, I'd grown up with the unconscious acceptance of the notion that feminism was an exclusively Western phenomenon. This was, of course, part of the insidious long-term effect of colonialism—the colonial possession of the mind. But what I had witnessed on that day in the Himalayas was indeed a home-grown, grassroots feminism; yet, in its rallying cry for collective self-determination and environmental protection, it went far beyond individualist Western conceptions to something larger and more profound.

The women who protected the trees were not privileged sentimental urbanites. For them the forest was necessary for survival; it was a place of immense practical as well as emotional and spiritual significance. As we learned up in those remote heights, the forests gave the villagers everything they needed: wood, fuel, fodder, fruits, water. This was brought home to us most dramatically in the village of Lasial, which perched atop a cliff at about 9,000 feet. Two years before our arrival, the only remaining natural forest near the village had been overexploited by the villagers. To prevent it from drying out, they self-imposed a ban on cutting anything but deadwood from the forest. They appointed a guard from amongst their number to make sure nobody flouted the ban. We saw the result of their efforts when they took us into their forest the next day. It was a mixed forest of oak and pine, with cascades of wild roses and clusters of rhododendrons; from its verdant interior flowed a broad stream of clear water. That people with no formal education could perform this ecological miracle was a revelation to my city-bred young self.

Walking us through a government pine plantation, the villagers pointed out the relative lack of undergrowth and the absence of water. The Forest Department, a legacy of British rule and an enabler of industrial logging, had a slogan: "What do the forests bear? Resin, Wood and Commerce!" To which the Chipko movement's rejoinder was: "What do the Forests Bear? Soil, Water, and Pure Air!"

The Chipko movement's sociological dimension included women's empowerment and fighting caste discrimination. Self-governance and economic independence of village communities were a central issue. This included access to forest produce such as wood for agricultural implements and homes. The destruction of the forests through mass felling and mono-culture caused great hardship to the people, especially women, who had to walk as much as 16 kilometers a day to get water. Men left in droves for cities in the plains as agriculture failed due to the degradation of the land from tree felling and monoculture, and the ones that stayed behind some-times gave in to alcoholism. We heard tales of hordes of women attacking and destroying illicit distilleries.

After decades of struggle, a 15-year moratorium was imposed by the gov-ernment on tree cutting in the Himalayas. The Forest Department learned a few lessons from the movement. Worldwide, the Chipko movement became the symbol of what an environmental movement should look like, and in being so depicted, things of key importance were lost. Instead of granting village communities their right to self-rule, including the right to manage their forests as they had done for millennia, the government imposed pater-nalistic, Western-inspired conservation schemes that drew the line firmly between human and nature, and lost the villagers many of their traditional forest rights. Disagreements between leaders, political uprisings, and the economic temptations of the dominant development model didn't help, least of all the villages involved in the struggle. The on-the-ground multiple threads of the movement were overtaken by a more simplistic Chipko-of-the-global-imagination, often presented as a naïve ecofeminism that essen-tialized Chipko women's connection to Nature instead of acknowledging the complex nexus of gender, caste, culture, history, ecology, and politics from which their agency emerged.

The strictly imposed boundary between the human and the natural continues to wreak havoc on the lives of indigenous people and rural communities the world over. Environmentalism that manifests in this form sequesters nature into national parks by removing the humans who have lived there traditionally, and polices the boundaries. This neat separation of human and natural denies the lessons of environmental history: that human and non-human lives and histories are deeply entangled. The Rights and Resources Institute and its partners report (Rights and Resources Institute et al. 2018) that indigenous people, despite being a mere 8% of the global population, manage about 80% of the world's biodiversity and almost 300,000 million tons of carbon. Despite increasing recognition from scientists and other scholars of the importance of traditional knowledge systems, indigenous communities continue to be at the receiving end of paternalistic and often brutal development policies. The United Nation's REDD Program (Reduction of Emissions from Deforestation and Forest Degradation), seeks to create a financial value for the carbon stored in forests, thereby offering incentives for developing countries to reduce emissions from forested lands. Despite gestures toward indigenous rights, the REDD initiative has been viewed with suspicion by indigenous groups; not only does it commodify nature, it also gives an excuse for governments and corporations to continue to grab land from native peoples.

Perhaps this parceling of the human from the non-human—an essential aspect of modernity—has its roots in the history of science itself. Because I am a physicist, I am particularly intrigued by the history of my field, and its complicity in the state of affairs today. In my current work on transdisciplinary pedagogy of climate change (Singh 2020), I use the term "Newtonian Paradigm," which is a way of referring to the mechanistic view of the universe that emerged from a Western European historical context. The mechanistic or clockwork universe arose from a particular entanglement of the sociopolitical and material—Europe's colonial imperatives, the history of clockmaking, and Newton's laws being some of the threads. From this paradigm arise the Industrial Revolution and the various socio-economic "isms" of our times; democracy and individualism, capitalistic economic theory with its core idea of social atomism—the human acting in rational self-interest—and of course the idea of Nature as something distinct from the human, all of which are aspects of modern industrial global culture. These are, of course, deeply gendered as well.

The Newtonian paradigm is both atomistic and reductionist. Its taxonomies are absolute and universal. Thus Nature and Culture, Myself and Other, Rationality and Emotionalism, Male and Female, Religious and Secular, Space and Time. Yet when we look closely, these terms are fluid, contextual, and do not always translate between cultures and situations. It is not that they aren't necessarily useful or important—but that they do not have meaning, *a priori*, without the proper context. What I mean here by context is not merely the socio-cultural matrix, but—since matter speaks—also the material—my interpretation of the physicist and philosopher Karen Barad's (2007) notion of the entanglement of matter and meaning. Categories and concepts arise from the cuts we make in the world of phenomena, through our intra-action with matter. Within those cuts (or those paradigms, if you prefer) such terms make sense. But other cuts are also possible, other paradigms in which such concepts may be entirely irrelevant. Much as I enjoy Newtonian physics within its domain of validity, extending its concepts to explain the behavior of black holes makes no sense. I am also aware that despite bearing the label female, I am not always so. Sometimes I feel like a "man," sometimes like a "woman," and often neither. When I am walking through a forest with no other humans nearby, am I a man or a woman, or even human? From my own upbringing I recall the ancient Sanskrit phrase "Neti, neti," "[I am] not this, not this," an attempt to open the consciousness through negation. The great Sufi poet Bulleh Shah sings "Who knows what I am?" Categories in certain contexts are all very well, but perhaps we shouldn't universalize them without thinking. Boundaries, especially those created by dominant paradigms, are worth interrogating.

So when we take a complex and multifaceted movement like the Chipko movement and call it feminist, or environmental, or even ecofeminist, perhaps we are using terms that are not context-independent, terms which might blind us to crucial aspects of the movement, in particular the various perspectives of the participants themselves. However, since the heyday of the movement, activists and scholars have been documenting multiple such grassroots efforts for self-determination, participatory democracy and ecological regeneration in India and around the world. There are hundreds of these in India alone: consider, for example, the community of Mendha Lekha village, where the inhabitants have declared local sovereignty, manage their forests, and take all decisions by consensus, involving every adult man and woman (Varma Patil and Sinha 2020). Such movements are culturally and geographically local, but not isolationist—many of them have a self-consciously planetary outlook and are beginning to talk to each other, reimagining the planet as a tapestry of alternatives that resist patriarchal capitalist dominance and domination. So far as I can tell, speculative fiction to date has not engaged with these real-life experiments, perhaps because their practitioners are marginalized, and most writers and critics of specific are not. But thanks to such efforts as Vikalp Sangam in India, and the Global Tapestry of Alternatives worldwide, these stories are coming to light (see, for example, Kothari et al. 2019). These movements have some common threads but they are all also different—complicating and broadening what we mean by ecology, gender, and feminism.

My Himalayan experience all those years ago, along with more recent accounts of grassroots social-ecological movements, have led me to an appreciation of an organic, non-exclusive, diverse collectivism that is manifested in the self-governance of communities deeply connected to their lands. Most understandings of collective or communitarian actions have, in the West, been caricatured as Soviet-style forced conformity, as though no other communitarian arrangements are possible. We see this in the great dystopias of science fiction, from *1984* to *The Giver*. While I consider these works necessary and important, what is left out is a whole universe of possibilities—illustrated, for example, by Ursula K. Le Guin's *The Dispossessed* and *Always Coming Home* (see Karl Zuelke's chapter in this volume) or Joan Slonczewski's *A Door into Ocean* (see Irene Sanz Alonso's chapter in this book). These are, unfortunately, exceptions. The Western sociological imagination has been limited by the overwhelming importance given to the individual in isolation from environmental and sociological context, which is also, of course gendered. We see, for example, the fallout of these limitations beautifully and relentlessly explored in Octavia Butler's *Parable of the Sower*, in a world where the delusion of an isolated utopic existence is shattered by the terror of the socio-environmental context (see Hatice Övgü Tüzün's chapter in this volume).

In the broad sense that I understand it, an appropriately complex ecofeminism sheds light on the crisis in which we find ourselves today: the horror of climate change, the brutality of neoliberal capitalism, the hardening of boundaries of exclusion between social groups, and the rise of right-wing fascist nationalists in multiple places around the globe. For all these reasons it is reassuring to me that in this volume the term "ecofeminism" is presented with an ambiguity and complexity that allows for a multifaceted examination. It is indeed a cause for celebration that scholars in this volume have examined the ecofeminist imagination as expressed in multiple works of speculative fiction, including those by the authors named above. A broad ecofeminist lens helps us to see, for example, that utopias and dystopias can exist simultaneously, side by side, in the real world, and that for some peoples especially indigenous or tribal people the world over, dystopia has been their context ever since their encounter with modern civilization. This is a consequence of the power structures that capitalistic systems erect and strengthen at the cost of multiple disposables—disposable people, disposable non-humans, disposable materials, disposable geographies. Thus no gated utopia is possible without multiple accompanying dystopias, without pushing out and leaving certain kinds of people, non-humans, and places outside its walls. The great challenge of speculative fiction is to imagine alternatives—not merely to technologies such as those based on fossil fuels for example—but to values, to social arrangements, to our relationship with the rest of Nature.

Climate change is a logical end result of Power's insistence on the Nature/Culture divide. As Amitav Ghosh has expressed in his book of essays, *The Great Derangement*, current literary forms have arisen from the very context that also gave us colonialism and climate change. I only partly agree with his take on science fiction not being up to the task (Singh 2017). Science fiction, or more broadly speculative fiction, often reflects prevailing social conditions rather than challenging them. But those who inhabit, literally and otherwise, other countries, cultures, imaginations, paradigms than the norm are uniquely placed to engage with the climate catastrophe in new and illuminating ways. The scholars in this volume present a wide array of authors who attempt such an engagement.

A recognition of the Newtonian paradigm as a paradigm rather than the default implies other possibilities. The current crisis of climate change and its attendant ills force us to question the legitimacy of multiple boundaries, not just Nature/Culture but also Science/Humanities, the "two cultures" of C. P. Snow. I am fascinated by the question of what a post-Newtonian science might look like. Although currently, science deals with many systems not truly amenable to a Newtonian analysis, from atoms and black holes to bodies, ecosystems, and global climate, my suspicion is that despite the sophistication of quantum theory and relativity, we are still interpreting these through a primarily Newtonian lens. Science as we know it is susceptible to co-optation by power—consider its role in colonialism, war, and destructive industries like fossil fuel extraction. I imagine a post-Newtonian science that is informed by indigenous knowledge systems and liberated from paternalistic, capitalist power structures. I imagine a science that is capable of engaging with the climate crisis in a way that connects scales of space and time, the social and the natural, the local and the global, the ethical and the technological. What better place to explore this than the vast canvas of speculative fiction?

I had read science fiction and fantasy avidly through my childhood and early teen years, then dropped the habit in my young adulthood. Later, as a card-carrying alien on American shores, I began to relate my experience of foreignness to my early reading of science fiction. During my ten-year exile from academia, I started to write it. Discovering Ursula Le Guin was a revelatory experience that allowed me to see people like me in a kaleidoscope of alternative futures. It gave me permission to see myself as a writer of a very different kind of science fiction than the Asimov and Clarke that I'd read growing up. Looking back after writing two collections of short stories, I find that what makes me feel at home in the genre is the chance to play in a wider universe than I've ever known, where boundaries are fluid and ever-shifting, where new concepts, languages, paradigms arise out of the context that one creates. As an example, some years ago I wrote a novella as part of a project, "Year Without a Winter," of Arizona State University's Center for Science and the Imagination. The anthology in which it appeared (Hannah et al. 2019) featured well-known writers like Nancy Kress, Nnedi Okorafor, and Tobias Buckell. Its purpose was to commemorate *Frankenstein*, science fiction matriarch Mary Shelley's groundbreaking work, in the climatic context in which it was written two hundred years ago—the "year without a summer," later found to be caused by the eruption of Mount Tambora in Indonesia. The "re-enactment of the dare" was held on a high mesa in

Arizona in 2016, where a few of us (project organizers and writers) sat atop a cliff top under lowering clouds on a moonless night, and read Shelley and Byron out loud as the rain pattered down on us, ceremoniously marking our own far more serious climatic era. In my novella, one of the characters struggles to understand a monster he is certain has been let loose in the world. It is both material and metaphoric, a destructive, demonic creature that engulfs the Earth, giving us climate change and war and conflict. And yet it also contains the seeds of other worlds, the possibility of its own destruction. No one attribute or definition encompasses it—it defies and surpasses all classifications. All he can do then, is to name it—the World Destroying World Machine, or Widdam—which is also the name of the story. For me, Widdam as a concept represents the combined pathologies of capitalism, patriarchy, and colonialism, ever fearful, ever hungry, its unexamined inner demons let loose upon the world.

This is only one example, from a writer's perspective, of what speculative fiction allows us to do. Having seen the monster through the eyes of my character, I now recognize it in various manifestations in the world. And I see the world itself differently as a result of my fictional explorations. My first climate change novella, *Entanglement*, which I wrote in 2013, is set in five different places around the globe. Writing it was an expansion of my consciousness—a painful and exhilarating process—to peoples, cultures, landscapes that were not my own. One of these places was the Canadian Arctic, where I "inhabited," in a manner of speaking, a woman scientist who had lost her Inuit roots. Studying methane outgassing in the shallow, melting seas of the Arctic Ocean, she had an encounter that changed her life. A few months after writing the story, I found myself on the Alaskan North Shore for an academic project on climate change. I talked to scientists, Inūpiaq whalers, scholars, and elders (none of these categories is mutually exclusive) and the experience changed *my* life. In a very real sense, my fictional character brought me there.

Standing on the shores of the frozen Arctic, I was very conscious of the multiple entanglements within which we live. The angle of sunlight due to the astronomical arrangement of the Sun and the Earth, including the Earth's tilt, gives rise to the long polar winters and summers and the ice caps that reflect so much of the sun's light back into space, thereby cooling the globe as a whole. The great tundra, a frozen wasteland to the foreigner, a place to call home for the Inūpiaq people, gives rise in turn to a culture that is defined by the ice, and a language so delicately tuned to the environment that it might well be one of the most precise in the world. The area is rich in oil and gas deposits, and the oil economy gives some measure of prosperity to the people in this harsh land. But it is also taking away what they hold most valuable—the ice, the whales, a way of life. The dilemma is between short-term prosperity and long-term uncertainty—between modernizing the economy and finding some combination of old and new ways to live with the land. In the great metropolises south of the North Pole, the Widdam insulates us from these realities and dilemmas. But the fact that we are dependent on multispecies others, on astronomical juxtapositions, and their resultant geographies is true in Boston and New Delhi and Beijing as much as it is on the Alaskan North Shore or the Chipko Himalayas. The same dilemmas confront us as do the Alaskan Inūpiat and the villagers of Lasial.

> *Na kata, na kata re*
> *Hara jangala*

Do not cut down the green forest, sings Ghanshyam Raturi, the poet of the Chipko movement. What he means, I think, is not that we can't cut a tree to build a house or make a plough, but that the *forest* must live if we are to live. A forest is not a collection of trees and a plantation is not a forest. What distinguishes the two is the degree of entanglement between species. There is much evidence emerging now that "pristine nature" is a fiction (Levis et al. 2017) and that indigenous people have for thousands of years shaped and been shaped by their landscapes. Western explorers and conquerors in the Amazon for example, with their preconceived notions of the boundary between farmland and wilderness, failed to recognize the unfenced multispecies vegetable gardens that native peoples planted in the forest as gardens. We are not separate—we are entangled. We live and die within the interdependent web of life. To question boundaries is to challenge Power. Perhaps we who inhabit modern industrial culture as its enablers and captives, we who are lost can begin to remember, through the broad and complex ecofeminist lens, the way back to the forest.

Vandana Singh

References

Barad, Karen. 2007. *Meeting the Universe Halfway: Quantum Physics and the Entanglement of Matter and Meaning.* Durham, NC: Duke University Press.

Guha, Ramchandra. 1989. *The Unquiet Woods: Ecological Change and Peasant Resistance in the Himalaya.* Oxford: Oxford University Press.

Hannah, Dehlia, Brenda Cooper, Joseph Eschrich, and Cynthia Selin, eds. 2019. *Year Without a Winter.* New York: Columbia University Press.

Kothari, Ashish, Ariel Salleh, Federico Demaria, Arturo Escobar, and Alberto Acosta, eds. 2019. *Pluriverse: A Post-Development Dictionary.* New Delhi: Tulika Books.

Levis, Carolina et al. 2017. "Persistent Effects of Pre-Columbian Plant Domestication on Amazonian Forest Composition." *Science* 355, no. 6328: 925-931. Accessed October 12, 2020. DOI: 10.1126/science.aal0157.

Rights and Resources Initiative, Woods Hole Research Center, Environmental Defense Fund, World Resources Institute. 2018. *A Global Baseline of Carbon Storage in Collective Lands: Indigenous and Local Community Contributions*

to Climate Change Mitigation. Accessed October 12, 2020. https://rightsa
ndresources.org/wp-content/uploads/2018/09/A-Global-Baseline_RRI_Sept-
2018.pdf.

Singh, Vandana. 2017. "The Unthinkability of Climate Change: Some Thoughts on
Amitav Ghosh's the Great Derangement." *Strange Horizons.* Accessed October
12, 2020. http://strangehorizons.com/non-fiction/reviews/the-unthinkability-of-c
limate-change-thoughts-on-amitav-ghoshs-the-great-derangement/.

Singh, Vandana. 2020. "Teaching Climate Change in a Physics Classroom: Towards
a Transdisciplinary Approach." *arXiv Preprint.* Accessed October 12, 2020.
https://arxiv.org/abs/2008.00281.

Varma Patil, Pallavi, and Sujit Sinha. 2020. "Reinventing Gandhian Ideas and
Practice of Consensual Democracy, Satyagraha, and Village Socialism in Today's
Context: The Case of Village Mendha Lekha, India." *Presented at the Seventh
South-South Forum on Sustainability*, Lingnan University, Hong Kong, July
8–17. Accessed October 12, 2020. https://our-global-u.org/oguorg/en/pallavi-va
rma-patil/.

Preface

Caught as we are in a grave climate crisis that seems more irreversible with every passing year, our literary portrayals of the future often feature the dystopian collapse of the world as we know it. Science fiction explores how we got here, while pointing toward a more hopeful path forward. From an ecofeminist perspective, a core cause of our current ecological catastrophe is the patriarchal domination of nature, playing out in parallel with the oppression of women. As an alternative to dystopian futures that seem increasingly inevitable, ecofeminist science fiction helps us conjure utopias that promote environmental sustainability based on more egalitarian human relationships.

Dystopias and Utopias on Earth and Beyond: Feminist Ecocriticism of Science Fiction explores the fictional worlds of such canonical novelists as Margaret Atwood, Octavia Butler, Ursula K. Le Guin, Doris Lessing, and Joan Slonczewski, as well as those of lesser-known science fiction writers, as they collectively probe humanity's greatest existential threats. Contributors from five continents provide compelling analyzes of far-future dystopias on Earth that are all too easy to imagine becoming reality if humankind's current trajectory continues, as well as provocative insights into science fiction utopias set on idyllic planets orbiting distant stars, which offer liberatory alternatives that might someday be actualized in the real world.

Throughout the book, contributors cross-reference each other's chapters, fostering a dialogue about the links between the destruction of the environment and the domination of women. In the process, these scholars offer tools to counteract those intertwined oppressions, helping create a foundation for a truly habitable world.

In her commencement speech at Bryn Mawr College in 1986, Ursula K. Le Guin captured the motivation underlying the works featured in this volume when she said, "When women speak truly they speak subversively—they can't help it: if you're underneath, if you're kept down, you break out, you subvert. We are volcanoes. When we women offer our experience as our truth, as human truth, all the maps change. There are new mountains. That's what I want—to hear you erupting. You young Mount St Helenses who don't know the power in you—I want to hear you."

Douglas A. Vakoch

Acknowledgments

For their innovative contributions that explore dystopias and utopias through the intersection of ecofeminism and science fiction, I thank the authors of the chapters of this volume: Nicole Anae, Izabel F. O. Brandão, Ildney Cavalcanti, Amy Chan Kit-sze, Michelle Deininger, Julia Kuznetski, Patrick D. Murphy, Hatice Övgü Tüzün, Iris Ralph, Irene Sanz Alonso, Gemma Scammell, Vandana Singh, Christy Tidwell, Debra Wain, and Karl Zuelke. I gratefully acknowledge the scholars who reviewed and commented on the full manuscript: Gerry Canavan, Serpil Oppermann, Eric C. Otto, John Charles Ryan, Joan Slonczewski, and Scott Slovic.

In my work as president of METI International, my colleagues have shared with me their insights about what it takes for civilizations to remain stable across the millennia—a prerequisite for the success of our organization's namesake Messaging Extraterrestrial Intelligence (METI), given the immense timescales of interstellar communication. It is rare to find a community that sees a natural link between sustainability and the search for life in the universe, as reflected in METI's strategic plan that affirms the "ways that ecofeminism can provide insights into fostering environmental sustainability on multigenerational timescales." This book's focus on environmental critique and engagement is informed by conversations with current and past members of METI's Board of Directors: Jacques Arnould, Jerome Barkow, Kim Binsted, Steven Dick, David Dunér, Abhik Gupta, Adam Korbitz, Derek Malone-France, Anson Mount, Alan Penny, Florence Raulin Cerceau, Dalia Rawson, Ian Roberts, Jill Stuart, John Traphagan, Ariel Waldman, Laura Welcher, and Sheri Wells-Jensen.

For presenting an early version of her chapter in our panel on ecofeminist science fiction in the academic track of the international science fiction convention Worldcon 76, I thank Iris Ralph, as well as those who joined her for the follow-up workshop at METI's headquarters in San Francisco: Abhik Gupta, Peter I-min Huang, Mike Matessa, Ted Peters, Katja Plemenitaš, Dalia Rawson, Vandana Singh, Scott Slovic, and Laura Welcher.

For collaborating on ways to increase accountability for environmental threats and disasters, I am grateful to Otabek Suleimanov, founder of the Stihia Festival.

I warmly acknowledge the insights I have gained in integrating sustainable actions into our everyday lives through the clients I work with as director of Green Psychotherapy, PC, a clinical psychology and ecotherapy practice in the San Francisco Bay Area.

My thanks go to Scott Slovic and Swarnalatha Rangarajan for including this book in Routledge Studies in World Literatures and the Environment. To Michelle Salyga at Routledge, I am indebted for her help in shaping this book and for shepherding it through the editorial process. Bryony Reece has my gratitude for moving the book swiftly and efficiently into production. Finally, I thank Stephanie Derbyshire for conscientiously overseeing all aspects of the production process, as the final manuscript was transformed into the published volume you are now reading.

I am grateful to Ursula K. Le Guin for *The Left Hand of Darkness*, the novel I assigned for a course in the psychology of women that I taught as a graduate student a quarter-century ago, which opened the possibility for me to start reimagining gender and nature.

Most importantly, I thank my wife Julie Bayless for helping me understand what it means to be an ecofeminist.

Douglas A. Vakoch
San Francisco, California

Introduction

Patrick D. Murphy

When Sir Thomas More introduced the term "utopia" in his book by the same name in 1516, he created a vision of a society that has overcome the woes he and his contemporaries saw around themselves. Although More wrote his novel in Latin with its title literally meaning "no place," as a word in the English language its meaning has split into two conflicting definitions: one, a place that cannot be actualized in reality, but perhaps might be strived for in this imperfect world of fallen human beings; two, a place, or way of life, that could be developed if founded on the right principles. Through the centuries, utopias have been constructed on a variety of foundations, including economic and religious principles.

Women's participation in writing utopias has generally been viewed as a modern, if not contemporary, phenomenon. Yet, the recovery of women's writing keeps pushing the dates back in time. In English, readers now have Margaret Cavendish's (1666) *The Blazing World* from the seventeenth century as the earliest known utopia by a female writer. It is noteworthy that some critics, such as Dale Spender (1986), have viewed Cavendish's work as a forerunner of modern science fiction (SF), while others note that Cavendish was recognized as an outspoken feminist in her day. Thus, even if women's participation in the utopian mode of imaginative literature is seen as a belated appearance, Cavendish's work nevertheless inaugurates at least a 450-year tradition of such writing. Of course, one should note that far more of women's work in this tradition consists of dystopian critiques than does men's work. I hope the reason for that imbalance requires no explanation in the days of "#MeToo."

Through much of its history, utopia has usually had a pastoral setting, as it did in the early twentieth century with Charlotte Perkins Gilman's (1915) *Herland*. And, indeed, with the rise of capitalism and mechanization, that pastoral orientation took on a clear political and economic antithetical orientation to contemporary life, as H. G. Wells (1895) has it play out in *The Time Machine*. The problem with nineteenth-century utopias for many contemporary readers tends to be their static, finished, "perfected" condition.

By the 1970s, science fiction writers tended to eschew the idea of utopia as a finished and "perfected" place. They did not abandon visions of a different kind of world in the near or far future, here or another planet, but began to represent unfinished and in-process "better" worlds rather than "perfect" ones. This change in orientation in utopian writing was driven by the new wave of feminist activism and authorship and its overlapping and commingling with the environmentalism springing out of the political activism of the 1960s. Writers such as Marge Piercy (1976) with her *Woman on the Edge of Time* envisioned feminist "eutopias," often in contrast to an existing dystopian society also represented in the novel. These are better places where the inhabitants are working through gender, economic, and political conflicts and differences. These books and stories tended to be feminist with an ecological orientation and should be understood as ecofeminist fictions whether or not their authors perceived them as such. At the same time, the most ecologically worked out "eutopia" of the 1970s also, and necessarily, showed significant feminist influence, Ernest Callenbach's (1974) *Ecotopia*. It, too, is portrayed as an unfinished work in progress with numerous environmental and social experiments underway with a fundamental participatory democracy deciding the fate of these various investigations into new ways to live non-exploitatively.

Still early in the twenty-first century, as people look toward the coming decades and centuries, it is easy to imagine the opposite of utopias: dystopias. In times of social upheaval, paired with a grave climate crisis that appears to be soon irreversible, dystopias have become increasingly prevalent in literary projections of possible futures. Indeed, the entire subgenre of climate fiction (cli-fi) is based on apocalyptic settings produced by climate change or more sudden environmental disasters. Often in these depleted environment novels, women suffer under harsh conditions of gender hierarchy. In doing so, these writers are looking back and learning from feminist dystopian stories of the 1970s, such as *Walk to the End of the World* by Suzy McKee Charnas (1974). Unlike the current cli-fi writers, however, the feminist dystopian novelists of the 1970s also often portrayed a feminist eutopia. Some, however, could only envision such a world as Gilman did back in 1915, one without men in it. That was the case for the planet of Whileaway envisioned by Joanna Russ (1975) in *The Female Man*.

Dystopias and Utopias on Earth and Beyond: Feminist Ecocriticism of Science Fiction examines these collective visions of future worlds, with a special emphasis on environmental threats and feminist solutions as explored through science fiction. Feminist ecocriticism provides a lens for understanding environmental degradation as a consequence of the patriarchal domination of nature and the attendant and inextricable oppression of women. Ecofeminist critiques can also be paired with liberatory antidotes, envisioning eutopias rather than utopias as alternatives to the dystopian near future promised by contemporary reactionary populism; or, in some cases, as more distant positive futures that follow the catastrophic devastation of environments and civilizations.

Part 1. Climate Change and Future Earth Dystopias

Treating climate change, with rare exceptions, for authors has resulted not in the portrayal of utopian worlds but dystopian ones. Unlike so much science fiction, cli-fi, as it is now labeled, tends to be set on Earth or at least within this solar system. This section includes five chapters addressing this kind of literature.

Hatice Övgü Tüzün opens this section with an essay on a well-established award-winning author, African American novelist and short story writer Octavia Butler, with a focus on her *Earthseed* novels. Of all her work, these novels develop most clearly Butler's spiritually based ecofeminist orientation, integrating it with her consistent anti-racist themes. She was the first SF writer ever to receive a MacArthur Foundation genius award and a trailblazer as an African American woman writing in a field dominated by white male authors. As Tüzün notes, Butler chooses to set her hyper-empathetic teenage African American protagonist in a post-apocalyptic California as the setting for these novels to develop the idea of a heterarchical "Earthseed spirituality." Perhaps the eeriest part of these near-future novels is the depiction of an authoritarian Trump-like American President. Butler's belief in the transformative potential of an ecocentric religious movement aligns her with the spiritual wing of ecofeminism and also serves as a precursor, if not direct influence, of the creation of Atwood's "God's Gardeners" in the MaddAddam trilogy.

The next two chapters treat Atwood's trilogy in detail, with Debra Wain focusing on "nourishment and feeding" and Izabel F. O. Brandão and Ildney Cavalcanti analyzing "ethics, gender, and ecology." Synthetic versus natural food production is a significant focus of the novels and Wain considers it through women's experience both in terms of oppression and empowerment, using in part Vandana Shiva's critique of the so-called "green revolution." Wain notes the despondent treatment developed through the first volume's male focalization and then the shift in the other two novels to female focalizers for the development of the narrative. As Atwood suggests, the technoscience approach to food production is doomed to failure and is already producing disastrous collateral damage through genetic engineering and the creation of a dizzying array of high-calorie non-nutritional junk food. Then, as do God's Gardeners, women must seize back the means of food production.

Brandão and Cavalcanti first discuss the issue of genre in relation to Atwood's novels to define them in terms of speculative fiction that presents a clearly identified dystopia in terms of both gender and ecology and their distinction from other current dystopias. They are particularly concerned about the representation of bodies and develop this argument by means of Stacy Alaimo's concept of "toxic bodies." They also consider the body as a mask for performative nonidentity, which Atwood particularly emphasizes in the second volume of her trilogy.

Julia Kuznetski treats the late Mara and Dann novels of an author who has gained recognition in both realist and science fiction literature, Doris Lessing. Kuznetski argues that the majority of SF reproduces the western binary paradigm of me/Other and me/outside force, but Lessing challenges these dichotomies through a feminist agenda that can be understood through the application of Stacy Alaimo's theory of transcorporeality. The world of Lessing's main characters is a far future post-technology back-to-basics one beset by the effects of climate change, particularly drought. The characters try to make sense of what has happened to the world in which they must struggle to survive. Kuznetski builds on the work of other critics, concurring that Lessing is writing a critique of western colonial discourse and producing a postcolonial parable with the setting being focused on North Africa. But unlike the critics she cites, Kuznetski emphasizes the importance of the ecocritical elements of Lessing's narratives.

Iris Ralph introduces readers to a 2015 novel by a Filipino-Australian writer, Merlinda Bobis, *Locust Girl*. It depicts the ecocide of Australia over two centuries as the result of patriarchal and masculinist fears and desires. Ralph provides a background first on science fiction as a literary mode arising from the development of modern science in the late seventeenth century and argues that a shift occurs in the last third of the twentieth century, concurrent with a massive influx of female writers into the field, to more attention to biology rather than engineering. *Locust Girl* is the story of climate refugees and migrants told from the point of view of a child and represents the potential for hybridity to generate alternative ecocentric forms of masculinity.

Part 2. Utopias on Earth and Beyond

Michelle Deininger and Gemma Scammell open this section with a shift in focus to a young adult story by Louise Lawrence, arguing that ecofeminist SF has the "power to reimagine the world and so transform it." Elizabeth Holden wrote under this pen name a series of Young Adult (YA) works in the 1970s and 1980s and considered the challenges of capitalism versus socialism and the impacts of technology on the environment. Deininger and Scammell argue that Holden's writing projected the idea that a dystopian disaster could lead to an ecotopian outcome in its aftermath. She successfully utilized both ecohorror and ecophobia, such as the overgrowth of plant life after civilization's collapse, a trope popular in British literature, to advance hopeful themes for her younger readers.

Stepping back in time, Nicole Anae introduces readers to late nineteenth- and early twentieth-century utopian works by Australian women writers, who may be unfamiliar to many other readers around the world. The first three texts she treats are all utopian texts written in 1883, 1888, and 1901, respectively. These novels are particularly striking for their prescience about ecofeminist concerns and themes. Augusta Dugdale's *A Few Hours in a Far-Off Age*, for instance, treats vegetarianism, a central concern of such ecofeminist and animal rights activists as Carol J. Adams, Marti Kheel, and Greta Gaard, promoting both anti-speciesism and gender equality. *A Week in the Future* promotes holistic science and, while not as radical as Dugdale, Catherine Helen Spence does provide a sexually progressive vision of the future. Mary Anne Moore-Bentley turns elsewhere to a parallel world of feminist empowerment in *A Woman of Mars*. In her novel, a Martian travels to Earth to emancipate women and regenerate humanity. All three novels critique the ideology of individualism and its illusory notions of masculine autonomy. Joyce Vincent's *The Celestial Hand* from 1901 is not a utopia at all but rather a harbinger of technological SF. It presents a critique of colonialism in the heyday of European imperial expansion.

Irene Sanz Alonso then examines Joan Slonczewski's seminal work, *A Door into Ocean*, using Carolyn Merchant's ecofeminist concept of partnership ethics to develop her discussion of the life entanglement of Slonczewski's "Sharers" on the moon planet Shora. Sanz Alonso points out the difficulty the author had getting an SF novel about a peaceful revolution by an environmentally sustainable community published, a work fundamentally standing in stark contrast to Frank Herbert's *Dune*. While Slonczewski uses the standard plot device of having an ignorant observer/participant who must be educated about the world portrayed in the novel, that world consists of a radically alternative heterarchy of species. Biological adaptation and mutation are proposed as a means of engagement with the rest of the natural world in opposition to technological transformations and the brute force evolution of the genetic engineering practiced today by agribusiness conglomerates.

In the next chapter, Amy Chan Kit-sze provides a re-reading of several of Ursula K. Le Guin's novels, developing her argument about the author's ecofeminist orientation by means of her use of the Daoist principle of *yin*. While Le Guin's indebtedness to Daoism is a well-established point in literary criticism, Chan develops her argument about it in a new direction through invoking Gilles Deleuze's concept of the "body without organs," as well as discussing how it counterbalances Confucianist emphasis on the masculine *yang*. Chan mainly discusses Le Guin's early works, *The Word for World is Forest*, published at the height of the Vietnam War and using both feminist and environmentalist strategies to attack the blatant colonialist racism of that war, as well as *The Left Hand of Darkness*. Influenced by the circulation of the manuscript of Russ's (1975) *The Female Man*, which was so radical Russ had difficulty in finding a publisher for it, Le Guin's novel helped launch the reconsideration of gender binaries in SF that occurred in the 1970s.

Continuing a consideration of Le Guin's oeuvre, Karl Zuelke analyzes the utopian community portrayed in *Always Coming Home*. Zuelke considers reciprocity in terms of plant languages and a concept of Earth others, through which Le Guin gives voice to "absent referents" elided in the value dualisms of contemporary society. Throughout, Zuelke incorporates the importance of listening to and appreciating the world in terms of "flowing" rather than perceiving the world as a set of inert and discrete objects that human beings name.

In the book's final chapter, Christy Tidwell addresses the writings of another influential writer from the 1970s, Sally Miller Gearhart, particularly her novel, *The Wanderground*. Reflecting the influence of radical feminism, Gearhart's novel portrays another all-female alternative society. Tidwell, however, would not label this one a utopia, because, unlike say *Herland* or *A Door into Ocean*, which Tidwell compares with the novel, Gerhart's society has rejected the potential benefits of science and technology, adopting a false romanticized view of nature, suggesting that it reflects an "overcorrection" of the ills of modern technological society, as do several other novels of the 1970s. As a result, Tidwell argues that the novel is more a "fantasy" than an extrapolation of actual social potential.

In contrast, Donna Young's lesser-known novel, *Retreat*, published in the same year as *Wanderground*, and ironically enough subtitled *A Fantasy*, offers a positive alternative narrative of scientific potential for such possibilities as parthenogenesis. Tidwell argues that while both novels present a story of human environmental reintegration, Young's novel does so in a much more productive way. Referencing Angelika Bammer, Tidwell argues for the importance of studying feminist utopian novels without ignoring their limitations, both to understand them as products of their age and as efforts to conceive of a non-oppressive world.

While dystopias are often discussed as cautionary tales with the premise that unless the readers change their ways or undertake significant political or social action they will be doomed to a nightmare society. In some works, that is the fate of all readers, male and female. In other feminist works, the emphasis often falls on the plight of women. In 1937, Katharine Burdekin published just such a novel, *Swastika Night*, envisioning the long-term dystopian gender effects of Hitler's rise to power. Today, the political, the economic, and the social are intertwined with the environmental, as demonstrated in Pat Murphy's (1989) *The City, Not Long After* or Starhawk's (1993) *The Fifth Sacred Thing*. Although they may present more of a sense of urgency about the need to redirect contemporary society in the face of a looming environmental crisis, utopian novels also call for such redirection. Perhaps "cautionary" is not quite the right word for these stories; perhaps "opportunity" or "possibility" tales would better serve. Doom and gloom does not always spur people to action; sometimes hope and potential does more to break inertia. In either case, the chapters contained here demonstrate the power and benefits to readers of the many literary efforts to paint a picture, for better or for worse, of what the world will/might look like sooner or later.

References

Burdekin, Katharine (Murray Constantine). [1937] 1993. *Swastika Night*. New York: Feminist Press.
Callenbach, Ernest. [1974] 2014. *Ecotopia*. San Francisco: Banyan Tree Books.
Charnas, Suzy McKee. [1974] 1979. *Walk to the End of the World*. New York: Mass Market.
Gilman, Charlotte Perkins. [1915] 1998. *Herland*. Mineola, NY: Dover.
More, Sir Thomas. [1516] 2003. *Utopia*. Translated by Paul Turner. New York: Penguin.
Murphy, Pat. [1989] 2006. *The City, Not Long After*. New York: Firebird.
Piercy, Marge. [1976] 1985. *Woman on the Edge of Time*. New York: Fawcett.
Russ, Joanna. [1975] 1986. *The Female Man*. Boston: Beacon.
Spender, Dale. 1986. *Mothers of the Novel*. London: Pandora Press.
Starhawk. 1993. *The Fifth Sacred Thing*. New York: Bantam.
Wells, H. G. [1895] 2017. *The Time Machine*. Oxford: Oxford University Press.

Part 1

Climate Change and Future Earth Dystopias

1   An Ecofeminist Reading of Octavia Butler's *Parable of the Sower* and *Parable of Talents*

Hatice Övgü Tüzün

A multiple recipient of the prestigious Hugo and Nebula awards, the African American writer Octavia Estelle Butler successfully employs the science fiction genre as a platform upon which she discusses contemporary issues, such as climate change, gender and racial discrimination, and class conflict in a futuristic setting. In the words of De Witt Douglas Kilgore and Ranu Samantrai (2010, 355), Butler's work

> pushes the genre to speak to our deepest, culturally burdened horrors as well as to our transcendent hopes. For Butler, the most intimate fear is located at the meeting point of race and sex, the former the licence for and the latter the tool by which a historically enfranchised class has controlled the bodies and destinies of peoples considered inferior.

Although Butler repeatedly identified feminists, science fiction fans, and black readers as her "fairly distinct audience" (McCaffery and McMenamin 2010, 10), her novels increasingly attract a wide and varied readership across the globe. In her critically acclaimed speculative science fiction novels *Parable of the Sower* (1993) and *Parable of the Talents* (2000), Butler employs an ecofeminist perspective to examine the conditions that cause and perpetuate the subordination of both women and nature in a post-apocalyptic setting.

Parable of the Sower comprises of journal entries written by the protagonist, Lauren Oya Olamina—a 15-year-old African American woman who has hyper-empathy syndrome, which is a psychosomatic disorder that makes her experience other people's feelings as her own. Events described in the novel begin in post-apocalyptic southern California, where the climate is warming, food is scarce, and violence and racial turmoil are rampant. When her Robledo community is eventually overrun, Lauren manages to escape with two other survivors, disguising herself as a man. She gradually develops her own belief system called Earthseed, which locates God in change, chaos, and uncertainty and aims to prepare humankind to take root among the stars and thus fulfil what Lauren calls their Destiny. Joined by several others during her arduous journey north, Lauren ends up founding a commune in the woods with a group of likeminded people who learn new and better forms of relating to each other and to the world around them. In *Parable of the Talents*, the commune gets smashed and many—including children and Lauren's husband—get killed. Although Lauren is forced to endure many hardships along the way, she lives to see the Destiny accomplished toward the end of her life.

Both *Earthseed* novels reflect Butler's perception of humanity as deeply flawed by a strong tendency for hierarchical thinking, which leads to intolerance and violence and is manifest in sexism, racism, and ethnocentrism. In her words, "the more hierarchical we become, the less likely we are to listen to our own intelligence or anyone else's" (Mehaffy and Keating 2010 106). Like ecofeminists, Butler strongly opposes the exploitation of the weak by the strong and offers a powerful critique of patriarchal society and its structures of domination. I would thus argue that the *Earthseed* novels are classic ecofeminist texts in their exploration of intersections of oppression and their visceral portrayal of connections between harmful practices that exploit the environment and social structures that oppress women among other groups. As Meghna Mudaliar (2021) suggests, science fiction as a genre has always been related to ecocritical ways of thinking. In this sense, Butler effectively employs the science-fictional space to promote an ecocritical and ecofeminist agenda. Drawing on theoretical debates in the field of ecofeminism, this chapter critically examines Butler's treatment of ecofeminist ideas in *Parable of the Sower* and *Parable of the Talents*.

Emerging as an intellectual and social movement in the 1970s as an offshoot of cultural feminism, ecofeminism seeks to expose connections between the gender problem and ecological degradation in order to address contemporary problems. Employing ecofeminism as a lens for examining intersections of repression, ecofeminist writers and thinkers draw attention to the systematic relationship between the subjugation of women and the exploitation of nature by capitalist patriarchy. So, as Aslı Değirmenci Altın (2021) notes, ecofeminist theory borrows from both feminist and ecocritical studies as it exposes subjugation and otherization of both humans and nonhumans on the planet. In Noël Sturgeon's definition (1997, 58),

> Ecofeminism is a movement that makes connections between environmentalisms and feminisms; more precisely, it articulates the theory that the ideologies that authorize injustices based on gender, race and class are related to the ideologies that sanction the exploitation and degradation of the environment.

As this definition suggests, social justice and environmental justice are inseparably linked, as we are all part of a living and an interconnectedly organic whole.

Butler's science fiction novels vigorously engage with these issues in a timely manner. In the words of Peter Stillman (2003, 15),

Butler presents the reader with "mental images" or "cognitive map" of future dystopias. Weaving together the imagined future development of contemporary tendencies such as increasing social divisions, economic inequality, global warming, and the political fantasies of the anti-government right (in *Sower*) and the religious right (in *Talents*), Butler generates detailed depictions of "social totalities" that contextualise the tendencies into concrete institutions, practices, and personal experiences.

Since most people tend to acclimatize to and accept many things they are exposed to, they often display a certain unwillingness to tackle dysfunctional and/or destructive patterns, face problems head-on, and take action accordingly. Warning her readers against complacency in the face of escalating sociopolitical cleavages and environmental degradation, Butler's fiction offers haunting portrayals of possible (and increasingly probable) future worlds that could come to be if we refuse to go beyond our circumstantial comfort zones. In this sense, Butler's dystopian future scenarios are cautionary tales that show us what might happen if we fail to address existing problems effectively *now* as a collective.

As Izabel F. O. Brandão and Ildney Cavalcanti note in their chapter on ecodystopic science fiction (this volume), the genre of dystopia flourishes throughout the twentieth century and reaches the new millennium with narratives offering "newest maps of hell." Butler offers one of the most nightmarish dystopic visions in contemporary science fiction through her haunting portrayal of the United States as a failed state where large numbers of people have been plundered along with nature. The novels also portray how the reckless squandering of natural resources has led to irreversible environmental degradation, wreaking havoc also on social relations and the political system. The increasing impotence of the state and the uncontested rule of rapacious capitalism have led to the widening gap between the poor and the rich. While a very small minority enjoys comfort and security in its secluded and heavily guarded communities, a large segment of the population—comprising mainly the dwindling middle classes and a larger number of poor and homeless people—live under appalling conditions. According to Lydia Rose and Teresa M. Bartoli (2021, 142), "ecofeminists recognize that quality of life decreases, not only for women, but children and people of color due to the exploitation of the environment." Similarly, throughout both novels, Butler particularly stresses how women, people of color, and the working classes receive the fewest resources and hold the least amount of power. These victims of societal injustice and oppression are systematically abused, neglected, impoverished, and dying of various diseases.

Parable of the Sower shows in graphic detail how the joint forces of militarism, capitalism, and multinational corporations are operating to destroy the environment. Butler herself remarks that ecology, especially global warming caused by profligate use of fossil fuels, is almost a character in *Parable of the Sower*. On the stage of a postmodern, post-industrial, post-revolutionary world – a world in which capitalism is devouring feudalism – in *Parable* a search for 'good ground' begins.

(Sears 2015, 28)

As Julia Kuznetski asserts in her chapter on Doris Lessing's *Mara and Dann* series (this volume), works of science fiction create fictional situations about a world that does not exist but is possible, especially if current trends continue. I would suggest that Butler's futuristic dystopia is a memorable example of such speculative fictions since it can be read as a cautionary tale showing what is very likely to happen to us and our world if we do not mend our ways and take constructive action. Although the so-called "apocalypse" in the background of events described in the novel is never explicitly explained, we know that it is not a single event, such as a nuclear war, an asteroid hit, or a deadly pandemic. Early in the *Parable of the Talents*, Lauren's husband Bankole explains—in some detail—that this man-made apocalypse was in fact a series of cascading events that gradually unfolded:

> I have read that the period of upheaval that journalists have begun to refer to as "the Apocalypse" or more commonly, more bitterly, the "Pox," lasted from 2015 to 2030 – a decade and a half of chaos. This is untrue. The Pox has been a much longer torment. It began well before 2015, perhaps even before the turn of the millennium. It has not ended. I have also read that the Pox was caused by accidentally coinciding climatic, economic, and sociological crises. It would be more honest to say that the Pox was caused by our own refusal to deal with obvious problems in those areas. We caused the problems: then we sat and watched as they grew into crises.
>
> (*PT* 8)

Bankole's summary roughly dates the beginning of the Pox to the time of the novel's publication, reiterating the point that Butler is indeed using the futuristic template to speak to her contemporary moment. Bankole further observes:

> I have watched education become a privilege of the rich than the basic necessity that it must be if civilized society is to survive. I have watched as convenience, profit, and inertia excused greater and more dangerous environmental degradation. I have watched poverty, hunger, and disease become inevitable for more and more people.
>
> (*PT* 8)

Here, Bankole becomes the spokesperson for a powerful message that is highlighted throughout the novel: it is mainly because humans were unable (or rather unwilling) to effectively address their current problems that the Pox came about and gradually became an irreversibly destructive force. Drawing on this point, I would argue that Butler's fictional construction of the Pox as "accidentally coinciding climatic, economic, and sociological crises" reflects her awareness of the complexity of living systems. From this perspective, I would also add that the novel successfully illustrates how the major problems (of our time) depicted in the *Earthseed* novels—environmental degradation, climate change, economic disparities, racial and gender discrimination—cannot be understood in isolation. Being systemic problems that are interconnected, they can be considered as various aspects of a single crisis (the Pox).

In a 1994 interview, Butler describes herself as "A pessimist if I'm not careful, a feminist, a Black, a former Baptist, an oil and water combination of ambition, laziness, insecurity, certainty, and drive" (Cobb 2010, 56). The protagonist of the *Earthseed* novels, Lauren, is very closely modeled after Butler to the point that she could be considered a stand-in for the writer herself. As Sandra Govan (2004, 246) suggests, the strikingly precocious Lauren "functions as the archetypal wise woman made young." *Parable of the Sower* depicts Lauren as a very young woman escaping her suburban enclave. As the book opens, we learn that although Lauren lost faith in her Baptist father's God a while ago, she still allows herself to be baptized. While her friends, neighbours, and family are relatively content with their life behind the walls of their small gated community, Lauren is haunted by a sense of impending doom and rightly predicts that sooner rather than later those walls will be breached. And when their commune is eventually attacked by outsiders, Lauren manages to escape and starts her arduous journey north, where she eventually starts her own community that she names Acorn.

The basis for Lauren's vision of an egalitarian and self-sustaining community is Earthseed, a belief system that gradually takes shape over the years: "With her bible, Earthseed: Book of the Living, Lauren creates a manual of praxis instead of mere faith and theory" (Hampton 2010, 92). Earthseed is thus part of a larger program that Lauren believes will increase humanity's chances of survival and assist their maturation as a species. It is, at the same time, an empowering creed that helps individuals uncover their hidden potential and thus become better versions of themselves. Emphasizing the significance of human agency in existentialist terms, Lauren says,

> We can choose. We can go on building and destroying until we either destroy ourselves or destroy the ability of our World to sustain us. Or we can make something more of ourselves. We can grow up. We can leave the nest.
>
> (*PT* 393)

On a personal level, Earthseed is undoubtedly Lauren's "positive obsession" that endows her existence with meaning and helps her survive the many challenges she faces throughout her life. Although her main motive is to instigate sociopolitical change, Lauren knows she will have a much better chance of realizing her goals if she can use the power of religion in the process:

> I must create not a dedicated little group of followers, not only a collection of communities as I had once imagined, but a movement. I must create a new fashion in faith – a fashion that can evolve into a new religion, a new guiding force, that can help humanity to put its great energy, competitiveness, and creativity to work doing the truly vast job of fulfilling the Destiny.
>
> (*PS* 267)

Religion, in this context, is a tool for "transforming the relation among diverse populations and between humans and the earth" (Mehaffy and Keating 2010 121). It can thus be argued that Lauren employs religion and spirituality to initiate and then support a systemic transformation. In Butler's own words,

> I wanted Lauren to envision, but then also to focus the Earthseed group toward, the goal of changing human attitudes about and treatment of the Earth and of each other. And a big part of that vision was to formulate not a national government but, instead, multiple communities, self-governing and – supporting, but also interactive with each other. In Lauren's religion, the Earthseed group's going back to the Earth, as at the end of Sower, means being alive again, literally and spiritually.
>
> (121)

As a new-age religion that is well-suited to the times in which we live, Earthseed is remarkably eclectic insofar as it combines spirituality with political, social, and even scientific insights. It is essentially a Darwinian religion that foregrounds evolution, change, and constant adaptation. Lacking a supernatural component, it also encourages its followers to orient themselves toward the universe with the idea of maximum flexibility. Earthseed strongly rejects the patriarchal conception of God as a transcendental being and proposes that "God is Change," urging people to "learn to shape God with forethought, care, and work; to educate and benefit their community, their families, and themselves; and to contribute to the Destiny" (*PS* 234). So Lauren's God is an unfolding event rather than a fixed, stable, unmovable entity that watches over his creations from above the skies. In the sequel to *Parable of the Sower*, Lauren's husband Bankole explains that "Some of the faces of her God are biological evolution, chaos theory, relativity theory, the uncertainty principle, and, of course, the second law of thermodynamics" (*PT* 46).

Lauren's construction of God as an infinitely malleable force that is intrinsically dynamic is most certainly a far cry from the image of God espoused by the monotheist tradition. Early in the novel, she says,

> A lot of people seem to believe in a big-daddy-God or a big-cop-God or a big-king-God. They believe in a kind of superperson. A few believe God is another word for nature. And nature turns out to mean just about anything they happen not to understand or feel in control of... So what is God? Just another name for whatever makes you feel special and protected.
>
> (*PS* 15)

All in all, Earthseed's conception of God is at the root of Lauren's wider program of opposing and subverting hegemonic patriarchal conceptions of knowledge and politics. Our conceptual frameworks are largely shaped by our social structures and a primary concern of ecofeminism is "making visible the various ways in which the dominations of women and nonhuman nature are sanctioned and perpetuated under patriarchy, and engaging in practices and developing analysis aimed at ending these dominations" (Warren 1997, 64).

Like ecofeminists, Lauren is acutely aware of the destructive significance of patriarchal religion for both nature and women, and she articulates a revolutionary consciousness through the teachings of Earthseed. Similar to spiritual ecofeminists, Lauren certainly sees "spirituality as a way to overcome and dismantle oppressive ideological frameworks as well as revalue female experiences and power" (Carroll 2018, 4). However, this revolutionary consciousness does not end up promoting the replacement of a patriarchal deity with a matriarchal one, since it calls into question all essentialist notions of divinity. Thus, Earthseed rejects not only the patriarchal conception of God that the monotheist tradition upholds but also the essentialist notion of an "earth mother goddess" based in cultural feminism (Melzer 2002, 36).

Lauren has the chance to put into practice many of the ideas she developed in Earthseed when she and a small group of followers start their commune, Acorn. As Claire Curtis (2010, 146) remarks, "The inhabitants of Acorn are motivated by an 'improve the earth' mentality, but it is one that will produce health and flourishing for the whole community." By founding Acorn, Lauren seeks to liberate men, women, and children from the structures of dominance that characterize patriarchy. Lauren writes,

> We'll have to be very careful how we allow our needs to shape us. But we must have arable land, a dependable water supply, and enough freedom from attack to let us establish ourselves and grow... We might be able to do it – grow our own food, grow ourselves and our neighbours into something brand new. Into Earthseed.
>
> (*PS* 223–224)

Although believing in Earthseed is not a precondition for living in Acorn, everybody who chooses to stay is to assume responsibility for healthcare, housework, teaching children, and other essential support work. As Mathias Nilges (2009, 1335) argues, Lauren's community "is presented to us as fundamentally progressive in its collective practices based upon change, in its celebration of diversity, and its acceptance of different sexual orientations." In this respect, Lauren's aim appears to be connecting those who are most vulnerable in a community which, in turn, can create a kind of strength that respects difference and does not scapegoat.

Ultimately, what Lauren successfully achieves with Acorn is nothing less than a nonviolent transformation of the structures of male dominance whereby balance and harmony between masculine and feminine values are restored. The earth-based sensibility that underpins Earthseed promotes an ecologically sustainable way of life. In this ecological community, those who had been dispossessed and overworked find a safe haven as well as new purpose. Acorn provides for them what Curtin (1997, 92) calls a caring context

> in which women and men can experience themselves as citizens in a broadly ecological community. This space, which is normally an ambiguous borderland, neither fully culture nor fully nature, can become a context in which the dualistic opposition between culture and nature is transformed.

Unlike other communes where people are unified primarily by place or property, Acorn is "a collective Project based on the conscious interdependence and agreement of its members, who must know, trust, and be able to work with each other for shared purposes" (Stillman 2003, 22). Since Acorn is also a very inclusive community, all differences are welcome and nobody suffers from discrimination. Hence, the tightly knit community of Acorn includes a diverse group of individuals including those who are gay, straight, white, Black, Latino, ex-slaves, and wanderers. In brief, Acorn is "an experiment in enlightened communalism a communalism that transcends differences in race, class, gender, and sexuality" (Phillips 2002, 309). *Earthseed: The Book of the Living* states:

> Embrace diversity.
> Unite –
> Or be divided
> robbed,
> ruled,
> killed,
> By those who see you as prey.
> Embrace diversity
> Or be destroyed.

(*PS* 176)

Lauren's ecofeminist perspective, informed by the theory of Earthseed and its practical application Acorn, effectively responds to many problems and questions we are currently dealing with by facing them holistically. Her remarkable ability to think in terms of relationships and patterns also allows her to see that all the major problems of her time are interrelated as well as mutually reinforcing. What is required, she comes to conclude, is a radical shift in our perceptions; we can only reconstruct the world by reconstructing our minds. Her vision of an emancipatory society is fundamentally informed by this outlook, which she promotes without asserting her power as a "leader" over others. It is important to note that Lauren "does not base her leadership on charisma or on the retention of power. Instead, she builds a group of equally powerful and self-conscious individuals, seeking to uncover leadership potential in others" (Agusti 2005, 358). Therefore, although Lauren provides guidance, assigns roles, and makes critical decisions, she never becomes an authoritarian ruler like President Jarrett, who rises to power in the election of 2032. Jarrett's authoritarian populism, and his promise to make "America Great Again" gains him mass support at a time when an overwhelming majority of American citizens have given in to despair. He successfully appeals to and inflames the worst impulses in people who he then mobilizes to further his own political agenda.

Jarrett, Lauren remarks,

> insists on being a throwback to some earlier, "simpler" time. The *Now* does not suit him. Religious tolerance does not suit him. The current state of the country does not suit him. He wants to take us all back to some magical time when everyone believed in the same God, worshipped him in the same way, and understood that their safety in the universe depended on completing the same religious rituals and stomping anyone who is different.
>
> (*PT* 19)

The kind of Christian fundamentalism espoused by Jarrett and his dedicated followers poses a striking contrast to the eclectic and inclusive philosophy of Earthseed. As a result, Lauren and her followers are soon designated as a threat by Jarrett's Christian crusaders who see them as heathen sinners. When a group of these Christian America Crusaders eventually attack and then take over Acorn, they turn it into a "Camp Christian Reeducation Facility." Demonizing Earthseed as a heathen belief system, these Christian fanatics go on to commit—on a regular basis—heinous crimes against the inhabitants of Acorn such as murder, rape, and physical as well as psychological torture. The children, including Lauren's daughter, are forcefully taken away from their families to be adopted by Christian Americans, while many—including Lauren's husband—are killed. The total destruction of the once flourishing Acorn in the hands of Christian fanatics shows how Utopias are always fragile, incomplete, and must constantly be fought for.

Lauren's husband Bankole had long feared the possibility of such an attack and urged Lauren to move with him to Halstead—a relatively well-off gated community where he would work as a doctor and she as a teacher. Although Bankole remained convinced that this opportunity was not to be missed since it would provide more safety and comfort to their nuclear family, Lauren never warmed up to the idea, thinking that in Halstead "there is mere existence." For Lauren, life is not about the pursuit of comfort and security but it should rather entail a stoic embrace of the harsh realities of existence and the search for meaning. That is to say, the purpose of life is to find a mode of being so meaningful that the fact that life is full of suffering becomes irrelevant. It is thus Lauren's unfaltering belief in her sense of mission and purpose that makes it possible for her to stay strong instead of giving up on her ideals even when all seems lost. And it is her extraordinary resilience as well as her cautious optimism that helps her endure the horrors of servitude under "Jarrett's Crusaders." Luckily, Lauren and the remaining inhabitants of Acorn eventually regain their freedom when a power failure disables their electronic slave collars, enabling them to overpower their captors. Having become even more adamant in striving toward her ambitious goals, Lauren gradually shifts her tactics by seeking alliances with rich and well-connected people in order to spread the message of Earthseed. By the end of the novel, Earthseed has attained a huge following and the first shuttles are launched into space:

> Earthseed was an unusual cult. It financed scientific exploration and inquiry, and technological creativity. It set up grade schools and eventually colleges, and offered full scholarships to poor but gifted students. The students who accepted had to agree to spend seven years of teaching, practicing medicine, or otherwise using their skills to improve life in the many Earthseed communities. Ultimately the intent was to help the communities to launch themselves toward the stars and to live on the distant worlds they found circling those stars.
>
> (*PT* 415–416)

All in all, the end of the novel marks the fulfillment of Lauren's lifelong dream, the accomplishment of the "Destiny," which was inspired by and rooted in Lauren's recognition that humans will need

> a new environment, another planet to be exact, on which to settle so that they can adapt into a healthier, diverse, and more peacefully coexistent species and spread their seed, to use the overarching organic metaphor that controls the novel series.
>
> (Allen 2009, 1360)

It is quite remarkable that, despite her extremely trying and often devastating experiences in the world, Lauren never loses faith in humanity, or perhaps rather in the belief that humans can evolve into better beings. Yet it certainly is not simply this unwavering faith in humanity or some kind of naive optimism that brings her success. Lauren clearly has the will to set her mind in motion and she continuously shows the ability to get things done. She is moreover portrayed as an ideal leader who employs her power in the service of altering the conditions of other people for the better. She serves a purpose beyond herself and inspires others to do the same. Most significantly, she constantly tries to articulate new possibilities for agency and action that have been denied to especially the disenfranchised members of the populace.

I agree with Rachel Sears' (2015, 28) suggestion that "Butler exposes a myriad of feminist concerns in her Parable novels; however, she champions the concerns of Ecofeminists unlike any dystopian novelist before her." Like ecofeminists, Butler stresses the importance of acknowledging that we are part of an interconnected system of life that supports our survival. In her discussion of Merlinda Bobi's *Locust Girl* as an example of ecofeminist science fiction, Iris Ralph (this volume) draws attention to the destructive effects of dominant masculine values, such as aggressive territorial expansionist behavior, confrontation as opposed to compromise, domination, competition, absolutism, and a deficit of empathy and compassion for the environment. The *Earthseed* novels also foreground the harmful effects of masculinist thinking and offer an alternative way of relating to the environment and others. As Earthseed teaches us, we should strive to live harmoniously and oppose all forms of domination. Relative to this point, both novels powerfully assert that environmental destruction and social injustice (racism, poverty, sexism) have a common cause—a particular kind of hierarchical and dualistic thinking that is rooted in oppressive patriarchy. Thus both novels strongly assert the point that, in order to address environmental destruction, we must challenge value-hierarchical frameworks and ways of thinking. In the words of Audre Lorde, "The future of our earth may depend upon the ability of all women to identify and develop new definitions of power and new patterns of relating across difference" (Melzer 2002, 32).

As her life and teachings aptly illustrate, Lauren is acutely aware of the fact that addressing environmental injustices requires addressing social injustices. Confronted with circumstances that are not of her making, she is rendered into a marginal and yet she uses her agency and resources to bring on a new world. She also motivates others to grow into their highest potential by liberating them from the ties and binds on their subjectivity and their agency. Similar to Butler, Lauren sees existence as an interconnected web. Thus, her critical intervention with the paradigm-shifting Earthseed is fundamentally shaped by a view of the world that respects all creation, holistic connections, and the value of collaboration. She is, in many ways, a spokesperson for Butler, who has always considered the vocation of writing as an instrument for instigating change on both an individual and societal level:

When I write a book, if I influence one person who goes on to influence others, then probably I've done something worthwhile if the influence is good. Nobody can see how long their books will last or how much influence they'll have, so I just assume that at least I can make a few people think. I don't know what will come of that, possibly nothing, but you never know what that one kid, for instance, sitting in the back of the room is going to wind up doing.

(Mehaffy and Keating 2010, 117)

Butler's work has contributed significantly to ongoing conversations on a variety of contemporary issues ranging from ecology and feminisms to forms of discrimination on the basis of gender, race, and class. As Michelle Deininger and Gemma Scammell (this volume) maintain, ecofeminist science fiction has the power to reimagine and transform the world. Given the increasing critical and popular interest in Butler's fiction as well as the uncanny prescience of her future visions, her work is more relevant than ever. Most important in relation to my purposes here is her advocacy of an ecofeminist future defined by Glynis Carr (2011, xvii) as "a world free of oppressions based on sex, race, class, and nation that is also environmentally sustainable and sound." As Butler strongly suggests in her *Earthseed* novels, working toward this goal entails embracing connecting struggles and exploring more ways to work and live together. In her words, "I don't think any of us can know how things will be in the future. We're creating the future, but we can't see it clearly. We can only try to make it better" (Williams 2010, 176).

This message has a particular urgency and resonance as I am writing these words in October 2020, at a time when the COVID-19 pandemic continues to wreak havoc all across the planet. The virus has clearly demonstrated the degree to which we are all interconnected and how much we indeed need to cooperate on a planet-wide scale. Having caused a rupture in the exterior order of our existence, it has also forced large numbers of people to re-examine and reconfigure their fundamental relationships with each other and with the environment. As modern economic structures—supported by vested economic interests—crumble down, millions of people have been shocked into new forms of awareness that may indeed mark a significant turning point in the history of our species. While repeated economic and environmental disasters in recent history were not enough to curb the appetites of multinational corporations or wake decision makers from their slumber, a small virus has brought the planet to the brink of wholescale systemic collapse. In this period of massive uncertainty, fear, and confusion, the story we tell ourselves about COVID-19 is of critical importance. A crisis of this scale *may* precipitate evolution and we can grow through what we go through.

As a pattern-seeking and storytelling species, our lives are defined and shaped in many ways by the narratives that surround us. Works of speculative science fiction obviously play a very vital role in this context; they encourage us to look at our problem from different perspectives so that we can shift our orientation to the problems and perceive them in new ways that would be impactful to us. They thus open people up to different points of view and bring them to new ways of thinking. Seen through this lens, both *Earthseed* novels make it abundantly clear that the only effective course of action is to adjust our systems and lifestyles to acknowledge that we are all interconnected. Butler shows us that even in the darkest places there is hope and that with clear-sightedness, determination, and will, we could perhaps find breakthroughs in breakdowns.

References

Agusti, Clara Escoda. 2005. "The Relationship between Community and Subjectivity in Octavia E. Butler's *Parable of the Sower.*" *Extrapolation* 46, no. 3: 351–359.

Allen, Marlene D. 2009. "Octavia Butler's Parable Novels and the 'Boomerang' of African American History." *Callaloo* 32, no. 4: 1353–1365.

Butler, Octavia. 1993. *Parable of the Sower*. New York: Grand Central Publishing.

Butler, Octavia. 2000. *Parable of the Talents*. New York: Aspect.

Carr, Glynis. 2011. "Foreword." In *Ecofeminism and Rhetoric: Critical Perspectives on Sex, Technology, and Discourse*, edited by Douglas A. Vakoch, ix–xix. New York: Berghahn Books.

Carroll, Valerie Padilla. 2018. "Introduction: Ecofeminist Dialogues." In *Ecofeminism in Dialogue*, edited by Douglas A. Vakoch and Sam Mickey, 1–12. Lanham, MD: Lexington Books.

Cobb, Jelani. 2010. "Interview with Octavia Butler." In *Conversations with Octavia Butler*, edited by Conseula Francis, 49–64. Jackson: University Press of Mississippi.

Curtin, Deane. 1997. "Women's Knowledge as Expert Knowledge: Indian Women and Ecodevelopment." In *Ecofeminism: Women, Culture, Nature*, edited by Karen J. Warren, 82–98. Indianapolis: Indiana University Press.

Curtis, Claire P. 2010. *Postapocalyptic Fiction and the Social Contract*. Lanham, MD: Lexington Books.

Değirmenci Altın, Aslı. 2021. "Anthropocentric and Androcentric Ideologies in Jeanette Winterson's *The Stone Gods*: An Ecofeminist Reading." In *Ecofeminist Science Fiction: International Perspectives on Gender, Ecology, and Literature*, edited by Douglas A. Vakoch, 63–74. Abingdon: Routledge.

Govan, Sandra. 2004. "The Parable of the Sower as Rendered by Octavia Butler: Lessons for Our Changing Times." *Femspec* 4, no. 2: 239–258.

Hampton, Gregory Jerome. 2010. *Changing Bodies in the Fiction of Octavia Butler*. Lanham, MD: Lexington Books.

Kilgore, De Witt Douglas, and Ranu Samantrai. 2010. "A Memorial to Octavia Butler." *Science-Fiction Studies* 37, no. 3: 353–361.

McCaffery, Larry, and Jim McMenamin. 2010. "An Interview with Octavia E. Butler." In *Conversations with Octavia Butler*, edited by Conseula Francis, 10–26. Jackson: University Press of Mississippi.

Mehaffy, Marilyn, and Ana Louise Keating. 2010. "'Radio Imagination.' Octavia Butler on the Poetics of Narrative Embodiment." In *Conversations with Octavia Butler*, edited by Conseula Francis, 98–122. Jackson: University Press of Mississippi.

Melzer, Patricia. 2002. "'All That You Touch You Change': Utopian Desire and the Concept of Change in Octavia Butler's Parable of the Sower and Parable of the Talents." *Fempsec* 3, no. 2: 31–52.

Mudaliar, Meghna. 2021. "Queering *Doctor Who* and *Supernatural*: An Ecofeminist Response to Bill Potts and Charlie Bradbury." In *Ecofeminist Science Fiction: International Perspectives on Gender, Ecology, and Literature*, edited by Douglas A. Vakoch, 87–98. Abingdon: Routledge.

Nilges, Mathias. 2009. "We Need the Stars: Change, Community, and the Absent Father in Octavia Butler's *Parable of the Sower* and *Parable of the Talents*." *Callaloo* 32, no. 4: 1332–1352.

Phillips, Jerry. 2002. "The Intuition of the Future: Utopia and Catastrophe in Octavia Butler's *Parable of the Sower*." *Novel – A Forum on Fiction* 35, no. 2–3: 299–311.

Robertson, Benjamin. 2010. "'Some Matching Strangeness': Biology, Politics and the Embrace of History in Octavia Butler's *Kindred*." *Science-Fiction Studies* 37, no. 3: 362–381.

Rose, Lydia, and Teresa M. Bartoli. 2021. "Hegemonic Masculinity and Tropes of Domination: An Ecofeminist Analysis of James Cameron's 2009 Film *Avatar*." In *Ecofeminist Science Fiction: International Perspectives on Gender, Ecology, and Literature*, edited by Douglas A. Vakoch, 141–156. Abingdon: Routledge.

Sears, Rachel. 2015. "Butler: To Take Root Among the Stars." *Plaza: Dialogues in Language and Literature* 5, no. 2: 22–31.

Stillman, Peter. 2003. "Dystopian Critiques, Utopian Possibilities, and Human Purposes in Octavia Butler's *Parables*." *Utopian Studies* 14, no. 1: 15–35.

Sturgeon, Noël. 1997. *Ecofeminist Natures: Race, Gender, Feminist Theory and Political Action*. New York: Routledge.

Warren, Karen J., ed. 1997. *Ecofeminism: Women, Culture, Nature*. Indianapolis: Indiana University Press.

Williams, Juan. 2010. "Octavia Butler." In *Conversations with Octavia Butler*, edited by Conseula Francis, 161–180. Jackson: University Press of Mississippi.

2 An Ecofeminist Treatment of Nourishment and Feeding in Margaret Atwood's *MaddAddam* Trilogy

Debra Wain

Current climate change literature and literary criticism focuses on the antici-pated consequences of climate change but of particular significance for this chapter are the impacts of a changed climate on food and food production. The climate-changed setting within Margaret Atwood's *MaddAddam* tril-ogy highlights these impacts as they pertain to women's traditional domes-tic roles, which are aligned with ecofeminist principles relating to the ways that women and the environment are connected. Women's responsibility for food preparation is not only a means of oppression; food choices can also be linked to autonomy and power, resistance, and may even be seen as political acts. When women prepare food, they wield power over food choices. These choices are socially and culturally influenced (Blend 2021) but they in turn impact the environment so women are closer to an "awareness of environ-mental hazard, whether it is by shopping for food … preparing that food for safe eating, or caring for the health of their children" (Buckingham-Hatfield 2000, 1). We see this power and responsibility reflected in real-world exam-ples of the slow food movement, the desire for organic produce, and environ-mentally and socially aligned arguments for a plant-based diet. These matters are all considered within Atwood's *MaddAddam* trilogy. For the purposes of this chapter, Atwood's *MaddAddam* trilogy will be considered in more spe-cific terms than the broader "science-fiction" (Brandão and Cavalcanti, this volume) and will be regarded as climate change fiction or cli-fi.

The gendered nature of food work has long signified the oppression of women from varied backgrounds and life experiences. Despite the advances made by feminism, women are expected, as Emily Matchar explains, to maintain work outside the home but still get 78% of the home-cooked meals on the table (2013). This women-can-do-it-all mentality comes to us thanks to what Arlie Hochschild (2012) refers to as feminism's stalled revolution whereby many women felt the pressure to undertake employment outside of the home but also be responsible for the home duties which resulted in mak-ing full equality unattainable (Cairns and Johnston 2015). Women's respon-sibility for the food eaten by their families and communities is impacted upon by the environment and changes that occur within it. An ecofeminist argument would also point out that women have a connection with the

Figure 2.1 Visual representation of intersecting notions of food, environment, and women.

environment which means they are impacted by climate change to a greater degree than men within their community but also that they are in a better position to make changes that impact the environment, its preservation and/ or destruction but, as discussed by Benay Blend (2021), we should guard against ideas that romanticize this connection. Atwood's novels included within the *MaddAddam* Trilogy: *Oryx and Crake* (2003), *The Year of the Flood* (2009), and *MaddAddam* (2013) bring together a climate-changed future setting; a focus on food and its impacts on the environment, society, and people; and an ecofeminist perspective. These ideas will be discussed as if intersections found upon a Venn diagram (Figure 2.1). Under sections covering these intersections, this chapter will look specifically at the ways in which such ideas come together within Atwood's *MaddAddam* trilogy.

Climate Change (Nature) and Women

When discussing Atwood's *MaddAddam* novels it is necessary to first consider the structure of the three texts. The initial novel, *Oryx and Crake*, is focalized through a character who thinks he could be the only surviving human after an apocalyptic event caused by his childhood friend, Crake; the second, *The Year of the Flood*, offers a female perspective and retells events mainly from the points of view of Toby and Ren; finally, there is further narration by Toby which is balanced by some narration from her male romantic interest, Zeb, in *MaddAddam*. The significance of this positioning of the reader lies in the content and attitudes within the novels and it is this positioning that is the basis for an ecofeminist reading of the trilogy. The second and third novels reframe the content of the first and refocus the reader on the aspects relating to an ecofeminist reading.

The world the surviving humans have inherited in the *MaddAddam* novels is a result of environmental destruction and climate change in conjunction with the classic science-fiction premise of scientific advancement as out-of-control and unchecked by ethics. The efforts made by science within the fiction relate directly to ecofeminist philosopher Vandana Shiva's (2002) criticism of the green revolution involving scientists in laboratories trying to ensure the world's population is fed through a techno-fix with no consideration of the social and ecological settings within which it would be put to use. The ramifications of this unchecked scientific progress for women and female children within the Kallar community, for example, were dire and it has "deepened the sex-bias against women" including, in its most extreme form, female infanticide (Shiva 2002, 119). Atwood depicts Western women and families mostly as a counterpoint to the realities faced by women in developing countries. These realities are introduced by the character, Oryx whose family sold her into sex slavery because they could not feed all of the children. Her lot was being "[s]old, or being thrown into the river, to float away to the sea; because there was only so much food to go around" (Atwood 2003, 135). Shiva's criticism of the green revolution's approach is based on the understanding that Science's ability to provide enough food does not improve outcomes for many women (2002).

Mary Mellor argues that environmental issues are gendered issues because men are "in a position to affect environmental decision-making" and women are "at the mercy of those decisions" (2003, 13). This aspect of ecofeminism is not addressed explicitly within Atwood's *MaddAddam* trilogy but rather through the more oblique approach of matching content with a particular point of view. The environmental destruction and the devastating anthropogenic environmental changes detailed in *Oryx and Crake* are equated with the actions of men through the two male protagonists and the focalization of the third person narrative through Jimmy (or Snowman). The tone of the narrative is one of angst, futility, and hopelessness. There is a noted change in Jimmy's attitude toward conservation and the environment. This is particularly evident in his attitude toward animals and animal cruelty relating to ideas of ethical eating. When he is younger, Jimmy identifies more strongly with his mother, so he can be read with a more feminine alignment. As a child, he is concerned about who has the right to eat whom, as noted in his concern for the pigoons, a genetically modified pig designed to provide replacement organs for humans. Jimmy identifies with the animals and recognizes parallels between their lack of autonomy and his:

> Jimmy didn't want to eat a pigoon because he thought of pigoons as creatures much like himself. Neither he nor they had a lot of say in what was going on.
>
> (Atwood 2003, 27)

Pigoons as a food source is later complicated, in *MaddAddam*, when the humans recognize them as beings capable of communication, a matter also discussed by Lesley Kordecki (2021).

In early adulthood, Jimmy is confronted by the spectacle of meat production taken to "horrific dystopian extremes" in the ChickiNobs laboratory where Crake studies (Bedford 2015, 78). The description of the modified animal by a tour guide as "a mouth opening at the top, they dump the nutrients in there. No eyes or beak or anything, they don't need those" (Atwood 2003, 238) is a Frankenstein-esque result of experimentation, the creation of something new that consists only of parts of the naturally formed whole. The ChickiNobs protein-monsters are grown in a laboratory, not a farm. Nature has been eradicated from the production process. Blend (2021) discusses similar manipulation of corn which takes on a sacrilegious aspect with its significance to the Ojibwe. The production of animals in a laboratory undermines the natural procreation of a species. This points to the excision of women from the generative process. Humanity as apart from the natural world or human exceptionalism (Galbreath 2010, 1) is also reflected in Atwood's description of the after-hours genetic engineering treated like a game that those who participated called "create-an-animal" (Atwood 2003, 57). Human exceptionalism is also addressed by Lesley Kordecki in discussing Mary Doria Russell's *The Sparrow* and in Sarah Bezan's discussion of speculative sex in Larissa Lai's *Salt Fish Girl* (2021). Atwood again subtly points to these activities being a masculine preoccupation: "[It] was so much fun, said the guys doing it; it made you feel like God" (Atwood 2003, 57).

The premises of the first two novels set up the masculine *nature as adversary* and desire "to conquer nature" (Mier 2010, 93) against the feminine *nature as nurturer* or "care taker, provider" (Alphonsa 2017, 33). The first is embodied in Jimmy's inability to survive without the processed foods that he has relied upon his whole life—the natural world is presented as hostile to his survival. He realizes that without the likes of canned Sveltana No-Meat Cocktail Sausages, SoyOBoy Burgers, JoltBars, and CrustaeSoy "he's slowly starving to death" (Atwood 2003, 175). This contrasts with the images of the God's Gardeners within *The Year of the Flood* which is narrated by female narrators, Toby and Ren. The Garden at the center of their eco-worship is both Eden and Ecology. The Saints' days that make up the calendar of sacred celebrations honor only a few Judeo-Christian identities and focus instead on cultural leaders, ecologists, biologists, conservation philosophers, and theorists who focused on human impacts, scale, and sustainability. Toby lists some when she discusses keeping track of the days and although the list includes both men and women, and the origins are not with Toby herself but with Adam One, the structure of the narrative colors this information as belonging to, or at least being aligned with, the female protagonist. This is reinforced by her continued acknowledgment of these festivals and feast days despite her religious doubts (Atwood 2009, 2).

The most explicit ecofeminist stance is provided by one of the protagonists of *Oryx and Crake*, and the character to which the narrative owes its post-apocalyptic trajectory. Crake is disdainful of the human response to crisis being so disconnected from what is natural. Of humans, he says, "[*Homo sapiens* is] one of the few species that doesn't limit reproduction in the face of dwindling resources ... the less we eat, the more we fuck" (Atwood 2009, 139). Such balances and disturbances are also discussed by Kordecki (2021). Crake's techno-fix for anthropogenic environmental destruction still sees humans as separate from, and dominant over, nature (Galbreath 2010). Unlike Judith Butler's "Pox" in *Parable of Talents* (2000, 8) discussed by Hatice Övgü Tüzün (this volume), Crake does act to address the current climatic and environmental problems by attempting to replace humanity with a post-human hybrid of his own design. A game of "create-an-animal" with the human genome as the base materials (Atwood 2003, 57).

Women and Food

Within both literary studies and food studies, food prepared and served within the family comes to symbolize security and comfort. Issues of food security are linked to these representations of food and impact on autonomy and control, self-determination and empowerment, especially as these things relate to the women who are "tied to the traditional connection between food, care, and femininity, including a relationship of obligation and responsibility around food" (Aarseth and Olsen 2008, 282). A number of studies discussing women's roles maintaining foodways practices show that women see the power inherent in the role even while acknowledging this gendered work has been responsible for the construction and signification of their oppression (Ashley et al. 2004; Avakian 2005; D'Sylva and Beagan 2011; Lockie 2001; Kalivas 2007). The commodification of nature and the techno-scientific commandeering of food production and preparation in Atwood's future world can be seen to impact women's value in this role. There is a patriarchal undermining of the value of food and cooking that is reflected in the devaluation of the environment and nature thus further linking the female characters and the environment.

Oryx and Crake presents a disruption to the traditional gendered work in relation to food production. The narrative focus on Jimmy as he grows up determines that many of the female characters act as mother figures, but these women are not generally depicted as nurturers. This could be read as a second-wave feminist move away from the home and into the public sphere or, alternatively, as reflecting a society-wide breakdown of the nuclear family which typifies the climate-changed reality of the narrative world. Both Jimmy's and Crake's mothers are presented as broken or consumed by the world they live in. Similarly, Oryx has been commodified and consumed by the "patriarchal market" as discussed by Brandão and Cavalcanti (this volume). The mothers do not cook or produce anything, they are themselves eaten up by their roles within their corporate compounds. They are depicted as "resources" in parallel with those of the natural environment and appreciated only for their "instrumental value" (Bedford 2015, 76). In Jimmy's mother's case, she is wracked by guilt over her part in scientific advances that she later regrets (Atwood 2003).

Despite this, kitchens remain important spaces as symbolic of family function, nurturing, and comfort. The lack of these qualities within the scenes of Jimmy's childhood adds to the reader's experience of the society, environment, and family as broken in Atwood's dystopic future world. When he came home from school, Jimmy would find his mother sitting at the kitchen table "a cup of coffee in front of her, untouched" (Atwood 2003, 35). The kitchen is a site of both connection and disconnection. It is the place where he finds her, but where she is also lost. Later Jimmy has two dreams of his mother, in both instances she is in the kitchen:

> Jimmy's in the kitchen of the house they lived in when he was five, sitting at the table. It's lunchtime. In front of him on a plate is a round of bread—a flat peanut butter head with a gleaming jelly smile, raisins for teeth. This thing fills him with dread.
>
> (Atwood 2003, 311)

After Jimmy's mother disappears, Jimmy's relationship with his father's new girlfriend, Ramona, is also depicted through food. The slightly defective nature of their relationship is reflected in the mass-produced food that Ramona provides: "she microwaved dinner just for herself and Jimmy" or made popcorn "pouring melted butter substitute onto it" for them to eat while watching DVDs (Atwood 2003, 76). Jimmy accepts these foods from Ramona but later must refuse the Crakers' offer of "several caecotrophs they'd kept specially for him." Jimmy's refusal is softened by "explain[ing] carefully that their food was not his food" (Atwood 2003, 187). This need to explain *carefully* reinforces the notion that such offers of food are imbued with social as well as environmental importance (Bell and Valentine 1997; Avakian 2005; Knoebel 2016).

Crake's mother is similarly disconnected from the provision of nourishment. She would prepare "something that would pass as a snack" such as "stale crackers" with "chewy orange-and-white marbled hunks of cheesefood" (Atwood 2003, 101). The dysfunction is evident in both the food itself and the fact that she would sometimes "stop in the middle of her preparations" and stand still staring as if she could see someone else in the room (Atwood 2003, 101). There is something distant and detached about Crake's mother; she too has been consumed and damaged by her life.

Examples of kitchens as spaces of absence and lack in *Oryx and Crake* is in contrast to feminine domesticity as a power role rather than a form of oppression (Ashley 2004; Matchar 2013). The autonomy of such roles lies within the food choices, in food preparation as a political act, and is related to environmental sustainability choices made by women (Matchar 2013). This means of regaining control is depicted in *The Year of the Flood*. Atwood's second novel in the trilogy reinforces the importance of women as food preparers—this role is re-established and honored by the God's Gardeners as a survival skill and as the "social glue" that holds the community together (Bell and Valentine 1997). Instead of outsourcing this responsibility to unethical corporations, the God's Gardeners celebrate, on a religious level, the activities necessary to feed themselves resulting in their autonomy and resistance against the *status quo*. Similar to the Gardener principles of their intentional community in *The Year of the Flood* and *MaddAddam*, Octavia Butler's protagonist, Lauren in *Parable of the Sower*, establishes "Earthseed" as a belief system as the basis of her sustainable community (Tüzün, this volume) both systems rely on the devotion of "faith" combined with the practicality of science and reason.

There are a number of scholars discussing the return of twenty-first-century women to domestic roles. Studies such as Matchar's *Homeward Bound* interviews, Ariel Knoebel's women in the alternative food movement, Monica White's women urban gardeners, and the craft-working activists studied by Jack Bratich and Heidi Brush, all suggest that women have real reasons—environmental, social, ethical, revolutionary—for choosing to participate in roles that were once assigned to, and expected of, women (Bratich and Brush 2011; Knoebel 2016; Machar 2013; White 2011). The results of such studies into women's reasons to re-embrace roles traditionally thought to be *women's work* encompass a number of contemporary issues that range from ecologically related food security concerns to health and well-being choices, to a disillusionment with the sexism of a patriarchal corporate workplace (Matchar 2013). Atwood's female characters in *Oryx and Crake* have been denied this choice, and therefore the opportunity to engage in social and environmental resistance. The results of having such options available are developed in *The Year of the Flood* which suggests that instead of shutting off these choices for women, we need to acknowledge their reasons for returning to them. Bratich and Brush look at this movement as a *"detourning"* (2011, 239) of these roles and the home, a rerouting or hijacking of old meanings and motives in order to see the power in embracing this autonomy.

Food and Climate Change

Food is used in fiction for a number of purposes, one of which includes its use as a symbolic representation of safety and well-being (Gopnik 2011). This is often linked to the previously discussed imagery of home and family.

In a cli-fi context, this notion of safety expands to encompass concepts of food security. Both the pre- and post-flood worlds of Atwood's trilogy depict food scarcity. The pre-flood world of *Oryx & Crake* is rife with scientific, genetic manipulations within food production designed to feed the population despite climate changes.

Techno-scientific solutions to food shortages are explored in the pre-flood world of *Oryx and Crake*. This male-dominated, transgenic approach is pursued in further descriptions of food at Watson-Crick. At lunch, Crake had the "kanga-lamb, a new Australian splice" which is presented as a solution to "methane-producing, ozone-destroying flatulence" produced by other animals reared for meat (Atwood 2003, 344). The pinnacle of this stance is to be seen in Crake's solution for the planet. He explains to Jimmy that "[a]s a species we're in deep trouble," that this trouble exceeds what is being reported and that "very soon, demand is going to exceed supply for everyone" (Atwood 2003, 347). Crake's solution is to exterminate humanity and replace it with the Crakers who have been engineered not only to survive in the environmental conditions that human impacts have created but also to not wreak the havoc that humanity has/is.

Jimmy recalls that his mother "rambled on" about "her grandfather's Florida grapefruit orchard that had dried up like a giant raisin when the rains had stopped coming" (Atwood 2003, 72). This links to a masculine commodification of the environment. It is no accident that Atwood uses a grandfather, as opposed to grandmother or grandparents, as an orchardist—the environment is depicted as a resource to be exploited by the patriarchal figure. This idea of exploitation is reflected in Jimmy and Crake's consumption of monstrously surreal television programs such as the "Queek Geek Show" which featured "the eating of live animals and birds, timed by stopwatches" for "prizes of hard-to-come-by foods" (Atwood 2003, 97).

In response to the environmental changes and the altered climate, food production has been taken out of the hands of nature (women) and put into the hands of science (men). Transgenic solutions are pursued within the science-driven compounds (Galbreath 2010). The narrative points out that the corporate site where the pigoons are raised and harvested "wasn't really a farm" (Atwood 2003, 25). The ChickieNobs laboratory is not a farm either. In contrast, Toby's narration of life with the God's Gardeners in *The Year of the Flood* includes images of sustainability where Toby learns cooking, gardening, and beekeeping. The respect inherent in these activities is seen as a positive and proactive response to the environmental crisis. Zeb, another God's Gardener, is a realist, teaching the Gardener children the hunting skills they will need if the environmental damage cannot be mitigated (Atwood 2009) which contrasts with the current sanitized presentation of meat (Galbreath 2010). *The Year of the Flood* acts as a climate change solution counterpoint to *Oryx and Crake*. The Gardeners' sustainability practices and spirituality linked to feast and Saints' days provide a framework for living on a damaged planet. The Saints' days and feast days link environmental awareness, history, sustainability, autonomy, and food. It is important to note that in *Oryx and Crake*, Atwood takes every opportunity to point out the monstrous nature of the manufactured food that is supposed to sustain the characters. This continues in *The Year of the Flood* until the point where Toby is taken in by the God's Gardeners when *real* food is presented as providing real sustenance and nourishment—physical, emotional, and spiritual (Atwood 2003; 2009; 2013). Finally, in *MaddAddam*, we are presented with images of nourishment in the form of breakfasts, "the most hopeful (or utopian) meal" that "repeatedly frame this account of civilization's destruction" (Boyd 2015, 161). According to Shelley Boyd, this is "in keeping with Atwood's theory that utopias and dystopias are not opposites but, rather, co-related" (2015, 161) and leads us to question the nature of nourishment in this post-apocalyptic context as it might reflect on our real choices today, which are also not opposites.

The quality of the food available to characters in *Oryx and Crake* is also used to represent affluence. Jimmy's poorly provisioned tertiary Arts institution, Martha Graham Academy, contrasts Crake's well-funded science institution, Watson-Crick Institute where "the food in Crake's dining hall was fantastic—real shrimps instead of the CrustaeSoy they got at Martha Graham, and real chicken" and "the desserts were heavy on the chocolate, real chocolate" (Atwood 2003, 244–245). Heather Eaton points out such disparity is evident where "the corporate world has colonized everywhere" and corporations "give millions to universities to develop biotech programs" while they allow programs such as liberal arts to dwindle (2003, 30–31) Maria Aline Ferreira notes that this typifies "the divide between the sciences and the humanities" and the hierarchy of the two that leaves the Arts "occupying an inferior place in the context of the overpowering technological corporations" (2015, 44). The commercial support of education as depicted by food quality in the novels is indicative of the process followed by the patriarchal techno-scientific approach to repairing climate change.

In the post-flood setting of Atwood's trilogy, food scarcity is more pronounced, and the food choices made by characters relate more to survival than to an abstract set of ethics. Toby attempts to stick to her veggie vows but is forced to cook up a meal of "land shrimp" (Atwood 2009) and Rebecca serves up "pig in three forms: bacon, ham, and chops" (Atwood 2013, 34) while Snowman is driven by more selfish desires. The reader is unsurprised by Snowman's attitudes to food and survival but the pragmatic changes to Gardener attitudes serve to underpin the seriousness of the situation, indicating that options for doing better or repairing the damage are gone.

Queering a Conclusion

None of the depictions relating specifically to an ecofeminist reading of Atwood's trilogy are explicit. The alignment of nature with women is achieved through the subtlety of the narrative positionings of the three novels. In addition to this, the conclusion of the series should be taken into consideration. In some ways, the return of the survivors to a village structure rather than a nuclear family structure, and a suggestion of dispensing with traditional monogamous couplings encouraged by Craker mating practices leads us then to a queering of the ecofeminist reading.

The only reference to non-heterosexual coupled relationships occurs in *Oryx and Crake* when Jimmy recalls his development of advertising media to sell the BlyssPluss pill: "Simulations of a man and a woman, ripping off their clothes, grinning like maniacs. Then a man and a man. Then a woman and a woman ... Then a threesome." (Atwood 2003, 367). However, the heteronormative couplings are not depicted as of value within the narratives and are, instead, indicative of the flawed system rife with abuses of nature. The narrative of Atwood's final pages of *MaddAddam* portrays a diminished role for binary opposites that are "exclusive (rather than inclusive)", "oppositional (rather than complementary)" and hierarchical (Warren 1987, 6). Again, it is the structure of the narrative that provides this option for reading.

The solutions offered up by Atwood suggests a blurring of boundaries whereby the human/nonhuman distinction becomes less clear. The Crakers are both genetically (and largely structurally) human but they also contain genetic specifications for, amongst other things, "UV-resistant skin, a built-in insect repellent, an unprecedented ability to digest unrefined plant material" (Atwood 2003, 358). The first two novels provide a distancing of these post-human hybrids by largely discussing them as a group, making them indistinct which aligns with Val Plumwood's "homogenisation of the other" (1993, 57). Similarly predicted post-human futures, as presented in Winterson's *The Stone Gods* and discussed by Aslı Değirmenci, in the literature of Louise Lawrence discussed by Michelle Deininger and Gemma Scammell, and in Larissa Lai's *Salt Fish Girl* discussed by Sarah Bezan (2021) can be specifically linked to the stance taken in Atwood's works. By the end of *MaddAddam*, Atwood has a Craker named Blackbeard provide the conclusion to the story. The Crakers have therefore taken on the autonomy of storytellers. The oppositions and discrete definitions of one body and the next are also challenged by the Crakers' ability to communicate with the pigoons. Not only does this present cross-species communication; it is also nonverbal, which further suggests a loosening of bodily boundaries (Atwood 2013).

Margaret Atwood's novels within the *MaddAddam* trilogy potentially queer the traditional ecofeminist reading and suggest that the future of the planet might be post-human.

References

Aarseth, Helene, and Bente Marianne Olsen. 2008. "Food and Masculinity in Dual Career Couples." *Journal of Gender Studies* 17, no. 4: 277–287.

Alphonsa, S.R.P.J. 2017. "An Ecofeminist Reading to Denise Levertov's Selected Poems." *India University Grants Commission, New Delhi Recognized Journal No. 41311.* 5, no. 6: 30–35.

Ashley, Bob, Joanne Hollows, Steve Jones, and Ben Taylor. 2004. *Food and Cultural Studies.* London: Routledge.

Atwood, Margaret. 2003. *Oryx & Crake.* London: Virago Press.

Atwood, Margaret. 2009. *The Year of the Flood.* London: Virago Press.

Atwood, Margaret. 2013. *MaddAddam.* London: Virago Press.

Avakian, Arlene Voski. 2005. "Shish Kebab Armenians?: Food and the Construction and Maintenance of Ethnic and Gender Identities among Armenian American Feminists." In *From Betty Crocker to Feminist Food Studies: Critical Perspectives on Women and Food*, edited by Arlene Voski Avakian and Barbara Haber, 257–280. Amherst: University of Massachusetts Press.

Bedford, Anna. 2015. "Survival in the Post-Apocalypse: Ecofeminism in *MaddAddam*." In *Margaret Atwood's Apocalypses*, edited by Karma Waltonen, 71–92. Newcastle upon Tyne: Cambridge Scholars Publishing.

Bell, David, and Gill Valentine. 1997. *Consuming Geographies: We Are Where We Eat.* London: Routledge.

Beoku-Betts, Josephine A. 1995. "'We Got Our Way of Cooking Things': Women, Food, and Preservation of Cultural Identity among the Gullah." *Gender & Society* 9, no. 5: 535–555.

Bezan, Sarah. 2021. "Speculative Sex: Queering Aqueous Natures and Biotechnological Futures in Larissa Lai's *Salt Fish Girl*." In *Ecofeminist Science Fiction: International Perspectives on Gender, Ecology, and Literature*, edited by Douglas A. Vakoch, 75–86. Abingdon: Routledge.

Blend, Benay. 2021. "Rethinking Resistance: An Ecofeminist Approach to Anti-Colonialism in Louise Erdrich's Future Home of the Living God and Oreet Ashery and Larissa Sansour's The Novel of Nonel and Vovel." In *Ecofeminist Science Fiction: International Perspectives on Gender, Ecology, and Literature*, edited by Douglas A. Vakoch, 171–188. Abingdon: Routledge.

Boyd, Shelley. 2015. "Ustopian Breakfasts: Margaret Atwood's *MaddAddam*." *Utopian Studies*, Special Issue: Utopia and Food 26, no. 1: 160–181.

Bratich, Jack Z., and Heidi M Brush. 2011. "Fabricating Activism: Craft-Work, Popular Culture, Gender." *Utopian Studies* 22, no. 2: 233–260.

Buckingham-Hatfield, Susan. 2000. *Gender and Environment.* New York: Routledge.

Butler, Octavia. 1993. *Parable of the Sower.* New York: Grand Central Publishing.

Butler, Octavia. 2000. *Parable of the Talents.* New York: Aspect.

Cairns, Kate, and Josée Johnston. 2015. *Food and Femininity.* London: Bloomsbury Publishing.

D'Sylva, Andrea, and Brenda L Beagan. 2011. "'Food Is Culture, But It's Also Power': The Role of Food in Ethnic and Gender Identity Construction among Goan Canadian Women." *Journal of Gender Studies* 20, no. 3: 37–41.

Eaton, Heather. 2003. "Can Ecofeminism Withstand Corporate Globalization?" In *Ecofeminism & Globalization: Exploring Culture, Context, and Religion*, edited by Heather Eaton and Lois Ann Lorentzen, 23–38. Lanham, MD: Rowman & Littlefield Publishing Group, Inc.

Ferreira, Maria Aline. 2015. "The Posthumanist and Biopolitical Turn in Post-Postmodernism." *European English Messenger* 24, no. 2: 42–48.

Galbreath, Marcy. 2010. "A Consuming Read: The Ethics of Food in Margaret Atwood's *Oryx and Crake*." Presented at Florida Gulf Coast University's 2nd International Humanities and Sustainability Conference, Fort Myers, Florida, October 7–9.

Gopnik, Adam. 2011. *The Table Comes First*. London: Quercus Books.

Hochschild, Arlie, and Anne Machung. 2012. *The Second Shift: Working Families and the Revolution at Home*. New York: Penguin.

Kalivas, Tina. 2007. "Remembering Cyprus: 'Traditional' Cypriot Cooking and Food Preparation Practices in the Memories of Greek Cypriot Emigrants." In *Dining on Turtles: Food Feasts and Drinking in History*, edited by Tanja Luckins and Diane Kirkby, 171–187. London: Palgrave MacMillan.

Knoebel, Ariel. 2016. "Alternative Food Movements in Modern-Day America." Paper presented ar the Dublin Gastronomy Symposium: Food and Revolution, Dublin, May 31.

Kordecki, Lesley. 2021. "The Runa and Female Otherness in Mary Doria Russell's *The Sparrow*." In *Ecofeminist Science Fiction: International Perspectives on Gender, Ecology, and Literature*, edited by Douglas A. Vakoch, 24–34. Abingdon: Routledge.

Lockie, Stewart. 2001. "Food, Place and Identity: Consuming Australia's 'Beef Capital.'" *Journal of Sociology* 37, no. 3: 239–255.

Matchar, Emily. 2013. *Homeward Bound: Why Women Are Embracing the New Domesticity*. New York: Simon and Schuster.

Mellor, Mary. 2003. "Gender and the Environment." In *Ecofeminism & Globalization: Exploring Culture, Context, and Religion*, edited by Heather Eaton and Lois Ann Lorentzen, 11–22. Lanham, MD: Rowman & Littlefield Publishing Group, Inc.

Mies, Maria. 2010. "Feminist Research: Science, Violence and Responsibility." In *Ecofeminism*, edited by Maria Mies and Vandana Shiva, 36–55. Jaipur: Rawat Publications.

Plumwood, Val. 1993. *Feminism and the Mastery of Nature*. New York: Routledge.

Shiva, Vandana. 2002. *Staying Alive: Women, Ecology and Development*. London: Zed Books Ltd.

Warren, Karen J. 1987. "Feminism and Ecology: Making Connections." *Environmental Ethics* 9, no. 1: 3–21.

White, Monica M. 2011. "Sisters of the Soil: Urban Gardening as Resistance in Detroit." *Race/Ethnicity: Multidisciplinary Global Contexts* 5, no. 1: 13–28.

3 Margaret Atwood's Ecodystopic SF

Approaching Ethics, Gender, and Ecology[1]

Izabel F. O. Brandão and Ildney Cavalcanti

Margaret Atwood's name evokes futuristic works, especially due to the success of her novel *The Handmaid's Tale* (1986), an acclaimed feminist dystopia which received several literary prizes and was recently adapted for closed TV.[2] In spite of the controversy raised by Ursula K. Le Guin (2009) and addressed by Atwood herself (2011) regarding the frontiers between science fiction (SF), speculative fiction, and fantasy,[3] the fact is that one finds in Atwood a blend of literary genres, a hybridity regarding different compositional modes: from saga to tragic love story; from SF to apocalyptic fiction; from myth and legend to scientific fabulation. One clearly sees her alignment with a body of speculative feminist fictions of the previous centuries, more perceptible in the last century as shown by Larbalestier (2006), who has pointed out some of the recurring themes dealt with by these fictions.[4] Hence, we situate her work in the moving terrain of postmodernist aesthetics, from which precise categorical fences have been removed, and suggest that the *MaddAddam* trilogy—*Oryx and Crake* (2003), *The Year of the Flood* (2009), and *MaddAddam* (2013)—may be read as SF according to Donna Haraway's (2016) view, that is, as a mix of science fact, science fiction, speculative fabulation, and speculative feminism. Indeed, in the *MaddAddam* novels scientific facts and fictions are intertwined and colored by futuristic speculations whose contents are clearly gendered, ecologic and dystopic, precisely what provokes our responses in the light of a feminist *and* ecocritical reading. On a more specific note, we focus on the juxtapositions of issues regarding ethics,[5] gender, and ecology in the portrayals of the main women characters, especially Oryx, in the first novel, and their alignment with contemporary theories about women's bodies, utopian bodies (Foucault, 2013), and the mascarade (Russo 1986; Grosz 1990; Butler 1990).

The discussion that follows is based on the dystopic principle of world reduction (Jameson 2005), and of the reduction of women in the world (Lefanu 1989), a common trace in feminist dystopias. We focus on ecodystopic traces (the gender politics underlying representation), as we deal with Atwood's problematizing of women's trajectories in the context of patriarchal ideology as still configured in the future depicted in the novel, the extent to which women's bodies reveal a potential identification with the oppressor, and the literary metaphors at play in the interactions within the human, the posthuman, and/or the more-than-human universe.[6] Bearing in mind gender and ecological tropes, we believe Atwood's work may raise provocative reflections as regards the future of humanity.

Along with the failure of the project of modernity and the growing hegemony of the anthropocentric, patriarchal, class-based, heteronormative, capitalist, neoliberal model of human relationality, we witness the Anthropocene, an era of uncertainties.[7] In agreement with Jenning (2019, 17) we stress that "Although Atwood does not explicitly define or refer to the Anthropocene (as a name or concept), cultural anxieties about extreme climate change—including fears of economic, political, and environmental collapse—permeate her trilogy."

If there is anything certain in contemporary times, it is the idea that our world has become a dystopia.[8] And in such context, characterized by dark horizons (Baccolinni and Moylan 2003), the art of fiction points toward the rise of dystopias as an appealing tendency to readers. Although dystopias have always been a component in literary history,[9] the genre flourishes throughout the twentieth century, with the rise of classical and critical dystopias (Moylan 2000; Cavalcanti 2003), and reaches the new millennium as a strong tendency that brings together and transfigures the worst facts which surround us, crystalizing them in (literary, filmic, serial, graphic) narratives which flood culture with their "newest maps of hell" (Suvin 2004).

The dialogues uniting Atwood's SF works and the intertextual web of dystopias are evident. Confinement, control, and surveillance (including the reiterated use of eyes as one of its central symbols, in a clear allusion to George Orwell's *Nineteen Eighty-Four* [1949]) in *The Handmaid's Tale*) and the creation of a "new species"—the Crakers, by the obsessed scientist Crake—combined with the trope of the survival of the last human being in a post-apocalyptic scenario, are some of the plot details that incorporate the dark tones of Mary Shelley's proto-dystopic fictions of the nineteenth century. The standardization of behavior imposed by a central and omniscient power, another recurring trace in classical utopias and dystopias, is reinvented by Atwood through control over the bodies—both human and nonhuman—and over linguistic expression (see, for instance, the imposition of communication scripts in *The Handmaid's Tale*). The author also revisits the tradition of dystopic satire, as evidenced by the epigraphs (Jonathan Swift in *The Handmaid's Tale* and in *Oryx and Crake*) and by the irony she employs, as will be stressed.

The *MaddAddam* trilogy is a feminist ecodystopia[10] that has been receiving much critical attention from a variety of perspectives. Following Oliveira Neto's and Cavalcanti's (2019, 368) view that "the exploration of the feminine body contributes to the dystopic rendering of the world as imagined in this speculative work," the present reading examines some characters of the first novel, oriented by the perception that the feminist ecodystopic princi-ple is activated by intersecting axes in dialogue with issues such as ethics, gender, and ecology.[11]

Oryx and Crake can be defined as an ecodystopic story in that, from a destroyed world, there is the possibility of rebuilding it, even if the reader cannot be sure of what will happen.[12] The main narrative is framed around Jimmy, rebaptised "Snowman" after the apocalypse, who shares with us his memories of the recent past. Because Oryx's perspective is viewed in a very short part of the novel,[13] the "truth" belongs to a man, apparently the "last" of his species, being the story but a portion of a reality that exists in the mind of a specific man in extreme circumstances of survival. Yet, this is the fraction of reality to be dealt with as it reaches us.[14]

It is through Jimmy that we meet the other characters: the Crakers (or Crake's children, the result of his seven-year experiment "Paradice Project"), a group of genetically manipulated beings that Snowman is forced to become responsible for after the apocalypse;[15] their creator, Crake (other-wise Glenn), Jimmy's best friend, a highly intelligent scientist, also respon-sible for the apocalypse with his BlyssPluss death pill which decimated all those in search of long-lasting pleasure; Oryx, an enigmatic woman of indef-inite age who was sold by her mother as a child due to rampant poverty;[16] Jimmy's parents, and many others.

Jimmy's parents are both scientists, but Sharon,[17] the mother, leaves the family and a protected environment for scientists, precisely because she disagrees with what her professional life has become. Her domestic life as well is not what she feels she deserves, especially because her husband has sold his soul to the industry they work for, which she defines as "immoral" and "sacrilegious" (Atwood 2004, 57), a detail so well observed by Martin (2019, 177) who notes that "the first person to denounce bio-experiments … is a woman."

His attitude suggests a failure of ethics "in favour of the proliferation of scientific advancement at any cost" (Evans 2010, 37). After escaping from the highly watched compound, she joins what can be called "resistance" and is killed by the CorpSecorps halfway through the novel. Jimmy loses track of his father, who remarries his assistant, Ramona. He later learns his father was also killed by the CorpSecorps, like Crake's father, another scientist who knew too much.[18]

As Lúcia de La Rocque and Claudia Camel (2009) point out in their dis-cussion of the novel, the scientific practices presented go against the politics propounded in the 1999 Letter of Budapest, in which the United Nations defend that science is to be for all. Atwood presents a science thoroughly engaged with unethical policies, the kind of science critics call "male sci-ence," which caters to the very few with money.[19]

The novel explores issues that relate to this concept of "science-as-usual" in horrifying ways, making abhorrent ideas appear "normal." Experiments with animals and people establish a limitless manipulation of the body. Crake's genetic experiments which culminate in the creation of the Crakers depend on the decimation of people through his death pill. This future may in fact be taken as an ironic illustration of Stacy Alaimo's (2008, 259) discussion of the "ethical space of trans-corporeality"[20] in relation to toxic bodies, such as ours, which "inherit" the chemical products that pollute the environment. Like "the traffic in toxins [that] may allow us to notice that carcinogenic chemicals are produced by some of the same companies that sell chemotherapy drugs" (260), in Atwood's dystopic world, patriarchal science creates and destroys for the sake of profit.

A clear view of the way science-as-usual works in the novel is the comparison between Jimmy's father's first and second wives. Sharon, the first wife, is an ethical scientist, who rejects her husband's selling himself to the biotechnological complex. It is not surprising that Atwood chooses to define her identity primarily as Jimmy's mother. The second wife, Ramona, is his assistant, "his right-hand man" (53), as he "jokes," and remains so in spite of being a competent lab technician. While Jimmy's mother leaves home to become an activist, Ramona stays behind fulfilling the role patriarchy wants for women. Ironically, she fails to become a mother, one of the most valued roles for women in patriarchy.

* * *

Recalling his friendship with Crake, their hacking of internet sites for fun, Jimmy reveals the special point of their friendship: Oryx, a character of indefinite age who cannot be called either "girl" or "woman," because the way she looks is never clear enough.[21] Atwood's portrayal of Oryx reminds readers of other women characters in dystopian novels—like Julia, in Orwell's *Nineteen Eighty-Four*, Clarisse McClellan in Ray Bradbury's (1953) *Fahrenheit 451*, and Marla, in Chuck Palahniuk's (1996) *Fight Club*—who play supporting roles to the male protagonists' counter-narratives.[22] Oryx, however, is more ambivalent. Her presence is always elusive, possibly indicating that she is not real in a material way. Since her image was "saved" by Crake from a porno site, and later she denies it is her ("I don't think this is me," 91), she might be devised as the idealized picture of a woman made to order: infantile, never to grow old.[23] Another recurring motif in contemporary feminist SF dystopias, such images, no matter how attractive, are fake, for they do not easily materialize.[24]

However, this idealized woman is merely a disguise, a mask Oryx wears, for this body is the product she offers to a patriarchal market that commodifies women.[25] Such commodifying of the body can be seen along with Alaimo's (2008, 249–250) understanding of "corporeal agency," or "bodies that resist the processes of normalization, or refuse to act, or act in ways that may be undesirable to those who inhabit them or to others," a concept she uses in relation to disability studies but which can be extended to Oryx's performance or identity mask.

Along with Mary Russo (1986, 223–224) we understand "femininity" as "a mask which masks nonidentity," as the psychoanalytical mascarade of presupposed dissimulation women learn to perform in order to survive.[26] More recently, this concept has also been dealt with by Cavalcanti (1999) in relation to survival strategies in feminist dystopias, and by Brandão (2014; 2018) in relation to the body as a mask in contemporary cinema and poetry. The latter's argument is particularly helpful for Atwood's novel in the sense of the body understood discursively as a cultural text, i.e., relational.[27] Such body, when seen in displacement, transformation, and repositioning, may "transform the mascarade into a power to be appropriated critically and positively by women" (Brandão 2014, 91). So we can understand Oryx's body as an ecodystopic body, for she "dresses" it according to the customer, to what is needed for her survival. No wonder she becomes a multitude of women, as we hear from Jimmy/Snowman:

> *Enter Oryx. Fatal moment. But which fatal moment? Enter Oryx as a young girl on a kiddie-porn site, flowers in her hair, whipped cream on her chin; or Enter Oryx, stark naked and pedagogical in the Crakers' inner sanctum; or Enter Oryx, towel around her hair, emerging from the shower, or Enter Oryx, in a pewtergrey silk pantsuit and demure half-high heels, carrying a briefcase, the image of a professional Compound globewise saleswoman? Which of these will it be, and how can he ever be sure there's a line connecting the first to the last? Was there only one Oryx, or was she legion?*
>
> (307–308)

The masks Oryx uses are related to "knowledge practices" (Alaimo 2008, 253), for hers is a body that reveals its limits and capacities, being therefore connected with culture, and with the environment. Such is her agency.

Most of what what we know about her is reported by Jimmy, who first describes Oryx as "three-dimensional (...) small-boned and exquisite, and naked like the rest of them, with nothing on her but a garland of flowers and a pink hair ribbon, frequent props on the sex-kiddie site" (90). But, although there is a pretense of innocence in the props such innocence disappears as the reader recalls her with whipped cream on her chin, the usual stuff used by porno sites that exploit children for commerce and profit. Is this really in the future? Oryx's ecodystopic body is indeed a meaningful text that reveals how women are sexually exploited from childhood in a patriarchal environment.

Atwood's irony is far from obvious. And subtle is her naming of the universities Jimmy and Crake attend. Crake, a numbers guy, goes to a top university, Watson Crick, whereas Jimmy, a words person, joins the low rate Martha

Graham, respectively a male and a female name. Numbers equal profit; words equal problems. Such dystopic choices show once more Atwood's use of irony to expose cultural imbalances most of us may be blind to.

Though he has affairs while in college, Jimmy remains tied to Oryx's image, the picture of someone he never forgot from his adolescence. When this picture "materializes," they become lovers, in fact, in a sort of "love triangle" with Crake, who is apparently unaware of it.[28]

Sold as a child to a man she called Uncle En, Oryx was forced to sell flowers and be exposed to (and exploited by) men. Uncle En "defended" her from violence (at least physical violence) and gave her candies. She never blamed him for anything. After he dies, Oryx is sold again to a man who makes porno movies. That is when Jimmy gets to know her on the computer. She was then about eight.

When they meet, Crake is possibly 26, maybe a little more, but Oryx's age is not mentioned. She might be 18, a prostitute, working for the Student Services. He falls in love with her, although he would never admit that. Oryx becomes his assistant, mediating between the world and the Crakers.[29] Among them she is always naked, her body yet again exposed, in order not to disrupt their natural world. Oryx's body is abused,[30] and her naked presence alongside the Crakers inside a glass cage—that prevents Crake's beings (and Oryx) from escaping—gives the idea of a spectacle put in sight for a voyeur.[31] Exposed to scrutiny, they (and their ecodystopic bodies) turn into odd creatures to be observed, reiterating how science-as-usual works in Atwood's dystopic world.

When Jimmy becomes Crake's assistant, to create an ad to sell his apocalyptic BlyssPluss, he meets Oryx in real life, and they become lovers, behind Crake's back. Their attachment is different, though, for she is not the prostitute she is with Crake, as she points out: "He has no time to play. Anyway, Crake is my boss. You are for fun" (312).

Although Jimmy is outraged about Oryx`s experience of exploitation, she does not seem to mind her past, what makes one wonder about the extent of the concept of exploitation. Women's complicity and even identification with the oppressor is not new. Confronted with Jimmy's anger, Oryx minimizes the trauma:

> "Oh Jimmy, you would like it better maybe if we all starved to death?" said Oryx, with her small rippling laugh. This was the laugh he feared most from her, because it disguised amused contempt. It chilled him: a cold breeze on a moonlit lake.
>
> (119)

In fact, one of her most distinctive features—her "small rippling laugh"—is ironic and subversive, a form of resistance, an attitude which absolves her from connivance with the oppressive system that exploits her.[32] It is her way of surviving such a system.[33]

Russo (1986), in discussing Bakhtin's notion of the grotesque body, wonders why he never questioned the hags' laughter in the Kerch terracotta figurines. The answer, in Oryx's case, is that her rippling laugh leads to the only kind of 'activism' she is able to perform.[34] Her "amused contempt" contrasts with the attitude of all those who rebel against the system and end up in death, such as Jimmy's mother, and later both his and Crake's fathers, who knew too much about the engineered diseases created by the system.[35]

* * *

In terms of ethics, gender, and ecology, Atwood's novel provides a clear and profound illustration of a possible dystopic "future." In such a picture, bodies have "leaky borders" (Alaimo 2008, 262), and this toxicity is part of the ethics of attempting to control the world.

Considering the body as a discursive marker of identity and the ecodystopic traces discussed in relation to the female characters of *Oryx and Crake*, we perceive that Atwood has envisaged a dystopic and hopeless world that is tragically part of our contemporary days. Jimmy, at the end of the novel, is intoxicated with all he has gone through: the decimated population; the killings of his loved ones; his injured and mistreated body; his being chased by the genetically modified animals; the Crakers, who depend on him for survival and who know next to nothing about the world; and the confrontation with possible enemies (human and nonhuman). His recollections are what may (re)connect the readers with a possibility of salvation. The glimpses of resistance, illustrated by Jimmy's mother and by Oryx, tenuously point toward hope. Their killing is part of the system trying to erase those who do not comply with its rules.

All the same, it is necessary to say that the attempts at resistance are different: Sharon dies facing the camera, as if asserting that she was defending freedom, as perceived in Jimmy's remarks upon seeing the images shown by the CorpSeCorps:

> Pan to close-up: the woman was looking right at him, right out of the frame: a blue-eyed look, direct, defiant, patient, wounded. But no tears. Then the sound came suddenly up *Goodbye. Remember Killer. I love you. Don't let me down.*
>
> (258, original italics)

Oryx's killing takes a different turn, for it is ambiguous. Her acquiescence to the system fails, either as a result of jealousy on the part of an obsessed scientist or as a necessary act, since Crake wanted only Jimmy to survive and look after his creation. And since Jimmy survives and indeed looks after them, the ambiguity is a persistent path in this ecodystopic novel.

As to a possible resistance of the subaltern Ramona, we have no clue. All we have are the next two novels of the trilogy to clear the mystery left at the end of *Oryx and Crake*. That is perhaps one of the reasons why Atwood has created the term *ustopia*, defined as "the perfect society and its opposite— because, in [her] view, each contains a latent version of the other" (Atwood 2011, 66).[36] Though *Oryx and Crake* contains all the elements of a possible destruction, yet there is a silence that the other two novels may fill. As for gender, ecology, and dystopia, the narrative goes on.

Notes

1 A Portuguese version of this chapter was read at the Conference "Minuto: Movências Interdisciplinares da Utopia," held at Ufal in Maceió, Brazil (May 26–30, 2018). We thank CNPq for making this research possible, and Professor Susana Funck for her second reading of this essay. Thanks also to Pedro Fortunato Oliveira Neto, Ildney Cavalcanti's PhD student who was our research assistant.

2 Created by Bruce Miller and directed by Reed Morano, for the streaming platform Hulu, with the first season launched in 2017.

3 "When it comes to genres, the borders are increasingly undefended, and things slip back and forth across them with insouciance" (Atwood 2011, 7).

4 In her introduction, Larbalestier (2006, xvii) stresses, among others, two themes explored by twentieth century women authors of SF: some of them are "set in post-apocalyptic futures" and "treat directly with scientific theory and practice."

5 We use the term ethics following Alaimo's (2008) understanding of a material ethics that includes us humans in a transcorporeal space which is also a posthuman space.

6 Our notion of the posthuman follows Cary Wolfe (2010, xvi) in the sense that posthumanism goes beyond "a thematics of the decentering of the human," privileging "*how* thinking confronts that thematics." We also share Andrew Pickering's view that the term is located in "a space in which the human actors are still there but now are inextricably entangled with the nonhuman, no longer at the center of the action and calling the shots" (quoted in Alaimo 2008 253). For more on posthumanism, and specifically in relation to the trilogy, see Ferreira (2015).

7 Christian Hummelsund Voie (2019), in discussing the material nature of the Anthropocene, considers that "all landscapes have to various degrees and extents become 'landscapes of strange agencies.' Thus there is a dystopian possibility of regarding every landscape as potential landscapes of fear." Atwood's novel can be placed within this sense of fear, considering its post-apocalyptic scenario. Moreover such landscapes recur in the other novels of the trilogy in an escalating way.

8 In her introduction to *Dystopia(n) Matters*, Fatima Vieira (2013, 1) stresses the pervasiveness of dystopia in our times by affirming: "[dystopia] has invaded the political dimension of many countries in the world."

9 See Claeys (2017) for a historical survey of proto-dystopias: works that precede the well-known classical dystopias of the twentieth century.

10 The term "eco(dys)topia" (Brandão 2017) stems from the ambivalence present in the conceptualization of utopia and leads to the understanding of the body as a discursive text that sees naturecultures (Haraway 2003) as interdependent, interconnected, and in permanent interaction. These resonances can be either positive or negative. The novel may be considered ecodystopic because of the suppression of desire and agency of a human corporeality in the portrayal of Oryx as well as other women characters. We also consider Foucault's (2013) idea

of the body as a *locus* of utopia, as the narrative implies a limitation on its full expression.

11 See Ralph's chapter in this book for an analysis of climate change in Merlinda Bobi's *Locust Girl* as resulting from our dystopic ecological context.

12 The Waterless Flood gives no clear evidence of the kind of world that emerges out of the apocalypse.

13 See Chapter 6.

14 The experience of reading the three novels of the trilogy, which allows us to "hear" other characters' points of view on the "facts" narrated by Snowman, provides evidence that his narration is grounded on some truth.

15 Crake's posthuman/transhuman creatures are created through "bioengineering to destroy humans and science, reverting humans (which is, essentially, what the Crakers are, based on their genome) to a pre-human status (humanity understood as a social and technological basis)" (Marques 2015, 139).

16 Wain in this book discusses the issue of food and nourishment, calling our attention to Oryx's family condition that led to her being sold.

17 Her name is mentioned only twice in the entire novel. The scientist is usually referred to as "Jimmy's mother."

18 Crake's mother is also depicted as a scientist, a diagnostician, but her presence in the narrative is very obscure. Readers get to know she had a tragic death by contamination by a bioform—"accidentally" or caused by "sabotage" (176).

19 The critics' definition of "male science" seconds Sandra Harding's (1991, 54) notion of "science-as-usual": "the whole scientific enterprise, its purposes, practices, and functions," i.e., a science complicit with patriarchy that either excludes women or places them in secondary positions, as in the case of Ramona, Jimmy's father's second wife and assistant.

20 In Hummel's (2019) discussion of *The Year of the Flood,* she associates Toby with Merleau-Ponty's notion of "strange kinship" (2) in that "humanity and animality [are] a lateral continuum" (2). This idea asks for constant "renegotiations between self, other and environment" (3). Regarding this specific detail, and to some extent, we would consider Toby as another version of Oryx: both have lost their identities and their former lives and renegotiate the terms of survival. Toby's body as it recovers can be seen "as a site of multiple ethical encounters with other life forms" (11). Here the understanding is that when different species meet, this is "an ethical encounter, an ecofeminist phenomenon that Stacy Alaimo has termed trans-corporeality" (12). The same can be said of Oryx's encounter with the Crakers, who despite being human are genetically engineered, which gives them the prerogative of a different species of human (posthuman, transhuman). This "ethical encounter" indeed forms a "strange kinship," for it cultivates "affinity across species" (14) and in which affect is also a latent part of its negotiations. Their dependence on Oryx at first and later, after her death, on Jimmy, shows that this encounter is both an ethical and transcorporeal practice. Atwood's trilogy provides some answers in the other two novels for some of the questions posed here.

21 Atwood's novel discloses one of her concerns about contemporary culture: "the mainstreaming of pornography and violence into the main culture [..., and] her uneasiness as she describes the degradation of culture in a society where violence and pornography have become cheap, and readily available, forms of entertainment" (Bouson 2009, 97). Along the same lines, Martín (2019, 177) has remarked: "Atwood had already dealt with the topic of pornography in a previous novel, *Bodily Harm* (1981), in which the protagonist is exposed, in a similar way, to hardcore pornography." We would add to this that in *The Handmaid's Tale*, pornography is also explored, through the lenses of SF, in the clandestine

brothel attended by the white male elite. Besides, apart from *Oryx and Crake*, the same theme is dealt with in *The Year of the Flood* and *MaddAddam*. See Oliveira Neto and Cavalcanti (2019) for an analysis of the multilayered figuration of women's enforced prostitution and extreme sexual exploitation in the trilogy.

22 See Moylan (2000) and Lima (2017) for commentaries on such characterization.

23 Oryx can be seen as the Jungian anima, usually the product of a heterosexual mind that appears as a kind of truth. See Carl Jung (1987), James Hillman (1985), and Sarah Nicholson (2013) on the anima concept. For a feminist reading of this archetype, see Susan Rowland (2002). This image is akin to the psychoanalytic notion of femininity, especially in view of the mascarade as performed by women. See Russo (1986), Butler (1990), and Grosz (1990).

24 In Jeanette Winterson's (2007) *The Stone Gods*, the technological procedure called "genetic fix" freezes women's bodies so that they will remain young.

25 The word Oryx indicates an association with an African animal under threat of extinction. Oryx and Crake are names brought from a computer game known as "Extinctathon" (40, 214), and the irony here is that, since Jimmy's narrative is a retrospect, both characters are already dead, extinct as it were.

26 Joan Rivière's study of the masquerade in the beginning of the twentieth century points to it as women's use of the social mask of "womanliness" in order "both to hide the possession of masculinity and to avert the reprisals expected if she was found to possess it" (quoted in Wright 1992, 243). More recently, Russo (1986), Butler (1990), and Grosz (1994) revisit and problematize the mascarade.

27 See Bordo (1993) as well as Gaard, Estok, and Opperman (2013).

28 As in previous fictions by Atwood, echoes of the Biblical narratives can be heard in this plot detail. See Ferreira (2015, 46) for a reading that highlights the revision of the Christian Trinity (with the addition of a woman).

29 Other contemporary SF dystopias in which women characters are figured as "teachers" of the "new species" echo here. In Marge Piercy's (1991) *Body of Glass*, Malka, an old scientist, is responsible for the socialization of the cyborg Yod, devised and constructed by Avram. The pattern is that a (male) scientist creates the beings, which are then socialized by women assistants, thus reiterating and problematizing the gender bias in the sciences. In this context, Oryx can be read as a nurturer (in relation to the Crakers); and as a harbinger of the apocalypse due to her role as the disseminator of the BlyssPlus pill, or the dry Flood planned by Crake. In the other novels of the trilogy, following an ascending trajectory—which contrasts with Oryx's guided actions—Toby gradually becomes the nurturer and the one to direct her agency towards the formation of "strange kinships" (see note 21 above).

30 See, in this respect, Romero's (2013, 166) concept of "site of abuse."

31 See the fragment: "Three times a day Jimmy checked on the Crakers, peering in at them like a voyeur. Scrap the simile: *he was a voyeur*" (339, our italics).

32 Oliveira Neto and Cavalcanti (2019, 382–383) also highlight the subversive quality of Oryx's laughter as a trace of resistance and a victory over censorship.

33 Along similar lines, Hall (2009, 194) affirms: "Oryx's self-definition as a subject who is acting upon other rather than an object who is acted upon."

34 Oryx's agency occurs in a dissimulated way, for when she denies that she is the girl in the picture, we are informed that: "Another woman in her place would have crumpled up the picture, cried, denounced him as a criminal, told him he understood nothing about her life, made a general scene. Instead she smoothed out the paper, running her fingers gently over the soft, scornful child's face that had – surely – once been hers" (92).

35 See Alaimo (2008, 260).

36 Jennings (2019, 18) consistently argues that "Atwood demonstrates that apocalyptic narratives constitute a flexible tradition within a wide-ranging canon, one that not only includes despair-inducing dystopias, but hope-inducing utopias [...] Bearing in mind how Atwood's term, ustopian, unfolds these contradictory impulses, it is perhaps more accurate to call the *MaddAddam* trilogy a counter-apocalypse."

References

Alaimo, Stacy. 2008. "Trans-Corporeal Feminisms and the Ethical Space of Nature." In *Material Feminisms*, edited by Stacy Alaimo and Susan Hekman, 237–264. Bloomington: Indiana University Press.

Atwood, Margaret. 1986. *The Handmaid's Tale*. Boston: Houghton Mifflin Company.

Atwood, Margaret. 2003. *Oryx and Crake*. New York: Anchor Books.

Atwood, Margaret. 2009. *The Year of the Flood*. New York: Doubleday.

Atwood, Margaret. 2011. *In Other Worlds – SF and the Human Imagination*. London: Virago.

Atwood, Margaret. 2013. *MaddAddam*. New York: Doubleday.

Baccolini, Raffaella, and Tom Moylan, eds. 2003. *Dark Horizons: Science Fiction and the Dystopian Imagination*. New York: Routledge.

Bordo, Susan. 1993. *Unbearable Weight: Feminism, Western Culture, and the Body*. Oakland: University of California Press.

Bouson, J. Brooks. 2009. "'It's Game over Forever': Atwood's Satiric Vision of a Bioengineered Posthuman Future in *Oryx and Crake*." In *Bloom's Modern Critical Views: Margaret Atwood*, edited by Harold Bloom, 93–110. New York: Bloom's Literary Criticism.

Bradbury, Ray. 1953. *Farenheit 451*. New York: Ballantine Books.

Brandão, Izabel. 2014. "Questões do corpo em 'La piel que habito', de Almodóvar: gênero e tecnologia como máscara." In *Transculturalidade e de(s)colonialidade nos estudos em Inglês no Brasil*, edited by Paulo Rogério Stella et al., 85–104. Maceió: Edufal.

Brandão, Izabel. 2017. "The Body, Discourse, and Poetry in Contemporary Black Women Poets: Eco(Dys)Topic Languages." Paper presented at the 13th Women's World & 11th Fazendo Gênero, Florianópolis, Brazil, July 30–August 4.

Brandão, Izabel. 2018. "Grace Nichols and Jackie Kay's Corporeal Black Venus: Feminist Ecocritical Realignments." In *Literature and Ecofeminism: Intersectional and International Voices*, edited by Douglas A. Vakoch and Sam Mickey, 185–196. New York: Routledge.

Butler, Judith. 1990. *Gender Trouble: Feminism and the Subversion of Identity*. New York: Routledge.

Cavalcanti, Ildney. 1999. "Articulating the Elsewhere: Utopia in Contemporary Feminist Dystopias." PhD diss. University of Strathclyde.

Cavalcanti, Ildney. 2003. "The Writing of Utopia and the Feminist Critical Dystopia: Suzy McKee Charnas's Holdfast Series." In *Dark Horizons: Science Fiction and the Dystopian Imagination*, edited by Raffaella Baccolini and Tom Moylan, 47–68. London: Routledge.

Claeys, Gregory. 2017. *Dystopia: A Natural History*. Oxford: Oxford University Press.

Evans, Shari. 2010. "'Not Unmarked': From Themed Space to a Feminist Ethics of Engagement in Atwood's *Oryx and Crake.*" *Femspec* 10, no. 2: 35–58.

Ferreira, M. Aline. 2015. "The Posthumanist and Biopolitical Turn in Postmodernism." *European English Messenger* 24, no. 2: 42–49.

Foucault, Michel. 2013. *O Corpo Utópico, as Heterotopias.* São Paulo: Edições n-1.

Gaard, Greta, Simon C. Estok, and Serpill Oppermann, eds. 2013. *International Perspectives in Feminist Ecocriticism.* New York: Routledge.

Grosz, Elizabeth. 1990. *Jacques Lacan: A Feminist Introduction.* London: Routledge.

Grosz, Elizabeth. 1994. *Volatile Bodies. Toward a Corporeal Feminism.* Bloomington and Indianapolis: Indiana University Press.

Hall, Susan L. 2009. "The Last Laugh: A Critique of the Object Economy in Margaret Atwood's *Oryx and Crake.*" *Contemporary Women's Writing* 4, no. 3: 179–196.

Haraway, Donna. 2003. *The Companion Species Manifesto: Dogs, People, and Significant Otherness.* Chicago: Prickly Paradigm Press.

Haraway, Donna. 2016. *Staying with the Trouble: Making Kin in the Chthulucene.* Durham, NC: Duke University Press.

Harding, Sandra. 1991. *Whose Science? Whose Knowledge?: Thinking from Women's Lives.* Ithaca, NY: Cornell University Press.

Hillman, James. 1985. *Anima: Anatomy of a Personified Notion.* Dallas, TX: Spring Publications Inc.

Hummel, Katherine E. 2019. "Strange Kinship Matters: Cultivating Ethics of Place in Margaret Atwood's *The Year of the Flood.*" *ISLE: Interdisciplinary Studies in Literature & Environment* 26, no. 4: 986–1005.

Jameson, Fredric. 2005. *Archaeologies of the Future: The Desire Called Utopia and Other Science Fictions.* London: Verso.

Jennings, Hope. 2019. "Anthropocene Feminism, Companion Species, and *The MaddAdam Trilogy.*" *Contemporary Women's Writing* 13, no. 1: 16–33.

Jung, Carl G. 1987. *Dictionary of Analytical Psychology.* London: Arc Paperbacks.

Larbalestier, Justine. 2006. *Daughters of Earth: Feminist Science Fiction in the Twentieth Century.* Middletown, CT: Wesleyan University Press.

La Rocque, Lúcia, and Claudia Kamel. 2009. "A literatura de ficção científica como veículo de divulgação científica na educação informal em ciência: questões de ética e gênero em discussão em *Oryx e Crake*, de Margaret Atwood." In *Gênero e hibridismo cultural: enfoques possíveis*, edited by Sandra Sacramento, 203–210. Ilhéus: Editus.

Lefanu, Sarah. 1989. *Feminism and Science Fiction.* Bloomington: Indiana University Press.

Le Guin, Ursula K. 2009. "*The Year of the Flood* by Margaret Atwood." *The Guardian*, August 29. Accessed January 9, 2021. https://www.theguardian.com/books/2009/aug/29/margaret-atwood-year-of-flood

Lima, Felipe Benicio. 2017. "Sob o signo de Janus: Uma Análise de Clube da Luta em suas relações com a ficção distópica." MA thesis. Universidade Federal de Alagoas.

de Marques, Eduardo Marks. 2015. "Children of Oryx, Children of Crake, Children of Men: Redefining the Post/Transhuman in Margaret Atwood's 'Ustopian' *MaddAddam* Trilogy." *Aletria, Belo Horizonte* 25, no. 3: 133–146.

Martín, Javier. 2019. "Dystopia, Feminism and Phallogocentrism in Margaret Atwood *Oryx and Crake.*" *Open Cultural Studies* 3: 174–181.

Moylan, Tom. 2000. *Scraps of the Untainted Sky: Science Fiction, Utopia, Dystopia.* Boulder, CO: Westview Press.

Nicholson, Sarah. 2013. *The Evolutionary Journey of Woman: From Goddess to Integral Feminism.* Tucson, AZ: Integral Publishers.

Oliveira Neto, Pedro Fortunato de, and Ildney Cavalcanti. 2019. "Corpos Femininos Distópicos em *MaddAddam,* de Margaret Atwood." In *Trânsitos Utópicos,* edited by Ildney Cavalcanti et al., 368–391. Maceió: Edufal.

Palahniuk, Chuck. 1996. *Fight Club.* New York: Norton.

Piercy, Marge. 1991. *Body of Glass.* London: Penguin.

Romero, Diana Villanueva. 2013. "'Savage Beauty': Representations of Women as Animals in PETA's Campaigns and Alexander McQueen's Fashion Shows." *Feminismo/s* 22: 147–175.

Rowland, Susan. 2002. *Jung: A Feminist Revision.* Oxford: Polity Press.

Russo, Mary. 1986. "Female Grotesques: Carnival and Theory." In *Feminist Studies/Critical Studies,* edited by Teresa de Lauretis, 213–229. Bloomington: Indiana University Press.

Suvin, Darko. 2004. *Nuovissime Mappe Dell'Inferno: Distopia Oggi.* Rome: Monolite Editrice.

Vieira, Fátima, ed. 2013. *Dystopia(n) Matters: On the Page, on Screen, on Stage.* Newcastle upon Tyne: Cambridge Scholars Publishing.

Voie, Christian Hummelsund. 2019. "Nature Writing in the Anthropocene." In *Routledge Handbook of Ecocriticism and Environmental Communication,* edited by Scott Slovic, Swarnalatha Rangarajan, and Vidya Sarveswaran, 199–210. London: Routledge.

Wolfe, Cary. 2010. *What is Posthumanism?* Minneapolis, MN: University of Minnesota Press.

Wright, Elizabeth. 1992. *Feminism and Psychoanalysis: A Critical Dictionary.* Oxford: Blackwell.

4 Ecofeminist (Post) Ice-Age Ecotopia

Doris Lessing's *Mara and Dann* Books

Julia Kuznetski

The year 2020 and early 2021 have been marked by events and processes that may be called both catastrophic and eye-opening. The deadly fires in Australia and the United States, the outbreak of the COVID-19 pandemic with the global death toll nearing two million in early 2021 (*BBC News* 2021), alongside multiple disasters associated with climate change, have prompted the view that "a frightening future is already here" (Berardelli 2020a). The deserted streets of the unprecedented global lockdown in the spring, or the infernal orange skies of a burning Oregon in September have provoked associations with something seen before—in science fictional films or dystopian novels, thus creating a unique bridge between reality and what it is so tempting to call "fantasy," were it not plausible and long in the making, something that writers and artists had intellectually conceived of and warned about even earlier, or perhaps more convincingly, than scientists did. Speaking of the highest temperature ever recorded on Earth in Death Valley in summer 2020 and the unprecedented wildfires in the United States, climate specialist Jeff Berardelli (2020b) refers explicitly to these weather conditions as "dystopian," being "exactly what scientists have been warning about for decades" (Ibid.). Significantly, while science has all the facts, which are often ignored, it is culture that gives us the key to understanding, by providing a different angle at the processes and, most importantly, by making us reconsider the position of the human as being not in confrontation, but a part of the cycle we have largely initiated. As Indian novelist Arundhati Roy (2020) insightfully notes, using the imagery of science fiction (SF), the current coronavirus crisis may be seen as a "portal," not taking us back to a provisional normality but "offer[ing] us a chance to rethink the doomsday machine we have built for ourselves" (Ibid.). To expand Roy's metaphor, the best vehicle for clearing through the portal is literary narratives, considering the profile of the current volume, stories of the dystopian genre.

This chapter focuses on Doris Lessing's "Mara and Dann" books,[1] namely her novels *Mara and Dann* (1999) and *The Story of General Dann and Mara's Daughter, Griot and the Snow Dog* (2005, 2006),[2] set in an imagined future past an ecological catastrophe caused by wars and climate change. As Donna Haraway (2001 [1984], 2269) reminds in "A Cyborg Manifesto," "the boundary between science fiction and reality is an optical illusion." This, as suggested above, is felt specially acutely in 2020 and will probably last beyond. Distinctly from fantasy, works of SF, particularly dystopian SF, create fictional situations about a world that does not exist, but is scientifically possible, especially if the trends of the current civilization continue, and it is hard to find a writer to speak more insightfully of an imminent ecological catastrophe than Lessing (1919–2013), who grew up in Southern Rhodesia (now Zimbabwe) and had lived through WWII, apartheid, atomic age, and several competing ideologies. This chapter aims at approaching the two books with the following research questions: (1) What genre conventions of SF, particularly dystopia and futuristic ecotopia are followed in the two books? (2) What ecofeminist turns can be observed, such as challenging binaries, centrisms, and the rationalist paradigm, and drawing attention to the materiality and vulnerability of nature while speaking of the possible catastrophic scenarios? (3) How is the homogeneity of still male-dominated SF disturbed and turned multidirectional in a narrative centered on a non-stereotypical cast of characters trying to make sense of the world they had been left? (4) Finally, what are the larger conclusions to be made about the current state of the Anthropocene and the place of the human among other species, drawing on Lessing's fictional predictions and the ideas of the theorists resorted to?

Twenty-First-Century Dystopian Science Fiction, Posthumanism, and Ecofeminism

Twenty-first-century scholars of SF have indicated a shift in focus and subject matter of the genre proliferating in the twentieth century and often concerned with space exploration, life on other planets, and (mostly warlike) interaction with *aliens*—which may be viewed as a metaphor for the Eurocentric *Other*. Christopher Cokinos (2010) summarizes this shift as "[i]nstead of Suns, the Earth," with a view that if SF is to remain sustainable as a genre, it has to come back to the planet Earth. Similarly, Udo Nattermann (2013, 112), with reference to Cokinos, holds that "the most promising future of science fiction might lie in its cooperation with ecological writing" and theorizes an "ecotopian dreaming" and ecotopian situatedness characterized by border regions, as well as physical permeability, social communication, and violence that designate twenty-first-century SF, transforming it into *Earth science fiction* (Nattermann 2013 113–114), with what we can see as strong dystopian characteristics. Izabel F. O. Brandão and Ildney Cavalcanti (this volume, 44), propose the term *eco(dys)topia*, to address "the ambivalence present in the conceptualization of utopia and leads to the understanding of the body as a discursive text that sees nature cultures … as interdependent, interconnected, and in permanent interaction." In discussing Lessing's work, while approaching body and place as interconnected, I will be employing the terms "ecofeminist dystopia" and "ecotopia," to illuminate both the ambivalence (often concerning gender but not exclusively) and the negative aspects of a narrative set in the future and orchestrated by quite feasible (and definitely not positive-utopian) ecological causes.

Speaking of the genre of dystopia, Douwe Fokkema (2011, 20) observes that such writing proliferates at times of "a dreadful sociopolitical reality," or a major crisis, starting with the fifteenth- to sixteenth-century Europe and going especially strong after the Russian Revolution and WWII. These early dystopias were mostly political, while later, as he continues, "apart from political dystopias, we may distinguish texts focussing on scientific, ecological and genetic issues, sometimes in combination" (403). These circumstances for the production of dystopias may be also said to apply to their reception. Thus, the *Mara and Dann* series may be placed alongside Jean Hegland's (1996) *Into the Forest*, Margaret Atwood's (1985) *The Handmaid's Tale*, and Steven Soderbergh's (2011) film *Contagion* that are currently enjoying a renewed popularity because of their portrayal if not of screaming reality, then of a reality eerily plausible. As Aaron S. Rosenfeld (2020) concludes in *Character and Dystopia: The Last Men*, contemporary dystopias are not so much characterized by the "warning" function of the early models of the genre, as by the descriptive function interwoven into the anxiety about the future, which is in fact no longer future but the present: "Environmental degradation, corporate oligarchy, the surveillance state, technological infiltration of the human, and the new authoritarianism no longer seem like problems that can be averted. They are here." (Rosenfeld 2020, 247). He also looks back at modern (early twentieth century) dystopias as forms of "wounded humanism" (236) presenting the human as a "deformed character," deprived of agency and "deformed at least in part through the removal of a functioning social sphere" (235). Rosenfeld sees such instances as "pessimistic" (235) and even comprising the essential horror of dystopian fiction, as contrasted to the elevation of the "interior self" of the preceding Realist tradition (41), in which "common man's quest" takes center stage, and "a will to separation between character and setting" is celebrated (41). The dystopian occurs when "outer penetrates inner world completely" and the "human subject [is forced] into a position of peripherality" (42). The problem we can see in this argument is the old tension of the human—outside, echoing the way. Chris Pak (2016) describes the nature of post-WWII European SF, while employing the term *terraforming* (2), to refer either to the colonization of space and transforming alien planets to conditions resembling those on Earth or, on the contrary, earth being transformed to either accommodate living species, particularly humans, or make the conditions unliveable for them. According to Pak (2016, 102–103), terraforming of the earth as a narrative trope and "proto-Gaian narratives," presenting the Earth as a living organism, have informed SF's ecological discourse. However, the "ecological" property is dubious here, as we can recognize the grand narrative of living earth as biomass that is too large and hostile for the terraforming man, jeopardizing his chances to survival, or threatening to undermine his centrality, and that biological threat (be it *Alien* or *Jurassic Park*) has to be countered (successfully) with powerful machinery. From an ecofeminist perspective, the loss of centrality of man and their merging with the setting does not make him "deformed" or deficient, however shifting the paradigm in the perception of what human is.

Thus, Lars Schmeink (2016), in a study of what he terms "biopunk dystopias" (*passim*), argues that the question of the human, their capacities and place in the order of things has been an instrumental question of SF ever since *Frankenstein* (33), a work that "anticipates the posthuman condition" (34), in which "the posthuman self" is viewed "as relational and extended" (44), and life and history as *zoe*-centric (after Rosi Braidotti; Schmeink 2016, 44), including *all life* on the planet, not only humans, and all history, also "a future without 'us'" (45). Such a shift in perspective signals a strong ecological and posthumanist potential for both SF and SF dystopia, including ecotopia, in which "periferality" of the human subject will be no longer seen as a threat, but as potential, countering what Stacy Alaimo, in a recent interview (Kuznetski and Alaimo, 2020), insightfully referred to as "popular accounts of the Anthropocene," presenting a "cartoonish" view "in which some transhistorical 'Man' acts upon the inert, external matter of the world."

Speaking of the place of women in this discourse, we can see the same problematics of representation. Namely, as Mary E. Papke (2006, 145) rightly notes, women in most SF written by male authors serve a merely instrumental role as "receptacles for male valor, scientific expertise, or, literally, for out-of-this-world sex"—created, as she argues, "for the pleasure of the readership, the vast majority of it male." What we can see in these examples is the reproduction of the western binary paradigm of man/woman and me/the Other, whereby the Other may be substituted by me/the outside force, mystical or fantastic. However, challenging dualisms is an important part of a feminist agenda, undertaken, as the contributors to Justine Larbalestier's edited collection *Daughters of Earth* (2006) find, in feminist SF. For instance, Papke (2006, 145) discusses the writings by women "draw attention to the writing of science fiction as a political act" by making their female characters "active subjects and not simply objects of lust or passive helpmates, though the extraordinary dilemmas they face are not always easily resolved or their worlds redeemed." This leads us to discuss how feminist SF and ecocriticism, as well as ecological dystopian writing can find a way toward each other, in the form of ecofeminist dystopia (or feminist ecotopia).

Greta Gaard (2017, 146–147) employs the term *cli-fi* to speak of a new genre emerging since 2011-2013, to refer to novels in which climate change is a fact and the characters are struggling to survive within the degraded environments.[3] She stresses, however (Ibid. 145), that true "feminist fiction confronting climate change has yet to be written," as the problem with existing *cli-fi* (Ibid. 152) is narrating the story from the point of view of the male heterosexual center and, focusing on effects rather than causes, they represent a "truncated narrative," often remaining confined to "the apocalyptic failure of techno-science solutions, and uninformed by the global climate justice movement" (Gaard 2017, 147). One of the causes of such degradation, as ecofeminist Val Plumwood (2002) stresses, is the dominating "rationalist paradigm," as well as the "centrisms" that deem nature secondary to culture and reason. As a result, nature, and alongside it, women and indigenous people are positioned at the other end of "reason and science," because connected more with the body and emotions. Thus, the archetypes of a white hero saving the earth and his submissive, secondary heroine are but a natural outcome of this dualist thinking—in Gaard's words (145), the "root causes" of climate change can be traced to "humanist, colonialist, antidemocratic, and anti-ecological beliefs and practices." In the same vein, Haraway (2001 [1984], 2296) points to the systemic western practices of domination of various others—women, people of color, nature, workers, animals—"whose task is to mirror the self" and proposes instead the concept of "companion species" (2008, 16–19) to refer to non-human others. Another possibility to dissolve dualist borders is Stacy Alaimo's (2010) *transcorporeality*, or reciprocal co-dependence of humans with their non-othered environment, more-than-human others, unstable inner self and the environments of their own bodies, which thus are seen as porous, vulnerable, and unfinished, a multiplicity of multiplicities. As I will argue, *transcorporeality* can be a useful tool for ecofeminist dystopian SF, especially as regards Lessing's writings. According to Gaard, fiction informed by such openness has the potential for presenting adequately a full picture of climate change and its effect on us. Speaking on the tensions of this interconnectedness, Blend (2021, 173) points to the somewhat paradoxical nature of SF as a "venue for undermining patriarchal, capitalist, and colonial practices at the same time from within a genre that celebrates technoscience, a product of all of the above," thus stressing the potential of the genre. In Gaard's view (2017, 158), it is namely *cli-fi* narratives that, being sensitive to the "immediacy of climate change, have the potential to present not just a techno-science story but rather to narrate our transcorporeality" as key to addressing these complex issues of identity and difference.[4]

Lessing's Prophetic Vision

Many of the ideas presented above, particularly those related to the causes of narrative time catastrophe, as well as transcorporeality as relatedness of the human body and the body of nature can be found in Lessing's novels under discussion. While conventional SF most often presents technological wonders of the future—super-weapons, space machines, synthetic food, artificial intelligence, instant communication, and transportation devices,

Lessing depicts a world past technological advances and back to antique-style pot-cooking on fire, scooping water from shallow wells, eating roots, drawing maps on goatskins, being ignorant about birth control, fighting with knives, and traveling on foot. Brother and sister Mara and Dann are survivors of a once-prosperous and highly developed Mahondi tribe in Ifrik, now swept by war and permanent draught. On the other side of the world, "Yerrup" is covered in ice right down to the "Middle Sea," now called "Bottom Sea," because nearly empty, "boiled away in some frenzy of heat" (Lessing 2006, 58). It is also called the "Divide" (Lessing 2006, 25) separating the ice from the draught, where formerly great cities, "built to last forever [are] now lying deep under water" in frozen marsh (Lessing 2006, 25). Change in climate has caused biological mutation (Lessing 1999, 67): "Animals that had eaten plants learned to chase humans for their flesh … rivers moved, disappeared … trees died … and insects, even scorpions, changed their natures." There are some remnants of a former civilization with advanced technology and learning that is currently redundant: the "sky-skimmers" for which there is no fuel; wonder-weapons that were once so powerful they could destroy the whole earth but that no one has the skill to use now; a wondrous material that does not wear away, warms and cools, takes up body shape and never gets dirty or stained; wonder-metal covering some buildings in ghost towns; sun-traps that that no one knows how to operate.

Both books are largely about characters trying to make sense of what had happened to the world, and the causes, as well as the possible lives and ways of the perished civilization. Knowledge is communicated through a few remaining books in the "sand libraries" and antique museums in the Center in a kind of reverse antiquity, displaying technological wonders of the past to a rather helpless present, as well as through female community members called Memories. The siblings, rescued from their perished city, are raised in the rivaling Rock community by such a Memory—Daima—who relates to Mara that

> Once, long ago, there was a civilization—a kind of way of living—that invented all kinds of things. They had science—that means, ways of thinking that try to find out how everything works—and they kept making new machines, and metals … There were machines so clever they could do everything … no one knows why all that came to an end. They say that there were so many wars because of those machines … And they invented that material that never wears out and the metal you see here that you can't break.
>
> (Lessing 1999, 37)

A peculiarity of the narrative is characters constantly telling each other stories about the past, as well as the present in different parts of a shrunk-up world. The quality of these stories is much like a fairy-tale: the time is a variation of "once upon a time"—"once, long ago" and the possibility of truth or fact is ruled out by the constant resorting to "They say" or "it is said"/"It is known that." It is that uncertainty about bits of knowledge, that fragmentation that drives Mara to further questions and Dann to walk further in pursuit of some sense of the world he cannot find. As a grown-up, he senses that the perpetual movement going through both books is he and Mara walking toward themselves, in pursuit of something they had to know.

> [T]he marshes, and beyond them ... scrub and sand and Ifrik drying into dust. He and Mara had walked through all that, walked from deserts into marshland, and both were on the way to their opposites, through slow changes you could hardly *see*, you had to *know*.
>
> (Lessing 2006, 21)

Lamia Tayeb (2009, 19) convincingly explores the narrative texture of *Mara and Dann* in terms of fairy-tale, myth, and romance as a critique of western colonial discourse (Ibid. 18) and a *postcolonial parable* (Ibid. 21). Tayeb demonstrates insightfully Lessing's skill of constructing a narrative of "*regression*" (Ibid. 23, emphasis in the original) to upset the Eurocentric myth of European supremacy, as well as Enlightenment ideas about history as a progression toward a "civilization" in which knowledge is a decisive power tool. However, she makes only a passing observation that Lessing "*also* projects a prophetic image of a post-apocalyptic human life on earth and ... evokes a modern universe lurching on the verge of ecological catastrophe" (Ibid., my emphasis), thus ignoring the deep ecological agenda of the novel. It is true that the action of *Mara and Dann*, and even more so of *General Dann*, is centered on permanent wars that are colonial in nature: tribes capture people from other tribes and turn them into slaves or soldiers. But the deep reason is expressed by wise Daima right at the outset (Lessing 1999, 36): "'There'll be another rebellion and more fighting. The worse things get with water and food, the more fighting'" and reiterated by Dann while walking through the dead landscape seeing extinction around (Ibid. 105):

> "there was a war"
> "What about"
> "Water. Who was to control the water from the spring that makes the stream that feeds the lake we were on"
> "Who won?"
> "Who cares? It's all drying up anyway."

In the twenty-first century, reports on the situation in East Africa have pointed to the increased frequency of draught in the region, and to the fact that "the global forces of climate change, forced migration, and volatile food supply converge, resulting in severe hunger and, at worst, famine." (Wainaina 2017). As of autumn 2019, Western, central, and some parts of Southern Africa, have been experiencing the lowest rainfall since 1981, making, for instance in Namibia, 2.4 million people "food insecure," with children being particularly vulnerable (Reliefweb). Climate change is increasingly evoked as being "a central force driving a continued rise in global hunger, with both droughts and flooding negatively impacting food production" (Ibid.) Therefore, the European refugee crisis of 2015 may also be seen as largely the result of wars and climate change on the African continent, only emphasizing the first rule of ecology, that everything is connected to everything else. What is more, the severe summers of 2018 and 2019 with temperature records breaking across Europe, and a scorching heat wave in the north from Ireland to Scandinavia, causing huge ice sheets to melt in Greenland (Fountain 2019), has been attributed to climate change by a number of scientists (Carrington 2018), who have underscored that "serious climate change is 'unfolding before our eyes'" (Ibid.). Thus, *Mara and Dann* and its sequel present a prophetic vision of the political, economic, and environmental landscape we are facing today. It also communicates the idea that the crisis of resources affects all and in the face of draught or all-pervading ice *all* living beings, as well as the landscape, are bodily vulnerable to the changes despite hierarchical divisions, which is perhaps among the most important messages of the book.

What is also prophetic is people's persistent blindness to warning signs and reluctance to take action. Hatice Övgü Tüzun (15, this volume) makes the same observation concerning the writings of Octavia Butler she scrutinizes: the current apocalyptic state is the result of people being "unable (or rather unwilling) to effectively address their current problems." In this sense, both Butler and Lessing use what Tüzün (14) calls a "futuristic template to speak [of their] contemporary moment." When Mara tells the complacent Chelops community how quickly climate change had happened (Lessing 1999, 200) and that already nearby regions are filling with sand and the draught will soon reach them (Ibid. 185), the people first smile, "wanting to smile it away" (Ibid.), or leave in "anger and indignation. They did not want to know all this." (Ibid. 200). The difference between Mara and the community is that she is speaking from her bodily experience of draught, and from knowledge and ability to make connections, while the Kin from a sense of established social structure that they would rather not break. In the sequel, it is Dann's turn to tell people in the still liveable islands by the Bottom Sea of Chelops, "now gone into dust and ashes" (Lessing 2006, 71), and feel how he is losing them as an audience, because "[t]heir imaginations had gone fat and soft with the comfort of their lives" (Lessing 2006, 54). We can explain this lack of curiosity about the past, history, and the causes of climate change as the universal human tendency of separating themselves from the physical reality of their environment. Stacy Alaimo warns of the falseness and danger of thinking in terms of "Man" vs. "the world," which may give the human a false sense of power while making them blind to their own vulnerability and the culture of risk (Kuznetski and Alaimo, 2020). This applies to climate change denial practiced by the neoliberalist far-right (notably, Trump withdrawing the United States from the Paris Agreement on climate change) and to ignoring the start of coronavirus pandemic in 2020 (Bolsonaro's infamously dismissing it as a "fantasy" and Boris Johnson taking a "similarly cavalier approach" until testing positive themselves, Lutz 2020). As old Felissa, one of the last Mahondis in the Centre, summarizes it to Mara, "it is true that people always have a tendency to believe that what they have is going to continue forever" (Lessing 1999, 373), a fallacy partially dictated by lack of knowledge of and interest in the past. For instance, the inhabitants of the island by the Bottom Sea never question its history, their argument being, "We have always been here" (Lessing 2006, 55). Speaking of the genre of dystopia, Rosenfeld (2020, 234) suggests that their "terrifying visions of the future are also visions of a world without a past," while "[d]ystopias are as much about making a connection to the past as to the future" to "prevent memory from ossifying into a toxic nostalgia." This explains the interest of Mara, Dann, Ali, and the female Memories in the past as not only the history of civilization and technology, but also of the environment. They are also among the characters falling outside mainstream SF, as discussed below.

Lessing's Characters: Breaking the "White Hero" Paradigm

Reviewing the then-emerging canon of feminist SF, as well as feminist SF criticism, Robin Roberts (1995, 190) points out in *Extrapolation* such commonly used tropes of the genre as fragmentation, instability, and apocalypse, borrowed from the postmodern tradition. Claire Curtis, in turn, scrutinizes a set of post-apocalyptic novels united by the idea of "starting over." In her view (2010, 2), "[p]ostapocalyptic accounts that reflect the modern view focus on the role of individuals in the recreation of community." The sense of community is quite provisional in *Mara and Dann*, with communities coming together for the sake of safety and survival, as when the Rock People go to fetch water together to fight it from the wild animals; or when the siblings join a pack of refugees marching North, staying together for safety from the animals, or boarding a packed boat for a possibility of movement, but being far apart in stealing food and coins from one another, attacking and marauding. In Chelops, the Hadrons kidnap Mahondi women for reproduction, and Mahondis control water while being slaves to the Hadrons. Kira, a former Hadron slave, contemplates taking slaves for farming the fertile lands at the end of *Mara and Dann* and in the sequel (Lessing 2006, 205) we learn that she is indeed now selling and buying slaves and plotting an invasion of the remaining habitable lands. As shown by Lessing, such a "social contract" is hardly a recreation of civilization or "starting over" for the sake of a better world. It is but a reproduction of the binary power paradigm in which, in Foucauldian terms, there is no master without a slave, and staying together is dictated by pure necessity. The focal characters, however, resist the "new social contract as reproduction of the old" logic by, first, not conforming to the dualist power paradigm and second, to the white hero paradigm of SF narratives.

First of all, instead of a frail white princess in the hands of some alien, a cliché in mainstream SF, we encounter Mara, as a confused child in the beginning and a resourceful survivor in the end. There is a hint that the siblings are "special," perhaps royal; they are ordered to forget their real names, Prince Shahmand and Princess Shahana (Lessing 1999, 369), as children, and pass through many identities in the course of the two books. However, there is no "happy ending" with the princess being returned to her castle of birth, for it is gone into the dry sands and Mara, as Dann observes in the sequel (2006, 278), "never danced in all her life. She was too busy—surviving." She is also harassed by Kulik while alone in the village, kidnapped for reproduction by the Hadrons, and nearly forced into incestuous reproduction with him by Felix and Felissa to reproduce the extinct royalty (Lessing 1996, 74–75). This emphasizes the vulnerability of women in a situation of crisis. For example, there have been alarming reports on the increase in domestic violence, particularly against women and girls during the COVID-19 lockdown, of women being pushed back into domestic roles, and even an increase in forced female genital mutilation (FGM) (Hodal 2020). Still, to Dann, his sister is "fierce Mara; indomitable and tenacious" (Lessing 2006, 71).

Further on, the instability characteristic of postmodern dystopia can be seen in the characters' bodies reacting to the landscape around. Thus, during severe draught Mara sees herself in a shallow water hole (a kind of *mirror stage*) as "so thin, only bones with skin stretched over them. Her eyes were deep in her face" and her hair, "greasy, solid clumps" (Lessing 1999, 75), which in the relative green of Chelops will become her own again— long, shiny and beautiful. If it is a cliché to link the cycles of the female body to the cycles of nature, then in Mara's case, her cycles and bodily functions are in correlation with lack or availability of water.

> She knelt and looked down between her thighs to see if perhaps that trickle of red blood was back, but the lips of her slit were pulled tight and wrinkled with dryness. Where she would be peeing was a burning that she had become so used to it seemed only part of the angry, hungry, itchy desperation of her whole body for water.
>
> (Ibid. 71–72)

Due to this alteration of her body, another change of identity becomes possible: skinny and with her hideous haircut, Mara joins the crowd of refugees as Maro, passing for Dann's brother for her own safety. Thus, cross-dressing, renaming, and physical changes in the body are simultaneously physical reactions and survival strategies, undermining gender and social categories and stressing the interdependence of the human body with its physical environment.

Secondly, Dann, who is ironically referred to as General Dann from the second half of the first book on, is but an unstable, vulnerable, probably bisexual, dependent, possibly bipolar boy and man, with incestuous love for Mara. Lessing brilliantly portrays Dann's childhood trauma, when he is locked up and tortured by a man from a rival tribe who had just murdered his parents. While Mara is able to cope with the experience, turning it into future strength, Dann is crashed to the point of developing a psychological disorder: because they are eventually rescued by that "bad" man's "good" brother, the boy retains forever a confusion at seeing two alike-looking men, unable to tell which is good and which is bad. He often experiences relapse, e.g., in the Towers, being abused and ill, he slaughters two men thinking them one, "the bad one" (Lessing 1999, 192). Then the strong and tall General becomes childish and speaks in a child's voice, (Ibid. 194), sucking his thumb (Ibid. 48) and becoming as if entranced; hallucinating about the "other man" pursuing him. In *General Dann*, we finally come to realize that "the other one" must be an abstract idea of evil, the other side of everyone, including himself, and probably his inner opponent, or part of a bipolar personality. Seeing Dann after one of his periods of "mind sickness" (Lessing 2006, 234), Griot senses that he looks "Himself. Who? Well, he wasn't *the other one*—whoever he was." Thus, such ecotopian elements as instability, permeability, violence, and danger in a place acquire a strong philosophical dimension.

As the full title of the second book suggests, Dann is in the company and within multidirectional stories of Mara's daughter Tamar, their more-than-human companion snow dog Ruff, and orphaned boy soldier and later story-teller Griot. Through this unusual cast of characters, the paradigm of the sane, autonomous, and singular white hero is undermined further. "Where there should have been General Dann, a strong healthy man, there was a sick man who was at that moment sleeping off a bout of poppy" (Lessing 2006, 121–122). What is more, Dann is aware of his condition, of "the other one" in him, when he confesses to Tamar (Lessing 2006, 268): "sometimes when I wake in the morning I don't know who I am, Dann or—the Other."

Dann's fluid, unstable psyche is best understood by Griot, who had served him faithfully and now, at the end of times, keeps the fidelity that he thinks of as *love* (Lessing 2006, 121, emphasis in the original). To match, Griot's own personality is far from conventional: a big, sturdy man with a healthy complexion, he is gentle, grieving his lost parents, and has an attachment for Dann that he calls love but that can be classified as a sexual or motherly feeling or both. Griot is rendered as having animal features, particularly green eyes exactly like the snow dog's, and it is through this animality that he is organically connected to Ruff and Dann. If Dann comes to be attached to Ruff after rescuing him from drowning in the marshes, Griot thinks of falling in love with Dann while nursing his "terribly scarred body ... like the wounded horse whose life he had saved" (Lessing 2006, 121).

Finally, Ruff is one of the many specimens migrating from the North because of ice melting. He has to find a way to survive in a changed climate, a more-than-human orphan joining a mix-race *ad hoc* community of orphans in Dann's camp, for they have all lost a parent (Tamar), or both parents (Dann, Griot, Ruff), or children (Ali). Interestingly, he is not humanized, but remains a beast, amiable to those who care for him, aggressive with outsiders. It is also Raff who *chooses* to leave the kind cabin-owner Kass and follow Dann, who had saved his life (Lessing 2006, 84) and then to adopt his orphaned niece Tamar (Lessing 2006, 207), thus showing agency and becoming a true "companion," in Haraway's terms. Dann allows him to be natural, does not train him to kill the way Kira does, and when they talk, there is harmony in which there are "whines and a man's voice" (Lessing 2006, 235).

In contrast, characters who are farthest from nature and seek to maintain a binary order are presented as negative and even ridiculous, from Kulik who reigns by terror to Kira who recreates slave-holding, forgetting she was a slave herself once. She and daughter Rhea, with their flashy looks and false locks, put up a show that is "off key, discordant, and the two of them ... like dolls that had been wound up and were running low" (Lessing 2006, 256). Lessing cleverly eschews both the "white-hero" trap and the "Amazon world with men no more" scenario, by making Kira, with her "platoon of female soldiers," "black dramatic eyes," and "imperious voice" (Ibid. 252–253) that render Dann speechless, perfectly ridiculous, sitting on her throne in one of the emptying museums, "sodden with poppy" (Ibid. 281). That the vicious Kira is finally defeated not by an army but by a plant signifies that even in a post-apocalyptic world, it is nature that has its way, voice, and agency, as rendered through the strong transcorporeal and animalistic motifs in the narrative.

Becoming Animal in a Futuristic Landscape

General Dann opens with an ecotopian setting of a man in a changed landscape: Dann bodily positioned "over an extremity," stretching over a rock that "could crumble and fall and he with it" (Lessing 2006, 5). The metaphor suggests yet another exposition of events in a world in which the human and the non-human, in this case, the material rock, are closely connected and, what is more, that in case of a catastrophe of the material world, man will "fall together with it." Dann finds this natural consequence of the connection no less than exhilarating (Ibid. 6).

In contrast, in the poignant scene with Rock People coming to fetch water, a typical anthropocentric attitude of terraforming as colonizing the last bits of liveable earth is portrayed. People and animals alike are suffering, undernourished, and dehydrated (Lessing 1999, 41–45), and they are depicted as fighting one another and each other, despite being enmeshed in a common environmental disaster.

> There were some trees marking where the water was, and a lot of animals of every kind clustered by the water, and this is why the villagers had to go to the water together ... Now everyone was standing around the biggest pool and beating it with sticks, and there were all kinds of wrigglings and heavings under the water, and dark shapes appeared and sank.
>
> (41)

We may note how the pool is referred to here, as just a surface with nothing there, but is in fact full of life, being home to a variety of non-human species that humans feel right to expel: "The crowd were now all standing round the pool they had beaten" (42). Notably, the scene puts human superiority into question by vivid parallels between human and non-human behavior in extreme circumstances. Thus, Dann keeps chanting "Water, water, I want the water" (43) as if entranced; a big water stinger tears live flesh from a helpless furry animal (42), while the ferocious tribe chief Kulik is "showing those big yellow teeth" (42), as if capable of doing the same; and, while Daima is busy keeping the children safe in the water from other humans, a woman nearly steals her precious water cans (43). Yet, in this situation of all species being reduced to their primary nature, the man with a stick is still trying to maintain his master position, driving all animals out of the water, thereafter emptying the pool for himself. The powerful and cruel patriarch Kulik, in addition to nearly drowning little Dann only to demonstrate his superiority, tramples all powerless and "senseless" others—women (Daima), children, nature, animals (their "milk beast" Mishka), and "mad" (neighbor Rabat).

Contrarily, Daima rescues a scorpion trapped in her dry cistern, where it had come looking for water, observing that "It's hungry ... just like everyone else" (45). In the same way, Mara perceives that the earth speaks: "the dead white trees with their white branches like arms: please, please, give us water" (Lessing 1999, 74); "the flowers ... emitting a high, almost audible scream for help, because she was ... identifying so strongly with a longing for rain" (143). She rolls her itching body in the sand "as she had seen animals do" (Ibid. 71), and it is the recognition of oneself in landscape and ability to adapt to its ways that helps the siblings survive and dooms the anthropocentric characters. Thus, Kulik's son is killed by a water stinger outside the village (70). Dann recounts their experiences through this bodily enmeshment with the physical world and the capacity to mutate and adapt rather than stick to invented rational rules that do not work in nature: "It seems we can be lizards in sand and then take to water like birds. All our early lives Mara and I were dying of draught and then we became water people" (Lessing 2006, 214). Such narrative turns to challenge the idea of human exceptionalism, distinction of categories and separateness, steering toward, as Schmeirk maintains (2016, 96), a "*zoe*-centric worldview" outside humanist subjectivity, thus engaging the readers "in critical dystopian thinking" (Ibid.).

Further on, Lessing abandons a Eurocentric view by giving the habitual geographical places alternative names (Yerrup for Europe, Middle Sea for the Mediterranean Sea, South Imrik for South America, and Ind for India), placing the Centre in North Africa and making Yerrup an anonymous, monolithic mass of ice-covered land, while Ifrik has its distinct territorial variation. Similarly, the characters are non-Europeoid, representing physical and linguistic diversity. A tiny surviving Europoid minority is referred to as Albs that "Yerrup had been filled with ... all with white fish skins" (Lessing 2006, 115). Interestingly, the Albs as Other are associated with nature (fish) here, as well as witchcraft (Ibid.)—a label people anywhere are quick to attach. What is more, physical properties are not linked to race, but rather depend on environmental conditions, just like the physiology of animals: "'you think that this is a Mahondi baby, and then you take another look ... Why?' 'Nobody knows. Why are those scorpions ... and the lizards, changing?'" (Lessing 1999, 251).

It is significant that Mara and Dann are constantly on the move, for it is through that movement that they perceive the real nature of the land around, which no geographical map can communicate. It is especially clear when Dann draws a map and measures the distance between the places they had walked with only two fingers (Lessing 1999, 95), while for the body, it is days. It is through this physical walking and direct encounter with the land that the siblings get in touch with their own, transcorporeal selves. In *Becoming Animal*, David Abram (2010, 85) describes the reciprocal connection of body and landscape and the ability of both for mutual influence:

> the depth of a terrain—the relation between the near and far aspects of that land—depends entirely upon where you are standing within that terrain. As you move, bodily, within that landscape, the depth of the scape alters around you.

Abram stresses (Ibid. 3) that by moving bodily within ever-changing landscape, "the flesh of the breathing world" (Ibid. 78), by growing deeply into our animality (Ibid. 10), one becomes fully human. He also holds the view (Ibid. 172) that "all things have the capacity for speech," meaning that language is not limited to humans, and there is no privilege for a certain, standard, written language. Oral speech, Abram stresses (Ibid. 265), moves us closer to nature: its rhythm may change depending on the season, and "even the calm solidity of a boulder we lean against can influence the weight of our spoken words." In *Mara and Dann*, such agents of orality are Daima,

Candice, and Mara herself; in *General Dann*, it is Griot, who learns singing from a black girl Nubis, teaching him *stories of her river* (Lessing 2006, 275, my emphasis), then making his own song of "Dann and Mara and the River Dragons" (Ibid.), and eventually singing only with voice and abandoning language. On the moorland hills, with "only the foxes and hawks to hear him" (Ibid. 276), he lets his voice go free till it turns into a howl, like the one the snow dog made, or one Dann imagines his "bad other" would make (Ibid. 274). In fact, through that elemental language, "sensible Griot" stops being sensible (in the Cartesian sense) and gets in touch with his natural self in that unstable and fragmented post-apocalyptic world. Interestingly, in *Locust Girl* as discussed by Ralph in this volume, singing serves as the climax of Amedea's early transcorporeal relationship with an insect, and her final passage to freedom, allowing her to burst into flames and turn into a flying creature able to rejuvenate her post-climate-catastrophe land in a narrative that Ralph reads as another specimen of *cli-fi*.

In Lessing's case, *Mara and Dann* books do what scholars of ecofeminist SF (Merrick 2008, 220) see as the genre's potential: resisting the reproduction of the Cartesian project of realist fiction as well as "the reinscription of mechanistic scientific narratives around 'nature/s.'" Rather than reproducing the patriarchal and Eurocentric bias of the "white hero" paradigm of conventional SF, Lessing's ecotopia refutes binaries and the primacy of rationality, and focuses instead on fluid, racially and sexually ambiguous characters in situations with no body-landscape or human-animal divisions. In a situation of terraforming as recreating a post-climate-catastrophe world with its pre-apocalyptic flaws, the focal protagonists adopt a transcorporeal and caring relationship with the changed environment and the non-human others on their way, which becomes their survival strategy. As suggested before, the larger project for *cli-fi*/ecotopian narratives, and particularly ecofeminism, is to help grasp the complexity of present-day crises by drawing attention to human enmeshment in all these environmental processes, not as a distanced and superior agent, but as a co-actor caught in the flux of material changes, aware of one's own precarity and thus sensitive to the vulnerability of other species as well as our own, to the planet at large, capable of imagining its possible futures, which are in no way distant from our troubled present.

Notes

1 The two novels will be treated namely as a continuous story, with alternating references to both books, cited as Lessing 1999 and Lessing 2006.
2 The edition cited here is 2006 Harper Perennial edition.
3 Gaard's examples are McEwan's *Solar* (2010), Kingsolver's *Flight Behaviour* (2012), McCarthy's *The Road* (2006), Butler's *Parable of the Sower* (1993), etc. We may upgrade this list, for example, with John Lanchester's *The Wall* (2019).
4 For a further and more detailed discussion of Gaard's cli-fi discourse, see Ralph in this volume.

References

Abram, David. 2010. *Becoming Animal: An Earthly Cosmology.* New York: Pantheon.

Alaimo, Stacy. 2010. *Bodily Natures: Science, Environment and the Material Self.* Bloomington: Indiana University Press.

Atwood, Margaret. 1985. *The Handmaid's Tale.* London: Vintage.

BBC News. 2021. "Covid-19 Pandemic: Tracking the Global Coronavirus Outbreak." January 5. Accessed January 8, 2021. https://www.bbc.com/news/world-51235105

Berardelli, Jeff. 2020a. "Climate Chaos: Extreme Heat, Wildfires and Record-Setting Storms Suggest a Frightening Future Is Already Here." *CBS News*, August 24. Accessed September 29, 2020. https://www.cbsnews.com/news/climate-change-heat-wave-wildfires-hurricanes-derecho/

Berardelli, Jeff. 2020b. "Wildfires and Weather Extremes: It's Not Coincidence, It's Climate Change." *CBS News*, September 17. Accessed September 30, 2020. https://www.cbsnews.com/news/wildfire-climate-change-extreme-weather/

Blend, Benay. 2021. "Rethinking Resistance: An Ecofeminist Approach to Anti-Colonialism in Louise Erdrich's *Future Home of the Living God* and Oreet Ashery and Larissa Sansour's *The Novel of Nonel and Vovel*." In *Ecofeminist Science Fiction: International Perspectives on Gender, Ecology, and Literature*, edited by Douglas A. Vakoch, 171–188. Abingdon: Routledge.

Carrington, Damian. 2018. "Heatwave Made Twice More Likely by Climate Change, Scientists Find." *The Guardian*, July 27. Accessed July 28, 2018. https://www.theguardian.com/environment/2018/jul/27/heatwave-made-more-than-twice-as-likely-by-climate-change-scientists-find

Cokinos, Christopher. 2010. "Instead of Suns, the Earth: Another Kind of Science Fiction." *Orion*, July/August, 64–67.

Contagion. 2011. Directed by Steven Soderbergh. Burbank, CA: Warner Bros.

Curtis, Claire P. 2010. *Post-Apocalyptic Fiction and the Social Contract.* New York: Lexington Books.

Fokkema, Douwe. 2011. *Perfect Worlds: Utopian Fiction in China and the West.* Amsterdam: Amsterdam University Press.

Fountian, Henry. 2019. "Europe's Heat Wave, Fueled by Climate Change, Moves to Greenland." *The New York Times*, August 2. Accessed September 30, 2020. https://www.nytimes.com/2019/08/02/climate/european-heatwave-climate-change.html

Gaard, Greta. 2017. *Critical Ecofeminism.* Lanham, MD: Lexington Books.

Haraway, Donna. [1984] 2001. "A Manifesto for Cyborgs: Science, Technology, and Socialist Feminism in the 1980s." In *The Norton Anthology of Theory and Criticism*, edited by Vincent B. Leitch. 2269–2299. New York: W. W. Norton and Company.

Haraway, Donna. 2008. *When Species Meet.* Minneapolis: Minnesota University Press.

Hegland, Jean. 1996. *Into the Forest.* New York: Dial Press.

Hodal, Kate. 2020. "Why Coronavirus Has Placed Millions More Girls at Risk of FGM." *The Guardian*, June 16. Accessed September 30, 2020. https://www.theguardian.com/global-development/2020/jun/16/coronavirus-millions-more-girls-risk-fgm

Kuznetski, Julia, and Stacy Alaimo. 2020. "Transcorporeality: An Interview with Stacy Alaimo. *Ecozon@: European Journal of Literature, Culture and Environment* 11, no. 2: 137–146. https://doi.org/10.37536/ecozona.2020.11.2.3478

Lanchester, John. 2019. *The Wall*. London: Faber and Faber.

Lessing, Doris. 1999. *Mara and Dann: An Adventure*. London: Flamingo.

Lessing, Doris. [2005] 2006. *The Story of General Dann and Mara's Daughter, Griot and the Snow Dog*. London: Harper Perennial.

Lutz, Eric. 2020. "Brazil's Bolsonaro Tests Positive for Virus He Dismissed as a 'Fantasy.'" *Vanity Fair*, July 7. Accessed September 24, 2020. https://www.vanityfair.com/news/2020/07/brazils-bolsonaro-tests-positive-for-virus-he-dismissed-as-a-fantasy

Merrick, Helen. 2008. "Queering Nature: Close Encounters with the Alien in Ecofeminist Science Fiction." In *Queer Universes: Sexualities in Science Fiction*, edited by Wendy G. Pearson, Veronica Hollinger, and Joan Gordon, 1–18. Liverpool: Liverpool University Press.

Nattermann, Udo. 2013. "Mundane Boundaries: Eco-political Elements in Three Science Fiction Stories." *ISLE* 20, no. 1: 112–124.

Pak, Chris. 2016. *Terraforming: Ecopolitical Transformations and Environmentalism in Science Fiction*. Liverpool: Liverpool University Press. Stable URL: http://www.jstor.org.ezproxy.tlu.ee/stable/j.ctt1gpcb56

Papke, Mary E. 2006. "A Space of Her Own: Pamela Zoline's 'The Heat Death of the Universe.'" In *Daughters of Earth: Feminist Science Fiction in the Twentieth Century*, edited by Justine Larbalestier, 130–159. Middletown, CT: Wesleyan University Press.

Plumwood, Val. 2002. *Environmental Culture: The Ecological Crisis of Reason*. London: Routledge.

Reliefweb. 2019. "Joint Call for Action to Address the Impacts of Climate Change and a Deepening Humanitarian Crisis in Southern Africa." November 14. Accessed September 25, 2020. https://reliefweb.int/report/zimbabwe/joint-call-a ction-address-impacts-climate-change-and-deepening-humanitarian-crisis

Roberts, Robin. 1995. "It's Still Science Fiction: Strategies of Feminist Science Fiction Criticism." *Extrapolation* 6, no. 3: 184–197.

Rosenfeld, Aaron S. 2020. *Character and Dystopia: The Last Men*. New York: Routledge.

Roy, Arundhati. 2020. "The Pandemic Is a Portal." *Financial Times*, April 3. Accessed September 29, 2020. https://www.ft.com/content/10d8f5e8-74eb-11ea-95fe-fcd274e920ca.

Schmeink, Lars. 2016. *Biopunk Dystopias: Genetic Engineering, Society and Science Fiction*, Liverpool: Liverpool University Press.

Tayeb, Lamia. 2009. "Arabian Nights Fairy-tale Turned Postcolonial Parable: Narrative Manoeuvres in Doris Lessing's *Mara and Dann*." *Doris Lessing Studies* 28, no. 2: 18–25.

Wainaina, Stephen. 2017. "Droughts in East Africa Becoming More Frequent, More Devastating." *African Arguments*. March 17. Accessed September 30, 2020. http://africanarguments.org/2017/03/17/

5 Ecofeminist Climate Fiction
Merlinda Bobis's *Locust Girl*

Iris Ralph

In Australian climate change contexts, *Locust Girl*, a climate fiction (cli-fi) novel by Filipino-Australian writer Merlinda Bobis, reads as a thinly disguised account of human agents and agencies that transformed Australia from a verdant continent with ample sources of water to a sunburnt and parched one after 1788. In global contexts, the novel describes the planet Earth as humans are transforming it from a cool green sphere into a hot red orb. Today, "1% of the world is a barely livable hot zone. By 2070, that portion could go up to 19%" (Lustgarten 2020a). The novel asks questions in particular about what specific human agents and agencies in Australia and beyond are most responsible for that change. In the implicit answers that the novel gives to those questions, it castigates what ecofeminists identify as *masculinist* beliefs and behaviors. That is the main subject of this chapter. The second main subject, which precedes the first, relates to questions about the genre of cli-fi. In addressing it, I briefly summarize the origins of literary realism, sci-fi (science fiction), and cli-fi, a genre that is the meeting halfway between literary realism and sci-fi, genres that traditionally have stood at opposite ends on the literary spectrum. *Locust Girl* exemplifies the new genre of cli-fi in its address of stark climatic realities generated by human activities. Even only half a century ago, those realities would not have been seen in literature outside of a sci-fi novel. They include skyrocketing temperatures, desertification, proliferation of fire, shrinking aquifers, species loss on a massive scale, loss of arable land, and condensation of human populations in and around mega cities.

Literary realism dates to the nineteenth century, when the words "realism" and "verisimilitude" first appear in literary criticism and writers become preoccupied with producing so-called faithful representations of reality (Mullan 2014). In North America, distinguished wielders of the form include William Dean Howells, Hamlin Garland, Rebecca Harding Davis, and Henry James. Across the Atlantic, famous purveyors are George Elliot, Charles Dickens, Charlotte and Emily Brontë, and Elizabeth Gaskell. In the southern regions of the globe, in Australia, Henry Lawson, Steele Rudd, Joseph Furphy, and Miles Franklin are key figures in the movement of nineteenth-century literary realism (Lamond).

Historically, literary realism, as its name reflects, speaks for the aim on behalf of its writers and readers to represent and engage with actual social, economic, and political phenomena. However, ecocritics fault the form on the grounds that it mostly focuses on *the human*. There is no sustained interest in or cynosure of *the environment*. Principal roles are given to human characters and secondary roles to other characters. The latter have limited agencies, to the extent that in the work of literary realism *the real* is eclipsed by or virtually synonymous with *the human*. Dominic Head sums up the genre's failings by saying that it is "peculiarly resistant to the operations of ecocritical inquiry" and any "green reading" of it thus demands at the outset, at the very least, "a vulgar ecocritical exploration of what is left out—of the genre's environmental bad faith" (2000, 237).

Even in the case of literary naturalism and regionalism, two late-nineteenth-century outcroppings of literary realism that do foreground ecogenic (nonhuman-made) environments, up until the 1980s the critical response to those genres reflects more interest in the human, or more interest in how humans are affectively and materially shaped by the (ecogenic) environment and less concern for how and why the (ecogenic) environment might be equally overdetermined (for example, bullied and threatened, not merely neutrally shaped and configured) by the human. In North America, literary naturalism is represented by such authors as Jack London, Stephen Crane, and Frank Norris. Sarah Orne Jewett, Mark Twain, and William Faulkner are famous figures in literary regionalism. Certainly, the two distinctive genres raise high the critical roof beam of *agency* as it applies to the shaping of the human by ecogenic environments. However, not until the emergence of ecocriticism in the 1980s do literary critics begin to show an interest in ecogenic environments in literature (for example, the Mississippi River that profoundly shaped Twain's writing or the coast of Maine where Jewett sets at least one of her most famous stories, *The Country of the Pointed Firs*) for reasons that reflect questions of environmental agency as that critically and morally attaches to questions of the *rights* of the environment. Before the late 1970s and early 1980s, when ecocriticism first emerges as a distinct area in literary studies, critics tend to reserve the question of *rights* (inclusive of suffrage and suffering) when addressing the human and overlook or dismiss that particular question when engaging with the (ecogenic) environment and the nonhuman species and ecosystems that support and make up that kind (and those kinds) of environments.

Much sci-fi, from its earliest formations and emergence alongside the birth of modern scientific inquiry in the seventeenth century (Stableford 2003, 15), to its dominant forms in the last two-thirds of the twentieth century, might be compared to nineteenth-century literary naturalism and regionalism because of its interest in nonhuman characters and agencies. Where that sci-fi greatly contrasts with those two literary relatives is in its dearth of ecogenic nonhuman characters and agencies. In that sci-fi, nonhuman characters typically are anthropogenic agents or else agents that hail from the otherworld of dreams or from the otherworld of extraterrestrial space. In that same sci-fi, explorations of strange new worlds—or *novum,* a term coined by sci-fi's "elder statesman" Darko Suvin (Roberts 2000, 7; Trexler and Johns-Putra 2011, 186)—tie to, further, manifest interest in the so-called hard sciences, in such subject areas as chemistry and physics, and the relative lack of interest in the soft sciences, in such subject areas as biology and psychology. These three main interests, or two main interests and third corollary interest—anthropogenic agents and agencies, extraterrestrial agents and agencies, and knowledge generated out of the hard sciences—are seen in the proliferation of spaceships, computers, mechanical robots, and computers. Interplanetary and interstellar travel and encounters with aliens also is subject matter that abounds in sci-fi up through the end of the last century (Roberts 2000, 15).

If, up through the 1990s, sci-fi shows as little interest in earthly ecogenic environments, so-called *natural* environments, as its generic opposite, literary realism, does, then more recently it takes a different flight. In the last two decades, sci-fi has turned more toward biology and the life sciences. Authors now explore biological intelligence and the brain, biological robots ("androids"), mutation and evolution, genetic engineering, sexuality and reproduction, and the environment and the biosphere (Slonczewski and Levy 2003, 174–175). The last two interests, the environment and the biosphere, shuttle sci-fi particularly in the direction of more down-to-earth realities, so to speak. One of those realities is climate change, a planetary progenitor of cli-fi.

The term "cli-fi" was coined less than a decade ago by Dan Bloom, a writer and blogger in Taiwan (Cranston 2019, 181). Bloom uses the term to distinguish any fiction that foregrounds "environmentalism and climate change issues" (Bloom 2013).[1] Adam Trexler and Adeline Johns-Putra, two prominent cli-fi scholars, further characterize cli-fi as a sub-genre of sci-fi that replaces off-the-planet settings with earthly venues, reflects interest in "the relationship between climate change and humanity in psychological and social terms," and represents climate change "not just as a meteorological or ecological crisis 'out there' but as something that is" vitally connected to the human and "filtered through our inner and outer lives" (2011, 196).[2] Trexler and Johns-Putra trace literary and cultural engagements with "worldwide environmental change" back to such ancient narratives as *Gilgamesh* and the biblical account of the flood; however, they emphasize that in its narrowest sense cli-fi refers to recent dystopic climate change narratives that address phenomena related to the escalation since the 1950s of the burning of fossil fuels, the rising of sea levels, rising temperatures, rising levels of greenhouse gases, shrinking sources of potable water, deforestation, desertification and so forth (2011, 186).[3] *Locust Girl* exemplifies cli-fi and it does so especially in the context of what ecofeminists are saying about climate change.

In the first section of the novel, entitled "Locust Girl," readers are introduced to the *Locust Girl's* eponymous heroine, nine-year-old Amedea. She lives with her father and mother and fellow country people in one of the seemingly endless camps, "missions," in a vast and arid territory. The people are controlled by the rulers of the so-called Five Kingdoms (Bobis 2015, 152). They eke out a bare existence, subsisting on rations and "sand porridge and locust" (3). When the rulers obliterate their country by fire, most of the people perish. Amedea is one of the few who survives. She hibernates deep below the Earth's surface. During that time, another lone survivor, a locust, buries itself in Amedea's forehead. Ten years later, the hybrid human-insect and "earth-other," "Locust Girl," is accidentally discovered by Beenabe, a sixteen-year old girl from a neighboring country who is lost and is trying to find her way back home.[4] The two girls make their way through a vast, parched, and denuded terrain in search of Beenabe's country. Along the way, desperately searching for water and grain (barley), they meet other displaced people, mostly children, women, and old men, presumably because the adult males of their population have died defending their people against the rulers of the Five Kingdoms. Most of the refugees have suffered great privation. Woman have lost their children. Many people are missing a body part because of the lucrative trade in heads, arms, legs, and so forth, a trade that is controlled by the senior-most government officials of the Five Kingdoms (the "Minister of Arms," the "Minister of Legs," the "Minster of Heads," and so forth). The people whom Amedea and Beenabe meet come from countries similar to their own, places that the rulers of the Five Kingdoms have destroyed, through both deliberate and sleight-of-hand genocidal and ecocidal policies. Vegetation is sparse. Water is in even more short supply, and there are few animal species. The only animal species that the rulers of the Five Kingdoms allow to survive in large numbers are the guri. The Five Kingdoms use them as a source of food, forcing women who are not officially or legally allowed to reside within the borders of the Five Kingdoms to kill the animals in regularly scheduled culls.

In the second section, "Singing," Amedea loses her beloved Beenabe not long after they reach Beenabe's country. Almost as soon as the two young women arrive, the rulers of the Five Kingdoms raze it to the ground. In the inferno, Amedea and Beenabe are separated. For three years after that, Amedea travels by foot in search of the borders of the Five Kingdoms, for, as rumors have it, there is where water, food, and work are plentiful. She meets many other displaced people who are also desperate to reach and cross the borders of the Five Kingdoms.

In the third and final section of *Locust Girl,* "Love," Amedea reaches the Five Kingdoms. There, she finds and is reunited with Beenabe, who now is a sex slave to officials of the Five Kingdoms. Not long afterward, the officials discover the two women together and charge them with the crimes of "singing," "disturbing the rooms," "spreading ill-rumours," "inspiring revolt," "sleeping in the impure rooms," "bringing in the plague," and "contaminating the Kingdoms" (Bobis 2015, 163). During the trial,

Amedea and Beenabe's friends, who are camped outside the borders of the Five Kingdoms, begin to sing. Amedea joins in with them. She "[gathers] all the unseen voices in [her] throat," which "[swells] with many more voices" until it can no longer "bear the strain," and her body "[bursts] and [catches] fire" (173). Everyone in the courtroom scatters. As she lights up in flames, Amedea transforms into a fully winged human-insect creature. She flies homeward. When she reaches her country, she sees that it has regenerated. She remembers that Beenabe had replanted the earth with seeds three years earlier, sometime after she and Beenabe were separated and before Beenabe was enslaved by the rulers of the Five Kingdoms. Amedea's country now is a vast plain of "green stubble as far as the eyes can see" (178). "I know our nature, I know our history," Amedea says. She continues: "how we love. How frail the heart, yet how enduring" (178-179).

Read in the context of its identity as a work of Australian literature, *Locust Girl* evokes current heated debates in Australia about the environmental impact of colonizer-settler people in Australia since it was claimed as a British colony in 1788. One side of those arguments is made by environmental historians, ecologists, and indigenous studies scholars. It is that Anglo-European newcomers to Australia transformed the continent in a remarkably short period of time, between 1788 and the present, from a loosely united amalgam of many small and relatively autonomous countries, where the human and the environment coexisted and where the environment was green for much of the year, to a country that now is dry across much of its length and breadth for many months in the year (Haebich 2019; Laudine 2019).[5] As that group of scholars also point out, many Australians take for granted or have been misled to believe that Australia's dry and sunburnt lineaments without exception predate by thousands of years the advent of European newcomers (Gammage 2011; Pascoe 2016; Rigby 2015; Rose 1996).

The arguments that environmental historians, ecologists, and indigenous studies scholars are making about the transformation of Australia since 1788 from a country where water and grasses were abundant to a country of parched earth, salinization of soils, soils prone to runoff, and shrinking aquifers, tie to a related argument, one articulated by ecofeminists, which is that the main protagonists of the baking and drying cake of the planet are key policymakers in governments and key stakeholders in both public and private institutions who either actively promote or passively condone *masculinist* values and behaviors. Greta Gaard, in a comprehensive and exhaustive account to date of ecofeminist theory and practice (2017), identifies and critiques those values and contrasts them with *ecofeminist* values. *Masculinist* values and the behaviors that reflect them refer to mainstream values and practices of competition, hierarchy, aggression, territorialism, confrontation, monopolization, and domination. *Ecofeminist* values and the practices that they define refer to cooperation, negotiation, compromise, nonhierarchical relations, empathy, sharing of space and place, listening, dialogue, and actively endeavoring to mitigate, avoidance, and reduce suffering and violent confrontation. The latter values and principles abound in the rhetoric of governments' abuses of the environment but are practiced far less and certainly not consistently or uniformly. In *Locust Girl,* the rulers of the Five Kingdoms behave mainly according to *masculinist* principles, and they assert that that is for the greater benefit. Under these *masculinist* principles and practices, the rulers rationalize, downplay, or deny the suffering that they cause to Amedea's people, Beenabe's people, and thousands of others. The rulers recognize neither the rights of ancient ecosystems nor the affective bonds that unite those ecosystems with the oldest human populations.

Throughout the world today, *masculinist* insensitivity to the bonds between human beings and ecogenic environments is triggering and driving climate change—drought, flood extreme weather, desertification, loss of arable land, loss of species, shrinking aquifers, and displacement of people. As ecofeminists argue, that insensitivity is not fully understood let alone addressed. Many of the world's most powerful political leaders and parties in effect dismiss outright the claim that their agendas are *masculinist.* A great deflection is occurring, and has been occurring. It is seen in the many public debates about people who are fleeing countries torn apart by political upheaval and civil war and crossing into others. Notwithstanding the new discourse of "climate migration" and the remarkable work of many scholars and activists who are pointing to and laying out the evidence for the links between climate change (or global warming) and patterns of migration in the present century, there is little discussion of the *masculinist* ideologies that are driving that flight and, behind that flight, the phenomenon of climate change (Lustgarten 2020b). There is little or no interest in the major role that discrimination against women plays and has been playing in the mainstream disregard for and disinterest in ecogenic environments. On the side of the debate that reflects governments' anti-immigration sentiments and arguments for an increase in "militarism," a *masculinist* "technoscience discourse" is particularly unquestioned, taken-for-granted, and assumed (Gaard 2017, 126, 140).

In identifying *masculinist* ideologies and practices as key drivers of climate change and the related phenomena of the migrations that humans are making today, the displacement of people, and the emptying of rural regions of human populations, ecofeminists who teach and study literature focus on, among many other literary genres, cli-fi and sci-fi literature. These scholars note that the most "prominent texts of climate change fiction and science fiction … are largely male-authored and nonfeminist at best, or antifeminist and sexist at worst" (Gaard 2017, 145).[6] Few of those texts address or climate change as it directly links to and betrays *masculinist agendas* and, beneath them, anthropocentric, "colonialist … antidemocratic, and antiecological beliefs and practices" (145). Such texts carry little social and environmentally transformative bites. Julia Kuznetski makes this point in "An Ecofeminist (Post) Ice-Age Dystopia: Doris Lessing's Mara and Dann Series" (this volume), where she observes that sci-fi from its beginnings has been a "eurocentric" and "white hero" genre, and one, moreover, that Ursula Le Guin—one of the historically few feminist authors of sci-fi literature—famously characterized as being "so self-contentedly, exclusively male, like a club, or a locker room" (quoted in Kuznetski, this volume). Mainstream sci-fi's obsession with the figure of the *alien* is one that betrays in particular fears of "the other" as that refers to women as well as to people who are not from western Europe whose cultural beliefs and practices are different from those of western Europeans (Kuznetski, this volume). Mainstream sci-fi's grand narratives also tend to revolve around representations of Earth and other planetary sites as spaces and places that are hostile to the human—specifically, "terraforming man"—and so spaces and places that jeopardize the survival of the human (Kuznetski, this volume). Popular sci-fi represents *masculinist* trends in "techno-science" typically in undiluted affirmative terms (Kuznetski, this volume).

Debra Wain, in "An Ecofeminist Treatment of Nourishment and Feeding in Margaret Atwood's MaddAddam Trilogy" (this volume) and Izabel F. O. Brandão and Ildney Cavalcanti, in "Margaret Atwood's Ecodystopic SF: Approaching Ethics, Gender, and Ecology" (also in this volume), similarly engage with mainstream *masculinist* beliefs about technology and science. The authors focus on the cli-fi and speculative fiction of Margaret Atwood. Wain examines Atwood's critique of *masculinist* techno-scientific food production and the links between that mode of food production and climate change. Citing the work of two Brazilian critics, Lúcia de La Rocque and Claudia Camel as well as a study by Sandra Harding, Brandão, and Cavalcanti address the *masculinist* biases in much scientific and technological research, research that amounts to "male science" (this volume).

In the area of food production, *masculinism* is as rampant as in other areas of human enterprise. Historically, food production is associated with women. In the last 50 years or so, food production was "taken out of the hand of nature (women) and put into the hands of science (men)" (this volume). Such seizure betrays both the *masculinist* hubris of believing that the human can control the environment (which includes plants that humans depend on for food) and the *masculinist* principles of monopolization and homogenization (which are seen in both the industrial farming of animals and in monocrop and cash crop agribusiness). Corporate food giants lead that theft and misappropriation (Gaard 2017, 132).

One of the most infamous global food giants is Monsanto, the subject of an incisive critique by Marie-Monique Robin entitled *The World According to Monsanto: Pollution, Politics, and Power*. It received the 2009 Rachel Carson Prize and also is the basis of a documentary film directed by Robin.

Robin's main argument is that industrial food giants such as Monsanto are making virtual vassals of farmers, stripping them of control over their crops as well as putting the fates of plants entirely in the hands of the human. The company allows the plants themselves little agencies of their own, agencies that in fact might be, and have been found in many cases to be, beneficial, or not only detrimental or useless, to humans. As ecofeminist and environmental justice scholar Rachel Stein describes one of Monsanto's *masculinist* principles and practices of monopolization, the company engineers seed stock that carries biological mechanisms, "terminator technologies," in order to make the stock sterile, and so farmers who purchase the stock cannot use what is left over for the next planting season (2010, 183). Instead, farmers must purchase new seed stock from Monsanto, and at prices that Monsanto dictates (183). The food conglomerate defends its right to destroy "plant reproductive capacities, so that neither farmers nor plants have access to free propagation outside of market property arrangements" (183). Moreover, it makes no effort to stop its bioengineered seeds from cross-pollinating with crops (in fields adjacent to where its bioengineered seeds are being grown) that are from older non-bioengineered seeds. Yet, its official rhetoric, like that of the Honorable Head in *Locust Girl*, is that it offers the most creative and productive solutions to ethical, sustainable food production and the science lab is the optimal environment for discovering those solutions.

Ecofeminists theorize the connections between food, hunger, and plants and animals. Hunger is a problem of unequal and unfair distribution of resources, not overpopulation. Global food giants oversee debt repayment programs and heavily invest in biotechnology corporations and industrialized animal food production. The debt repayment programs, which are euphemistically called "structural adjustments," require "developing countries to produce cash crops for export rather than food crops for subsistence as a way to pay off debt" (Gaard 2017, 132). Those same food giants "promote high-yield seeds which require expensive inputs of fertilizer and monocropping techniques that displace subsistence foods, destroy biodiversity, and lower water quality" (132). The displacement, destruction, and compromise of quality in turn produce more hunger and more debt (132). Industrialized animal food production, foremost of which is the production of meat and dairy, plays particular havoc with a broad range of interlocking justices: "species justice, environmental justice, reproductive justice and food justice" (132).

The term *masculinist* commonly carries negative connotations in ecofeminist critical contexts, and I have used it in those same senses here. I thus also use the term (as well as *masculinism*) in contrast with these terms: "masculine," "masculinity," and "masculinities." In ecofeminist discourse, these words carry meanings that include but are not limited to the typically negative meanings associated with *masculinist*. *Masculinist,* refers to dominant and mainstream forms of masculinity. A significant one of those forms is "white, human heteromasculinity," (Gaard 2017, 161). It refers to unquestioned equivalences between planetary progress, the human species, and Euro-Western heterosexuality (161). *Masculinist* contrasts with other forms of masculinity. Those other forms include "ecomasculinities" and "ecosexualities" (161). As Gaard notes, early ecofeminist studies, those published between the 1970s and 1990s, pointed to these alternative masculinities in the work of challenging

> monotheistic patriarchal religions that worship a sky god and remove spirituality and the sacred from the earth, placing hell beneath our feet and heaven in the sky, deifying men, and valuing men's associated attributes over the values, attributes, and bodies of women, children, nonhuman animals, and the rest of nature
>
> (185)

Gaard here draws on Judith Halberstam's groundbreaking study *Female Masculinity* (1998) in her own work of identifying ecocentric practices of masculinity that contrast with dominant, *masculinist*, forms of masculinity. The former practices are distinguished as "female masculinities" as well as "ecomasculinities" (Gaard 2017, 167).

Both "female masculinities" and "ecomasculinites" (Gaard 2017, 167) are seen in the critical work of "theory-building" that challenges dominant *masculinist* theoretical frameworks and in the work of "interrupting/contesting" the *masculinist* rhetoric of "corporate media" (167); they are seen also in the critical work of addressing "the ecopolitical relation between butch identities and veganism" and in the work of theorizing links between "climate justice and the material realities of economically marginalized women, people of color, queers, and nonhuman animals" (167). In the area of food justice, "female masculinities" and "ecomasculinities" are reflected in the efforts of "the budding ecoqueer movement" to expand alternative food movements, which have been predominantly white, heteromale, and middle class in their formation (132). "Female masculinities" and "ecomasculinities" also are reflected in posthumanist and critical animal studies and call for governments to recognize the affective entanglements that morally bind humans and other animals to each other; to free up "excessive land space now used by industrialized animal agriculture"; to promote "small-scale farming and community gardens"; and to cease "the artificial insemination of female animals on factory farms" (138). "Female masculinities" and "ecomasculinities" emphasize that climate change affects women and children more severely than any other human population (123).

In other words, "masculinity has not always been defined in opposition to ecology" (Gaard 2017, 165). The affinities between masculinity and ecology trace back to ancient indigenous cultures such as those in what are now the states of Arizona and New Mexico in the United States. The oldest human populations of this region of the planet worshipped the earth god, Kokopelli, "a 3,000-year-old Hopi symbol of fertility, replenishment, music, dance, and mischief" (165). Kokopelli continues to be worshipped today but is a marginalized god, overtaken by the *masculinist* gods of science and technology. Similarly, in many parts of Europe, people pay homage to the earth god, Green Man. Often "pictured as a male head disgorging vegetation from his mouth, ears, [and] eyes"—the deity traces back to ancient (pre-Roman conquest) Celtic beliefs and other European ecomasculine and ecosexual belief systems (165). In Greek mythology, Pan, that most underestimated and ridiculed of deities, is an earth god (Ralph 2011).

Ecofeminists argue that instead of striving for a "genderless society," it would be more productive and strategic to "[theorize] the ecological articulations of a diversity of genders and sexualities" (Garrd 2017, 167). These same scholars especially focus on "ecomasculinities" (167) because of the tendency among scholars to reductively construct and understand masculine gender identity as being, by definition, "*anti*ecological" (167). Normative, Western-European, *heterosexual* masculinities emphasize abstraction and individualism. They are predicated on notions of "maturity-as-separation" as well as notions of "male self-identity and self-esteem," and on high moral estimations of "dominance, conquest, workplace achievement, economic accumulation, elite consumption patterns and behaviours, physical strength, sexual prowess, animal 'meat' hunting and/or eating, and competitiveness" (163). In contrast, feminist and queer masculinities recognize in effect that "all human identities and moral conduct are best understood 'in terms of networks or webs of historical and concrete relationships'" (Warren 1990, quoted in Gaard, 168). Such masculinities challenge a dominant, *masculinist* "ethic of daring"; they speak for a marginalized, ecofeminist "ethic of caring" (Gaard 168). That ethic emphasizes love, tolerance, forgiveness, friendship, trust, compassion, consideration, reciprocity, and "cooperation with human and more-than-human life" (Pulé quoted in Gaard, 168).

Feminist and queer masculinities are largely unstudied and underestimated despite the fact that they play a vital role in the climate justice movement, ecojustice movement, as well as other activism struggles against "climate-changing forces of economic 'development'" based on "ecosystem destruction, species loss, homophobia, and the loneliness of humanism" (Gaard 2017, 186). Bobis's cli-fi novel speaks for those kinds of masculinities and speaks against *masculinism* in its narrative of two young women, possibly lovers, who struggle to survive in a *masculinist* world. Although younger than Amedea (by three years), Beenabe is physically bigger and stronger than Amedea. She also is more experienced and plays the role of protector and defender of Amedea. She also does not recoil against the trans-species being of Amedea when she first discovers the nineteen-year-old hybrid human-insect buried beneath the crust of the Earth. She represents what Gaaard calls the feminist masculine, queer masculine, and ecomasculine revolts against "species loss, homophobia, and the loneliness of humanism" (2017, 186). Amedea's figure complements Beenabe; her character speaks for the profound symbiotic relationships between humans and what Gaard calls "earth others" (Gaard 2017, 22), and for what could be possible if governments were to recognize and promote feminist masculinities, queer masculinities, ecomasculinities, and other non-*masculinist* beliefs and behaviors. Amedea represents that vision in particular in her trans-species bonds with a lone winged insect, the sole survivor of a species that has been wiped out by the Five Kingdoms.

Insects, by far the most successful planetary species, "are multitudinous almost beyond our imagining" (McCarthy 2017). They "thrive in soil, water, and air," "have triumphed for hundreds of millions of years in every continent bar Antarctica" and "in every habitat but the ocean" (McCarthy 2017). Their planetary success has seemed "staggering, unparalleled and seemingly endless" (McCarthy 2017). However, winged insects are disappearing at alarming rates. One study, part of a series of studies in the past five years, found that "the biomass of flying insects" in Germany has dropped by three-quarters since 1989 (McCarthy 2017). Perhaps, one should find hope in the fact that scientists now at least are concurring that it is human activity—generations of "blithely accepted" industrialized farming that has poured "a vast tide of poisons ... over the land year after year after year" since the 1950s (McCarthy 2017)—that is causing the attrition. As ecofeminists critically narrow down that "human activity," it betrays *masculinist* assumptions, beliefs, prerogatives, and practices.

In bringing together ecofeminist theory and Bobis's cli-fi novel *Locust Girl*, and in doing so first by situating cli-fi between the two once genres of literary realism and sci-fi, I have aimed in this chapter to critically foreground recent developments in ecofeminism that overlap with queer ecology, climate justice, environmental justice, and environmental rights. I also have sought to bring attention to a relatively little known work of Australian cli-fi that complements and articulates key concerns that scholars address under the critical inquiry of ecofeminism.

Notes

1 Bloom singles out Taiwanese writer Mingyi Wu's *The Man with the Compound Eyes* (複眼人) (2011) as an inaugural work of cli-fi.
2 See, also, Trexler (2014).
3 For examples of early cli-fi (beginning in the 1950s) that directly and specifically deal with climate change and for the distinction between popular or formulaic cli-fi fiction and so-called literary and "more serious" cli-fi, see Trexler and Johns-Putra (2011).
4 The term "earth other" is from Gaard (2017, 22).
5 Haebich's argument is in specific context of the history of Anglo-European colonization and settlement of Western Australia; it readily applies to or represents the history of colonization and settlement of much of the Australian continent and its islands after 1788 by Anglo-European newcomers.

6 At the same time, as Sarah Lefanu argues in an early work of feminist sci-fi criticism, the genre's "plasticity…makes possible, and encourages (despite the colonization by male writers) the inscription of women as subjects free from the constraints of mundane fiction; it offers the possibilities of interrogating that very inscription, questioning the basis of gendered subjectivity (1988, 9). For more on the absence of women in as well as the contribution that feminism has made to sci-fi, see Hollinger (1999, 254).

References

Bloom, Dan. 2013. "'Cli-fi' All the Rage among Literati and Academia." *Taipei Times*, July 12, 8.

Bobis, Merlinda. 2015. *Locust Girl*. North Melbourne, VIC: Spinifex Press.

Cranston, CA. 2019. "Reconstructing Representations: 'Australia' as Ecocritical Androgyny." In *Ecocritical Concerns and the Australian Continent*, edited by Beate Neumeier and Helen Tiffin, 163–189. Lanham, MD: Lexington.

Gaard, Greta. 2017. *Critical Ecofeminism*. Lanham, MD: Lexington.

Gammage, Bill. 2011. *The Biggest Estate on Earth: How Aborigines Made Australia*. Sydney: Allen and Unwin.

Haebich, Ann. 2019. "Biological Colonization in the Land of Flowers." In *Ecocritical Concerns and the Australian Continent*, edited by Beate Neumeier and Helen Tiffin, 75–90. Lanham, MD: Lexington.

Halberstam, Judith. 1998. *Female Masculinity*. Durham, NC: Duke University Press.

Head, Dominic. 2000. "Ecocriticism and the Novel." In *The Green Studies Reader: From Romanticism to Ecocriticism*, edited by Laurence Coupe, 235–241. London: Routledge.

Hollinger, Veronica. 1999. "Contemporary Trends in Science Fiction Criticism, 1980–1999." *Science-Fiction Studies* 26: 232–262.

Jewett, Sarah Orne. [1896] 1997. *The Country of the Pointed Firs*. New York: Simon & Schuster.

Lamond, Julieanne. 2011. "Stella vs. Miles: Women Writers and Literary Value in Australia." *Meanjin Quarterly* 70, no. 3: 32–39. Accessed July 25, 2020. https://meanjin.com.au/essays/stella-vs-miles-women-writers-and-literary-value-in-australia

Laudine, Catherine. 2019. "From Reverence to Rampage: Care for Country versus Ruthless Exploitation." In *Ecocritical Concerns and the Australian Continent*, edited by Beate Neumeier and Helen Tiffin, 43–56. Lanham, MD: Lexington.

Lefanu, Sarah. 1988. *The Chinks of the World Machine: Feminism and Science Fiction*. London: Women's Press.

Lustgarten, Abram. 2020a. "The Great Climate Migration." *New York Times*, July 23. Accessed October 4, 2020. https://www.nytimes.com/interactive/2020/07/23/magazine/climate-migration.html

Lustgarten, Abram. 2020b. "How Climate Migration Will Reshape America." *New York Times*, September 15. Accessed October 4, 2020. https://www.nytimes.com/interactive/2020/09/15/magazine/climate-crisis-migration-america.html.

McCarthy, Michael 2017. "A Giant Insect Ecosystem Is Collapsing." *The Guardian*, October 21. Accessed August 30, 2020. https://www.theguardian.com/environment/2017/oct/21/insects-giant-ecosystem-collapsing-human-activity-catastrophe

Mullan, John. 2014. "Realism (The Novel 1832–1880)." *Discovering Literature: Romantics and Victorians*. British Library. Accessed October 3, 2020. https://www w.bl.uk/romantics-and-victorians/articles/realism

Pascoe, Bruce. 2016. *Dark Emu: Black Seeds: Agriculture or Accident?* Broome, WA: Magabala Books.

Pulé, Paul M. 2009. "Caring for Society and Environment: Towards Ecological Masculinism." Paper Presented at the Villanova University Sustainability Conference, April. Accessed October 1, 2020. http://www.paulpule.com.au/Eco logical_Masculinism.pdf

Pulé, Paul M. 2007. "Ecology and Environmental Studies." In *Routledge International Encyclopedia of Men and Masculinities*, edited by Michael Flood, Judith Kegan Gardiner, Bob Pease, and Keith Pringle, 158–162. New York: Routledge.

Ralph, Iris. 2011. "*Paterson*, Pan, Satyrs, and Deep Ecology." *NTU Studies in Language and Literature* 25: 81–104.

Rigby, Kate. 2015. *Dancing with Disaster: Environmental Histories, Narratives, and Ethics for Perilous Times*. Charlottesville: University of Virginia Press.

Roberts, Adam. 2000. *Science Fiction*. Oxon: Routledge.

Robin, Marie-Monique. 2010. *The World According to Monsanto: Pollution, Politics, and Power*. North Melbourne, VIC: Spinifex Press.

Rose, Deborah Bird. 1996. *Nourishing Terrains: Australian Aboriginal Views of Landscape and Wilderness*. Canberra: Australian Heritage Commission. Accessed October 3, 2020. https://www.academia.edu/4539641/Nourishing_Terrains_Au stralian_Aboriginal_views_of_Landscape_and_Wilderness_Australian_Heritage _Commission_Canberra_1996.Slonczewski

Slonczewski, Joan, and Michael Levy. 2003. "Science Fiction and the Life Sciences." In *The Cambridge Companion to Science Fiction*, edited by Edward James and Farah Mendlesohn, 174–185. Cambridge: Cambridge University Press.

Stableford, Brian. 2003. "Science Fiction before the Genre." In *The Cambridge Companion to Science Fiction*, edited by Edward James and Farah Mendlesohn, 15–31. Cambridge: Cambridge University Press.

Stein, Rachel. 2010. "Bad Seed: Imperiled Biological and Social Diversity in Ruth Ozeki's *All Over Creation*." In *Postcolonial Green Environmental Politics and World Narratives*, edited by Bonnie Roos and Alex Hunt, 177–193. Charlottesville: University of Virginia Press.

Trexler, Adam. 2014. "Mediating Climate Change: Ecocriticism, Science Studies, and *The Hungry Tide*." In *The Oxford Handbook of Ecocriticism*, edited by Greg Garrard, 205–224. Oxford: Oxford University Press.

Trexler, Adam, and Adeline Johns-Putra. 2011. "Climate Change in Literature and Literary Criticism." *WIREs Clim Change* 2: 185–200. Accessed May 10, 2020. doi:10.1002/wcc.105. https://www.researchgate.net/publication/230451233 _Climate_change_in_literature_and_literary_criticism.

Warren, Karen. 1990. "The Power and the Promise of Ecological Feminism." *Environmental Ethics* 12: 125–144.

Wu, Mingyi (吳明益). [2010] 2013. *The Man with the Compound Eyes* (複眼人). Translated by Darryl Sterk. London: Harvill-Secker.

Part 2
Utopias on Earth and Beyond

6 "Extinction is Forever"

Ecofeminism and Apocalypse in Louise Lawrence's Young Adult Short Fiction

Michelle Deininger and Gemma Scammell

Introduction

Ecofeminism, at its heart, identifies parallels between the patriarchal domination of women and the exploitation of the environment. The term is credited to Françoise d'Eaubonne whose *Le Féminisme ou la Mort [Feminism or Death]* (1974) highlighted a "direct link between the oppression of women and the oppression of nature" (Tong 1998, 251). Despite the existing debate over the exact scope of the term, and the relationship between activism and scholarship, this chapter takes the position that there are compelling parallels between feminist and environmental issues that need to be acknowledged and explored. Furthermore, this chapter argues that science fiction is a form of environmental literature *par excellence*. There is, we would argue, much more at stake than publishing tastes or the constraints of genre labels when it comes to ecofeminist science fiction, a type of writing that could easily fall through the cracks of "serious" literary criticism. This kind of fiction has the power to reimagine the world and so transform it. Moreover, ecofeminist science fiction gives writers the opportunity to explore different types of knowledge and understandings in imagined futures beyond the reckoning of today's ethical or moral codes. As Natalie Rosinsky argues, drawing on the work of Carol Christ, fantasy genres may be "as significant a form of discourse for women seeking to shape a 'sacred story' of transcendence, questioning for self and spiritual awareness, as more conventionally realistic, serious modes" (1984, 3). Julia Kuznetski (this volume) engages with Donna Harroway's *A Cyborg Manifesto* (1991) to argue that the boundary between science fiction and reality is merely an illusion and that ecofeminist science fiction has the potential to present a realistic picture of how climate change will affect our everyday lives if nothing is done to prevent it.

Louise Lawrence (1943–2013) published prolifically over her lifetime, from her first novel *Andra* (1971) to her ebook-only novel *The Witch and the Weathermage* (2013), which was published only weeks before her death. Born Elizabeth Rhoda Wintle Holden, she used the pseudonym of Louise Lawrence throughout her writing career. Very little has been written about her and her short stories are rarely explored from an academic standpoint.

What is striking about her writing, looking back over her apocalyptic and futuristic worlds, is that her fictions, which are deeply rooted in an ecofeminist agenda, engage with the issues of living in what we now call the Anthropocene—the term for the period in which humanity's impact on the planet's geology, ecosystems and climate, reached its tipping point. The type of fiction Lawrence was writing from the 1970s onward could be termed as "cli-fi"—a new genre of fiction accredited to 2011 in which climate change is the primary theme. As Kuznetski (this volume) explains, the character struggles in this type of fiction center around the degraded environment they live in. Climate change and environmental disaster is something we can readily identify with. The summer of 2020 saw mass forest fires sweep through Australia while 2018 saw multiple protests across the globe from young adults in the *Friday's for Future* campaign, organized by the environmental activist Greta Thunberg. Thunberg also attended the 2018 United Nations Climate Change Conference, where she publicly criticised world leaders for their lack of action in combating carbon emissions.

As a term, the Anthropocene takes into account the altered atmospheric changes from carbon emissions, oceans polluted by plastic waste and the mass extinctions of both plants and animals. This coincides with the start of the nuclear age and the "Great Acceleration," a period which saw a substantial increase in carbon emissions, species extinction, concrete, plastic and metal waste, along with a population boom. These environmental and ecological concerns made their first appearance in literature in the 1960s when the world suddenly became aware of "global warming, deforestation, desertification, the disappearance of species, the destruction of the outer ozone layer (leading to increased skin cancer), and other alarming environmental changes" (Lippit 2005, 129). The 1990s, known as "The Decade of the Environment" following the Earth Summit of 1992—an event which brought together world leaders to acknowledge and address anthropogenic issues—also saw the use of Lawrence's nuclear war novel, *Children of the Dust* (1985), as part of the National Curriculum, as a set text for GCSE examinations in English Literature. The novel portrays the world in various states of ecological decline, while engaging with ecofeminism, deep ecology, capitalism as an ideology of mass consumer waste, and in some cases, utopian outcomes that draw parallels with socialist ideology. The novel remains on the National Curriculum recommended reading list for students at Key Stage 4, aged 14–16 years in England and is, lamentably, one of the few examples of her writing to still be in print.

More recently, themes of deep ecology, environmental disaster, and climate change have been at the forefront of young adult fiction. Examples include Suzanne Collins' *The Hunger Games* (2008), which features a dystopic future where nuclear war has destroyed most of the planet, leaving only 13 districts suitable for habitation. Justin D'Ath's *Shædow Master* (2003) sees the 15-year-old Aqua-Ora renounce the throne and become a

Shædow Master (a spirit capable of healing and sustaining the ecosystem), a transformation that brings harmony to multiple races and the environment. Philip Reeve's *Mortal Engines Quartet* (2001, 2003, 2005, 2006)—recently made into a film (2018)—features a world where cities are mobile engines struggling to survive in a barren wasteland caused by warfare. These novels paint a bleak picture of what life could look like as a result of world war and mass consumption of the planet's dwindling resources. The worlds that Louise Lawrence imagined are, in many ways, precursors to these highly successful young adult novels and were path breaking in their exploration of the impact of human destruction on the environment.

This chapter will argue that Lawrence's young adult science fiction engages with the three key themes considered by Patrick D. Murphy (2000) as essential frontiers for ecocritical analysis, as they:

> provide factual information about nature and human-nature interactions ... provide analogous depictions of ecosystems and human interaction with such systems ... [and finally, they] demonstrate the disastrous consequences of exploitive relationships between humans and other humans, humans and other sentient beings, and humans and ecosystems in which they are an exotic.
>
> (2000, 41)

Lawrence is able to fully realize these themes through her use of the short story form, which has often been considered a genre concerned with non-hegemonic experience. Clare Hanson (1985) examines the short story as a tool for engaging with key ideological factors, arguing that:

> The short story is a vehicle for different kinds of knowledge, knowledge which may be in some way at odds with the 'story' of dominant culture. The formal properties of the short story—disjunction, inconclusiveness, obliquity—connect with its ideological marginality and with the fact that the form may be used to express something suppressed/repressed in mainstream literature.
>
> (1985, 6)

Building upon *Children of the Dust* (1985) Lawrence continues to engage with the two political ideologies of capitalism and socialism in her short story collection *Extinction is Forever* (1990), which is the main focus of this chapter. "The Death Flower," which is discussed later in the chapter, consists of a technologically advanced civilization represented by the Galactic Council, who "ruled over the whole Federation of Planets, great men gathered together, representative of worlds" (Lawrence 1990, 86). This Council is intent on committing genocide in order to save a planet, X33, from itself once it develops nuclear technology. X33 is continually contrasted with

X21, the planet Merion, the home of a small, socialist society whose simple and non-technological lifestyle is portrayed as a type of utopia. The story throws a critical light on issues of deep ecology and morality by showing Merion as a paradise with the severely reduced human population living in harmony with the surrounding ecology. Furthermore, the text highlights the role of the mentor-mentee relationship from an ecofeminist standpoint. This relationship is a key part of Lawrence's oeuvre and is perhaps most obvious in her chilling yet cautionary dedication at the beginning of *Children of the Dust*: "for the children that they may never know the dust" (1985).

Louise Lawrence's Ecofeminist Utopias and Dystopias

Lawrence utilized science fiction to engage with ecofeminist issues that were, when she was writing in the 1980s, underexplored, especially in the fields of young adult fiction and the short story. Through the use of utopian and dystopian imagery, settings and plot lines, we are presented with the reoccurring trope that society needs to firstly experience a dystopia of apocalyptic proportions before it can truly achieve a utopian way of life. The utopias Lawrence describes demonstrate a society in which the indigenous people live in harmony with each other and the environment. She repeatedly explores this kind of story—from the post-industrial, depleted world of "The Inheritors," in *Extinction is Forever*, to a fully-fledged exploration of a society so dependent on fossil fuels that social cohesion and industrial infrastructure collapse in her novel *The Disinherited* (1994). This novel, set in Cardiff and Penarth (south Wales), explores a future in which society failed to utilize clean energy and so depleted fossil fuels to near extinction levels. This utter failure to consider the long-term effects fossil fuel usage has on the planet has recently been brought to the forefront by *The New York Times* in their article "The Trump Administration Is Reversing 100 Environmental Rules. Here's the Full List" (Popovich, Albeck-Ripka, and Pierre-Louis 2020). The reversal of these rules looks to undo the environmental protections brought into effect by President Obama and sees America taking a clear step backward in its use and reliance on fossil fuels. *The Disinherited* provides a glimpse of what America could look like should it continue to ignore climate change. In these two fictions, both set in the same area of industrial south Wales, these dystopias have the potential to become utopias if capitalism is abandoned in favor of environmental harmony. It is this push toward this vision of the future, characterized by community and co-operation rather than violence and greed, that makes Lawrence's fictions inherently ecofeminist.

Lawrence's young adult science fiction was written during a period in which science fiction (SF) saw a revitalization of utopias, accredited to "the re-emergence of feminism in the later 1960s … the Civil Rights movement, the New Left, the ecological movement the anti-war protests of the early

1970s and the emerging gay and lesbian movements" (James 2003, 225). Lawrence was by no means the only author writing consciously utopian novels focused on a concern for the environment. She was joined by Angela Carter's *Heroes and Villains* (1969), Ernest Callenbach's *Ecotopia* (1975), and Sheri S. Tepper's *The Gate to Women's Country* (1988), yet she has been strangely overlooked from a critical standpoint. Lawrence's fictions throw a crucial light on ecofeminist issues by portraying varying levels of dystopian futures that could happen, should we continue marching to the beat of capitalism's ideology of mass consumerism and waste. Accompanying these futuristic outcomes is the eventual prospect of a utopian lifestyle that sees the ecofeminist aspirations of a society living in peace and harmony with all life forms, including the surrounding ecosystem. Lawrence's use of the science fiction genre to explore ecofeminist themes sees her "not merely writing light, diversionary, or 'escapist' fiction but … analysing and responding to vital contemporary issues" (Rosinsky 1984, 3).

More recently, with the outbreak of COVID-19, we have seen a change in the way we live forced upon us by the need for sudden, large-scale lockdowns. These lockdowns have resulted in a lowering of carbon emissions following a huge reduction in international flights and, on a more local level, a reduction in car pollution caused by people working from home. This reduction is tempered, however, by the continuing impacts of consumerism and mass waste, crystallized in the form of single-use plastic. Lockdown, however, has given local wildlife a chance to bloom with an increase in animal activity as a direct result of the reduction of human movement. As Professor Martin Wikelski argues, "relatively minor changes to our lifestyles and transport networks can potentially have significant benefits for both ecosystems and humans" (*Science Daily* 2020). The shock waves of COVID-19 are microcosms, in some respects, of the cataclysmic changes that would force transformation in many of Lawrence's worlds. Whether humanity will make the same choices as the characters in her fictions, who choose community over consumerism, remains to be seen.

Lawrence's utopias are frequently concerned with issues of morality. Lawrence emphasizes this by continually raising the notion of human rights, using her fictions to call these ideals into question. "Rigel Light" sees the colonization of an alien planet, in which the inhabitants' infants are forced into slavery. The exploitation of these indigenous children sits in line with the capitalist ideology which is "predicated on the pursuits of profit […] part of profit maximization involves minimizing costs" (Lippit 2005, 130–131). As Vandana Singh (this volume) highlights in the foreword, the exploitation of indigenous peoples is a direct consequence of the power structures created by capitalism, which is precisely what the humans on Rigel Three enact upon their colonization of the planet. The human conquerors collect the seemingly abandoned offspring of the indigenous inhabitants and lock them inside a compound with electrified fencing. These children are then forced to work as slaves in the fields, farming Earth-like foods for the surrounding colonies of human workers. At times, the human characters are able to receive psychic messages from the infants' parents—something that is mistakenly thought of as a type of attack—but eventually, the human colonizers realize that the indigenous inhabitants are not simply attacking out of aggression, but are trying to reach and free their offspring. This sudden realization that these children were not abandoned and that they had actually stolen them and forced them into slavery causes the human population to consider the morality of their actions and to seek immediate redemption by opening the electrified gates and setting the children free. Stephanie Lahar (1996) takes the subject of morality to be a key feature of ecofeminism, regarding it as "a prescriptive psychological and social model that includes an idea of future potential and how best to unfold it, not just an analysis of how things were in the past or are currently" (1996, 8–9). Lahar warns "that Ethical systems based only in abstracted values fail to draw real commitments and can too easily be used as tools of manipulation and deception—for example, to rationalize military aggression in the basis of furthering democracy" (1996, 9). This is precisely what happens in Lawrence's debut novel *Andra* (1971), where a totalitarian government risks the future of its youth in order to maintain order in an underground world, created in the wake of nuclear disaster. Lawrence revisits this topic again in *Children of the Dust*; in the middle section of the novel, the military leader of one of the few surviving underground bunkers insists on totalitarian rule, as a necessity to safeguard the democracy of the future. In this case, "it is a matter no longer only of dictatorial control but now also of democratic process, [...] people allow themselves to be controlled, [...] supposedly for the people's own protection" (Kaplan 2016, 31). In Lawrence's fiction, however, these militarized societies crumble in front of the reader's eyes, and a new era begins to take shape, often led by strong female characters.

Lawrence furthers her engagement with ecofeminist issues by examining the role of capitalism in her dystopic and eventual utopic outcomes. Lawrence's depiction of capitalism parallels that of Henri Lefebvre by acknowledging its domination of "not just industrialisation or the reproduction of the labour force, but also the intensity of the administrative and political colonisation of lived experience" (Butler 2014, 51). Capitalism, then, is an all-encompassing ideology. E. Ann Kaplan argues in *Climate Trauma: Foreseeing the Future in Dystopian Film and Fiction* (2016) that "as drastic climate change renders the end of the world a potential reality, we have to revise our leftist thinking" (2016, 5). Kaplan explores the links between capitalism and environmental degradation and highlights the need for political change. Lawrence continually revisits socialist communities in her fictions, often achieved after mass environmental damage caused by a capitalist society. As Lawrence warns continually in her fictions, "the end result can only be the destruction of that environment and of all the species that rely upon it" (Lippit 2005, 130). Several of Lawrence's stories engage directly with this such as, the utopian planet Merion in "The Death Flower," which had previously been a capitalist economy, the exploitation of children in the name of capitalism in "Rigel Light," and the acute global climate change in "The Inheritors," which examines a shift from capitalism to a more communal, socialist way of life.

Engaging with themes of deep ecology, where human life is just one of many parts of a global ecosystem, Lawrence's fiction portrays mass-scale death, and often complete extinction of the human population through nuclear fallout. These dystopian settings pave the way for a utopian way of life for the remaining or new species, one in which humanity is forced to recognize and learn from past mistakes. Lawrence engages with the population problem theorized by deep ecologists, in which she recognizes that the "relevance of the size of the human population in the consideration of global environmental destruction and species depletion cannot be denied" (Cuomo 1994, 91). The title story, "Extinction is Forever," sees the protagonist, Stephen, theorize upon his discovery of a future in which mankind has been wiped out by a nuclear holocaust, that each life form has a "suicide instinct triggered naturally whenever the species put too great a strain upon the environment" (Lawrence 1990, 39). This hypothesis is further echoed in "The Death Flower" where the eponymous plant is described as instigating "a kind of natural selection [...] because those who were left were the ones who learned to adapt" (Lawrence 1990, 93). These engagements with deep ecology continue in Lawrence's other works, such as *Children of the Dust*, which concludes with a severely reduced human population, expected to die out imminently, leaving the new race of humanoids, now imbued with almost magical powers, to live in harmony with the surrounding ecosystem.

Mentor–Mentee Relationships

While Louise Lawrence utilizes the tropes of utopia and dystopia to explore wider social and ecological issues, it is also at the level of form and theme that her writing has transformative power. *Extinction is Forever* is, above all, a collection of cautionary tales, or modern-day fables, which warn their young adult audience about the dangers of mistreating and devaluing the natural world. If humanity is to survive, the stories foretell, it cannot continue to ignore the consequences of environmental destruction. Hatice Övgü Tüzün (this volume) examines the work of Octavia Butler (1993 and 2000), which allows us to identify a similar trend in ecofeminist science fiction in that Butler, too, engages with a parable type of story, creating cautionary tales in the form of dystopic future scenarios. These dystopian settings, like Lawrence's, serve as a warning of what our future may look like should we continue to ignore climate change. Two of the collection's stories, "Extinction is Forever" and "Rigel Light," were originally published in an important anthology entitled *Out of Time: Stories of the Future* (1984), which was edited by the influential "youth literature" and education critic Aidan Chambers. When *Extinction is Forever* was published as a collection in 1990, events such as the Chernobyl disaster (1986) and the terrifying possibilities of the Cold War were still fresh in popular memory. Each story has a clear purpose—in some way, each story aims to shape and change the reader's understanding of current and future ecological issues. Most importantly, Lawrence deploys the trope of the mentor-mentee relationship to educate and transform readers' understanding of global issues that remain, especially now, politically pressing.

In the title story, "Extinction is Forever," the reader is presented with several versions of the mentor-mentee relationship, in two distinct time frames. Kermondley is a teacher figure in the post-apocalyptic world where a new species of humanity now lives—an aquatic race with recognizable human features. Kermondley imparts knowledge of history to his students, including the inquisitive and empathic Vanya, partly by showing them the ruins of the long-lost human civilization of London. In a parallel scenario, in the world of 2005 (set 20 years ahead of the time Lawrence wrote the story), Stephen is the student of Professor Goddard, in a physics department at the University of London. While Kermondley teaches Vanya about the nuclear holocaust, Goddard is equipping Stephen to travel to the thirty-first century to see how the future of humanity will unfold, to prove whether nuclear catastrophe is inevitable. As readers, we know what Stephen will find even before we encounter him in the story. Moments before Stephen leaves 2005, he is watching a march comprised of peace campaigners, making their way to Trafalgar square. Goddard asks, speaking of the protestors: "Are they right to demand the abolition of nuclear weapons? ... Or is it, as the government claims, only the threat of nuclear war that guarantees world peace?" (Lawrence 1990, 37). What Stephen records as he travels through time is thoroughly bleak and answers those questions beyond doubt:

> He had seen the white clouds mushroom over England and the black ash falling on the land. He had witnessed the whimpering aftermath of a war they said would never happen, the hell of human dying and genetic decline. What new life was born sickened and failed ... plant, animal and human. It seemed that nothing survived.
>
> (37–38)

The beauty of Lawrence's story is that it forces the reader to view the world through a different lens and to understand the complexities of human experiences and prejudices from a variety of viewpoints. Even in the naming of the characters, Lawrence points toward a future where the patriarchal constraints of the world of 2005 will no longer hold sway. Vanya, for example, is often a masculine name while Kermondley sounds more like a place name or a surname. Stephen, by contrast, evokes the martyrdom of St Stephen, while it seems no coincidence that Professor Goddard wields god-like power through the knowledge that the time machine can bring.

Stephen's terrible vision of the future is an inevitable fact of capitalist expansion by the time that Vanya is learning about the planet's past. While the suffering caused by nuclear contamination is terrible, the new life that emerges is full of hope. Vanya epitomizes this hope as she has empathy for the humanity that she is distantly related to, symbolized by the lone figure of Stephen, an alien himself in this new world. Through Kermondley's teaching, Vanya is able to recognize that "The Ancients were not simply a legendary race, just marble statues in the sea-museums, cold carved forms of men and women, artworks and artifacts and strange-sounding names [...] as real and alive as she was now" (Lawrence 1990, 36). It quickly becomes clear that Vanya's whole existence is threatened by Stephen's desire to return to 2005, in order to give the government proof of the nuclear devastation. This is where the story turns darker and opens up an important ethical debate— is Stephen's right to alter his future more important than Vanya's right to life? The story, we discover, has a clear answer—the humanity of 2005 cannot sacrifice the lives of the human hybrids of the future. There is, as with Benay Blend's (2021) discussion of Louise Erdrich's *The Future Home of the Living God* (2017), a beauty in this post-apocalyptic world that has an intrinsic value of its own. Following her vandalization of Stephen's time machine effectively trapping him in the future, Vanya bitterly says, "One nuclear war guaranteed" to which Kermondley reminds her, "The Ancients still have a choice" and it is this knowledge that drives the story (Lawrence 1990, 47). Lawrence is arguing, effectively, that all the technology in the world will not save the human race—it is education. What makes this element of the story ecofeminist, and so many of the others in the collection, is that it is about dismantling patriarchal systems of power and thought and that for there to be a future at all, a new way of thinking—about the world, its resources, and its inhabitants—must evolve.

"The Death Flower": Ecophobia and Ecohorror

Themes of mentorship, learning, and education run deeply through "The Death Flower," one of Lawrence's most disturbing stories, a tale that explores facets of ecophobia and ecohorror. The story begins at the Academy, where students train for intergalactic missions. Pilot Hal-Arrison must take a trip to X21, the planet Merion, accompanied by the botanist Dr Largo and the student, Ky. Ky is there to learn and observe as part of his training, but unaware that he is being pulled into the calculating plans of Dr Largo. Ky is the innocent who learns the truth about the societies he visits, following the path of the young adult reader Lawrence's fiction aimed to educate. In a scene similar to Stephen's view of history unfolding, Ky's first vision of both the planet and the plant of the story's title tracks a familiar story. Rather than nuclear devastation, Ky sees a dead world; it is this process, of gradually perceiving the horrors of adult life and the wreckage caused to the environment by humanity that frames the experience of the Academy's employees and the wider work of the Galactic Council:

> Clouds obscured his view. Then they emerged and below was a landscape of rolling hills and dead vegetation, a forest perhaps, dry, brown and leafless. [...] For hundreds of miles the jungle went on, brown matted colour [...] Nothing was alive on this part of Merion ... But Ky saw something on the land beneath the undergrowth. He saw perhaps shapes of fields, bare earth sucked clean of sustenance, a few ruined buildings, then fallen walls and a pattern of streets.
>
> (Lawrence 1990, 79)

Dawn Keetley's (2016) discussion of plant horror is particularly pertinent here as she describes how "plants do not only mass, swarm, and crowd, they hijack—as is apparent in apocalyptic visions of vegetation overgrowing a ruined built environment" (2016, 15). There are the vestiges of a civilization beneath the plant matter, but nature has retaken this space so that human handiwork is barely visible. When Ky asks if the reason for the devastation is atomic war, Hal-Arrison says "Just war [...] And poverty and pollution, the mass slaughter of animals for food, rape and murder and violence ... whatever else is acceptable in an unenlightened civilization. They never reached the atomic stage on Merion" (Lawrence 1990, 79). Part of Ky's education is to learn to value this matted brown vegetation in a different way, much as Vanya must come to understand her ancestors from a different perspective. In many ways, the reader is caught up in the process of gradual perception, as the ending of the story forcefully reminds us. Merion's past is inextricably linked to the fate of X33, a planet that is known to be "decadent and unstable," populated by a "renegade civilisation," and so much of a preoccupation within the Galactic Council that X33 has become part of the curriculum at the Academy, and "what to do about it became every student's problem" (Lawrence 1990, 79). Later, when Ky has landed on Merion, he begins to understand the dangers of this seemingly dead plant matter. When he approaches it, he senses it as much as sees it: "Something was alive out there in the tangled darkness, something terrible and formless, watching and waiting and knowing he was there" (1990, 82). As an outsider, Ky's perceptions of this plant matter echo the anthropocentric and androcentric views of the settler character, Davidson, in Ursula K. Le Guin's *The Word for World is Forest* (1972), as discussed by Deirdre Byrne (2021). In fact, both texts are fundamentally concerned with depicting different ways of living, of being—in Le Guin's story, Byrne (2021) argues that it is the forested world of Athshe that shapes the social, emotional, and cognitive practices of its inhabitants. Similarly, in Lawrence's story, the vegetation that covers huge swathes of the planet's surface shapes the way communities are formed and built.

Ky's perceptions also have a dimension which closely links to Simon C. Estok's (2011) definition of ecophobia as "an irrational and groundless fear or hatred of the natural world" (2011, 4). The plant that Ky has seen from the viewing platform of his ship, and then later, on the planet's surface, is the death flower of the story's title. It feeds on negative human emotions, such as rage and jealousy. As this plant is repeatedly described as being female, there is a deep connection between the fears associated with women in patriarchy and the horror incited by the plant in the story. Lawrence weaves together associations with fairy tale, myth, and legend as the death flower is a vampiric plant which required "blood in order to germinate, emotional terror, some blundering creature to impale itself on her spikes" (1990, 83). The seeds are well hidden within the plant's roots and perhaps evoke the seeds of the pomegranate, associated in Greek myth with Persephone's journey into hell. At the same time, the plant has much in common with parasitic plants that derive nutrition from other living plants, but in this case, the nutrition is derived directly from human emotion, as well as blood. The plant has caused a huge shift in the way the people of Merion live their lives, as well as their culture, artwork, and communal interactions as they have "altered their natures to defy her" (Lawrence 1990, 83). We might also want to trace an intertextual connection with Nathaniel Hawthorne's short story, "Rappaccini's Daughter" (1844), in which Beatrice, the daughter of the story's title, becomes impervious to plant poisons after she cares for her father's medicinal garden. In the process, however, she becomes poisonous to others, including her beloved, Giovanni. The story, suffice to say, does not have a happy ending. "The Death Flower" has some strong parallels with Hawthorne's story but instead of just one character becoming poisonous, the whole of humanity has the potential to become poisonous *to itself*. Nature, embodied by the death flower offers, instead of fear, the potential for a different way of being in contrast to the Galactic Council, ruled as it is by supposedly "great men" (Lawrence 1990, 86). What Lawrence repeatedly reminds us is that evil is something of human construction, rather than it being embodied by the unknown and potentially horrifying natural world. When the people of Merion choose to live in harmony with nature and each other the plant has no power over them, and this horror dissipates.

Merion's death flower is sleeping, but Dr Largo has decided to use Ky as human bait to reawaken the plant and to enable it to germinate. As Elizabeth Parker notes, plants are seen as "utterly mundane ... undervalued objects which exist only to serve humankind ... They are seen as entirely inanimate and wholly devoid of any sentience or agency" (2016, 215). Much of the death flower's power lies in the way it undermines these associations—it is a "sensate plant" that feeds on "all the stupidity and wrongness and wretchedness until no one was left but the wise" (Lawrence 1990, 85). Later in the story, when Ky is attacked by Dr Largo, an attack which forces the Death Flower to awaken, Ky is hurt so badly by the plant that he almost dies. It is at the point of death that he realizes, as is often the case in Lawrence's fiction, that the good of the many far outweighs the desires of the individual. He returns to his life, irreparably altered, and tries to make his peace with the way of life on Merion. He almost succeeds but he realizes that there is still the issue of X33 to contend with. Dr Largo, the reader discovers, was harvesting the seeds so he could use them on X33, thus ensuring the planet does not become an atomic-wielding power. Even if Ky opts out of this course of action, something that he has the opportunity to do several times, he knows that the fate of the people of Merion rests with him—his inaction will likely result in Merion being attacked by X33 in the future, especially as Merion's culture has rejected capitalism. Filled as it is with riches, including precious stones and metals, it is one of the first places X33, as a colonial power, is likely to try to conquer. Unlike Merion, X33's dominant ideology is capitalism. The survival of which:

> depends on their being able to extend their reach to space in its entirety: to land (in the process of absorbing the towns and agriculture ...) to the *underground* resources lying deep in the earth and beneath the sea-bed—energy, raw materials, and so on; and lastly to what might be called the *above-ground* sphere [... other] planets.
>
> (Lefebvre 1991, 325)

What Lawrence withholds until the very last page is that X33 is not some exotic or mysterious planet, outside of the reader's understanding or sphere of knowledge. As Ky comes to accept by the very end: "On X33, over Asia, Europe and America, over all the continents someone had to scatter the seeds of the death flower" (Lawrence 1990, 110). While this course of action is left somewhat open-ended as the story draws to a close, it is clear that in reality, this act of genocide is the only way to ensure peace. The people of X33 can either adapt, as did the people of Merion, or they can die. In Lawrence's worldview, this is the choice facing her late twentieth-century readers—to embrace a way of living that eschews violence, and, ultimately, ecological damage, however difficult that might be to carry out.

Conclusions

Louise Lawrence was already writing ecofeminist science fiction before the term had been fully coined or realized. She had the foresight to see where the world was headed and warned, repeatedly, throughout her large body of fiction, that the only way to save humanity and to overthrow patriarchal structures was to change the way we value the planet and our own place upon it. She was, in short, a visionary. Her stories and novels were published by influential young adult publishing imprints, such as Bodley Head (*Extinction is Forever* and *Children of the Dust*) and later, were reprinted by Lion Teen Tracks. Her writing, through these accessible and affordable imprints, had the potential to both terrify and educate her young adult readers in ways that government advertising campaigns or lobbying by environmental charities were unable to match. Her characters face impossible decisions, in worlds where time is fast running out, but even in the bleakest dystopia, Lawrence will give the reader a glimmer of hope or a brief moment of spiritual certainty. It is this hope, coupled with the power to transform, that connects everything that she wrote. In "Extinction is Forever," the words themselves are constantly repeated—on the peace campaigners' banners (banners that would not look out of place in one of Greta Thunberg's environmental protests) and in the internal thoughts of the characters. It is no coincidence that Professor Goddard, a man whose life had "not amounted to much" and sends his student to certain death, fails to read the banner tied to the railings outside the physics department: "EXTINCTION IS FOREVER" (Lawrence 1990, 48). If we fail to heed Lawrence's warnings, who knows how long it will be before these words are our own epitaph.

References

Blend, Benay. 2021. "Rethinking Resistance: An Ecofeminist Approach to Anti-Colonialism in Louise Erdrich's *Future Home of the Living God*, and Oreet Ashery and Larissa Sansour's *The Novel of Nonel and Vovel*." In *Ecofeminist Science Fiction: International Perspectives on Gender, Ecology, and Literature*, edited by Douglas A. Vakoch, 171–188. Abingdon: Routledge.

Butler, Octavia. 1993. *Parable of the Sower*. New York: Grand Central Publishing.

Butler, Octavia. 2000. *Parable of the Talents*. New York: Aspect.

Butler, Chris. 2014. *Henri Lefebvre: Spatial Politics, Everyday Life and the Right to the City*. Oxon: Routledge.

Byrne, Deirdre. 2021. "The Road to Sinshan: Ecophilia in Ursula K. Le Guin's Early Hainish Novels." In *Ecofeminist Science Fiction: International Perspectives on Gender, Ecology, and Literature*, edited by Douglas A. Vakoch, 189–203. Abingdon: Routledge.

Callenbach, Ernest. 1975. *Ecotopia*. New York: Bantam Books.

Carter, Angela. 1969. *Heroes and Villains*. London: William Heinemann Ltd.

Chambers, Aiden, ed. 1984. *Out of Time: Stories of the Future*. London: Bodley Head.

Collins, Suzanne. 2008. *The Hunger Games*. Scholastic Press: New York.

Cuomo, Christine J. 1994. "Ecofeminism, Deep Ecology, and Human Population." In *Ecological Feminism: Environmental Philosophies*, edited by Karen J. Warren, 88–105. London: Routledge.

D'Ath, Justin. 2003. *Shædow Master*. Crows Nest, New South Wales: Allen & Unwin.

d'Eaubonne, Françoise. 1974. *Le Féminisme ou la Mort*. Paris: Pierre Horay.

Erdrich, Louise. 2017. *The Future Home of the Living God*. New York: Harper Collins.

Estok, Simon C. 2011. *Ecocriticism and Shakespeare: Reading Ecophobia*. Basingstoke: Palgrave Macmillan.

Hanson, Clare. 1985. *Short Stories and Short Fictions, 1880–1980*. London: Palgrave Macmillan.

Haraway, Donna. 1991. "A Cyborg Manifesto: Science, Technology, and Socialist-Feminism in the LateTwentieth Century." In *Simians, Cyborgs and Women: The Reinvention of Nature*, 149–181. New York: Routledge.

Hawthorne, Nathaniel. 1844. "Rappaccini's Daughter." In *Mosses from an Old Manse*. London: Wiley & Putnam.

James, Edward, and Farah Mendlesohn, eds. 2003. *The Cambridge Companion to Science Fiction*. Cambridge: Cambridge University Press.

Kaplan, E. Ann. 2016. *Climate Trauma: Foreseeing the Future in Dystopian Film and Fiction*. New Brunswick, NJ: Rutgers University Press.

Keetley, Dawn. 2016. "Introduction: Six Theses on Plant Horror; or, Why Are Plants Horrifying?" In *Plant Horror: Approaches to the Monstrous Vegetal in Fiction and Film*, edited by Dawn Keetley and Angela Tenga, 1–30. London: Palgrave Macmillan.

Lahar, Stephanie. 1996. "Ecofeminist Theory and Grassroots Politics." In *Ecological Feminist Philosophies*, edited by Karen J. Warren, 1–18. Bloomington: Indiana University Press.

Lawrence, Louise. 1971. *Andra*. London: Collins. Reprint, 1991.

Lawrence, Louise. 1985. *Children of the Dust*. Berkshire: Red Fox. Reprint, 2002.

Lawrence, Louise. 1990. *Extinction is Forever*. London: Bodley Head.

Lawrence, Louise. 1994. *The Disinherited*. Berkshire: Red Fox. Reprint, 1996.

Lawrence, Louise. 2013. *The Witch and the Weathermage*. Self-published: Kindle edition.

Lefebvre, Henri. 1991. *The Production of Space*. Oxford: Blackwell.

Le Guin, Ursula K. 1972. *The Word for World is Forest*. New York: Tor.

Lippit, Victor D. 2005. *Capitalism*. Abingdon: Routledge.

McCulloch, Gillian. 2002. *The Deconstruction of Dualism in Theology: With Special Reference to Ecofeminist Theology and New Age Spirituality*. Milton Keynes: Paternoster.

Murphy, Patrick D. 2000. *Farther Afield in the Study of Nature-Oriented Literature*. Charlottesville: University Press of Virginia.

Otto, Eric C. 2012. *Green Speculations: Science Fiction and Transformative Environmentalism*. Columbus: Ohio State University Press.

Parker, Elizabeth. 2016. "'Just a Piece of Wood': Jan Švankmajer's Otesánek and the EcoGothic." In *Plant Horror: Approaches to the Monstrous Vegetal in Fiction and Film*, edited by Dawn Keetley and Angela Tenga, 215–225. London: Palgrave Macmillan.

Popovich, Nadja, Livia Albeck-Ripka, and Kendra Pierre-Louis. 2020. "The Trump Administration Is Reversing 100 Environmental Rules. Here's the Full List." *New York Times*, July 15. Accessed September 19, 2020. https://www.nytimes.com/interactive/2020/climate/trump-environment-rollbacks.html

Reeve, Philip. 2001. *The Mortal Engines*. London: Scholastic Inc.

Reeve, Philip. 2003. *Predator's Gold*. London: Scholastic Inc.

Reeve, Philip. 2005. *Infernal Devices*. London: Scholastic Inc.

Reeve, Philip. 2006. *A Darkling Plain*. London: Scholastic Inc.

Rosinsky, Natalie M. 1984. *Feminist Futures: Contemporary Women's Speculative Fiction*. Ann Arbor, MI: UMI Research Press.

Science Daily. 2020. "COVID-19 Lockdown Reveals Human Impact on Wildlife." June 22. Accessed 10 October 2020. https://www.sciencedaily.com/releases/2020/06/200622133020.htm

Seed, David, ed. 2008. *A Companion to Science Fiction*. Oxford: Blackwell Publishing.

Sullivan III, C. W, ed. 1993. *Science Fiction for Young Readers*. London: Greenwood Publishing Group.

Tepper, Sheri S. 1988. *The Gate to Women's Country*. London: Orion Book Company Group.

Tong, Rosemarie P. 1998. *Feminist Thought: A More Comprehensive Introduction*. 2nd ed. Oxford: Westview Press.

Wagner-Lawlor, Jennifer A. 2013. *Postmodern Utopias and Feminist Fictions*. Cambridge: Cambridge University Press.

Warren, Karen, ed. 1994. *Ecological Feminism: Environmental Philosophies*. London: Routledge.

Warren, Karen, ed. 1996. *Ecological Feminist Philosophies*. Bloomington: Indiana University Press.

White, Donna R. 1999. *Dancing with Dragons: Ursula K. Le Guin and the Critics*. Columbia, SC: Camden House.

7   Ecofeminist Utopian Speculations
     in Henrietta Dugdale's *A Few
     Hours in a Far-Off Age* (1883);
     Catherine Helen Spence's
     A Week in the Future (1888);
     Mary Anne Moore-Bentley's
     *A Woman of Mars; Or, Australia's
     Enfranchised Woman* (1901);
     and Joyce Vincent's *The Celestial
     Hand: A Sensational Story* (1903)

Nicole Anae

More and more, the value of literary science fiction (SF) continues to attract serious scholarly attention in offering feminists a speculative probe for investigating the promise and capability of women. Nowhere is the richness of the convergence between speculating on women's futurity and a concern with the environment more apparent than in a relatively under-explored subset of Australian women's writing of the late nineteenth and early twentieth centuries. Henrietta Dugdale's *A Few Hours in a Far-Off Age* (1883) and Catherine Helen Spence's *A Week in the Future* (1888) were published in the late Australian colonial period; the closing decades of the nineteenth-century fin-de-siècle. Mary Anne Moore-Bentley's *A Woman of Mars; Or, Australia's Enfranchised Woman* (1901) and Joyce Vincent's *The Celestial Hand: A Sensational Story* (1903) were published subsequent to Australia becoming an independent nation—on January 1, 1901, also known as "Federation"—after the British Parliament passed self-governing legislation for Australia's six colonies under the Commonwealth of Australia. This is significant because between both periods, we see the intersection of changes in national identity, a growing political consciousness, in the form of the women's suffrage movement, concerns around environmental crisis, and the concept of a utopian life world (and its counterpoint), finding a productive literary response in the beginnings of a genre now recognized as science fiction (SF). Indeed, what makes these works particularly unique is the way in which these women writers apply allegory to challenge traditions of colonial SF—with its emphasis on the colonial mastery of the land, colonial conquest, and oppression (Blend 2018, 36 & 38), "the acquisition of land, nature and nonhuman and human

Others, and in profiting from them," and the representation of "patriarchal colonial scientific 'progress'" (Bedford 2018, 16 & 19)—toward a distinctly ecofeminist similitude. Formative SF of this kind,

> placing the ideal society in an extra-empirical world ... instantly turns itself into an allegory, into a narrative, that is, that speaks about the utopian ideal not directly, as in utopian fiction, but indirectly, through the meticulous construction of an intermediary fictional world.
>
> (Paschalidis 2000, 46)

* * *

Henrietta Dugdale's *A Few Hours in a Far-Off Age* (1883)

Henrietta Dugdale's (Figure 7.1) dedication of her novel to Mr Justice Higinbotham (*Judge of the Supreme Court in the Colony of Victoria*)—in earnest admiration for his brave attacks against "the greatest obstacle to

Figure 7.1 Henrietta Dugdale as pictured in Melbourne's *Table Talk* in 1899 ("Mrs. Dugdale" 1899, 6). Renowned for her "persistent advocacy of 'women's rights'" ("Mrs. Dugdale" 1886, 55), Dugdale was president of the first Victorian Women's Suffrage Society, formed on May 7, 1884. Contemporaneous with Dugdale's feminism was the activism of Catherine Helen Spence (1825–1910), a prominent advocate of women's rights, Australia's first female professional journalist, and the first Australian woman to write a novel, *Clara Morison* (1856).

human advancement; the most irrational, fiercest, and most powerful of our world's monsters—the only Devil—MALE IGNORANCE"—perfectly articulated Dugdale's (1827–1918) own interest in critiquing the social "principles" (3) for gender equality in realizing her dream for "the future of a higher world" (Dugdale 1883, 85). In this early example of SF's roots in colonialism and European expansion—a colonial voyage of discovery, to apply Bedford's phrase (2018, 17)—we see through the eyes of an unnamed narrator from the late nineteenth-century the idyllic futurist society that is "Alethia." This utopia developed because of a change in the earth's orbit, precipitating "a long glacial period" (Dugdale 1883, 23) some "two millions of years ago" (38) in which the continent of "ancient Australia" (23) disappeared and a new landmass ascended in its place. The unnamed narrator, not "dressed in my earth body" (76) freely integrates with the Alethians. She finds herself in an "immense building" (5)—dedicated to "gallery instruction" (102), a form of learning about human anthropological history—where she joins an Alethian family as an unseen observer of this wondrous socio-technologically advanced world.

Abolished in this future-world are all forms of industry exploiting earth's natural resources, including mining, *"the use of coal as fertiliser"* (97), as well as eliminating the animal exploitation industry; "No suffering animals, urged by cruelty to overtax their strength" (6), and no *"devour*[ing of animal] *flesh"* (91), including terminating the commercial manufacture of leather (72). Alethians are vegans consuming a diet consisting of a modest vegetarian meal twice daily: a selection of "five or six absurdly small loaves, three different kinds of fruit that has evidently been stored from summer (all new sorts) and a vessel of water" (81).

Observing this future utopian paradise, the narrator perceives that environmentalist philosophy underlies the social, economic, and spiritual harmony of Alethian society itself. Even the city in which the visitor from a far-distant past first finds herself harmonizes with the environment. Its architecture—itself "truly grand works of art" (5)—includes "[v]ery few prominent angles, only sufficient to make the curves more beautiful" (6) where "Every dwelling has around it a certain quantity of land, in which are growths of use and decoration. No sign of poverty in home or people" (74). Allegory of this kind in late nineteenth-century SF linking urbanization and human settlement to care for the environment clearly espouses a basic tenet of ecofeminism: that the way humans treat nature and the way humans treat the human and nonhuman Other are intimately related (Bedford 2018, 20). From this position, the ecofeminist implications of Dugdale's literary SF do not suggest a "single issue" movement, but "rests on the notion that liberation of all oppressed groups must be addressed simultaneously" (Gaard 1993, 5). Without eliminating practices exploiting the earth's resources, there can be no equality. Without equity, there can be no liberty, and without liberty, there can be no social congruence.

Alethians coexist with nonhuman life forms described as a dog-like animal with a tiger's skin. While the visitor from the past remains undetected by one Alethian family as an unseen voyeur, only the nonhuman life form they coexist with, named Leoni, has the perceptual acuity to recognize the narrator's presence. Leoni's gaze, "with an expression of contempt and dread" (Dugdale 1883, 85) suggests to the narrator that the animal identifies the narrator for what they are: a human from the bygone, "half-barbarous time" (92) of "brutish" oppression, subjugation, and violence. Allegorically, the motif of Leoni's sentience, vigilance, and intelligence in Dugdale's *A Few Hours in a Far-Off Age* represents a significant interspecies speculation linking progressive futurism with an unenlightened past; "Can Leoni know there is in this pure life a remnant—or visitor, or whatever my presence here may mean—from the ignorant ages?" (78). This representation of human/animal interaction challenging our interpretation and hierarchies of environment, and the paralleling of the feminine and the masculine between the two species is also a question Lesley Kordecki explores (2021). By hypothesizing a utopia eradicating the exploitation and conquest of nonhuman animals, itself challenging a common trope of colonial SF, Dugdale also envisions a form of anti-speciesism—"extending moral consideration to non-human nature and promoting representative thinking beyond species boundaries" (Smith 2003, 70)—long before it formerly existed as an ecofeminist concept. Here too, the inherent ideologies concerning the nonhuman Other underlying Dugdale's early example of ecofeminist SF represent a precursor to the more contemporary questions of reproduction, utilitarianism, and speciesism explored in further detail by Imelda Martín Junquera (2021).

Catherine Helen Spence's *A Week in the Future* (1888)

Catherine Helen Spence (Figure 7.2) offers in her "social-political novel" (Viva 1896, 1268) a vision of futurity set in the year 1988. Like Dugdale, Spence too presents an early example of SF's roots in colonialism and European expansion—a colonial voyage of discovery (Bedford 2018, 17)—but also like Dugdale, departs from colonial traditions of SF, particularly with respect to representations of capitalism and industrialization. The novel's heroine, spinster Emily Bethel, after a long period of caring for her aged mother, discovers from her doctor—Dr. Brown—that she has a terminal heart condition with only a few years left to live. Brown prescribes a calm existence avoiding all fatigue, excitement, and worry, to which Emily replies

> I would give the year or two of life you promise me for ONE WEEK IN THE FUTURE. A solid week ... to see all their doings, and to breathe in their atmosphere, so as to imbibe their real spirit.
> (Spence 2006, "Chapter 1 Introductory")

Thus, two days later, from Adelaide, South Australia, 1888, Emily awakens one century into the future: London 1998, rationalizing her choice by claiming "I need all my past knowledge [of London] to throw light on the new

Figure 7.2 Illustration of Catherine Helen Spence ("Miss C. H. Spence" 1899, 5), dubbed "the Australian Harriet Martineau" (Source: Viva 1896, 1268). Following the fin-de-siècle, Spence's utopian vision is taken up and pushed toward more other worldly expression by Mary Ann Moore-Bentley (1865–1953): a woman making history in 1903 as among the first female candidates to stand for Federal election (albeit unsuccessfully).

revelations" (Spence 2006, "Chapter 1 Introductory"). This application of allegory in colonial SF effectively illustrates Sarah Bezan's claim (2021) that feminist interpretations of embodiment intersect with past, present, and future states. Unlike the disembodied narrator of Dugdale's *A Few Hours in a Far-Off Age*, Emily appears in the future "not like a spirit at all, but just in this habit as I am, like a middle-aged or rather an elderly single woman, who surely can never be altogether out of date in any century" (Spence 2006, "Chapter 1 Introductory").

Allegory also operates in the gift Florrie Henderson makes her aunt of *Scientific Meliorism and the Evolution of Happiness* to indicate how heavily Spence drew on Clapperton's work (Spence 2005, 268). Whether in her dreaming or in her new futurist reality, Emily does as Clapperton did "gather[ing] from other authors and other observers, and had worked out for herself from the signs of the times into a foreshadowing of the society of the future." Just as Christy Tidwell (this volume) argues that ecofeminist science fictional history of the 1960s and 70s has much to teach modern readers, so too is this the case with respect to ecofeminist science fictional history of the late 1890s and early 1900s. Motivating the "scientific meliorist," according to Clare (1993, iv) was "the conviction that science has a major role to play in dispelling myth and obfuscation and establishing a more substantial understanding upon which politicians and legislators can operate." Spence's *A Week in the Future* illustrates the way in which late-nineteenth-century suffragists writing colonial SF allegorized ideologies around science as a driver of social reform into early feminist utopian speculations. Importantly, Spence's utopia owes its debt to science in acknowledging human sexual desire, according to women reproductive rights and access to birth control, and providing society with a biological mechanism for regulating population growth as "Science has put it into the power of the married people to regulate their families." Spence's self-described "social speculation" (Spence 1893, 5) therefore not only approached social justice issues using a form of speculative fiction nowadays characterized as SF, but also hinted at how to achieve her utopian ideal.

Unemployment and the "working-classes" no longer exist, and the value of money ceases to determine "one's enjoyment of life" as the economic tendency is toward "equalisation." The system of "co-operation and combination" prevent the accumulation of capital in single hands." Superseding individual housing are "Associated Homes," a communal, environmentally sensitive system of shareholder housing, where up to 20 families share one large residence. Just like Dugdale, allegory of this kind linking urbanization and human settlement to care for the environment also clearly espouses a basic tenet of ecofeminism: the inextricable link between the human treatment of nature and the human and nonhuman Other.

Spence's vision, however, perpetuates the gendering of domestic arrangements in the organization of cooperative agriculturalism, where the service was done "exclusively by women" (Spence 2006, "Chapter 2 Tuesday"). With women rests the task of providing clothing for the community. Women also work in factories and cotton mills, the difference being they now maintain a fiscal concern in the profits (Spence 2006, "Chapter 2 Tuesday"). It is, however, by design that Spence necessarily refers to the aspects of social and economic organization of her own time. The backdrop thus contextualized makes it possible to advance her ideas regarding how to achieve her futuristic ideal. While her speculations of the future rest on critiquing familiar aspects of the nineteenth-century social and economic organization toward reconfiguring a twentieth-century ideal founded on cooperation and community collaboration, hers is nonetheless a decisive future-world proclaiming "Woman is no longer degraded as the slave or the toy of man, but takes her equal place in all relations of life" (Spence 2006, "Chapter 8 Sunday").

Mary Ann Moore-Bentley's *A Woman of Mars* (1901)

Mary Ann Moore-Bentley's (Figure 7.3) novel portrays a feminist red planet that considers women's rights as "the bedrock foundation upon which a

Figure 7.3 Photographic illustration of Moore-Bentley published in the *Nepean Times* in 1903. Some commenters claimed that the success of *A Woman of Mars* gained for Moore-Bentley the title of "the Australian Marie Corelli" after the hugely popular best-selling English novelist and mystic ("Mrs. Moore-Bentley's Books" 1903, 13). Speculations that Martians were attempting to communicate with Earth using light signals ("Is Mars Signalling?" 1901, 4), together with advances in telescopic technologies and astronomical observations conducted at the Sydney Observatory, fuelled the fin-de-siècle imaginary around interplanetary space and extra-terrestrial life. That Moore-Bentley names her Martian protagonist "Vesta" bears more than a coincidental relationship to the name of a real-life mystic of the period named Vesta La Viesta. Could it be that Moore-Bentley had known of, or read something about, New York clairvoyant Mrs Almira Gaylord Beach (a.k.a "Madame La Viesta"), whose appearances at the Cosmological Center in 1904 detailed her interplanetary travels to Mars and Venus by means of astral projection?

statesman [sic] must seek to establish a happy, progressive, social State" (1901, 89). Following both Dugdale and Spence, Moore-Bentley too presents a clear example of a common SF theme—human contact with other life beings and the struggle to understand human progress and its costs— while again, like Dugdale and Spence, distorting the traditions of colonial SF with an ecofeminist twist. The opening prelude to the novel depicts the soul of a deceased Australian woman traveling through space accompanied by Castor, an angel (Figure 7.4). Castor interrupts their journey upward so the woman, Margeurite Des Vaux Fairfax, can experience life on Mars first hand. "I perceive," said Castor, "that sociology upon earth is merely in its homogeneous stage of evolutionary progress ... with fixed functions of distribution and uniformity of action, being very indefinite" ("Recent Publications" 1901b, 12).

Figure 7.4 This illustration titled "On the Way to Mars," from a story called "A Trip to Mars," sardonically published by the *Melbourne Punch* under the pseudonym "Terah Firmer," in 1898, represents a vision of astral travel not unlike that imaged by Moore-Bentley (Firmer 1898, 5).

Soon after her arrival, Margeurite realizes that the Martians are uniquely superior to Earth's humans. Indeed, Castor acknowledges the assentation of the Martians to a state of "human perfection" (Moore-Bentley 1901, 89). The Martian Prime Minister assigns his daughter, Vesta, to visit Earth tasked with ensuring "the emancipation of Woman and the regeneration of the [human] race" (Moore-Bentley 1901, 35). Vesta travels to Earth using a flying machine operated via remote control (44); easily managing Earth's gravitational field given "the Martians are masters of all such phenomena" (44). Vesta commences her mission in Sydney, Australia, and through her observations, makes comparative claims regarding contemporary social and cultural conditions in contrast to Martian evolutionary philosophies: "It appears to me that woman in some remote period of human development, has evolved intelligence sufficient to degrade a natural instinct, thereby deteriorating her species" (Petro 1901, 6). Man, meanwhile, "during his moral and intellectual development, availed himself of many barbarous methods for coping with over-population," including infanticide and abortion (Petro 1901, 6). Vesta expresses her shock at the subjugation of Earth's women claiming, "What cruel fiend seduced her? What subtle influence made her first betray the divine trust and prostitute the holiest of all things created, that highly wrought, finely constructed, beautifully designed masterpiece of all Nature's machinery, Woman?" (Moore-Bentley 1901, 76). Thus inspired, Vesta successfully transforms the Australian industry into a perfect model of rational organization within five years. She emancipates Earth's female population and regenerates the entire human race, thus espousing, like Dugdale and Spence, the ideal that the key to realizing social change toward emancipation is the subordination of individualism for the good of the state.

Importantly, Moore-Bentley's allegorization of Mars as a spiritually fertile, almost separatist feminine space encouraging female interspecies, interplanetary, exchange itself presents an inherently ecofeminist political statement well ahead of its time. As Eric Otto argues, "[t]o posit a separatist, feminist space where a spiritual ecological conscience can thrive is a key theoretical move for ecofeminist science fiction" (2012, 22). Mars as a utopian civilization and Vesta's significance as a feminine envoy tasked with Australia's transformation into a model of equality represents a social critique allegorizing women's experiences of alienation, subjugation, and exploitation. Allegory thus applied not only posits a central claim of ecofeminism—that a connection exists between social-environmental change and the disenfranchisement of women—but itself positions a literary challenge against the themes of colonial mastery of the environment, Imperial conquest, and colonial subjugation characterizing the very traditions of colonial SF.

Pushing further Moore-Bentley's literary speculations concerning astral projection and flying machines was Joyce Vincent's *The Celestial Hand* (1903), which, unlike Dugdale, Spence, and Moore-Bentley, does not profess a utopian ideal of women's emancipation. However, hers is nonetheless significant as speculative SF for two separate, but interrelated reasons. First, the novel presents a compelling literary example converging the preoccupations of fin-de-siècle popular culture with all things fantastical, including advanced weaponry and technological warfare. Second, *The Celestial Hand* tracks both the convergence of advanced scientific technologies and the manipulation of conventional tropes of "Yellow Peril" fiction—"narratives demonizing the Chinese as a sub-human horde of dangerous pests, sometimes under the ideologically freighted moniker Celestial (a reference to China as the celestial empire)" (Roberts 2016, 269)—in the representation of global warfare as environmental violence. Modern-day literary works focusing on interplanetary war, dystopian futurism, and environmental apocalypse are also taken up by Michelle Deininger and Gemma Scammell (this volume), as well as Deirdre Byrne (2021) and Asli Değirmenci (2021) respectively.

Joyce Vincent's *The Celestial Hand: A Sensational Story* (1903)

In Joyce Vincent's futuristic story, invading forces, led by "a scientist-warrior" ("A Thrilling 'Shocker'" 1903, 7) named Amarbal, use Sydney, Australia, as a base camp for launching a bid for global domination. Amarbal, of an ancient but reclusive "Akkaadian race," possesses "much knowledge of the relation of the spiritual to the material world, and of Nature's secrets, which had never been obtained, and never would be obtained, by the Western world" (176). This knowledge he uses to devise advanced technologies and mechanized weaponry far superior to anything the world has ever seen (Figure 7.5).

In Vincent's representation of technologically advanced systems of warfare, Amarbal's scientific methods impact the environment in ways never before imagined; "thousands of flashes of light rained down on the earth from the sky, explosions took place in all directions, choking bluish fumes rose from the ground, and covered everything like a pall" (199). Amarbal has even developed technologies to manipulate environmental factors—such as increasing the amount of oxygen in the atmosphere—as a devastating military tactic; "faces became flushed, pulses rose to 120; maniacal gestures were indulged in; soldiers seized their rifles and discharged them in all directions; cannon boomed out; machine guns spluttered, and generally Pandemonium reigned" (204).

Via allegory, Vincent's *The Celestial Hand* fuses threatening technologies and advanced science with a central claim of ecofeminism—that a connection exists between environmental violence and the disenfranchisement of the Other—a position itself clearly contesting the tropes of colonial supremacy of the land, Imperial annexation, and colonial suppression characterizing traditions of colonial SF. From this perspective, it is possible to

Figure 7.5 Vincent's flying machines perfectly accorded with the ideological fascination with advancing technologies and developments in mechanization among Australians of the fin-de-siècle; a richly visual traditional preoccupation with national defense as indicated by the above illustration published in the *Australian Town and Country Journal* (1895). In this sense, Vincent's *The Celestial Hand* communicates with Roberts's (2016, 19) definition of SF in a Heideggerean sense as "technology fiction" in which we acknowledge technology "as a mode of enframing the world, a manifestation of a fundamentally philosophical outlook."

view the inevitable and unsurprising defeat of Amarbal's invasion efforts, even despite the superiority of his scientific technologies and the size of his legions, as highly satirical. Amarbal's inventions—high-velocity projectiles (102), "strange, low-lying craft" (151), "death-dealing gas" (161), and the world's largest gun (234), among others—and his "supernatural powers" (234)—astral projection (133), telepathy (134–135), and levitation (253)—were no match against the forces of "right." The battle was, after all, inherently ideological; "a fight for national as well as individual life, and every man felt that each foe cut down was a menace to civilisation removed" (223). That this discourse of Imperialism was characteristic of its time perhaps accounts for the fact that a machine of Imperial invention—called "'Devastator,' the crowning glory of the British" (214)—perpetrated the greatest environmental violence and devastation:

This fearful machine, by electricity or other means not made known, generated heat to the extent of 3000 degrees, and sent sheets of flame roaring across the country in the direction of the opposing army ... beneath the fiery breath of the monster, which at once demonstrated itself as the most terrible instrument of destruction yet invented. Nothing living could stand against it.

(214)

Rieder argues that, "while staying within the ideological and epistemological framework of colonial discourse, [SF] exaggerates and exploits its internal divisions" (2008, 10). In this sense, *The Celestial Hand* clearly offers a "reversal of perspective" example of colonial SF. Vincent invites her readership to engage with questions of colonialism and its aftermath foregrounding Australia's own reality as the product of Imperial colonization. It is against this backdrop that Vincent encourages readers to compare the "Celestial" invasion of Australia with European attempts to colonize parts of Asia, particularly those identified as geographically strategic for European powers in the early twentieth century, "thus demanding that the colonizers imagine themselves as the colonized, or the about-to-be-colonized" (Rieder 2008, 5).

Whatever modern-day scholars theorize concerning the novel's racist learnings, the sheer imaginary scope of the work's interest in representations of futurism—"modern chemistry, engineering science, and theosophy" ("Review" 1903, 6)—was ground breaking. Significantly, that reviewers commonly mistook her for a male writer ("Literary Notes" 1903, 3; "Recent Publications" 1903, 47; "A Thrilling 'Shocker'" 1903, 7)—a trend which persists in contemporary critical work with remarkable regularity (Blackford et al. 1999, 39; Roberts 2016, 269; Wong 2015, 262)—overtly stresses the masculinization of the literary theme of advancing technologies and developments in mechanization. While like Moore-Bentley's *A Woman of Mars* (1901), which some reviewers also mistook as a work of fiction by a male writer ("Recent Publications" 1901a, 1), the trend itself in Vincent's case tacitly suggests the continuation of male biases in the gendering of a work considered not only ahead of its time, but what one critic described as "one huge sensation from start to finish" ("Literature" 1903, 7). In this sense too, that reviews noted the influences of Jules Verne ("Review" 1903, 47) and H. G. Wells ("Current Literature" 1903, 6), as well as Kenneth Mackay's *The Yellow Wave* (1895) and M. P. Shiel's *The Yellow Danger* (1898) ("New Novels" 1903, 49), suggests Vincent's novel experiments with traditions of colonial SF and "Yellow Peril" tropes. Vincent's novel combines Verne's material limitation to technological devices with Wells' expansion of a mystically nuanced imaginary into "speculative and universal directions" (Roberts 2016, 20). From this perspective, Vincent does not represent Amarbal as a "sub-human" (Roberts 2016, 269) antihero of Yellow Peril or colonial SF type, but rather significantly, contextualizes his so-called "holy war against the European nations", to coin Roberts (2016,

179), against a backdrop of technological ingenuity, "[h]ypnotism and other occult sciences" ("Literature" 1903, 7) as a counter-response to, among other things, white appropriation and Imperial colonialism. Amarbal, as the Other, exploits and imitates Imperial practices of colonialism and the crisis implications of environmental warfare—a context in which, to quote Jairus Victor Grove, "[t]he quantitative and then annihilative mode of warfare also says something about the creeping entanglements between war and other ecological orders such as the economy, resource extraction, urbanization, and scientific innovation" (2019, 83)—thereby revealing and subjecting to the latter their own forms of suppression and exploitation. Amarbal's forces invade early twentieth-century Australia just as the English invaded Australia more than a century before, "not just because they are arrogant colonists invading a technologically inferior civilization" (Rieder 2008, 5), but because with his superior machines and instrumentals of warfare, Amarbal historicizes white Imperialism's past and personifies its future. Thus, as an early example of "reverse perspective" colonial SF, the conclusion of *The Celestial Hand* preserves the structures of British Imperialism and colonialism, while challenging the inviolability of colonialism's ideological paradigms from within.

Conclusion

The pivotal role played by women in the development of SF prior to the twentieth century remains relatively under-recognized in the scholarship. Even less scholarship exists exploring the development of the genre of feminist SF in the late nineteenth to early twentieth centuries. This chapter has aimed to broaden the research on ecofeminist SF generally by paying particular attention to four novels belonging to a relatively under-explored subset of Australian women's writing: Dugdale's *A Few Hours in a Far-Off Age* (1883), Spence's *A Week in the Future* (1888), Moore-Bentley's *A Woman of Mars* (1901), and Vincent's *The Celestial Hand* (19031903). Offering a close re-reading of these works reveals that Australian women writers of this period conceivably played a precursor role in the development of ecofeminist SF in recognizing correlations between the containment of women and the containment of the environment. Each of these speculative works challenges traditions of colonial SF by exploiting a set of narrative strategies privileging allegory to cypher and decipher social conventions that gesture toward an imagined future while simultaneously focusing on the environment of this alterative world as a cultural change agent. They apply allegory as a kind of nexus, since it offers the opportunity of narrative dislocation, exposing the text to multiple readings, and in the process, meticulously constructing "an intermediary fictional world" (Paschalidis 2000, 46) emblematic of future ecofeminist similitudes. From this position, this chapter has shed new light on both the contributions made by female writers typically under-represented in the critical scholarship about SF, such as Australian women of the late nineteenth century, as well as carries forward the research on the emergence of ecofeminist SF as an influential genre of critical social commentary and women's empowerment. What is most powerfully underscored in this chapter is the way in which the contributions of these women—Henrietta Dugdale, Catherine Helen Spence, Mary Anne Moore-Bentley, and Joyce Vincent—can lay claim to both "opening up new understandings of the stories" themselves, as much as contributing innovative and remarkable insight into examinations of "feminist SF in its first century of existence" (Larbalestier 2006, xviii).

References

"An Interesting Celestial Neighbor, Mars." 1893. *Illustrated Sydney News*, February 18. Accessed September 25, 2020. https://trove.nla.gov.au/newspaper/article/64032645.

"A Thrilling 'Shocker.'" 1903. *Cumberland Argus and Fruitgrowers Advocate [Parramatta]*, November 14. Accessed September 25, 2020. https://trove.nla.gov.au/newspaper/article/85684328.

Bedford, Anna. 2018. "Ecofeminist, Post-colonial, and Anti-capitalist Possibilities in Nalo Hopkinson's *Brown Girl in the Ring*." In *Ecofeminism in Dialogue*, edited by Douglas A. Vakoch and Sam Mickey, 15–30. Lanham, MD: Lexington Books.

Bezan, Sarah. 2021. "Speculative Sex: Queering Aqueous Natures and Biotechnological Futures in Larissa Lai's *Salt Fish Girl*." In *Ecofeminist Science Fiction: International Perspectives on Gender, Ecology, and Literature*, edited by Douglas A. Vakoch, 75–86. Abingdon: Routledge.

Blackford, Russell, Van Ikin, and Sean McMullen. 1999. *Strange Constellations: A History of Australian Science Fiction*. Westport, CT: Greenwood Publishing Group.

Blend, Benay. 2018. "'I Learnt All the Words and Broke Them Up/To Make a Single Word: Homeland': An Eco-Postcolonial Perspective of Resistance in Palestinian Women's Literature." In *Ecofeminism in Dialogue*, edited by Douglas A. Vakoch and Sam Mickey, 31–44. Lanham, MD: Lexington Books.

Byrne, Deirdre. 2021. "The Road to Sinshan: Ecophilia in Ursula K. Le Guin's Early Hainish Novels." In *Ecofeminist Science Fiction: International Perspectives on Gender, Ecology, and Literature*, edited by Douglas A. Vakoch, 189–203. Abingdon: Routledge.

Clapperton, Jane Hume. 1885. *Scientific Meliorism and the Evolution of Happiness*. London: Kegan Paul.

Clare, Anthony. 1993. "Foreword." In *Violence in Society*, edited by Pamela Jane Taylor, iii–iv. Royal College of Physicians of London. Lavenham: The Lavenham Press.

"Current Literature." 1903. *Morning Bulletin [Rockhampton]*, October 23. Accessed January 7, 2021. https://trove.nla.gov.au/newspaper/article/53000389

Değirmenci Altın, Aslı. 2021. "Anthropocentric and Androcentric Ideologies in Jeanette Winterson's *The Stone Gods*: An Ecofeminist Reading." In *Ecofeminist Science Fiction: International Perspectives on Gender, Ecology, and Literature*, edited by Douglas A. Vakoch, 63–74. Abingdon: Routledge.

Dillon, Grace. 2012. *Walking the Clouds: An Anthology of Indigenous Science Fiction*. Tucson: University of Arizona Press.

Dugdale, Henrietta A. 1883. *A Few Hours in a Far-Off Age*. Melbourne: McCarron, Bird & Co.

"Federal Elections. Mrs. H. Moore-Bentley." 1903. *Nepean Times [Penrith]*, November 7. Accessed September 18, 2020. https://trove.nla.gov.au/newspaper/article/100917612.

Firmer, Terah. 1898. "A Trip to Mars." *Melbourne Punch*, December 22. Accessed October 12, 2020. https://trove.nla.gov.au/newspaper/article/180222135/20433312.

Gaard, Greta, ed. 1993. *Ecofeminism: Women, Animal, Nature*. Philadelphia: Temple University Press.

Grove, Jairus Victor. 2019. *Savage Ecology: War and Geopolitics at the End of the World*. Durham, NC: Duke University Press.

"Is Mars Signalling?." 1901. *Evening News*, February 23. Accessed September 21, 2020. https://trove.nla.gov.au/newspaper/article/114021362.

Kordecki, Lesley. 2021. "The Runa and Female Otherness in Mary Doria Russell's *The Sparrow*." In *Ecofeminist Science Fiction: International Perspectives on Gender, Ecology, and Literature*, edited by Douglas A. Vakoch, 24–34. Abingdon: Routledge.

Larbalestier, Justine, ed. 2006. *Daughters of Earth: Feminist Science Fiction in the Twentieth Century*. Middletown, CT: Wesleyan University Press.

"Literary Notes." 1903. *The Bendigo Independent [Sydney]*, October 22. Accessed January 6, 2021. https://trove.nla.gov.au/newspaper/article/223411273

"Literature." 1903. *Examiner [Launceston]*, November 4. Accessed September 28, 2020. https://trove.nla.gov.au/newspaper/article/35570072.

Martín Junquera, Imelda. 2021. "Reproduction, Utilitarianism, and Speciesism in *Sleep Dealer* and *Westworld*." In *Ecofeminist Science Fiction: International Perspectives on Gender, Ecology, and Literature*, edited by Douglas A. Vakoch, 35–46. Abingdon: Routledge.

"Miss C. H. Spence. An Interview by a Special Representative." 1893. *South Australian Register [Adelaide]*, April 4. Accessed January 6, 2021. https://trove.nla.gov.au/newspaper/article/48524233

"Miss C. H. Spence. Philanthropist and Reformer." 1899. *The Express and Telegraph [Adelaide]*, August 12. Accessed September 12, 2020. https://trove.nla.gov.au/newspaper/article/209574859.

Moore-Bentley, Mary. 1901. *A Woman of Mars, Or Australia's Enfranchised Woman*. London: Edwards Dunlop.

"Mrs. Dugdale." 1886. *Melbourne Punch*, March 25. Accessed September 30, 2020. https://trove.nla.gov.au/newspaper/article/174567720.

"Mrs. Dugdale." 1899. *Table Talk [Melbourne]*, October 20. Accessed September 30, 2020. https://trove.nla.gov.au/newspaper/article/145918328.

"Mrs. Moore-Bentley's Books." 1903. *Windsor and Richmond Gazette*, November 7. Accessed September 20, 2018. https://trove.nla.gov.au/newspaper/article/86221329.

"New Novels." *Australasian*, October 17. Accessed September 28, 2020. https://trove.nla.gov.au/newspaper/article/138693055/11341039.

Otto, Eric C. 2012. "Ecofeminist Theories of Liberation in the Science Fiction of Sally Miller Gearhart, Ursula K. Le Guin, and Joan Slonczewski." In *Feminist*

Ecocriticism: Environment, Woman, and Literature, edited by Douglas A. Vakoch, 13–38. Lanham, MD: Lexington Books.

Paschalidis, Gregory. 2000. "Modernity as a Project and as Self-Criticism: The Historical Dialogue between Science Fiction and Utopia." In *Science Fiction, Critical Frontiers*, edited by Karen Sayer and John Moore, 35–47. London: Macmillan.

Petro, Altiora. 1901. "Woman's Whims." *Truth [Brisbane]*, March 24. Accessed September 26, 2020. https://trove.nla.gov.au/newspaper/article/200507520.

"Recent Publications." 1901a. *Evening News [Sydney]*, March 16. Accessed January 6, 2021. https://trove.nla.gov.au/newspaper/article/114020924.

"Recent Publications." 1901b. *Sunday Times [Sydney]*, April 7. Accessed January 6, 2021. https://trove.nla.gov.au/newspaper/article/125883120.

"Recent Publications." 1903. *Chronicle [Adelaide]*, October 24. Accessed January 7, 2021. https://trove.nla.gov.au/newspaper/article/87869943

"Review." 1903. *Maitland Daily Mercury*, October 14. Accessed January 7, 2021. https://trove.nla.gov.au/newspaper/article/126241719.

Rieder, John. 2008. *Colonialism and the Emergence of Science Fiction*. Middleton, CT: Wesleyan University Press.

Roberts, Adam. 2016. *The History of Science Fiction*. 2nd ed. London: Palgrave Macmillan.

Smith, Graham. 2003. *Deliberative Democracy and the Environment*. London: Routledge.

Spence, Catherine Helen. 2006. *A Week in the Future. Serialized in The Centennial Magazine: An Australian Monthly*. Accessed January 6, 2021. http://gutenberg.net.au/ebooks06/0603381h.html.

Spence, Catherine Helen. 2005. *Ever Yours: Catherine Helen Spence's An Autobiography*, edited by Susan Magarey. Kent Town: Wakefield Press.

"The 'Penny Dreadful' in Excelsis." 1895. *Australian Town and Country Journal [Sydney]*, February 22. Accessed September 21, 2020. https://trove.nla.gov.au/newspaper/article/71225915/5241807.

Vincent, Joyce. 1903. *The Celestial Hand: A Sensational Story*. Melbourne: J. C. MacCartie & Co.

Viva. 1896. "Gossip." *Sydney Mail and New South Wales Advertiser*, June 20. Accessed September 15, 2020. https://trove.nla.gov.au/newspaper/article/162830821.

Wong, Edlie L. 2015. *Racial Reconstructions: Black Inclusion, Chinese Exclusion, and the Fictions of Citizenship*. London: New York University Press.

8 Alien Ecofeminist Societies

"Sharers" in Joan Slonczewski's *A Door into Ocean*

Irene Sanz Alonso

From its origins, ecofeminism has been a complex movement in the sense that it encompasses political activism as well as theoretical works in philosophy, literary criticism, and science and technology, including as well poetry, novels, and art (Plumwood 1993, 48; Warren 2000, xiii). Its multi-disciplinary conception is also reflected in the two main fields of action of the ecofeminist movement. The first one is the idea "that there are important connections—historical, experiential, symbolic, theoretical—between the domination of women and the domination of nature, an understanding of which is crucial to both feminism and environmental ethics" (Warren 1996, 19). But these patterns of domination, as Warren comments, affect not only women and nature but also all those social groups labeled as the other, for example, ethnic minorities, children and nonhuman animals (2000, 1). For this reason, ecofeminists believe that in order to end with unjustified forms of oppression it is necessary to analyze how all these patterns are interconnected and interrelated (Warren 2000, 1–2). The second main concern of ecofeminism is to propose and devise alternative ways of relating with the other which do not reproduce oppressive patterns but which highlight respect, understanding, and interconnectedness.

Taking into account the two main concerns of ecofeminism noted above, different authors have dealt with the contrast between the current social systems that sanction oppressive attitudes, and the desirable social infrastructures that would improve our lifestyle as well as the well-being of the other creatures we share our planet with. In this sense, Karen Warren distinguishes between healthy and unhealthy social systems and she posits that the health of a system is determined both by how well it meets the needs of humans as social and ecological selves, and by how well it provides for the flourishing or well-being of the environment on which human social and ecological needs depend. On the contrary, unhealthy social systems tend to be closed, highly rigid, and characterized by power-over hierarchies (2000, 205). In the ecofeminist attempt of substituting unhealthy social systems with healthy ones, Linda Vance highlights that such a social model would encourage values such as "diversity, interdependence, sustainability, cooperation, and renewal" (1993, 134).

From a different perspective, Carolyn Merchant uses the concept of partnership ethics instead of that of a healthy social system. In this social model, which somehow reproduces the social systems of prehistoric societies, human and nonhuman creatures enjoy an equal position, thus eliminating oppressive patterns and coexisting in a "more nearly equal relationship" (1996, 8; 56). In her description of a partnership ethic, Merchant points out four essential ideas. The first one is the "enquiry between human and nonhuman communities," that is, to learn from one another about each group's needs and well-being—something that is essential to satisfy every group's needs as commented in Warren's description of healthy social systems. The second one is the "moral consideration for humans and nonhuman nature," something neglected in the anthropocentric and rationalist models according to which human beings are positioned on top of the hierarchy of living beings. The third idea is the "respect for cultural diversity and biodiversity," since oppressive systems tend to neglect richness and uniqueness through the homogenization of human and nonhuman others. Finally, the partnership ethic includes "women, minorities, and nonhuman nature in the code of ethical accountability" (1996, 217). One of the most interesting aspects of this partnership ethic is that it is based on the heterarchy of its members since they all occupy the same position as equal partners. Another interesting assumption from this ethic is that despite its ecocentric character, the needs of human beings are also taken into account, but just as much as the other partners'. Merchant's model is as inclusive as the ecofeminist movement because it encompasses feminist, social, ecological, and scientific concerns. From the social point of view, this ethic encourages alternative economic systems which promote the wellness of the environment rather than its exploitation and subsequent degradation. And from the scientific perspective, science is understood in as much as it can foster discoveries that help humans cooperate with nature (Merchant 1996, 222).

One of the most interesting ways in which ecofeminist philosophy can reach larger audiences is through literature. Approaching literary works using an ecofeminist lens enables readers and critics to analyze—and understand—the underlying oppressive patterns that permeate the social systems in which we live today, and that authors usually portray in their writings. If we focus our analysis on science fiction in particular we find that these social systems are sometimes taken to the extreme through the use of dystopias. For this reason, science fiction works are especially interesting for ecofeminism because we can both experience what it is to live in a dystopic situation, and what alternative social systems have to offer. This interesting idea is also highlighted in Nicole Anae's article in this volume when she notices how speculative genres such as fantasy and science fiction enable authors to explore women's potential. Using the extrapolative character of the genre, writers invite readers to envision from the outsider's vantage point of view their own society, thus creating a separation that helps them understand critically the underlying social infrastructure. This way, patterns of domination that often go unnoticed in our everyday lives can be perceived critically. This is precisely what Joan Slonczewski does in *A Door into Ocean* (1986) by presenting two opposing civilizations, Valans and Sharers, and how their differing lifestyles reproduce both patterns of domination and desirable alternative ways of relating with the other. Using Karen Warren's, Val Plumwood's, and Carolyn Merchant's ideas on ecofeminism, this work aims at exploring how Slonczewski portrays what unhealthy and healthy societies consist of and how individuals can move from the former to the latter.

Despite receiving the John W. Campbell Memorial Award for Best Science Fiction Novel in 1987, *A Door into Ocean* was rejected by several publishers because of its defense of peace and non-violent resistance at a time when the Cold War was still a threat: "Before *A Door into Ocean* there was absolutely nobody writing about peaceful revolution. In fact, people told me that it was unpatriotic. Peace revolutions take 20 years, they don't happen overnight" (Slonczewski 2014, n.p.). Therefore, inspired by the circumstances that characterized the times when the novel was written, Slonczewski decided to propose an alternative and peaceful way of facing a conflict. Apart from the two confronting societies that Slonczewski portrays, the other prominent characteristic in the novel is the setting. Sharers, a society without males that trade sea silk products with other planets, inhabit an ocean moon called Shora. One of the reasons why Slonczewski decided to set her novel on a planet completely covered by water was that she envisioned the work "as a kind of response to Frank Herbert's *Dune* and to Ursula Le Guin's *The Word for World is Forest*" (2001). Herbert's *Dune* (2005) depicts violent confrontations between mostly male characters that want to increase their power, setting the story on a desert planet. Besides, in the series of *Dune* we can see how the decisions we make can have disastrous consequences for the environment. For this reason, Slonczewski created Shora and Sharers, who face war and a militaristic process of colonization through non-violent resistance, and who understand that even the smallest action can unbalance the equilibrium of the planet.

At the beginning of the novel, we see how a male Valan, Spinel, travels to Shora to live among Sharers, a distressing situation until he becomes used to Sharers's ways. Little by little we can perceive his transformation and how he embraces Sharers' beliefs and lifestyle. Once Valans realize the power and mineral richness of Shora, as well as her powerful scientific knowledge, they start the invasion of the planet, opposed by Sharers' non-violent resistance. Throughout the novel we can perceive how the different protagonists face extreme situations that make them reflect on their attitudes toward others—whether human or nonhuman—and toward the environment. Besides, by presenting two extremely different civilizations Slonczewski invites readers to analyze Valans' and Sharers' social structures as compared to their own in order to be more critical from their role as outsiders.

Because of the multiple topics covered in the novel—from politics to religion, feminism, and violence—several authors have analyzed the work using different approaches, especially if we consider that *A Door into Ocean* is a very influential work in science fiction, as Christy Tidwell comments in her chapter in this volume. Tidwell herself has a very interesting work analyzing how feminist science is portrayed in the novel, showing how Sharers are able to combine lived experience and laboratory science (see Tidwell 2020). Religion is another important aspect in Slonczewski's life and work, and the influence of Quakerism in the portrayal of Sharers is evident as exposed in Edward F. Higgins's (2001) article "Quaker Ethos as Science Praxis in Joan L. Slonczewski's *A Door into Ocean*." Apart from science and religion, another essential topic in the novel is that of feminist utopias and Susan Stratton's (2001) article "Intersubjectivity and Difference in Feminist Ecotopias" deals with this novel as compared to other feminist ecotopias. Finally, and although the role of ecology in Sharers' social system is part of the analysis carried on later from an ecofeminist perspective, it is interesting to point out Edrie Sobstyl's (1999) "All the Sisters of Shora: An Anarcha/Ecofeminist Reading of Slonczewski's *A Door into Ocean*," which approaches the novel using Murray Bookchin's ideas on social ecology.

From an ecofeminist point of view and, more specifically, considering Warren's ideas on healthy and unhealthy social systems we can see that the two models can be clearly associated with Sharers and Valans, respectively. On the one hand, Sharers live in harmony with their ecosystem and treat the other inhabitants of the planet as part of an interconnected web of life represented by Shora, the planet herself. Politically and socially, they reach decisions by consensus, and so they all participate in each other's life and decide what is best for their community. On the other hand, Valans live in a strict hierarchical system in which some elite controls the power while most of the population tries to survive by working for those in the higher classes. Their relationship with nature is based on the exploitation of resources for their benefit, creating artificial cities and robots, and conquering new places when resources are exhausted. Therefore, the contrast between the two civilizations is very clear and one of the main characteristics of the novel. This polarization is only breached by some of the protagonists, whose personal decisions in times of conflict determine that being part of a social system or other is a matter of choice.

When the Valan boy Spinel arrives in Shora he is surprised by its impressive landscape:

> Something nagged at him; something was missing, he did not know what. As he watched the sea, it came to him. There were no landmarks of any kind, just the flat horizon. It was hardly safe, out on the open sea in such a small craft, and with what navigation?
>
> (Slonczewski 1986, 53)

When he starts to live among Sharers he realizes that it is not only Sharers' appearance that catches his attention—and his curiosity—but also their life-style and habits. Because of the ecosystem they live in, and after years of evolution, Sharers have developed webbed fingers and toes; and thanks to a Shoran microbe that enables them to swim underwater for longer periods, their skin is purplish blue. Although Spinel asks for a remedy so that his skin does not change, he never uses it, and little by little he learns to appreciate Sharers' uniqueness and how healthy their social system is. For example, he finds it fascinating how Sharers treat their food since although most of them are vegetarian, some do eat fish. Those who eat fish and other living creatures give thanks for their food because they think of them as part of their cycle of life: "Their voices wove eerily with the roar of the sea. Spinel watched, mystified, until Lady Nisi leaned over to whisper, 'We sing for the fish, for those sharers of our sea who die that we may feed'" (Slonczewski 1986, 84).

As we can see, Sharers conceive their role in Shora as that of a link within a chain and, for that reason, they treat all the other creatures on the planet with respect and understanding. Chris Pak reflects on this and highlights that by understanding their dependence on other animals, their relationship with them "is not one of dominance but of symbiosis" (2017, 125). This approach contrasts with the traditional anthropocentric vision of Western societies in which humans' ability to reason, as a result of the evolutionary process, has placed them on top of their artificially created hierarchy of creatures on Earth. In this sense, biologist Lynn Margulis comments that the idea that human beings are the most evolved creatures lacks any scientific support: "All beings alive today are equally evolved. All have survived over three thousand million years of evolution from common bacterial ancestors. There are no 'higher' beings, no 'lower animals,' no angels and no gods" (1998, 3). For this reason, Margulis posits that because all species occupy the same level, we should focus more on the similarities between species and not on our differences, that uniqueness "should inspire awe, not repulsion" (1998, 4). This idea is also present in "God, Gaia and Biophilia", an article written together with her son Dorion Sagan, when the authors state that humans should think of themselves as just another part of the chain of life on Earth (1993, 351). It is precisely this equal status among all the inhabitants of our planet which enables healthy social systems to flourish because if no member enjoys a superior position, all creatures' wellness is provided for.

The idea of a planet as an interconnected web of life in which all elements play a role is closely related to James Lovelock's Gaia hypothesis. As a sci-entist herself, Slonczewski was probably familiar with this approach, and in *A Door into Ocean* we can see Gaia represented in the ocean moon Shora. Both Gaia and Shora can be described as having a dual nature because even though they are planets geological and biologically speaking, they are also thought of as superior beings that hold together a network of life forms. This conception is at the base of Sharers' philosophy of life since they see their planet as a living creature and they realize that their survival depends on the survival of all the other elements that conform to the web of life that Shora is, even of the lesser beings. Therefore, the balance of Shora—and of any other ecosystem—is essentially based on the recognition of the interdependence and interconnection of the members of that ecosystem. In the Gaia hypothesis, Lovelock comments on this interconnectedness of life from a scientific point of view: "the atmosphere, the oceans, the climate and the crust of the Earth are regulated at a state comfortable for life because of the behavior of living organisms" (Lovelock 1991, 10). The main problem of this hypothesis for environmentalists is that since according to Lovelock the Earth would be able to heal itself and recover its balance in case we damaged it, then there would be no need to be careful with the Earth and its resources. In *A Door into Ocean* this controversial aspect is counteracted by Sharers's practices since they are aware that her actions can seriously affect the well-being of Shora.

The relationship of Sharers with their environment, the planet Shora, is very interesting from an ecofeminist point of view. If we consider the definition of a healthy social system we can see that Sharers take care of all the inhabitants of the planet so that its equilibrium is maintained. Similarly, if we relate Sharers with the characteristics of partnership ethics we can conclude that their vast scientific knowledge is used to understand and cooperate with nature, rather than to subject it to their personal interests. This is clearly seen when Valans invade Shora and start to use pests to control some of the dangerous creatures that live in the waters of the plant. Sharers are horrified to see how those pests alter the ecosystem and "threaten not only the livelihood but the very center of being of every Sharer of Shora" (Slonczewski 1986, 90). Sharers find this intromission—and form of colonization of a hostile ecosystem—especially serious because they, who are expert genetic engineers, have never used their biochemical knowledge to kill the most dangerous species: "the people of Shora, who call themselves 'Sharers,' claim to resist terraforming their planet, preferring even to be eaten alive by predators rather than harm the balance of nature" (Slonczewski and Levy 2008, 184). A clear example of this can be seen with the seaswallowers—sea creatures that travel across Shora twice a year—which threaten Sharers' lives by destroying the rafts where they live. They could easily create a pest or some chemical substance to repel these creatures, but they choose not to intervene: "'Sharers know their own limits; that, perhaps, is their greatest strength. They don't like to alter the life balance. Something worse *might replace seaswallowers* ...' Every 'lesser sharer' had its purpose, Sharers claimed" (Slonczewski 1986, 90). This is precisely what happens when Valans use their artificial pests without considering the consequences:

> The overcrowded raft seedlings festered and oozed scum that poisoned fish and octopus, while fleshborers devoured what little remained. Then mudworms bloomed and turned the sea brown, without fish to

consume them; and fanwings that skimmed the sea for food sickened from the mudworms, until flocks of their bodies drifted on the raft seedlings. The one thing worse than swallower time was the time when swallowers failed to appear.

(Slonczewski 1986, 287)

This episode illustrates very clearly why Sharers try to avoid altering the equilibrium of the planet. Besides, their attitude toward this type of practices may be directly related to a famous quote from Frank Herbert's *Dune*, a novel that served as an inspiration to Slonczewski, stated by Pardot Kynes, a planetologist: "That's why the highest function of ecology is the understanding of consequences" (Herbert 2005, 482). Therefore, Valans' invasive and manipulative attitude toward the environment contrasts with Sharers' respect, a contrast that is even voiced by one of these women when she is talking to Spinel: "What's the use, if you can't even manage your own planet properly? Everything is plentiful the first time you share it, but once we come to need it, it vanishes" (Slonczewski 1986, 71). This non-interference stemming from the understanding of the rules of nature is also examined in Amy Chan Kit-Sze's chapter in this volume when she analyzes the concept of *wuwei* in the lifestyle of Gethenians in Ursula K. Le Guin's *The Left Hand of Darkness*.

Regarding the management of natural resources, and the relationship with the environment in general, both Valans and Sharers can be described as very advanced from a scientific point of view. However, their view on how scientific knowledge should be used differs completely since whereas Valans see science as a tool to control nature, Sharers see it as a way of understanding their role in the ecosystem; then, for Sharers "science is a science of life, their intellectual supremacy in biology used not to destroy but to nurture ecological systems" (Otto 2012, 32). It is in fact their supremacy in biochemistry and genetics what Valans see as a threat and one of the reasons why they decide to invade the planet.

When Valans arrive in Shora in order to conquer the planet, they unsuccessfully try to locate Sharers' laboratories. Valans' scientific facilities resemble human ones—as we can see in one description of the Valan headquarters on Shora—so that when they look for the places where Sharers carry out their experiments they are unable to find them because they expect, as Edrie Sobstyl points out, laboratories "often shiny, typically with switches, or dials and lights that flash" (1999, 144). However, Sharers' laboratories—or life-shaping rooms, as they call them—are underwater infrastructures that are part of the rafts where they live. These rafts are described as houses with different panels made of woven sea silk and whose walls are decorated with fungus.[1] The author herself explains that these rafts are inspired by mangrove forests: "Mangrove trees hold soil and support the world's most fertile wetland ecosystems in South America, Asia, and Australia. In these watery forests, people gather crabs and fish while sometimes living upon 'floating villages,' much as the Sharers do" (Slonczewski 2001, n.p.). Despite the apparent simplicity of Sharers' life-shaping rooms, every cell in the raft contains all the genetic knowledge Sharers possess, so that if Valans wanted to eliminate it, they would have to destroy the whole raft.

> There's work space, there's plumbing. No glassware, bottled chemicals, or autoclaves, much less recognizable analytic hardware. But those vines you saw, they form galls whose cavities can be inoculated with pure cultures of microorganisms. Other vines are specialized secretors for enzymes, organic reagents, acids, you name it.
>
> (Slonczewski 1986, 215)

When some Valan scientists realize where Sharers' laboratories are, they understand that for these alien women scientific research is not an independent discipline studied by a small elite, but part of their everyday life and open to everyone. In fact, before the conflict between Valans and Sharers reaches its peak, some Valan scientists work together with Sharers in order to learn from them new procedures.

Even though Slonczewski does not offer specific details about how Sharers are able to perform genetic engineering in such a highly specialized way, we are aware that science plays an important role in their life. This can be very shocking for the reader—as well as for Valans—because they are described as a primitive society whose life depends on hunting and trading but with a deep knowledge of biochemical processes. As Jane Donawerth notes, these women are able to "redesign bacteria and viruses for healing," and this enables them to regrow lost limbs, as well as to restore the balance of Shora when Valans create plagues against clickflies andseaswallowers (1997, 12). Besides, science is not seen as a competition and when new things are discovered, the information is passed from one Sharer to another through clickflies, insects that are able to carry genetic information. As a consequence, and as Jane Donawerth comments, we can consider that for Sharers science is seen as a communal activity in which they share learning as if it were any other social issue (1997, 11). Then, Sharers see science as an essential part of life, but their knowledge is not based on exploitation, but on understanding: "Their ecofeminist technology is based on ways of working with the natural capacities of other species and a sense of themselves as part of a larger web of life" (Vint 2010, 447).

As we can see from the previous analysis, Slonczewski presents two opposing societies—Sharers and Valans—that can be easily associated with Karen Warren's description of healthy and unhealthy social systems, respectively. However, the most interesting aspect of the novel is not this polarized vision but how the author crosses the boundary between the two civilizations in a way that results as very enriching from an ecofeminist point of view. Feminist utopias like the one in Shora have usually criticized on the grounds that they see everything male-ish as negative, and thus they tend to offer a very limited view. As Stone-Blackburn posits, they offer the possibility for women to develop their potential without the constraints of patriarchy, but they also tend to "raise and leave unanswered is whether male violence can be eliminated without eliminating men" (1994, n.p.). In *A Door into Ocean,* however, Slonczewski includes both how a male Valan arrives in a feminist utopia with its man-less alternative evolution, and a patriarchal society with several prominent female protagonists; so, she sets out a complex setting in which the most interesting characters are those in between the two worlds. Besides, by considering the evolution of male characters in feminist atmospheres as well as that of female characters in a strict hierarchical patriarchy, the novel rejects the essentialist criticism against ecofeminist philosophy by showing that the ability to live according to ecofeminist values is not determined by origin nor by sex, but by personal choice. In this sense, Peter Fitting comments that although in Slonczewski's novel there is a clear distinction between male and female values, "this distinction is not ultimately tied to biological sex" (1992, 40).

In order to illustrate this Slonczewski uses three different characters. The first one, Nisi, a Valan woman, who has spent long periods of time in Shora but who finally decides to use violence to defend Shora, which goes against Sharers' philosophy and betrays their way of life. The second one is another Valan woman, Jade, whose ruthless behavior when torturing Sharers positions her as one of the most violent characters in the novel. In this sense Eric Otto comments that "given the cultural atmosphere a woman can embody the worst of masculine aggressiveness" and as such, Jade "challenges essentialist notions of femininity and the idea that violence and hostility are sex specific" (Otto 2012, 35). Finally, we have one of the most interesting characters, Spinel, who after having lived most of his life according to Valan values decides to leave behind his planet and to settle permanently among Sharers. For Edward F. Higgins, Spinel functions:

> as a symbolic bridge between the two worlds that must take place on an individual scale if there is to be a recognition of mutual humanity between Valedon and Shora [...]. He must, as it were, get into an alien skin to experience Shoran humanity as well as to be recognized as human himself by the ocean world sisters.
>
> (Higgins 2001, n.p.)

This transformation starts when he rejects the drug that would stop his body from turning purplish blue, which becomes both a physical and psychological transformation. When he decides to stay on Shora, this process is complete and as Chris Pak points out, by living in a close relationship with other creatures—both human and nonhuman—he is able to revise his inherited hierarchical way of classifying beings and "to reconsider the basis of his culture's orientation to nature" (Pak 2017, 125).

Therefore, Slonczewski portrays in her novel two societies that end up facing a violent conflict in opposing ways. Valedon, a patriarchal civilization, is characterized as an unhealthy social system because of its rigid hierarchical organization. Besides, it does not provide for the wellness of others and the environment is seen as a resource to be exploited through science. As a contrast, Sharers represent healthy social values such as respect, peacefulness, and understanding. For them, the environment is part of themselves just as they are part of the environment. This polarization could be considered simplistic at first sight, but Slonczewski complicates it by using three different characters who show that regardless of the origin and the sex, the set of values according to which we decide to live our lives is a personal decision. In this sense, Spinel is the most interesting character because he is able to ignore his prejudices and learn to appreciate alternative lifestyles, even though he has to face the rejection of some of the Sharers who see him with suspicion because he is a Valan man. Since the beginning of the novel, one of the Sharers is able to see through him: "It is true that Shora knew no men before traders came. But that does not prove that a man can't become a Sharer" (Slonczewski 1986, 23); and little by little we see that her words become true because he ends up rejecting Valedon in favor of Shora: "But there were rafts beyond the horizon, where he belonged. Maybe the land beyond death was like that, a living raft on the infinite sea" (Slonczewski 1986, 296). As a science fiction novel, *A Door into Ocean* helps us analyze underlying oppressive patterns that can be present in our own cultural system, but it also shows that with effort and commitment alternative ways of life are possible. At the end of the novel, the reader understands that the life we live is not completely determined by our origins or the system that has been imposed on us, but by the choices we make when we consider their consequences for us and others.

Note

1 Parisa Hassanzadegan (2019) offers an interesting overview of existing projects together with her own designs to illustrate the architectural environment behind *A Door into Ocean* that can be very useful to envision Slonczewski's Shora.

References

Donawerth, Jane. 1997. *Frankenstein's Daughters*. New York: Syracuse University Press.

Fitting, Peter. 1992. "Reconsiderations of the Separatist Paradigm in Recent Feminist Science Fiction." *Science-Fiction Studies* 19: 32–48.

Hassanzadegan, Parisa. 2019. *A Journey to Shora: Expressing the Architectural Environment Behind A Door into Ocean*. Master's Thesis. University of Waterloo. Accessed September, 20 2020. https://uwspace.uwaterloo.ca/handle/10012/14695.

Herbert, Frank. 2005. *Dune*. New York: Ace Books.

Higgins, Edward F. 2001. "Quaker Ethos as Science Praxis in Joan L. Slonczewski's *A Door into Ocean.*" Accessed September 22, 2020. http://www.davidmswitzer.com/slonczewski/higgins.html

Lovelock, James. 1991. "Mother Earth: Myth or Science?" In *From Gaia to Selfish Genes: Selected Writings in the Life Sciences*, edited by Connie Barlow, 3–19. Cambridge, MA: MIT Press.

Margulis, Lynn. 1998. *Symbiotic Planet: A New Look at Evolution.* New York: Basic Books.

Merchant, Carolyn. 1996. *Earthcare: Women and the Environment.* New York: Routledge.

Otto, Eric C. 2012. "Ecofeminist Theories of Liberation in the Science Fiction of Sally Miller Gearhart, Ursula K. Le Guin, and Joan Slonczewski." In *Feminist Ecocriticism: Environment, Women, and Literature*, edited by Douglas A. Vakoch, 13–37. Lanham, MD: Lexington Books.

Pak, Chris. 2017. "'Then Came Pantropy': Grotesque Bodies, Multispecies Flourishing, and Human-Animal Relationships in Joan Slonczewski's *A Door into Ocean.*" *Science-Fiction Studies* 44: 122–136.

Plumwood, Val. 1993. "Feminism and Ecofeminism: Beyond the Dualistic Assumptions of Women, Men and Nature." *Society and Nature* 2, no. 1: 36–51.

Sagan, Dorion and Lynn Margulis. 1993. "God, Gaia and Biophilia." In *The Biophilia Hypothesis*, edited by Stephen R. Keller and Edward O. Wilson, 345–364. Washington, DC: Island Press.

Slonczewski, Joan.1986. *A Door into Ocean.* New York: Tom Doherty Associates, LLC.

Slonczewski, Joan. 2001. *A Door into Ocean Study Guide.* Accessed September 20, 2020. http://biology.kenyon.edu/slonc/books/adoor_art/adoor_study.htm

Slonczewski, Joan. 2014. "Joan Slonczewski: Field of Discovery". *Locus Magazine.* 9 March 2014. Accessed 2 Janruary 2021. https://locusmag.com/2014/03/joan-slonczewski-field-of-discovery/

Slonczewski, Joan, and Michael Levy. 2008. "Science Fiction and the Life Sciences." In *The Cambridge Companion to Science Fiction*, edited by Edward James and Farah Mendlesohn, 174–185. Cambridge: Cambridge University Press

Sobstyl, Edrie. 1999. "All the Sisters of Shora: An Anarcha/Ecofeminist Reading of Slonczewski´s *A Door Into Ocean.*" *Anarchist Studies* 7, no. 2: 127–153.

Stone-Blackburn, Susan. 1994. "Single-Sexed Utopias and Our Two-Sexed Reality." Accessed September 23, 2020. http://www.davidmswitzer.com/slonczewski/stone-blackburn.html

Stratton, Susan. 2001. "Intersubjectivity and Difference in Feminist Ecotopias." *Femspec* 3, no. 1: 33–43.

Tidwell, Christy. 2020. "*A Door into Ocean* as a Model for Feminist Science." In *Posthuman Biopolitics: The Science Fiction of Joan Slonczewski*, edited by Bruce Clarke, 47–64. Cham: Palgrave Macmillan.

Vance, Linda. 1993. "Ecofeminism and the Politics of Reality." In *Ecofeminism: Women, Animals, Nature*, edited by Greta Gaard, 118–145. Philadelphia: Temple University Press.

Vint, Sherryl. 2010. "Animal Studies in the Era of Biopower." *Science-Fiction Studies* 37: 444–455.

Warren, Karen. 2000. *Ecofeminist Philosophy*. Lanham, MD: Rowman and Littlefield.

Warren, Karen. 1996. "The Power and the Promise of Ecological Feminism." In *Ecological Feminist Philosophies*, edited by Karen J. Warren, 19–41. Bloomington: Indiana University Press.

9   Re-reading Ursula K. Le Guin's SF

The Daoist *Yin* Principle in Ecofeminist Novels

Amy Chan Kit-Sze

Introduction

One of the thoughts that run through Ursula K. Le Guin's science fiction is Daoist philosophy. Le Guin herself has rendered a translation of the Daoist classic, *Daodejing*, which she hopes to be "accessible to a present-day, unwise, unpowerful, and perhaps unmale reader" (Le Guin 2011, "Introduction" paragraph 6). In fact, a lot of the critics of Le Guin have commented on the interconnection of Daoism and ecology in her novels (notably Bain, Barbour, Cogell, Porter, Suvin, which are highly relevant to my article here). However, most of them could only read the general Daoist ideas in her novels, such as *yin-yang*, ecology, balance, and the most famous butterfly dream. Darko Suvin (1975) even downplays the Daoist elements in Le Guin's novels. Prettyman (2014) criticizes and Suvin (1975) and Jameson (2007) downplay the Daoist elements in Le Guin's novels, but Jameson's reading of the Daoist elements in Le Guin is nonetheless general. Main concepts in Daoism indeed not only run through Le Guin's novels but play a significant and fundamental role in shaping the worlds in her novels. As Bain writes, "Tao is the universal base upon which societies and individual characters act" (1980, 209). For example, in *The Lathe of Heaven (LH)*, *The Left Hand of Darkness (LHD)*, and *The Word for World Is Forest (WWF)*, the Daoist concepts of *zuo-wang*坐忘 (sitting in forgetfulness) and *wuwei*無為 (non-doing) are used to describe the non-human or future human characters in the novels. In *WWF*, the little green beings on the planet of Athshe show a Daoist sensitivity to the environment. The *yin* principle of Daoism, as I will argue in this chapter, runs through all the worlds in her novels. Moreover, the worlds built upon the *yin* principle, such as Athshe in *WWF*, are usually portrayed as a utopia. Daoist philosophy is considered to be a *yin* or a feminine philosophy in the Chinese tradition as compared to Confucian philosophy (*yang* and masculine), which was appropriated and commended by the kings and emperors throughout Chinese history. As Wong explains, *yin* and *yang* are originally "an emergent process of fluid and rotational connectivities" (Wong 2016) and it is Confucianism that allocated *"yin* and *yang* with various and contrastive values ... Henceforth, Confucianism is described as a *yang* school of thinking and practice, whereas Daoism has kept its major tenet as a philosophy valorizing *yin* characteristics" (ibid.).

Besides the *yin* principle, I would also like to bring in the Deleuzian concepts of Body without Organs and becoming to the discussion as these two concepts shed new light on the interpretation of the *yin* principle in Daoist thought. Altogether, the basic components in this paper, namely, Daoist *yin*-principle, ecological thought, Deleuzian philosophy, and Le Guin's SF, finally coalesce into a multispecies community best described by Donna J. Haraway's most recent "reworlding" of SF which embraces science fiction, speculative feminism, speculative fabulation, science fantasy, and string figures. By reading some of Le Guin's novels from the Daoist perspective, this paper attempts to bring out the ecological and feminine Daoist thought embedded in her novels.

Wuwei, Wuyu, and *Wuzhi*

In Le Guin's *The Left Hand of Darkness*, the narrator is an envoy sent from Earth to a planet called Gethen.[1] After spending some time with the Gethenians, he comments that "Gethenians could make their vehicles go faster, but they do not. If asked why not, they answer 'Why?'" (*LHD*, 52). Moreover, he says, "The people of Winter, who always live in Year One, feel that progress is less important than presence" (ibid.). There is a religion called Handdara, and according to the narrator's understanding, "[t]he Handdara is a religion without institution, without priests, without hierarchy, without vows, without creed ..." (*LHD*, 57). As an envoy from Earth who doesn't know much about the religion, he doesn't even know whether there is a God. People here do practice "the Handdara discipline of Presence, which is a kind of trance—the Handdarata, given to negatives, call it an untrance—involving self-loss (self-augmentation?) through extreme sensual receptiveness and awareness ... tending towards the experience of Immanence" (*LHD*, 60). After spending some time with the Handdarata, he comments,

> [i]t was an introverted life, self-sufficient, stagnant, steeped in that singular "ignorance" prized by the Handdarata and obedient to their rule of inactivity or non-interference ... Under that nation's politics and parades and passions runs an old darkness, passive, anarchic, silent, the fecund darkness of the Handdara.
>
> (*LHD*, 63)

These ideas of non-doing and non-interference are central ideas in Daoist thought—*Wuwei* (non-doing), *wuyu* (without desire), and *wuzhi* (not-knowing). *Wu*, generally understood as a negation, can be translated as not, non-, or without. However, Laozi's philosophy is more complicated than that. According to Ames and Hall, *wuwei* is noncoercive action that is in accordance with the *de* of things.[2] Another scholar, W. T. Chan, shares a similar thought. He comments that *wuwei* does "not mean literally 'inactivity' but rather 'taking no action that is contrary to Nature'—in other words, letting Nature take its own course" (Chan 1963, 136). In Chapter 37 of *Daodejing*, it is said that:

> The Way never does anything, and everything gets done.
>
> If those in power could hold to the Way,
>
> the ten thousand things would look after themselves. (Le Guin's translation)[3]

道常無為而無不為。侯王若能守之，萬物將自化。

The Gethenians exhibit this *wuwei* attitude by privileging presence over progress. The fact that they are always living in Year One tells us that they live "in the moment." From the envoy's observation, "Winter hasn't achieved in thirty centuries what Terra once achieved in thirty decades. Neither has Winter ever paid the price that Terra paid" (*LHD*, 105). Nevertheless, they have done something over a period of time: "Slow as their material and technological advance had been, little as they valued 'progress' in itself, they had finally, in the last five or ten or fifteen centuries, got a little ahead of Nature" (*LHD*, 109). It is not that the Gethenians have not done anything to improve their living condition, rather they act in accordance with the rules of Nature. The place they live in is called Winter and just as the name suggests, it is freezingly cold throughout the year. There is no heating, no warm bed or hot bath. They simply live in the cold weather without doing anything about it for 30 centuries. As Byrne (2021) points out, Le Guin herself is critical of the predominance of the "yang" civilization that privileges progress. This certainly sheds light on how we could reshape our world in the post-COVID-19 period.

The Gethenians believe that "[t]he only thing that makes life possible is permanent, intolerable uncertainty: not knowing what comes next" (*LHD*, 75). Moreover, they think that "[i]gnorance is the ground of thought" (ibid.). That brings our discussion to the second *wu*-form, that is, *wuzhi* (not-knowing). *Wuzhi* is not ignorance; instead, it is "unprincipled knowing" (Ames and Hall 2003, 41). Knowledge, as we understand it, is dependent upon ontological presence. Our knowledge of things is determined by rules of discrimination, for example, "[r]ules of thumb, habits of mind and action, established customs, fixed standards, received methods, stipulated concepts and categories, commandments, principles, laws of nature, conventions ..." (ibid.). With these discriminations, categories, patterns, or principles, we can only perceive and live in the world patterned by them. Therefore, Laozi asks us to know the world without any pre-structure (in Heidegger's word). While *wuwei* means noncoercive action that is in accordance with the *de* of things, *wuzhi* is an understanding "with a sense of the *de* of a thing" (Ames and Hall 2003, 40). *De*, being part of the title of *Daodejing*, means "a particular uniqueness and focus" (Ames and Hall 2003, 41) of a thing. An unprincipled knowing can be further interpreted as a process of becoming in our knowledge making. In other words, our knowledge of things neither comes from some pre-determined structures nor does it remain unchanged; instead, it is always in a becoming process.

In *The Word for World Is Forest* (WWF), a military-controlled logging team from Earth colonized a planet called Athshe and named the colony "New Tahiti." The inhabitants on Athshe are small green beings (the colonizers do not see them as human) which are called "creechie" by the colonizers. The anthropologist, Dr. Lyubov, describes them as follows:

> They're a static, stable, uniform society. They have no history. Perfectly integrated, and wholly unprogressive. You might say that like the forest they live in, they've attained a climax state. But I don't mean to imply that they're incapable of adaptation.
>
> (*WWF*, 74)

Like the Gethenians, the small green people have a different sense of time from human beings (perhaps I should say intelligent life forms from Earth or Terra). In addition, they also do not treasure progress. The narrator says that,

> For this world, New Tahiti, was literally made for men. Cleaned up and cleaned out, the dark forests cut down for open fields of grain, the primeval murk and savagery and ignorance wiped out, it would be a paradise, a real Eden.
>
> (*WWF*, 12)

The novel has a very strong anti-imperialism and anti-war tone. What the colonizers do on Athshe is exactly the same as what they did in their colonies for centuries. When Kees, an Army officer from the Central, complains to Captain Davidson that his men hunt antlers illegally, Captain Davidson just says that it's his men that he looked after, not the animals and he doesn't see any harm for his men to have some "extra-legal" (*WWF*, 13) recreation. Kees confronts him by asking whether he wants to make the planet into Earth's image, he answers,

> When I say Earth, Kees, I mean people. Men. You worry about deer and trees and fiberweed, fine, that's your thing. But I like to see things in perspective, from the top down, and the top, so far, is humans. We're

here now; and so this world's going to go our way. Like it or not, it's a fact you have to face; it happens to be the way things are.

(*WWF*, 14)

The anthropologist, Dr. Lyubov, holds a different view. He reports to the old Colonel at the Central, that what the logging team is doing annihilates the planet: "If the forest perishes, its fauna may go with it. The Athshean word for world is also the word for forest. I submit, Commander Yung, that though the colony may not be in imminent danger, the planet is—" (*WWF*, 86). The worldview and attitude of the inhabitants of Athshe can certainly be compared with the Daoist philosophy.

In Chapter 3 of *Daodejing*, Laozi talks about how a sage ruler should govern. Three of the *wu*-forms are included in this chapter. All of them are related to the way of good government. First, the sage ruler has to empty the hearts and minds of the people of knowledge as we understand it. Second, the people should also desire things without the desire to possess or to control. Third, the way to achieve the first two *wu*-forms is *wuwei*—noncoercive action. The idea of a ruler should be *wuwei* and is reiterated in Chapter 57: "We do things noncoercively (*wuwei*) /And the common people develop along their own lines" (我無為，而民自化) (Ames and Hall 2003, 166).

Zhuangzi, another classic of Daoism, is also based on the *wu*-form. One of the most prominent *wu*-forms in *Zhuangzi* is *wuyong* 無用 (no-use). According to *Zhuangzi*, being no-use is a way to enjoy the natural course of life. In Chapter 4, "Way of the Human World" 〈人間世〉, a carpenter sees a huge oak tree that could shelter thousands of oxen. He does not even care to look at it. The apprentice is puzzled because he has never seen such a marvelous timber. When he asks his master why he doesn't bother to even take a look, the carpenter says,

> Forget it! Don't talk about it! It is a useless tree. A boat made from it would sink; a coffin made from it would rot; a vessel made from it would split; a door made from it would sweat; and a beam made from it would be infested. The timber is worthless and useless. That's why it can stand so many years.

(Wang 1999, 65)

已矣，勿言之矣！散木也，以為舟則沈，以為棺槨則速腐，以為器則速毀，以為門戶則液樠，以為柱則蠹。是不材之木也，無所可用，故能若是之壽。

When the carpenter goes to sleep that night, the oak tree appears in his dream, asking him what trees he compares it to. It then says that all those fruit trees are torn off as soon as they are ripe. It said, "It is their utility that makes their life miserable. That is why they cannot live out their life-span but die a premature death" (ibid.). It continues to say that, "For a long time I have been trying to be useless ... Now that I am useless, my useless-ness is of the greatest use to me" (ibid, 65; 67). 且予求無所可用久矣……乃今得之，為予大用。This is the gist of the Daoist idea of "the usefulness of uselessness." Only when all people look down on it and consider it use-less, then the tree is the most useful to itself because it can live out its natural course of life and prevent itself from a pre-mature death. The idea of useless-ness is also briefly mentioned in *LHD*. The narrator is introduced to Faxe, a Foreteller and a leader in the Handdara religion. According to Faxe, the art of Foretelling was created by the Handdara "[t]o exhibit the perfect useless-ness of knowing the answer to the wrong question" (*LHD*, 74). However, contrary to what Faxe says, knowing the answer to the wrong question is not perfectly useless. In fact, it acts as a plot-mover (or, shall we say it is a kind of self-fulfilling prophecy?) in the case of Lord Berosy and his lover, Herbor (*LHD*, 45–48).

Zuo-wang and the Body without Organs

In Chapter 6 of *Daodejing*, there is the famous story of Yan Hui talking with Confucius about "sit and forget." Yan Hui told Confucius that he had made some progress by forgetting the ethical codes, music, humaneness, and righteousness, but Confucius told him it was not good enough. Finally, after some time, Yan Hui said he could sit and forget.

> Confucius asked in astonishment, "What is 'sit and forget'?"
>
> Yan Hui said, "I cast off my limb and trunk, give up my hearing and sight, leave my physical form and deprive myself of my mind. In this way, I can identify myself with Tao. This is the so-called 'sitting and forgetting.'"
>
> (Wang 1999, 211)

> 仲尼蹴然曰：「何謂坐忘？」顏回曰：「墮肢體，黜聰明，離形去知，同於大通，此謂坐忘。」

This "sitting and forgetting" or *zuo-wang* brings us back to the Handdara's principle of presence—untrance or self-loss. Le Guin aptly calls it a prin-ciple of "presence" because unlike our common sense understanding of the practice of meditation, it is not a loss of consciousness in the realm of the unknown. As Lu Ch'ang-keng comments (quoted in Chan), "To forget means to have one's mind in all things but not to have any mind about oneself, and to have one's feelings in accord with all things but not to have any feelings of oneself" (Chan 1963, 201). Most scholars comment that this practice of *zuo-wang* amply demonstrates the Daoist concept of "*tian-ren he-yi*" 天人合一(heaven and human become one).

We may analyze it from a more critical perspective. Yan Hui told Confucius that he had forgotten *ren yi li le*仁義禮樂 (humaneness, right-eousness, ceremonies, and music). The first two belong to the fundamental ethical codes in Confucianism according to which people should comply with; the latter two are two of the six skills that an educated man should acquire. When put together, we may say that these four features are sym-bols of the rules and codes people have to abide by should they want to be accepted by the genteel class. To forget about all these is to free oneself from the rules and codes imposed by Confucianism. However, as Moeller queries, "If it is a philosophy of absolute forgetting—how can one talk and think about it?" (Moeller 2001, 103). If Yan Hui has cast off his limbs and lost his senses, who is talking there? It is at this point that we can bring in Deleuze and Guattari's concept of Body without Organs. "BwO is not at all the opposite of the organs. The organs are not its enemies. The enemy is the organism. The BwO is opposed not to the organs but to that organization of the organs called the organism" (Deleuze and Guattari 2000, 158). In other words, the BwO is a non-formed, non-organized, or destratified body that is in a state of constant flux. The BwO can be seen as a process that is directed toward a course of continual becoming and not geared towards any teleological point of completion. The construction of BwO is a pursuit of lines of flight which allows for destratification, deterritorialization, and reterritorialization.

Deleuze and Guattari claim that "The BwO is the egg" (ibid, 164). In *Anti-Oedipus*, Deleuze and Guattari expand the BwO image by comparing its real potentials to the egg:

> The body without organs is an egg: it is crisscrossed with axes and thresholds, with latitudes and longitudes and geodesic lines, traversed by gradients marking the transitions and the becomings, the destina-tions of the subject developing along these particular vectors.
>
> (Deleuze and Guattari 1994, 19)

For Deleuze and Guattari, the BwO is like a fertilized egg with a vast reser-voir of potential traits, connections, affects, movements, etc. This collection of potentials is what Deleuze and Guattari call the BwO. As Delanda points out, "[e]mbryological development is all about rates of change which are coupled and uncoupled through the action of genes and gene products - these processes of embryological development can be viewed as 'computer programs'" (Delanda 2002, 96).

To read Yan Hui's story of *zuo-wang* as a process of attaining a BwO is probably more creative than just saying by sitting and forgetting, humans can become one with nature. By opening up the body to lines of flight, there is a possibility of openings and spaces for the creation of new modes of experience. However, absolute forgetting is not possible. Similarly, it is not possible for one to have a zero BwO because an empty BwO is a dead body. In Yan Hui's case, by forgoing the constraints imposed by Confucianism, he enters into a process of transformation. In fact, at the end of this story, Confucius says to Yan Hui, "When you become one with the Great Universal you will have no partiality, and when you are part of the process of transformation, you will have no constancy (rigidity)" (Chan 1963, 201). 同則無好也，化則無常也。

The *Yin* Principle and Becoming-Woman

The most well-known feature of *The Left Hand of Darkness* (*LHD*) is certainly the issue of gender. The Gethenians are gender-neutral for 22 days in a month and only develop a sexual drive during kemmer (a period of heat). When two Gethenians in kemmer get together, one of them will develop a hormonal dominance, either toward the male or female, and the other will assume the opposite sex. If the female one gets pregnant, she will remain female till the birth of the child. Theoretically, every Gethenian can be a mother or father of their children.[4] To be exact, the Gethenians are not androgynous. In Le Guin's words, they are "hermaphroditic neuters" (*LHD*, 50). The narrator is deeply troubled by the sex of the Gethenians because as a human from Earth, he simply cannot look at another living being but as a man or a woman. It is not till the end of the novel that the narrator finally trusts Estraven, who turns out to be the only character that has the same belief as him, that is, they are not to serve any ruler or any nations, but humankind. And that mistrust originates from the fact that he doesn't know what to make of Estraven since Estraven can neither be classified as male or female. He admits that it is "almost impossible for our imagination to accept" (*LHD*, 101). On the other hand, he agrees that it is perhaps better to be neuters since there will be "no division of humanity into strong and weak halves" (*LHD*, 100) and "[o]ne is respected and judged only as a human being" (ibid., 101).

The title of the book *The Left Hand of Darkness* comes from a line in the novel: "Light is the left hand of darkness" (*LHD*, 252) that has a strong overtone of the *yin-yang* principle in Daoism. When the narrator tries to explain *yin-yang* to Estraven, he draws the symbol on his notebook and says,

> It's found on Earth, and on Hain-Davenent, and on Chiffewar. It is yin and yang. Light is the left hand of darkness … how did it go? Light, dark. Fear, courage. Cold, warmth. Female, male. It is yourself, Therem. Both and one. A shadow on snow.
>
> (*LHD*, 287)

The *yin-yang* principle aptly describes the sex of the Gethenians: they have both sexes in them. And when *yin* gets stronger, then the *yang* recedes, and vice versa. Nevertheless, they are dependent on each other. It is said in *Daodejing* that "Everything carries *yin* on its shoulders and *yang* in its arms/

And blends these vital energies (*qi*) together to make them harmonious (*he*)" (Chapter 42). 萬物負陰而抱陽，沖氣以為和。The idea of co-dependence is also mentioned in Chapter 2:

> Difficult and easy complement each other,
> Long and short set each other off,
> High and low complete each other,
> Refined notes and raw sounds harmonize (*he*) with each other,
> And before and after lend sequence to each other—
> This is really how it all works. (Ames and Hall 2003, 80)
> 有無之相生也，
> 難易之相成也，
> 長短之相形也，
> 高下之相盈也，
> 音聲之相和也，
> 前後次相隨，
> 恆也。

The idea of *yin-yang* is so well-known now that I don't need to elaborate on it. Instead, I am more interested in the *yin*-principle. In Chapter 8, water is celebrated as the highest efficacy. In Chapter 61, the feminine power is celebrated as more superior than the male. It says,

> A great state is like the lower reaches of water's downward flow.
> It is the female of the world.
> In the intercourse of the world,
> The female is always able to use her equilibrium (*jing*) to best the male.
> 大國者下流，天下之交，天下之牝。牝常以靜勝牡，以靜為下。

In Chapter 34, it is said that "Way-making (*dao*) is an easy-flowing stream / Which can run in any direction" 大道汜兮，其可左右. *Dao* is being compared to a river here that can flow freely in any direction. The power of water is further elaborated in Chapters 66, 76 & 78.

By stating that the most virtuous men should be like water and by comparing water to female and *Dao* to water, *Daodejing* suggests that rulers should follow the *yin* principle because it is the symbol of life and where the power lies. As Moeller comments,

> The perfect ruler has to copy the strategy of water and the feminine … Like water and the feminine, the ideal ruler is supposed to naturally "conceive" all energy around him and thus be the source of life. Water and femininity are at the *center* of the circle of procreation.
>
> (Moeller 2001, 39)

In *The Left Hand of Darkness*, King Argaven is initially very suspicious of the intention of the envoy. He thinks Ekumen wants to annex power from them or to exert control on them by inviting the Gethenians to form an alliance. He even orders to exile Estraven (the then prime minister) for treason because he tries to persuade the king that they should join the alliance. However, at the end of the novel, he agrees to join the alliance. The question is what causes the change. In between the exile of Estraven and the envoy's return to Karhide, the King has got pregnant, given birth to and then lost his (or her) heir. Apparently, being female for nine or ten months has changed his (or her) mind. He eventually comes to see that joining Ekumen will bring benefits to his country and his people.

This becoming-woman of King Argaven seems to make him a wiser ruler. In fact, the concept of becoming-woman according to Deleuze and Guattari does not literally mean one has to turn oneself into a woman; instead, it means one has to begin the becoming process with becoming-woman since woman is a minoritarian and all becomings have to pass through the process of becoming-woman to attain becoming-immanent. Moreover, the construction of a BwO is inseparable from becoming-woman. A body is a molar entity. To construct a BwO means to destratify the body, deterritorialize and reterritorialize it, and also to turn it into molecular. The *yin*-principle in Daoism and the becoming-woman concept in Deleuzian philosophy do share a lot in common: a body is hard while a BwO is soft (for there is no organization); a body is *yang*, and a BwO is *yin*. The idea of "hermaphroditic neuters" and how the hormonal dominance of male and female decides who is man or woman during kemmer are interesting examples of Deleuze and Guattari's idea of a thousand tiny sexes.

Conclusion

In *Staying with the Trouble: Making Kin in the Chthulucene*, Donna J. Haraway adapts the concept of becoming and advocates the concept of becoming-with instead. She argues that the companion species have been becoming-with people for several thousand years. Now we have to come together, to stay with the trouble because, according to Haraway, we have entered the epoch of Cthulucene (not just the Anthropocene because it is a time of consequences)[5] where all refugees from environmental disasters (both human and non-human) will come together. She asks us to make kin (instead of babies), to "reworld, reimagine, relive, and reconnect with each other, in multispecies well-being" (Haraway 2016, 50–51). She prefers to call the human species the "com-post" to posthuman.

As this re-reading of Ursula Le Guin's ecofeminist science fiction novels has shown, Le Guin's novels do not only embody ecological and feminist ideas but also celebrate the *yin*-principle of Daoism which in turn is connected to the Deleuzian philosophy. SF—science fiction, speculative feminism, speculative fabulation, science fantasy, and Haraway's string figures; Deleuzian philosophy of becoming and Body without Organs; and Daoist *yin-yang* and *wu-* forms all can come together to form a compost and shed light on how human species could survive the Anthropocene by becoming-with other multispecies. In fact, there are still more Daoist ideas in Le Guin's novels that can be pursued, for example the concept of time (which is related also to the concept of deep time in the Anthropocene) and the motif of dreaming (also a well-known story in *Zhuangzi*). But this has to wait for another paper.

Notes

1 Ekumen is an interplanetary group in Le Guin's science fictional universe. In *The Left Hand of Darkness*, it is revealed that there are 83 planets in Ekumen. The narrator of *LHD* is sent to Gethen to persuade the king there to join Ekumen.
2 Ames and Hall write that, "*wuwei*無為," often translated (unfortunately) as "no action" or "non-action," really involves the absence of any course of action that interferes with the particular focus (de) of those things contained within one's field of influence. Actions uncompromised by stored knowledge or ingrained habits are relatively unmediated: they are accommodating and spontaneous. As such, these actions are the result of deferential responses to the item or the event in accordance with which, or in relation to which, one is acting. These actions are *ziran*自然, "spontaneous" and "self-so-ing," and as such, are nonassertive actions. (Ames and Hall 2003, 39)
3 Ames and Hall use a recently discovered version of the *Daodejing* written on bamboo and this line in Chapter 37 reads in a different way. Therefore, Le Guin's translation is used instead.
4 For a detailed description of the sex features of the Gethenians, please go to *The Left Hand of Darkness* (Le Guin 2010, 96–103).
5 Haraway writes, "These times called the Anthropocene are times of multispecies, including human, urgency: of great mass death and extinction; of onrushing disasters, whose unpredictable specificities are foolishly taken as unknowability itself; of refusing to be present in and to onrushing catastrophe in time; of unprecedented looking away." (Haraway 2016, 35)

References

Ames, Roger T., and David L. Hall. 2003. *Dao De Jing: Making This Life Significant: A Philosophical Translation*. New York: Ballantine Books.
Bain, Dena C. 1980. "The Tao Te Ching as Background to the Novels of Ursula K. Le Guin." *Extrapolation* 21, no. 3: 209–222.
Barbour, Douglas. 1973. "The Lathe of Heaven: Taoist Dream." *Algol* 21: 22–24.
Bryne, Deirdre. 2021. "The Road to Sinshan: Ecophilia in Ursula K. Le Guin's Early Hainish Novels." In *Ecofeminist Science Fiction: International Perspectives on Gender, Ecology, and Literature*, edited by Douglas A. Vakoch, 189–203. Abingdon: Routledge.
Chan, Wing Tsit. 1963. *A Source Book in Chinese Philosophy*. Princeton, NJ: Princeton University Press.
Cogell, Elizabeth. 1979. "Taoist Configurations: *The Dispossessed*." In *Ursula K. Le Guin: Voyager to Inner Lands and Outer Space*, edited by Joe De Bolt, 153–179. New York: Kennikat.

Colebrook, Claire. 2016. "'A Grandiose Time of Coexistence': Stratigraphy of the Anthropocene." *Deleuze Studies* 10, no. 4: 440–454.

Delanda, Manuel. 2002. *Intensive Science and Virtual Philosophy*. London: Continuum.

Delanda, Manuel. 2016. *Assemblage Theory*. Edinburgh: Edinburgh University Press.

Deleuze, Gilles. 1994. *Difference and Repetition*. Translated by Paul Patton. New York: Columbia University Press.

Deleuze, Gilles. 2007. *Two Regimes of Madness: Texts and Interviews 1975–1995*. Edited by David Lapoujade. Translated by Ames Hodges and Mike Taormina. New York: Semiotxt(e).

Deleuze, Gilles, and Felix Guattari. 1994. *Anti-Oedipus: Capitalism and Schizophrenia*. 3rd ed. Minneapolis: University of Minnesota Press.

Deleuze, Gilles, and Felix Guattari. 2000. *A Thousand Plateaus: Capitalism and Schizophrenia*. 8th ed. Translated by Brian Massumi. Minneapolis: University of Minnesota Press.

Haraway, Donna J. 2016. *Staying with the Trouble: Making Kin in the Chthulucene*. Durham, NC: Duke University Press.

Jameson, Fredric. 2007. *Archaeologies of the Future: The Desire Called Utopia and Other Science Fictions*. New York: Verso.

Le Guin, Ursula K. 2010. *The Left Hand of Darkness*. New York: Ace Books.

Le Guin, Ursula K. 2011. *Lao Tzu: Tao Te Ching: A Book about the Way and the Power of the Way*. Boston: Shambala.

Moeller, Hans Georg. 2001. *Daoism Explained: From the Dream of the Butterfly to the Fishnet Allegory*. Chicago: Open Court.

Porter, David L. 1975. "The Politics of Le Guin's Opus." *Science-Fiction Studies* 2, no. 7: 243–248.

Prettyman, Gib. 2014. "Daoism, Ecology, and World Reduction in Le Guin's Utopian Fictions." In *Green Planets: Ecology and Science Fiction*, edited by Gerry Canavan and Kim Stanley Robinson, 56–76. Middletown, CT: Wesleyan University Press.

Saldanha, Arun, and Hannah Stark. 2016. "A New Earth: Deleuze and Guattari in the Anthropocene." *Deleuze Studies* 10, no. 4: 427–439.

Suvin, Darko. 1975. "Parables of De-Alienation: Le Guin's Widdershins Dance." *Science-Fiction Studies* 2, no. 7: 265–274.

Wang, Rongpei. 1999. *Zhuangzi I*. Translated by Rongpei Wang, Xuqing Qin, and Yongchang Sun. Beijing: Hunan People's Publishing House.

Watson, Burton. 1968. *The Complete Works of Chuang Tzu*. New York: Columbia University Press.

Williams, James. 2011. *Gilles Deleuze's Philosophy of Time: A Critical Introduction and Guide*. Edinburgh: Edinburgh University Press.

Wong, Kin Yuen. 2016. "Yin-Yang." In *The Wiley Blackwell Encyclopedia of Gender and Sexuality Studies*, edited by Nancy A. Naples, Renee C. Hoogland, Maithree Wickramasinghe, and Wai Ching Angela Wong. New York: John Wiley & Sons. Accessed October 12, 2020. https://doi.org/10.1002/9781118663219.wbegss092.

10 Keeping Grows; Giving Flows

Reciprocal Relations and the Gift of *Always Coming Home*

Karl Zuelke

There is a tree in our yard, a crabapple. Every year, during a week some-time just before—or just after—or straddling—April 15, it explodes into an extravagant blooming pinkness: tens of thousands of individual pink five-petaled flowers, humming with bees of a dozen species, perfuming the air with its deep pink fragrance, proclaiming almost out loud that this is to be The Week of Pink so hold on to your hats! This tree grows upright, 30 feet tall, in the narrow space between our house and the neighbors'. But not long ago the crabapple nearly died of grief.

This is—admittedly—an odd statement, certainly one that risks ridicule. Grief is an emotion, and trees don't experience emotions, being alive though without consciousness. However, the Kesh, the imagined future inhabitants of Ursula Le Guin's novel, *Always Coming Home*, wouldn't think twice about a claim regarding the spirit of natural forms of life, the spirit ani-mating all elements of the natural world. At one point in the novel, Stone Telling, the novel's central character, narrates a moment in her past when she had sat by a stream talking to Spear, a man who had chosen the unusual life-path (for the Kesh) of becoming a warrior:

> I thought then, I think now, that the person who looked straight at me had come from inside him, that day, and he had forgotten about being the Warrior who had turned away and the Man and the Self. He had sat by the dry creekbed and the soul of the water had come into him. I stopped being afraid of him, and began talking to him, I do not know about what, and he answered, and so we talked for some while, trust-fully and quietly.
>
> (1985, 181)

For Stone Telling, it is the soul of the water entering Spear that facilitates a moment of deep communication, which years later she can't recall the sub-ject of, but of which she recalls the tone and the feelings clearly. The water has a soul, and the inspiriting presence of that soul provides for a memora-ble moment of trust and intimacy. But to empathize with a tree feeling grief, we need to take a critical step where we can acknowledge the soul of a plant.

The crabapple in my yard had been growing for some 20 years in intimate association with a box elder. The crabapple was probably the elder of the two, but box elders are quick-growing pioneers and prolific seeders, and they're quick to take advantage of a spot of bare soil and patch of sunlight, and this one did, and it took off. The trunks of the two trees were less than a foot apart; their branches intertwined; they had spent 20 years together growing in the same space, sharing sun, soil, and water, though the box elder had finally grown taller and fuller than the crabapple. Then a hard winter froze out half of the box elder, which are nervous and flighty as trees go anyway, quick to take hold and grow up fast, and just as quick to check out. The soft brittle wood of the dead branches threatened the power line leading to our house, and it just seemed apparent that this particular tree's time had come. So we made the decision to have the box elder cut down in the fall, with special instructions to the sawyers to please be extra careful with the crabapple, and they were. Not a scratch on it. But beginning the following summer, it began to decline.

For two springs, the bloom we waited for was sparse, scraggly, and the follow-up establishment of foliage was scrappy as well. It was hard to look at the meager foliage of the crabapple tree those two seasons following the death of the box elder and not say to oneself, "poor thing." The crabapple seemed bereft. It didn't feel like growing. It grieved. I'm happy to report that it looks now to have recovered, and as I write in May, after a bustling bloom back in April, the foliage is thick and healthy, green and red, and clearly ready to get on with things. It is already filling in the spaces once occupied by its buddy, and I'm no longer worried about it.

Such a pronouncement, about a grief-stricken crabapple tree, will ring with utter absurdity to many readers, and that is understandable. Christy Tidwell (this volume, 154), in her response to a tree telling a character to "Go well," makes the reasonable claim that, "Despite growing scientific evidence that plants and trees do communicate, they do not do so in anything approaching this way." We mostly function in an everyday Euro-Western milieu wherein the "language" of trees is only in the opening stage of being recognized. Greta Gaard refers to Robin Wall Kimmerer's claim, coming from Kimmerer's indigenous frame of reference, that plants do indeed communicate, with each other, certainly, and even with ourselves, if we would only listen. Kimmerer, a botanist of Potawatomi ancestry, acknowledges that "Until quite recently no one seriously explored the possibility that plants might 'speak' to one another" (2013, 19). But, Kimmerer notes, "In the old times, our elders say, the trees talked to each other" (2013, 19). Now, operating from the standpoint of a Euro-Western scientist, Kimmerer is able to claim that,

There is now compelling evidence that our elders were right—the trees *are* talking to one another. They communicate via pheromones, hormonelike compounds that are wafted on the breeze, laden with meaning.

Scientists have identified specific compounds that one tree will release when it is under the stress of insect attack—gypsy moths gorging on its leaves or bark beetles under its skin. The tree sends out a distress call … Trees appear to be talking about mutual defense … There is so much we cannot yet sense with our limited human capacity. Tree conversations are still far above our heads.

(2013, 19–20)

Pheromones as a plant "language" has entered the scientific world-view, and science is uncovering other modes of plant communication as well. For example, an article in *Ecology Letters* reports that, "Evidence is emerging that mycelial networks have potential to transport signalling compounds" (Zdenka et al. 2013, 835). Underground fungal networks even function, in some characterizations, as a kind of internet:

It's an information superhighway that speeds up interactions between a large, diverse population of individuals. It allows individuals who may be widely separated to communicate and help each other out … No, we're not talking about the internet, we're talking about fungi.

(Fleming 2014)

So plant communication is being established by the scientific community as a measurable biochemical phenomenon, one that can even lead into a metaphoric comparison with the complexity of our own electronic internet. But, soul? Emotions?

Greta Gaard extends the avenues of nature/human communication along the lines suggested by Kimmerer's indigenous insights, and she takes it far beyond the relatively constrained pathway of pheromones and chemical receptors that science has begun to explore. Gaard tells of a moment when she entered a grove of oak trees where she might rest and read in their midst:

Book in hand, I entered the grove and walked rather aimlessly looking for a suitable tree trunk against which I could lean comfortably. "Over here" one tree *messaged* me with the image that "there's a curve in this trunk that will just fit your back." Compliant and curious, I walked over to the tree of reference and on the other side, which I hadn't been able to see, I discovered a long vertical hollow, well formed for holding my body upright at rest. But then I ruined the moment, as my amazed thoughts shouted, "Trees don't talk!"

And in that instant, the grove of trees turned into wood.

(Gaard 2017, xix)

That tragic, irrevocable moment when Gaard felt the living, communicating trees turn to wood—only a step, it's easy to see, away from someone else commodifying them into board feet of lumber (if that's an avenue one's perception is liable to …)—demonstrates how prey persons raised in the Euro-Western tradition are to the silencing of what Val Plumwood has termed "earthothers," a term, Gaard notes, that includes humans as well as plants and animals (Gaard 2017, xxvi). "Clearly, Euro-Western culture is so permeated by Cartesian rationalism that children are taught at an early age not to receive" (Gaard 2017, xix). Before that moment when she "remembers" that trees don't talk, however, the tree had extended her an offer of kindness. Gaard goes on to describe another moment when, in listening and observing, she was

> looking attentively at the river and rocks, when—the English language offers no exact words for what follows, because it doesn't recognize these phenomena—the rocks *showed themselves to me*: as I watched, *the rocks flowed* … what the rocks had showed me was their story, their history, their becoming.
>
> (Gaard 2017, xxi)

In this incident, she avoids backsliding into the Euro-Western conceptualization whereby many earthothers "don't talk!" For Gaard, from then on, because of the communication she experienced with the rocks, "My understanding had been irrevocably changed: *all rock is flow*" (Gaard 2017, xxi). So, we can still learn to listen to the stories nature has to tell. Gaard claims, "This rich community of indigenous, feminist, and trans-species listening theory is our birthright as earth citizens" (Gaard, 2017, xviii). Listening, the means by which this birthright is realized, Gaard maintains, is one of the hallmarks of feminist scholarship (Gaard 2017, xvii).

Talking trees, rocks communicating elements of their history to an observer, these are vivid reminders of the distance Euro-Western conceptions of rational causality have moved from the widespread indigenous understanding of humans as listening members of a speaking, inspirited community of diverse earthothers. Science, as Kimmerer shows above, has only just begun an exploration into plant communication, initiating a Kuhnian paradigm shift within the science that acknowledges a level of active agency in plants never considered before, though as Kimmerer also demonstrates above, indigenous insight has been way ahead of science in this regard. With this shift, the dominant conception that insists plants don't talk has accommodated in a particular circumscribed manner an indigenous understanding. But the science remains the dominant mode of understanding, representative of a value dualism with hierarchical dominant and subordinate elements—plants don't talk. And should we discover that they do exchange pheromone messages, they still don't offer comfortable seats out of kindness, and they do not grieve. There is a hierarchical value dualism in play, the dominant half of which would maintain that the concept of grieving trees is absurd. Grieving trees thus occupy the conceptual space Josephine Donovan would identify as the "absent referent," (1998, 74), a term arising out of poststructuralist language theory, where "the refer-ent refers to the real or material entity signified by the linguistic signal, the word" (Donovan 1998, 75). Donovan summarizes an insight of Carol Adams, who notes that in terms of carnivorous eating, the term "meat" is often the signifier and "animal" or "cow" is thus made the absent referent. The term "meat" deadens the aliveness of the animal, rendering it into an "it" (Adams 1990, 40–62). This is reflective of "the ontology of domina-tion that supports carnivorism" (Donovan 1998, 75). "The living being of the actual cow is thus repressed as the signifier *meat* takes over, inscribing the referent as an exchange object within a symbolic commerce, which legitimizes the actual commerce of the meat market exchange" (Donovan 1998, 75). A hierarchical value dualism is thus established, with linguistic roots, where the value of the life of a cow is rendered subordinate to the value of the dead cow's meat in a market system perpetuated by a logic of domination. We see the same movement in the sudden ontological trans-formation of "speaking tree" to "wood," a signifier that suppresses the living, communicating tree. In my nervousness at ascribing grief to the struggle of a tree to recover from the shock of losing a close associate, I recognize an internalization of Karen J. Warren's understanding of the logic of domination "that 'justifies' domination and subordination" and that "assumes that superiority justifies subordination" (Warren 2000, 47). While the assumptions underlying a logic of domination are problematic, the recognition of a value dualism has value. Warren makes the assertion that "Contrary to what many feminists and ecofeminists have claimed, there may be nothing inherently problematic about hierarchical thinking (even value-hierarchical thinking), value dualisms, and conceptions and relations of power and privilege" (Warren 2000, 47), as long as hierar-chical thinking doesn't privilege a logic of domination. We understand that value dualisms exist, and we recognize that a logic of domination privileges male over female, cultural over natural, and Euro-Western over indigenous. Ecofeminism begins in a recognition of such, with the aim of deconstructing the extant logic of domination: the fact of the domi-nance and oppression of Euro-Western, patriarchal influences over nature, women, and diverse earthothers does not in itself justify that dominance. In the words of Eric C. Otto,

> for Warren and other ecofeminists, the projects of feminism and envi-ronmentalism must notice the similarities between this androcentric logic and the cultural logic that constructs a culture/nature opposition, places a higher value on culture, and as a result authorizes human domi-nation over nonhuman nature.
>
> (Otto 2012, 13)

Ursula K. Le Guin's *Always Coming Home* is structured around the indig-enous/civilized complex of value dualisms that my discussion about plant communication is intended to introduce, and it is remarkable in the way that it works to give voice to the absent referent of an indigenous society living in community with the plants, animals, and landscape of its setting. The novel is presented as an archeology of the future, an exploration of the culture of the Kesh, who inhabit a valley in what was once Northern California in a post-apocalyptic future. The novel includes the story of Stone Telling, a young Kesh woman of the valley who travels with her father to a life for a number of years among the Condor people, who are attempting to re-establish the civilized, warlike, domineering, patriarchal consumer culture the reader recognizes as reminiscent of ours at present day. Beyond this central narrative of departure and return from what the Kesh perceive as the upsidedown and backward world of the Condors, the novel is filled with artifacts of Kesh culture and daily life, including songs, stories, recipes, drawings, iconography, history, folktales. The novel is filled with descriptions of the technology and arts and the making of the Kesh. Le Guin creates a complex and detailed system of tradition, technology, story, and ceremony that encompass the Kesh's lives. There are descriptions of techniques for pottery making, musical instruments, foods, winemaking, clothing, houses, and the book includes a glossary that provides definitions for words that would not readily translate into English. There are detailed descriptions of local plants and their uses. The kinship affinity of the Kesh with all the inhabitants of the valley is reinforced through linguistic features of the Kesh language. A poem, "The Blue Rock's Song" exemplifies how the demarcation between rock, trees, and people of the valley is fluid:

> I am coherent, mysterious, and solid.
> I sit on dirt in sunlight between the live oaks.
> Once I was a sun, again I will be dark.
> Now I am between those great things for a while
> along with other people, here in the Valley.

> (112)

A schematic chart shows the nine organizational houses into which inhabitants of the valley are grouped, though with the caveat that "the actual listing and charting of the nine divisions and their various members and functions would strike the Valley mind as somewhat childish and—in fixing and 'locking' the information—as risky and inappropriate" (44). The grouping of the houses shows that distinctions between plants, minerals, animals, and people are much less important than their shared life as members of the valley community. The chart divides the nine houses into "The Five Houses of the Earth" and "The Four Houses of the Sky." The inhabitants of the Houses of the Earth are "the earth itself, the moon, all rocks and landforms, all fresh waters, individual animals and human beings currently alive, plants used by human beings, domestic and ground-living birds, game and domestic animals" (45). The inhabitants of the four Houses of the Sky include birds, fish, animals not hunted for food (which are listed, including puma, coyote, woodrat, vole, otter, fox, bat, etc.), and "human beings as the species, people, tribe, or nation; the dead, the unborn; all beings in stories or dreams; the oceans, the sun, the stars" (46).

The Kesh have returned to a nature-centered, indigenous way of life, and that the animals, trees, rocks, and people of the valley would communicate as they live together is simply a given. The lifestyle that the Kesh have developed is integrated harmoniously into the local ecology, and to accomplish this, their lifestyle is by necessity appropriately respectful of the local resources and not consumptive of them. The Kesh

> have created a rural potlatch society many generations after our runaway industrial society has ended. All of the Kesh's relations—with the world as a whole, with each other, with their arts—are based on participation and reciprocity, a constant circulation of giving and receiving.
>
> (LeClair 1989, 207)

This circulation of giving and receiving models natural systems that are ordered by processes of life, death, decay, and the systemic reintegration of physical resources. Furthermore, the Kesh's intimate involvement in a cycle of reciprocal relations depends to a great extent on their recognizing the value of the diverse earthothers that populate their valley. Dierdre Byrne calls attention to a quote from a Kesh document, "A Treatise on Practices," from "The Back of the Book" section of *Always Coming Home*: "The image of the other's pain is the center of being human" (478). Byrne (2021, 201) claims that

> The impulse of an ethical compassion that is encapsulated in these words includes marginalized others (nonhuman nature and women) is profoundly feminist, albeit not restricted to biological women, and gives expression to a *zoe*-centred care, that is more important attention than ever in the Anthropocene.

This same "A Treatise on Practices" also asserts that "If the image of the other's gift is lost, the killer's mind is lost, if the image of pain is lost, the killer is lost" (478). The Condors are portrayed as representative examples of the killers that this Kesh document warns against. They are developed both as a stark contrast to the ecologically integrated Kesh, but also to recall our own society and its power and vulnerabilities, its lack of a Kesh-like empathy for others, ultimately its failings. The Condors, as well, throw a sharp light on the gendered dominance of patriarchal modes of relation, both theirs and ours. As Stone Telling soon finds upon her arrival in her new Condor home, women are rarely permitted to leave their houses, they are held in tyrannical subjugation by male members of their society, and they are forbidden to even speak. The men, meanwhile, organize into military units and make war on neighboring societies in their quest for land, resources, and the wealth they strive to accumulate. As Stone Telling observes, "People who make life into a war fight it first with people of the other sex" (368).

The Condor, like all other societies, have access to the "Exchanges," interfaces with a vast cybernetic information network, created in the distant past by our fallen technological society, now self-perpetuating and extending well beyond the confines of the earth. Enormous amounts of information are available—essentially all knowledge ever created by humans. The Condors turn to the Exchanges for technological information leading to new and more effective weapons systems, which they use to build a machine called Destroyer (a tank) and flying machines called Nestlings. While noisy, powerful, and magnificent, the resources needed to build and fuel the machines are difficult to obtain. The Destroyer, which was to lead a conquering army in a path called The Way of Destruction, is so heavy that it falls through some weak ground, lodging in an underground crevice, and is lost. The Nestlings, fueled with alcohol fermented from "grain and shit," are rendered inoperable when one person, probably a slave, sets fire to the fuel dump. More fuel is manufactured from grain stores and the harvest of that autumn, including potatoes and turnips, so that the storehouses of the city are wiped out. In the end, the machines are too consumptive of Condor resources to be successful, and this eventually leads to a decline in the power and vitality of Condor society. While our present-day industrial society is sustained by access to energy resources that are depleted by the time of the Condors, their example nevertheless underscores its wastefulness and ultimate ecological futility.

The Condors function in the novel as a graphic example of the wastefulness and futility of their lifestyle, and by extension ours. At one point Stone Telling, in her recollection of her life with the Condors, remarks that, "However willfully I tried, it was difficult for me to become entirely a Condor person. I became as sick as I could, but I was not willing to die" (193). Still, it is the Kesh and their lifestyle and philosophy which are the novel's primary focus. While the novel, through Stone Telling's memoir, critiques the Condors, and by extension, us, its purpose is to offer the reader an entry into the reciprocal set of relations that characterize the Kesh life. The novel, in that sense, is intended as a gift to the reader. The first edition was actually packaged in a way that accentuates the book as an artifact, with a large-format paperback volume in a box along with a cassette recording of Kesh music and poetry. But a book, as Le Guin reminds us, is much more than an artifact. It is a relation.

The novel features several sections with a character named Pandora, partially a stand-in for Le Guin herself. As the Pandora sections unfold, the reader participates in Pandora's learning and growth, about herself, the Kesh, the societies she is creating, and the one she is part of. In a conversation with a Kesh Archivist—an author/character relationship given voice—Pandora declares that, "I never did like smartass utopians ... People who have the answers are boring," to which the Archivist replies,

> This is a mere dream dreamed in a bad time, an Up Yours to the people who ride snowmobiles, make nuclear weapons, and run prison camps by a middle-aged housewife, a critique of civilization possible only to the civilized, an affirmation pretending to be a rejection, a glass of milk for the soul ulcered by acid rain, a piece of pacifist jeanjacquerie, and a cannibal dance among the savages in the ungodly garden of the farthest West.
>
> (316)

The rejection the Archivist refers to is Le Guin's and the reader's response to the story marked by the pathetic futility, the sickness, and upside-downness, of the warlike Condors and the present-day "savages" who inhabit the "ungodly garden of the farthest West." But, as the Archivist is aware, this is ultimately pretense. The book's deeper purpose is in affirmation, of the Kesh, but beyond them, an affirmation of the reciprocal, ecological, matriarchal lifeways the Kesh exemplify—and that the Condors as well as ourselves have rendered silent. The obvious approach is to make an offering, as the Kesh would understand. Tom LeClair's treatment of the novel proposes to show

> that Le Guin is neither a Luddite nor a Utopian but a careful proponent of appropriate technology in a local ecosystem; that this "mere dream" is based on thorough knowledge of neolithic communities and systems principles; that Le Guin is not a nostalgist praising "primitive" life but a synthesizer of past, present, and futures; and that this "middle-aged housewife" has presented a profound feminist model of selfhood and human relations—all of which make *Always Coming Home* a novel of reformulated mastery and a needed gift.
>
> (221–222)

There is a richness in this giving, the Kesh would affirm. The Kesh word, *ambad*, is defined in the glossary: "giving, the act of giving; generosity; wealth. To give; to be rich, wealthy; to be generous" (510). The gift comes, though, not so much as the book itself, nor the stories it conveys, but in the establishment of a relationship. As the Archivist reminds Pandora, "A book is an act; it takes place in time, not just in space. It is not information, but relation" (315). And it is quite possible, according to the book's opening "A First Note" section, to have a relationship with an imaginary future, or imaginary text from the future, as well as with the past:

> The fact that it hasn't yet been written, the mere absence of a text to translate, doesn't make all that much difference. What was and what

may be lie, like children whose faces we cannot see, in the arms of silence. All we ever have is here, now.

(n.p.)

The hope of all ecofeminist writers and critics, I believe, is to encourage and enable what Iris Murdoch calls a "reverent sympathy with the rest of creation" (74). Commenting on Murdoch's ideas, Josephine Donovan observes that, "Murdoch maintains that great art teaches one to *see* the world, the particulars of the world in all their diversity ... and therefore allows to come into being entities that would otherwise remain concealed" (Donovan 1998, 92). Murdoch stresses *seeing* as the mode by which we apprehend the particulars of creation, but listening is just as critical in bringing into the realm of awareness those absent referents that we, as well as the Condors, render invisible and silent. Greta Gaard stresses that,

> Feminist communication scholars have looked not only at whose speech merits attention, but also at who listens. Speaking is associated with power, knowledge, and dominance, while listening is associated with subordination. Not surprisingly, feminist scholarship emphasizes *listening* as a hallmark of good scholarship—listening to one's research subjects, to the oppressed, to one's activist and scholarly community— and creating structures for collaboration, whereby the research subjects themselves can set the agenda, express needs, and benefit from the scholarly endeavor.
>
> (Gaard 2017, xvii)

I would maintain that *listening* is as critical to an archeology of the future as it is to feminist ethnographers of the present-day listening to their subjects, and *Always Coming Home* provides an extraordinary opportunity for this by creating a multiple, complex, rich diversity of sources to which the reader may actively listen. Jim Jose maintains that Le Guin's fiction "has been concerned with exploring alternative social formations and relations" (Jose, 180). Given our present society, many of the destructive patriarchal norms of which ecofeminism seeks to resist or controvert, it is clear that the egalitarian Kesh society—inclusive even of the soul of water, capable of producing a poem spoken by a rock as a functioning member of the Kesh community—certainly merits consideration as an "alternative." Entirely in service to Le Guin's presentation of a social alternative, Jones notes as well that Le Guin "has always placed a high premium on the problem of communication" (Jones 1991, 180). For Jones, "The social context in which it occurs can never be ignored. In Le Guin's writing, each implies the other" (Jones 1991, 180). The entities involved in the communication are critical (Kesh, tree, rocks, water), but the extension of multiple instances of communication into a web takes on even more importance. The Condors refuse to allow women to even speak, so women's participation as actors in a vibrant, inclusive community is not allowed. The earthothers of nature are silenced by the Condors and are thus opened to commodification and exploitation, ultimately to exhaustion. The Kesh, in contrast, acknowledges widespread, inclusive participation in a diverse weblike community of communicating entities. They exist ontologically enmeshed in an ecology, a system of relationships. For *Always Coming Home*, this has ramifications that extend beyond the confines of the novel. According to Rafail Nudelman, in Le Guin's fiction, "The essence of what is expressed is indicated by the nature of the means of expression; the form of the sign is the meaning" (Nudelman 1975, 180). The web of interrelation is finally the meaning, to which the reader listens but within which she or he also participates.

The web of relationships in which the reader becomes an element in reading *Always Coming Home* encourage a conceptual reordering of the world that brings back into being elements of our own, analogous society and creation that have been subordinated and therefore forgotten by the dominant patriarchal paradigm. This is critical, because quite simply, when we truly understand that the tree speaks, or the tree grieves, and that it is part of our community, it will not revert in our estimation to wood, and we are less likely to destroy it in order to sell it. *All rock is flow*, Gaard heard the rocks tell her. Stone Telling speaks in *Always Coming Home* as well, and in listening to the stone tell her story, to offer the gift and flow of her story and her world, we can rescue her resonant future world, with such clear connections to elements—silenced and therefore forgotten elements—of our own.

References

Adams, Carol J. 1990. *The Sexual Politics of Meat: A Feminist-Vegetarian Critical Theory*. New York: Continuum.

Byrne, Deirdre. 2021. "The Road to Sinshan: Ecophilia in Ursula K. Le Guin's Early Hainish Novels." In *Ecofeminist Science Fiction: International Perspectives on Gender, Ecology, and Literature*, edited by Douglas A. Vakoch, 189–203 Abingdon: Routledge.

Donovan, Josephine. 1998. "Ecofeminist Literary Criticism: Reading the Orange." In *Ecofeminist Literary Criticism: Theory, Interpretation, Pedagogy*, edited by Greta Gaard and Patrick D. Murphy, 74–96. Urbana: University of Illinois Press.

Fleming, Nic. 2014. "Plants Talk to Each Other Using an Internet of Fungus." *BBC*, November 11. Accessed October 13, 2020. http://www.bbc.com/earth/story/20141111-plants-have-a-hidden-internet

Gaard, Greta. 2017. *Critical Ecofeminism*. Lanham, MD: Lexington Books.

Jose, Jim. 1991. "Reflections on the Politics of Le Guin's Narrative Shifts." *Science-Fiction Studies* 18: 180–197.

Kimmerer, Robin Wall. 2013. *Braiding Sweetgrass: Indigenous Wisdom, Scientific Knowledge, and the Teachings of Plants*. Minneapolis, MN: Milkweed Editions.

LeClair, Tom. 1989. *The Art of Excess: Mastery in Contemporary American Fiction*. Urbana: University of Illinois Press.

Le Guin, Ursula K. 1985. *Always Coming Home*. New York: Harper & Row.

Murdoch, Iris. 1993. *Metaphysics as a Guide to Morals*. New York: Viking Penguin.

Nudelman, Rafail. 1975. "An Approach to the Structure of Le Guin's SF." *Science-Fiction Studies* 2: 210–220.

Otto, Eric C. 2012. "Ecofeminist Theories of Liberation in the Science Fiction of Sally Miller Gearhart, Ursula K. Le Guin, and Joan Slonczewski." In *Feminist Ecocriticism: Environment, Women, and Literature*, edited by Douglas A. Vakoch, 13–37. Lanham, MD: Lexington Books.

Warren, Karen J. 2000. *Ecofeminist Philosophy: A Western Perspective on What It Is and Why It Matters*. Lanham, MD: Rowman & Littlefield.

Zdenka, Babikova, Lucy Gilbert, Toby J. A. Bruce, Michael Birkett, John C. Caulfield, Christine Woodcock, John A. Pickett, and David Johnson. 2013. "Underground Signals Carried through Common Mycelial Networks Warn Neighbouring Plants of Aphid Attack." *Ecology Letters* 16: 835–843. Accessed October 13, 2020. doi:10.1111/ele.12115

11 "The Revolt of the Mother"

Romanticizing Nature and Rejecting Science in Sally Miller Gearhart's *The Wanderground* and Other Feminist Utopias

Christy Tidwell

The 1970s saw both the feminist movement and the environmental movement gaining momentum in the United States. The second wave feminist movement began in the 1960s, marked by the publication of Betty Friedan's *The Feminine Mystique* (1963) and the formation of The National Organization for Women (1966), and grew through the 1970s. Several influential feminist works were published in 1970, consciousness-raising groups became more common in the 1970s, and significant steps were taken over the course of the decade to give women more legal rights and protections, including Title IX (1972), Roe v. Wade (1973), the Equal Credit Opportunity Act (1974), and the Pregnancy Discrimination Act (1978). The environmental movement also came to public attention in the 1960s with the publication of Rachel Carson's *Silent Spring* (1962) and gained momentum in the 1970s. In 1970, the first Earth Day took place; the Natural Resources Defense Council was created; the Clean Air Act was passed; and the Environmental Protection Agency was founded. As Chaia Heller writes,

> Awareness of the ecological crisis peaked in 1972 when the astronauts first photographed the planet, showing thick furrows of smog scattered over the beautiful blue and green ball. "The planet is dying" became the common cry. Suddenly the planet, personified as "Mother Earth," captured national, sentimental attention.
>
> (1993, 219)

Further environmental action followed quickly, including the passage of the Federal Water Pollution Act (1972), the Marine Mammal Protection Act (1972), and the Endangered Species Act (1973).

Unsurprisingly, these massive political shifts significantly impacted science fiction (SF). Although women SF writers had long been addressing issues of gender in their work, much more explicitly feminist science fiction began to appear in the late 1960s and became even more common throughout the 1970s. Science fiction with environmental themes certainly predates the 1960s and 1970s, but during this period, in response to the same warnings and events that prompted environmental legislation, science fiction describing environmental catastrophes and dystopian futures began to appear more frequently.

Feminist and environmental science fiction largely developed separately, however. Most feminist SF did not engage with environmental issues, and most environmental SF did not address gender. These concerns did converge in a handful of ecofeminist science fiction texts during the 1970s and 1980s, though: Dorothy Bryant's *The Kin of Ata Are Waiting for You* (1976; first published in 1971 as *The Comforter*), Sally Miller Gearhart's *The Wanderground: Stories of the Hill Women* (1979), Donna J. Young's *Retreat: As It Was!* (1979), Joan Slonczewski's *A Door into Ocean* (1986), and Judy Grahn's *Mundane's World* (1988). While Slonczewski's *A Door into Ocean* remains widely read and influential in science fiction studies and Gearhart's *The Wanderground* is occasionally written about as a primary ecofeminist science fiction or utopian text,[1] the other novels mentioned here are largely forgotten. This is a shame, as this moment of ecofeminist science fictional history has much to teach modern readers.[2]

Slonczewski and Gearhart illustrate two very different approaches to ecofeminist science fiction. This is not surprising, because ecofeminism is not a unified discourse. Some definitions of ecofeminism are quite broad, describing it as "politically engaged discourse that analyzes conceptual connections between the manipulation of women and the nonhuman" (Buell, Heise, and Thornber 2011, 425), emphasizing the connection between women and nature without stating exactly what it entails and without necessarily calling for the rejection of either masculinity or science. Other forms of ecofeminism, however, are more absolute. As Catriona Sandilands writes of Mary Daly and her book *Gyn/Ecology* (1978),

> For her, the relationship between women and nature and biology was simple: where women embody the essence of life in all forms, patriarchal culture threatens to kill it through a legion of violent methods from clitoridectomy to language … Daly's text signaled a larger trend in 1970s feminism. Many feminists were beginning to explore the idea that women's difference from men might itself be a source of strength and that reproduction and nature might hold the key to women's power, not just women's oppression.
>
> (1999, 9)

Gearhart's *The Wanderground* illustrates this trend clearly. The novel imagines a harmonious separatist lifestyle for women (the women live in the Wanderground, the spaces outside of the City, while the men remain in the cities); they are so separate, in fact, that men and women are considered to be "no longer of the same species" (Gearhart 1979, 115). And this gender separatism is accompanied by a rejection of the creations of men, including science and technology. There is no technology in the Wanderground, after all, only in the City.[3] Slonczewski, on the other hand, creates a model of feminist science in her novel,[4] a world in which both women and the natural world escape the oppression of patriarchal and industrial society while still embracing science. Slonczewski does this in part by refusing the familiar binaries associated with gender (in which women are associated with nature, peace, emotion, and men with civilization, war, rationality).

Most of the 1970s and 1980s ecofeminist SF novels mentioned above follow the version of ecofeminism presented by Gearhart rather than by Slonczewski, romanticizing nature while rejecting science. These ecofeminist texts represent science as dangerous and unambiguously masculine, echoing arguments from some feminist science studies scholars who argue that "the science we have is highly incorporated into the projects of a bourgeois, racist, and masculine-dominant state, military, and industrial complex" (Harding 1986, 138). These ecofeminist utopias envision worlds in which, for the safety of all, science is eliminated or significantly minimized. While this may have been an understandable position for these radical ecofeminist SF writers to take, *The Wanderground* ultimately reveals the limitations of this version of ecofeminist thought. Rejecting sexism and oppression is one thing; rejecting all science and technology is dangerous and disempowering—for both women and the environment. *The Wanderground* and other ecofeminist novels like *The Kin of Ata Are Waiting for You* and *Mundane's World* are often left out of histories of feminist SF and histories of environmental SF, but they are worth remembering: they illustrate the temptation to turn away from science, and they can, especially when placed in their larger context, be read as a warning against such a rejection.

Most analyses of *The Wanderground* focus on its separatism and gender essentialism. Eric C. Otto recounts June Howard's critique of *The Wanderground*, noting that "From Howard's point of view *The Wanderground* promises nothing transformative and is actually dangerous in its maintenance of ahistorical gender divisions" (2012, 85). Although Otto complicates this, finding that "[t]he apparent essentialism of Gearhart's book thus borders on being 'a positive tool of liberation'" (83), he ultimately argues that "the women maintain their essentialism" and observes that the novel "defines men as inherently oppressive and liberated women as ecologically conscious" (87). Similarly, Jeana DelRosso describes it as "a text that wants to bond women telepathically through the power of their uteruses" (1999, 221). This gender essentialism is, as Howard notes, dangerous; the novel is also dangerous in its romanticization of nonhuman nature and its rejection of science, which go hand in hand.

Its romanticization of nature is illustrated most clearly in the connection between the hill women (as the women of the Wanderground are known), nonhuman animals, and the natural world itself. This connection begins with the earth's dramatic action to protect women from men: "the Revolt of the Mother" (Gearhart 1979, 158). "Once upon a time ... there was one rape too many," one character says, and then "[t]he earth finally said 'no.'" (158). From this point on, men's weapons and technology no longer work outside the City. Neither do their penises, making literal the critique of technology as a representation of phallic power; men who leave the City and try to rape the hill women simply fail. In this enforced impotence, the earth and the women ally themselves against technology and against men.

The women's alliance with nature extends beyond "the Revolt of the Mother" as well, challenging anthropocentric (and patriarchal) models of dominance. The women can communicate with animals psychically (through a mode of communication called "mindstretch"), and one early scene describing the death of a pony dramatizes this connection. While the pony lies dying, Krueva, who is responsible for it, senses the approach of a bobcat. Synchronizing her breaths to the pony's, "[t]ogether they built the dome against the cat. Together they bonded for protection against the approaching fear" (55). This protective bond is built upon Krueva's ability to communicate with nonhuman animals; she also tries to protect the pony by asking the cat not to eat it. The pony says, however, "I am ready. I've done all that was important for me to do. And I don't want to wear out my welcome ... I commend my body to my sister, the cat. May she feed well" (57). DelRosso writes, "The pony's final message, 'I commend my body,' strikes a Christ-like chord; indeed the pony sacrifices itself to sustain others, and in dying moves back into oneness with nature" (1999, 220). DelRosso sees this as "one of the more extreme—and perhaps more effective—ways that Gearhart attempts to undermine the Western notions" that place human above nonhuman (1999, 220).

This openness to other species' thoughts and feelings is appealing; however, in this form, such challenges to anthropocentrism function more as a romantic fantasy than as a useful alternative. As Susan Stratton writes, Gearhart's "depiction of the interactions between women and animals produces something of a Disney world ... [The animals] are rather excessively attentive to human wishes and surprisingly considerate of each other" (2001, 37). Thus, Gearhart's approach seems to be an overcorrection. Interspecies communication is a real possibility and one that deserves serious attention, but this is not a useful or realistic representation of that process, focused as it is on human thoughts and desires.

This romantic idea of communication with nature extends beyond the ability to speak to nonhuman animals and allows the hill women to speak with trees and water, too. For instance, when one of the hill women wishes to swim through an underground portion of a river, she pauses and asks permission before diving in, saying, "Earthsister ... I want to join you." The water replies, "Join" (Gearhart 1979, 12). As she exits the water, she is assisted by a tree root and promptly thanks the tree:

"Thank you," she said in mindstretch to the tree.
"Again if you need me," responded the tree.
"Stay well," she chanted inside.
"Go well," said the tree.

(13)

Despite growing scientific evidence that plants and trees do communicate, they do not do so in anything approaching this way. Other mammals have modes of communication that we can understand directly if we choose to (though this is not what Gearhart demonstrates), but the modes of communication used by plants are more difficult for humans to understand and take place in different registers. Plants communicate not through spoken (or even psychic) language but through chemistry (e.g., the emission of volatile organic compounds [Ueda, Kikuta, and Matsuda 2012]), which requires science to help humans observe and interpret it.[5]

Science here can be defined expansively and inclusively and still provide concrete, non-magical tools for understanding plant communication. Robin Wall Kimmerer's (2013) *Braiding Sweetgrass: Indigenous Wisdom, Scientific Knowledge, and the Teachings of Plants*, for instance, provides a compelling and thorough argument for the possibility of listening to plants through scientific techniques like measuring VOC emissions as well as through traditional ecological knowledges (TEK) and Indigenous science. Kimmerer discusses the knowledge gained from working closely with sweetgrass over lifetimes and generations, saying,

My colleagues might scoff at the notion of basket makers as scientists, but when Lena and her daughters take 50 percent of the sweetgrass, observe the result, evaluate their findings, and then create management guidelines from them, that sounds a lot like experimental science to me. Generations of data collection and validation through time builds up to well-tested theories.

(2013, 159)

The observation skills required for both Indigenous science and traditional science produce detailed, well-grounded knowledge of plants and the natural world and reveal forms of communication that take very different shapes from our own. Thus, it's not that Gearhart's idea of women communicating with the natural world is so far-fetched, but that Gearhart's representations of interspecies communication overlook the real—nonhuman—modes of communication that exist as well as the interventions or attention required for such connections to take place. Jeffrey Lockwood writes that "[e]cofeminism is, to some extent, irrevocably linked to the science of ecology, at least insofar as many of the concerns raised by ecofeminists arise from the findings of ecologists" (Lockwood 2012, 130), but this imagined communication between human and nonhuman nature does not build on either Euro-Western science or Indigenous ecological knowledge.

Further, these representations of interspecies connection seem to primarily concern themselves with the women's rather than the animals' or plants' desires. Gearhart may, therefore, truly value the natural world, but the romanticization of the natural world seen here becomes another form of control. As Heller writes, "romantic love is a love based on the lover's desires, rather than on the identity and desires of the beloved" (1993, 222). As such, it "reduc[es] woman from her full range of human potential to a tiny list of male desires" (222). The same could be said about the romanticization of nature: it reduces the natural world from a full range to a tiny list of desired behaviors. Thus, Gearhart's approach remains quite limited and anthropocentric, as it only acknowledges *some* of the natural world's abilities and/or desires.

The problem is not only that Gearhart is incorrect or unrealistic in her representation of the nonhuman world, however, but that this romanticization of nature encourages the reader to think anti-scientifically. Angelika Bammer argues,

> [t]he emancipatory potential of utopias is thus precisely *not* to be found on the level of representation ... , but rather on the level of discursive practice ... such texts ... force us to think critically not only about what we think, but how we have learned to think it.
>
> (2015, 24)

To take Gearhart's utopian model seriously, therefore, we must also take seriously modes of thought that are unscientific.

The novel's embrace of parapsychology, pseudoscience, and magic underscores this. For instance, the mindstretch that takes place between the hill women and the nonhuman world is a primary mode of communication between the women, and they have built a protective psychic net between themselves and the men of the City. The novel's use of psychic communication is not uncommon for midcentury SF, but by the late 1970s, most mainstream SF was beginning to move away from such forms of parapsychology, seeing that scientific attempts to test these ideas were either inconclusive or disproved such phenomena. Therefore, Gearhart's use of psychic communication may have been read differently in 1979 than it is now, but in either case, it represents an attempt to separate the women's abilities from science.

The women's abilities are further separated from science through Gearhart's location of their power in an invented power—called the lonth—that allows the hill women to transcend the limits of the body. This creation means that women's power does not come from external sources (like scientific knowledge or technological advances) but instead from within; it doesn't come from abilities that real women might be able to share and develop but from what is essentially magic. One of the functions of the lonth is to make flight possible. To fly, one of the hill women uses a breathing technique and then transfers some part of her consciousness "to her lower abdomen and … to her lonth there her suspension and her breathing" (Gearhart 1979, 105). Then, she uses visualization techniques to help guide her body's progress, gradually giving over more and more control to her lonth until "[s]he was using no conscious physical movement whatsoever. Her lonth moved her immobile body, made it sweep and slide, coast and skim" (106). Such a complete abandonment of the laws of physics indirectly reinforces Gearhart's rejection of scientific thought.

The novel rejection of science is even more explicit in its accompanying criticism of technology (the result of the scientific process) and embrace of magic. As one character says,

> That's the mistake the men made, sisterlove, and made over and over again. Just because it was possible they thought it had to be done. They came near to destroying the earth—and may yet—with that notion. Most of us like to think that even long ago women could have built what's been called "western civilization"; we knew how to do all of it but rejected most such ideas as unnecessary or destructive.
>
> (145)

According to the hill women, science and technology have done nothing but harm and the world is better off without them. Instead of relying upon science, they use magic: "Women who scanned the heavens and those who read raindrops or the bottoms of tea cups—any who on any occasion had discovered some danger sign—listed and described the omens" (127). Given that the women survive by using these methods, the novel clearly endorses such magical thinking.

There are legitimate critiques of technology here, and it is tempting to embrace the fantasy and the fun of imagining a world beyond masculin-ist science and technology. However, Gearhart's fictional arguments reflect her nonfictional arguments about "the hegemony of scientific reason" (Schweickart 1983, 201), precluding a simply metaphorical reading of the novel. Gearhart criticizes the idea that we might "accept without question the prescription of the reasoned scientist above that of the counterculture healer" (1983, 175), suggesting that "[u]ntil we accept such avenues of knowing as equal to reason and scientific method, we cannot hope to enjoy the full possibilities of human knowledge" (175). As noted earlier, some of the ideas Gearhart adopts—specifically regarding communication between human and nonhuman—are supported by both Indigenous and non-Indig-enous science, and both of these scientific knowledges are "reasoned" and based on tried and tested methodologies.[6] And it's unclear at this point who exactly the "counterculture healer" is that Gearhart wishes readers to embrace. What *is* clear is that accepting such avenues of knowing leads to dangerous places (e.g., the rejection of safe treatments like vaccines) and sets up a troubling dichotomy between "the reasoned scientist" (implied to be

Western, white, and male) and "the counterculture healer" (by implication more likely to be Indigenous and/or female).

Gearhart is not alone in building her ecofeminist utopia on the rejection of science; Dorothy Bryant's (1976) *The Kin of Ata Are Waiting for You* and Judy Grahn's (1988) *Mundane's World* do so, too. In *The Kin of Ata*, the people of Ata live simply on the land, minimize the difference between the sexes, and privilege their dreams above all else. They believe that dreams have messages that must be followed and that following one's dreams leads to a life of peace and harmony while denying one's dreams leads to nightmares and pain. *The Kin of Ata* seems to sidestep the topic of science altogether, but it actually takes a strong anti-science stance, primarily through privileging personal knowledge over testable knowledge. For instance, the narrator believes the farming techniques of the community are random and primitive and tries to improve them through the rational application of agricultural practices, but eventually he realizes that there is already a plan. Rather, there are many plans. Like everything else in Ata, planting is done according to people's dreams, and this method seems to work: "crops flourished where dreams directed they be planted," indicating that the people "operated with knowledge far deeper than I could ever reach" (Bryant 1976, 158) and that they did not need science or rationality. Cheris Kramarae and Jana Kramer argue that in *The Kin of Ata* "there is little conflict because there is no single truth, no one reality ... People can't *know*, they can only dream and act as their dreams suggest" (1987, 37). This is both a crucial element of the novel's utopian vision and a repudiation of scientific thought. If, after all, knowledge is purely personal and comes not from a shared reality but from the suggestions of dreams, there is no place for science.

Judy Grahn's *Mundane's World* likewise reinforces this rejection of science. As in *The Kin of Ata*, knowledge is personal; as in *The Wanderground*, communication flows freely between humans and the natural world. *Mundane's World* is, as Grahn says, "an ecotopia, and as much future as past" (2007); the city itself has no contemporary technology, instead relying on technologies associated with women (e.g., weaving, cooking, plant medicine). *Mundane's World* does not include explicit repudiations of science in the text itself; however, Grahn says about the writing of this book, "I had been educated in science and practical medicine (I was a laboratory technician) and had lost connection with the life of the earth, and the earth as a being. Writing this novel—*ecopsychology*—restored that sensibility for me" (2007). This indicates that instead of being an expansion of science to include women's knowledges, this novel is a denial of science. For Grahn, immersion in scientific practice is a harmful separation from the earth, while nature is vital but cannot be understood scientifically.

Gearhart, Bryant, and Grahn hope to escape the dangers of a science that they perceive "to be in complicity with misogynistic violence and with the domination of women in patriarchy" (Schweickart 1983, 204).[7] To do so, they align themselves ever more closely with nature and magic. However, this turn to magic and rejection of science does not in fact rescue women but disempowers them. As Jennifer Burwell writes,

> a feminist utopian impulse founded on Woman's difference continues to draw on a logic of exclusion and threatens to consolidate women's position on the margins of the social space without challenging the social structures and logics that place them there.
>
> (1997, xiv)

Similarly, Jean Pfaelzer writes, "the representation of women's separate space perpetuates the paradoxical image of women's original space: the home—*eu*topia, the good place; and *ou*topia, the unreal place. Hence, irrelevant and invisible" (1988, 291–292). Thus, this embrace of magic rather than science further marginalizes women and prevents them from taking part in scientific exploration or from most effectively understanding and defending the natural world. This is the warning of such texts for readers today.

Donna J. Young's *Retreat: As It Was!* (1979) provides an alternative to this ecofeminist rejection of science. In *Retreat*, women live in environmentally friendly communities and have developed an unusual form of reproductive science in which they procreate through parthenogenesis or through sharing genes.[8] This text, like *The Wanderground*, emphasizes connectedness and a closer relationship with nature. The central community is a "collection of buildings that seemed to blend into the landscape instead of rising from it" (Young 1979, 2), characters can "perceive the inner feelings of other creatures" (4), and they "don't have too many surface transports … because [they] don't want too many machines cluttering up a beautiful world such as this one" (9). At the same time, gene sharing is seen as the height of the community's cultural and scientific development. In many feminist texts featuring parthenogenesis or other alternative reproductive sciences, the science is glossed over or turned into fantasy. For instance, in *Mundane's World*, Grahn describes the conception of children as the result of dreams: some women "dreamed their children from stars, domesticated plants or people," while one "dreamed hers from a strange wild bush growing deep in some rocky hills east of the city" (1988, 11). But Young provides a scientific narrative to support gene sharing. In the process of gene sharing, the two women involved fast until they are extremely weak and their "bodies have been deprived enough to activate [their] Patterners" (1979, 59). The Patterner is

> a small appendage to your intestinal tract. It doesn't do anything your whole life until it's signaled by the deprivation of your body. Then it snatches the next available foreign substance that passes through the

intestines, analyzes it, and prints the gene pattern, if it's from another of our race, on your cells.

(59)

After this deprivation triggers the Patterner, the women engage in oral sex and hopefully swallow enough cells from each other to allow gene printing to take place. The science is entirely imaginary, but it is embraced as real science, part of a full and naturalistic understanding of the human body.[9]

The visions of feminist utopia provided in these anti-science texts can be seductive. What woman wouldn't want to live in a world in which she could communicate with nonhuman nature clearly and easily, in which an entire community coexists peacefully and without strife, in which women's work (present and historical) is truly valued? However, these particular worlds are built upon dangerous ideas, and that danger cannot be overlooked. This anti-science ideology creates a gulf between women and science, thereby eliminating the possibility of a more feminist science in favor of a separation that is not realistic or sustainable.[10] It encourages a rejection of technology that actively harms women in particular—through the removal of birth control, of safe medical treatment, of labor-saving devices that allow women to engage with the worlds of work and politics. It leads to ways of thinking that support the anti-vaccination movement, which harms children and reinforces ableist ideologies. And it closes off a powerful tool for environmental protection: scientific understanding. After all, the environmental legislation noted in the introduction to this chapter grew out of findings by ecologists.

These ecofeminist SF novels are not solely responsible for the results of anti-scientific thought, of course, but they serve—even now—as a reminder of the risk inherent in romanticizing nature and rejecting science. Bammer writes,

> the past is critical for utopian thinking: not only do the unmet needs of the past mark the futures that we long and strive for, but the unresolved issues of the past obscure our vision of what those futures could and ought to be.
>
> (2015, xxxiv)

The desires for space outside of patriarchy and for greater connection with the natural are still unmet needs, but the years between 1979 and the present (two decades into the twenty-first century) help us see the limits of Gearhart's vision of this utopian future. As Alexis Lothian argues, however, "the failures of speculative fictions' radical possibilities do not invalidate their meaning, their interest, or their capacity to make a difference" (2018, 20). This means that *The Wanderground* (and the other texts discussed here) can serve both as a dream of a better future and as a warning against creating a feminist future by rejecting science.

Notes

1 The novel "became a cult text of sorts, particularly in American cultural feminist and lesbian separatist circles," and the first edition sold out in months (Bammer 2015, 125).

2 Given the anti-science stance of most of these ecofeminist utopias, some might consider them fantasy rather than science fiction. Although science is typically one of the defining characteristics of science fiction as a genre, I still read these novels as science fiction. In part, this is due to their status as utopias, which is a subset of science fiction rather than fantasy; more significantly, however, these authors take their fantastic ideas seriously, seeing these worlds as ones that we could potentially get to from here. Gearhart, for instance, stated in a 1980 interview that "a lot of women … have nevertheless experienced those telepathic things in their lives" and argued that "there are practical things that we can do that can develop our psychic powers" (24).

3 Sarah Lefanu writes that "Sally Miller Gearhart [rejects] all traditional science and technology as being impossibly male-tainted" (1989, 59), and Debra Benita Shaw argues that, in *The Wanderground*, "men are identified with technology and women with nature in a way which proposes a complete polarisation of the genders and the lifestyles appropriate to each" (2000, 131); thus, the utopia of *The Wanderground* is predicated both upon the separation of the sexes and the rejection of science.

4 I have written more fully about this elsewhere ("*A Door into Ocean* as a Model for Feminist Science" in *Posthuman Biopolitics: The Science Fiction of Joan Slonczewski*, 2020), and Irene Sanz Alonzo's chapter in this volume provides another reading of *A Door into Ocean* that describes Slonczewski's positive representation of science in the novel.

5 See Karl Zuelke's chapter in this volume for more information about and another perspective on plant communication, one that privileges indigenous knowledges rather than Euro-Western ones.

6 In this essay, Gearhart includes a brief acknowledgment of other cultures' attitudes toward the earth and technology, but it relies heavily both on a vague sense of non-Western indigeneity as well as on the sense of the disappearing (or already disappeared) Native. She writes, "To be sure, some groups of human beings have related well to the earth, have developed a consciousness worthy of our intellectual gifts. But, precisely because they refused technology, they became vulnerable to those who didn't. Technology leads to power, domination, control" (1983, 180). This erases both Indigenous people and their uses of technology and their scientific knowledge.

7 This sense of science as harmful is also reflected in Margaret Atwood's *MaddAddam* books, as Izabel F. O. Brandão and Ildney Cavalcanti highlight elsewhere in this volume.

8 In this way, Young's novel builds on the foundation laid by Charlotte Perkins Gilman's *Herland* (1915).

9 Sarah Bezan's (2021) "Speculative Sex: Queering Aqueous Natures and Biotechnological Futures in Larissa Lai's *Salt Fish Girl*" illustrates the extension of this possibility into contemporary ecofeminist and material feminist science fiction. In Larissa Lai's *Salt Fish Girl*, as Bezan argues, women find a way outside of masculinist science without rejecting scientific knowledge entirely, and elements that at first may appear fantastic or pseudoscientific are instead anchored in an understanding and acceptance of the body's and the world's materiality.

10 And it creates the same kind of gulf between Euro-Western science and Indigenous knowledges by adopting the appearance of Indigenous engagement with the natural world without allowing it to be acknowledged as science, too.

References

Bammer, Angelika. 2015. *Partial Visions: Feminism and Utopianism in the 1970s.* Oxford: Peter Lang.

Bezan, Sarah. 2021. "Speculative Sex: Queering Aqueous Natures and Biotechnological Futures in Larissa Lai's *Salt Fish Girl.*" In *Ecofeminist Science Fiction: International Perspectives on Gender, Ecology, and Literature*, edited by Douglas A. Vakoch, 75–86. Abingdon: Routledge.

Bryant, Dorothy. 1976. *The Kin of Ata Are Waiting for You* (originally published in 1971 as *The Comforter*). Berkeley, CA: Moon Books/Random House.

Buell, Lawrence, Ursula K. Heise, and Karen Thornber. 2011. "Literature and Environment." *Annual Review of Environment and Resources* 36: 417–440.

Burwell, Jennifer. 1997. *Notes on Nowhere: Feminism, Utopian Logic, and Social Transformation.* Minneapolis, MN: University of Minnesota Press.

Carson, Rachel. 1962. *Silent Spring.* Boston, MA: Houghton Mifflin Company.

DelRosso, Jeana. 1999. "The Womanization of Utopias: Sally Miller Gearhart's Rhetorical Fiction." *Extrapolation* 40, no. 3: 213–323.

Friedan, Betty. 1963. *The Feminine Mystique.* New York: W. W. Norton & Company.

Gearhart, Sally. 1980. "Discovering the Wanderground: An Interview with Sally Gearhart." Interview by Susanna Sturgis. *Off Our Backs* 10, no. 1 (January): 24–25, 27.

Gearhart, Sally M. 1979. *The Wanderground: Stories of the Hill Women.* Watertown, MA: Persephone Press.

Gearhart, Sally M. 1983. "An End to Technology: A Modest Proposal." In *Machina Ex Dea: Feminist Perspectives on Technology*, edited by Joan Rothschild, 171–182. New York: Pergamon Press.

Gilman, Charlotte Perkins. [1915] 1979. New York: Pantheon Books.

Grahn, Judy. 1988. *Mundane's World.* Freedom, CA: Crossing Press.

Grahn, Judy. 2007. "Judy Grahn in Cyberspace: Books." Accessed January 12, 2010. http://www.judygrahn.org/books.html.

Harding, Sandra. 1986. *The Science Question in Feminism.* Ithaca, NY: Cornell University Press.

Heller, Chaia. 1993. "For the Love of Nature: Ecology and the Cult of the Romantic." In *Ecofeminism: Women, Animals, Nature*, edited by Greta Gaard, 219–242. Philadelphia, PA: Temple University Press.

Kimmerer, Robin Wall. 2013. *Braiding Sweetgrass: Indigenous Wisdom, Scientific Knowledge, and the Teachings of Plants.* Minneapolis, MN: Milkweed Editions.

Kramarae, Cheris, and Jana Kramer. 1987. "Feminist's Novel Approaches to Conflict." *Women and Language* 11, no. 1 (Winter): 36–39.

Lefanu, Sarah. 1989. *Feminism and Science Fiction.* Bloomington, IN: Indiana University Press.

Lockwood, Jeffrey A. 2012. "Afterword. Ecofeminism: The Ironic Philosophy." In *Feminist Ecocriticism: Environment, Women, and Literature*, edited by Douglas A. Vakoch, 123–135. Lanham, MD: Lexington Books.

Lothian, Alexis. 2018. *Old Futures: Speculative Fiction and Queer Possibility.* New York: New York University Press.

Otto, Eric C. 2012. *Green Speculations: Science Fiction and Transformative Environmentalism.* Columbus, OH: Ohio State University Press.

Pfaelzer, Jean. 1988. "The Changing of the Avant Garde: The Feminist Utopia." *Science-Fiction Studies* 15, no. 3 (November): 282–94.

Sandilands, Catriona. 1999. *The Good-Natured Feminist: Ecofeminism and the Quest for Democracy*. Minneapolis, MN: University of Minnesota Press.

Schweickart, Patrocinio. 1983. "What If... Science and Technology in Feminist Utopias." In *Machina Ex Dea: Feminist Perspectives on Technology*, edited by Joan Rothschild, 198–211. New York: Pergamon Press.

Shaw, Debra Benita. 2000. *Women, Science and Fiction: The Frankenstein Inheritance*. New York: Palgrave.

Slonczewski, Joan. 1986. *A Door into Ocean*. New York: Arbor House.

Stratton, Susan. 2001. "Intersubjectivity and Difference in Feminist Ecotopias." *Femspec* 3, no. 1: 33–43.

Tidwell, Christy. 2020. "A Door into Ocean as a Model for Feminist Science." In *Posthuman Biopolitics: The Science Fiction of Joan Slonczewski*, edited by Bruce Clarke, 47–64. Cham, Switzerland: Palgrave Macmillan.

Ueda, Hirokazu, Yukio Kikuta, and Kazuhiko Matsuda. 2012. "Plant Communication: Mediated by Individual or Blended VOCs?" *Plant Signaling & Behavior* 7, no. 2 (February 1): 222–226. doi:10.4161/psb.18765.

Young, Donna J. 1979. *Retreat: As It Was!* Weatherby Lake, MO: Naiad Press.

Index

Page numbers in *italic* denote figures

For Product Safety Concerns and Information please contact our EU
representative GPSR@taylorandfrancis.com
Taylor & Francis Verlag GmbH, Kaufingerstraße 24, 80331 München, Germany